DRAGONS AND DEMONS

KING'S DARK TIDINGS

BOOK 5

KEL KADE

This is a work of fiction. All characters, places, and events in this novel are fictitious. Opinions and beliefs expressed by the characters do not reflect the author's opinions and beliefs.

This book is intended for adult readers. It contains graphic violence, creative language, and sexual innuendo. This book does not contain explicit sexual content.

BOOKS BY KEL KADE

Sign up for Kel Kade's newsletter for updates or visit my website!

ACKNOWLEDGEMENT

Thank you to my most patient and understanding daughter who has encouraged and supported me throughout this writing process. Also, thanks to my friend and fellow author, Ben Hale, for his support and positivity. Gratitude to my family for giving me the space to write when I need to. Thank you to my readers for sharing my world with me.

Map of the Souelian Sea

Map of Ashai

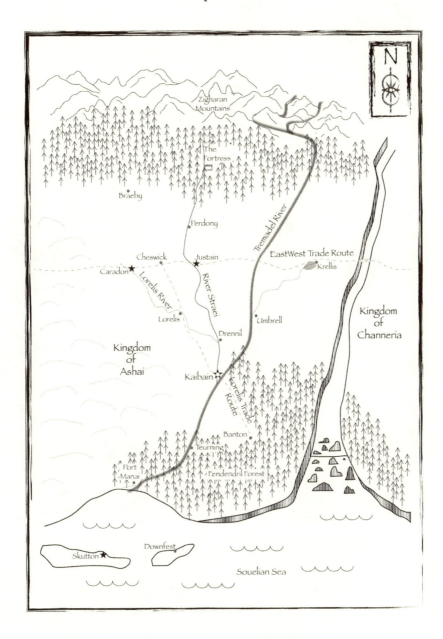

PROLOGUE

Swirling eddies of dark blue and grey broke apart as the waves crashed against the cliffs. Rezkin could feel the spray of the ocean on his face, could smell the salt in the air. He turned his head. There, seated on a large rock, was a woman. He saw her form, her dress, her face—he knew he had— but he could not remember her. All he could recall were the white strands that blew past her silver eyes. She gazed out to sea before turning toward her companion.

"Will he live (concerned)?" Her voice was melodic and clear. It seemed to be in harmony with the sounds of the ebbing ocean, the wind whipping through the trees, and the birds flitting around the rocks.

"I am not sure (indifferent)," said her companion.

"Will you give it back to him if he does?"

Her companion, who Rezkin could not see clearly, held up a leather lace wrapped around a small stone. "What choice do I have (irritated)?"

"Why did you take it (curious)?"

"He would not have survived wearing it (irritated)."

"Why does he wear it if it weakens him (curious)?"

"I do not know. If he lives, you may ask him (angry)."

"I do not care that much. I was just curious (indifferent)."

The woman shifted, and Rezkin caught a glimpse of her silver-eyed gaze once again. He wanted to see more. He wanted to know her face.

"I sense him (concerned)," she said.

"His energy suffuses the island. It has accepted him (frustrated)."

"No, it is more than that. I feel like he is watching us (anxious)."

"He cannot. He sleeps."

"We shall see soon enough (unconvinced)."

1

"Is there any change?" said Frisha.

"No," replied Healer Jespia. The healer's expression softened, and she gripped Frisha's hand. "I told you before. The fever has gone on for too long. He should not have survived this long. I'm afraid the only change we should expect is death."

Frisha glanced to where Rezkin lay in the bed. His skin was paler than usual, and beads of sweat gathered on his face. She knew his sheets would be damp from sweat as well and needed changing, just as they had at least twice per day for the past week that he had been unconscious. She looked back to the aged healer.

"No. He's stronger than any man I've met. He'll pull through. What did Wesson say about trying to kill the tiny invaders in his body?"

Jespia shook her head. "He refused, afraid he would do more damage than good, but it no longer matters. We've discovered that his sickness is caused by poison."

"Poison? From what? Something on the island?"

"We do not know. It is not contained in anything we have encountered. You said he was fine when you last spoke?"

"Yes," said Frisha with a pang of regret. Then she added, "I mean, he was cold and distant, but I think that was to be expected given the circumstances."

Jespia huffed. "Yes, you and Lord Tieran surprised us all."

"Was it really such a surprise?" Frisha said defensively. She pointed toward Rezkin. "He was never there for me—emotionally, I mean. Tieran overcame his doubts about himself and about *me* and fell in love. We work well together, don't you think?"

Jespia frowned. "I cannot deny that you *work* well together, but it is difficult for me to see how you fell for that spoilt"—she paused. Taking a deep breath, she said, "Never mind. It would be folly to speak poorly of the man who would be our next king."

Frisha knew what Jespia was thinking. It was what everyone was thinking. How could she fall for someone whom everyone thought to be a spoilt, self-absorbed lord when she had Rezkin, a selfless leader who gave everything to secure sanctuary for his people? They had no idea who Rezkin really was, though, and Tieran was transparent. He was exactly the man she thought him to be, and she believed he deserved more credit for his potential than people gave him.

With another glance at Rezkin, Frisha thanked Jespia and left the room. She nodded at Kai and Farson who stood guard over their liege. Two of the four strikers currently on the island watched him at all times preventing anyone but a few select from entering. They had debated even allowing *her* to see him considering how their relationship had ended. Frisha's stomach knotted at the thought. Her own guilt and doubts gnawed at her. She tried to shake the concerns, telling herself that she had no reason to feel such things. Rezkin was many things, but a devoted lover, he was not. She could never have the life she dreamt of with him. It was better that they remain only friends.

She left the healers' wing, passed the intersection that led to the living quarters then wended her way through several corridors, across the dining hall and up to the next level. She stopped in front of a newly constructed wooden door with iron bars blocking a head-sized window. Suddenly, a face appeared on the other side only inches from her own. Brandt gripped the bars. His disheveled hair and scraggly beard made him appear a mad man. The pain and fear in his eyes did nothing to appease Frisha's anger.

"What did you do to him?" she shouted. "Tell me! What was the poison?"

"Please, Frisha. You know me," pleaded Brandt. "You know I would never hurt him. He is our emperor and more importantly a friend. You have to believe me. Whatever was done to him was not done by my hand. If anything, it was *him*." Brandt pointed a finger through the gap in the bars toward a similar door across the corridor.

Frisha huffed, then turned toward the other door. She peered into the room beyond. Like the other, it possessed a bed, a bucket, and little more. Sitting on the bed with his back against the far wall was Brandt. *Another* Brandt. He looked identical to the one with whom she had just been speaking.

"Tell me now," she yelled. "What was the poison?"

Brandt ran a hand over his face and looked at her with weary eyes. "I have told you. *I* am the real Brandt, and I did nothing to Rezkin." He stood and crossed the room to peer through the window at the other Brandt. "How can you all not see that *he* is the imposter?" Looking back toward Frisha, he said, "I know nothing about poisons, anyhow."

"Oh, don't give me that. You've always known more than you want people to think. Rezkin even said so." Disheartened, she backed away and glanced between the two Brandts. "But that isn't the problem here, is it? Even if one of you is the real Brandt and didn't poison him, the other probably did."

"How do you know that?" said the Brandt on the left.

"Yes," said the one on the right. "What makes you think it was either one of us? Maybe it was someone else, someone who is not locked up."

"Maybe the real threat is still out there," added Brandt-on-the-left.

"The two of you are in agreement, now?" said Frisha.

Brandt-on-the-left's face screwed up. "I know not who *he* is"—he pointed across the corridor—"but he is not wrong."

"Yes," said Brandt-on-the-right. "Just because he is impersonating me for some reason, that does not mean he is the poisoner."

Frisha gripped her hair and screamed with frustration. "Why would anyone impersonate you except to get close to *him*? And there being two of you just *happens* to have occurred right when Rezkin gets poisoned."

Brandt-on-the-left said, "No, it was going on much longer than that. You know what I was doing for the past few months. I was with you and Rezkin. All that time, Rezkin was good and well. What was *he* doing back here?" He jabbed a finger toward the other door.

"I was doing exactly what I was supposed to be doing," said Brandt-on-the-right. "Tieran had me looking after the princess and helping with other tasks since *Frisha* ran off and left him to do them all."

Frisha stubbornly placed her hands on her hips. "*I* am not the one on trial here."

"What trial? You have already decided we are guilty. How many other people on this island could have poisoned him?" said Brandt-on-the-right. "How many people did you bring back from other lands? How many of them were less than trustworthy?"

Frisha silently fumed. The Brandts were right. With Xa, also known as Lus, and Connovan, the former Rez, the island had two assassins she knew about, and how many more? Was it only a coincidence that two Brandts had been discovered right when Rezkin fell ill?

As she turned and walked away, she wished more than anything that Tam were there to tell her everything would be okay. Tam was probably dead, though, and it was all Rezkin's fault. She was furious with him for what he had done to Tam and even more so for failing to go after him immediately. He had no right to be sick. He was the indomitable Dark Tidings. He was the Rez. He was the Maker-forsaken Raven, and he should be out there wreaking havoc on their enemies, not lying in bed stricken by a simple fever. After wandering aimlessly, she found herself back in front of his door in the healers' wing just as she broke down and began to cry. Was this *her* fault? Had she distracted him so badly that he had failed to avoid an attack? What she did know was that Rezkin had to pull through or she would never forgive him—or herself.

Kai cleared his throat. "Lady Frisha, perhaps you should get some rest. I could have someone escort you to your room—"

"No," she said, wiping her tears. "I'm fine. I just—I don't know what to do."

Farson said, "What makes you think there is anything *you* can do?"

She scowled at the surly striker. "Well, *you're* not helping any. I don't know why they even let you guard him."

His expression became stoney. "I am a striker."

"Yet he insists you will kill him the first chance you get."

He motioned into the dark room lit only by a single candle. "He is still alive."

Frisha looked back into the room. She could see the end of the bed from where she stood. She swallowed hard and said, "For how long?" Her gaze passed between them. "What will we do? What if—"

"I will not have you saying such things," said Kai, "especially while standing within earshot of him."

She nodded solemnly, then turned back down the corridor.

Kai glanced at Farson as Frisha disappeared around a turn. "I am going in to check on him."

"You think *she* did something? She is a mouse."

"No, I just need to see that he is still alive with my own eyes."

Farson shook his head but did not protest.

Kai turned into the dark room and stepped silently to the bedside. When he looked down upon the man who lay still as a corpse, he no longer saw the indomitable warlord who had taken half the Souelian. There, wrapped in linen sheets, was a young man who looked older than his years but was still barely more than a boy. The hardened warrior who struck terror into the darkest of souls appeared peaceful—peaceful as the dead. Kai frowned and cautiously lifted his hand toward his sleeping king. He pressed his fingers to the side of Rezkin's neck. His own heart began to race as he realized he could not feel a pulse. He shifted his fingers and pressed harder. Just as he opened his mouth to shout for the healer, he felt it. The tiniest flutter that would not have been noticeable had he not been searching so hard. He released a breath but felt no relief.

"Get the healer!" he called to Farson.

Farson did not wait a breath before he shot down the corridor.

Kai glanced up when the other striker returned mere minutes later with Healer Jespia thrown over his shoulder. The woman pounded on his back shouting, "Put me down, you brute!"

She rocked as her feet settled on the ground, but Farson forestalled her tirade by spinning her around to face Kai. Her eyes widened when she realized they were standing over Rezkin's bed. Before she said anything, Lord Tieran, who had apparently been talking to Jespia when she was snatched, came skidding into the room.

"What is it? Tell me now!" he said.

Kai raised a hand toward Rezkin. "I can barely feel a pulse, and I have not seen him take a breath."

Healer Jespia placed one hand on Rezkin's chest and the other on his forehead. She hummed under her breath and moved her hands across his skin. She shook her head and grumbled, then moved them again. After a few minutes, she straightened and took a few steps backward so she could face them all at the same time.

"We have done all we know to do for him. I am afraid he is past waking now. You should prepare yourselves. He will go at any moment."

No one spoke. No one breathed, but they all turned to stare down at Rezkin. They were so intent on their king that they jumped when two of the shielreyah suddenly appeared on the other side of the bed. The wispy wraiths looked down at Rezkin then back up to Tieran.

"He comes," they said in unison.

Tieran stared at them silently for a moment, then said, "Wha —who?"

Rezkin suddenly shot up in the bed with a great gasp. He grabbed the person closest to him, which happened to be Tieran, and tackled him to the floor. He grappled Tieran until he was wrapped in a cocoon of sheets. Kai snagged Jespia by the arm, and he and Farson both backed away from the fray to opposite corners of the room so as not to appear a threat.

"I yield," shouted Tieran. "Rezkin, it is me, Tieran! I yield."

Rezkin paused. His breathing was erratic, and his limbs shook with restraint. He slowly stood and backed into the far corner away from everyone else. With his back pressed to the stone, his eyes darted back and forth. His pupils were dilated, but it was rather dark in the room, so Kai did not know if that was an issue. Rezkin wiped a hand down his face, and paused, seemingly noting the sweat that he had swept from his brow. Finally, his gaze fell on the elven wraiths.

"Is there a threat?" he said.

"No, *Syek-lyé.*"

Rezkin's gaze took in Kai and Jespia, then Tieran, who was still wrapped in the bedsheets on the floor, and then landed on Farson. "What is happening?"

Farson took a step forward. "You have been ill. We thought you were about to die, but you suddenly woke."

Rezkin glanced down at himself. "Where are my weapons? My clothes?"

"You have been unconscious for a week," said Farson. "You have had a high fever. Your clothes and weapons were stripped from you so that the healers could care for your properly." He nodded toward the woman. "If it is okay with you, Healer Jespia can get you something to put on now."

Rezkin nodded then looked down at Tieran as Jespia hurried out of the room. "Tieran?" he said. "What are you doing down there?"

"What—what am *I* doing down here? *You* put me down here. Would you kindly get me out of this?" Tieran's struggles with the bedsheets were in vain.

Rezkin nodded toward Kai, and Kai knelt beside the bundle of Tieran to unravel him. Once freed, Tieran lurched toward Rezkin and threw his arms around him. "Thank the Maker, Rez. I thought you were going to leave me to clean up your mess."

"Lord Tieran," said Kai, keeping his voice steady and low. "Perhaps you should back away from Rezkin. He is still … adjusting."

Tieran backed up a step and looked at Rezkin who was staring at his cousin with a predatory gaze. Tieran ran his hands down the front of his shirt and backed away several more steps as he said, "Uh, sorry, Rez, I did not mean to overstep. Ah … please refrain from killing me."

Rezkin glanced at each of the others again, then looked back at Tieran. He said, "Are you going to marry her?"

"What?"

Rezkin took an aggressive step toward him and practically growled, "Are you going to marry her?"

Tieran backpedaled and threw up his hands. "Stop! I mean, I, um … do not know."

"Why?" snapped Rezkin. "Is she not good enough for you?"

"No, no, it is not that. I *will* marry her … if she will have me."

Rezkin's shoulders relaxed, and he stepped back into the corner again. Healer Jespia shuffled into the room bearing a stack of black clothing. Nestled atop the stack was a gold crown. She settled the stack on the bed and placed a pair of black boots on the floor. Then she asked Rezkin to sit on the bed so she could assess his condition before he dressed.

She looked toward Kai and said, "Shoo, all of you out. There are too many people in here." She glanced at the shielreyah and said, "You, too. Out."

The shielreyah took one last look at Rezkin then vanished in a wisp of light. Farson moved toward the door with Tieran on his heals, but Kai hung back.

"Someone should stay with you," he said with a pointed look for the healer. "He is still out of sorts."

Healer Jespia nodded curtly then turned to Rezkin expectantly. Rezkin slowly walked forward and sat on the bed. He watched the healer's every motion with avid attention and glanced at Kai frequently.

. . .

"What was wrong with me?" Rezkin said, his voice soft so as not to startle the healer who was leaning over him.

Kai said, "It seems you were poisoned. None one could identify it."

"I take it you do not know who poisoned me?"

"No, and we do not know how it got into your system, either."

Rezkin had a vague memory of a pain in his neck just before he collapsed into the corveua. "It was a dart."

"A dart?"

"A blow dart."

"Surely not," said Jespia. "Blow darts are very small, and you were near unto death. It would have been very strong poison indeed."

"Perhaps a venom?" said Farson from the doorway.

Rezkin nodded. "It is possible, but as you know, I am immune or resistant to the poisons and venoms that could have taken effect that quickly. This had to be something new."

Jespia put her hands on her hips and looked down at him with a frown. "Well, you seem well enough now, though I cannot explain it." With a shrug, she said, "Sometimes this happens. People pull through by some miracle of the Maker. I would suggest you take it easy for at least a week—no strenuous activity and plenty of sleep—but I doubt you will take the advice."

Rezkin stood and began dressing. He pulled on the black pants, then held up the black long-sleeved tunic embroidered with green and gold lightning bolts and looked at the woman quizzically.

"Lady Frisha left those for you," said Jespia. "She said you should look your best when you wake to reassure your people."

"And the crown?" he said, holding it up so the candlelight glinted off its golden curves.

She smirked. "You have your grandfather to thank for that."

Rezkin considered leaving it. A crown was impractical for any rigorous activity. Then he reconsidered her words. Frisha thought he needed to look the part of the king for his people. He ran his fingers through his hair, and Kai grunted. Rezkin glanced up to find the striker holding out a brush. With nothing to tie his hair back, it hung loose around his shoulders. The crown settled uncomfortably over his brow. He did not care for the metal ring or its weight upon his head, but he wore it anyway because it was expected of him.

"Where are my weapons?" He did not ask about the small stone he had grown accustomed to wearing around his neck.

"We put them in your quarters," said Kai. "We figured you would not want weapons lying around for anyone to pick up and use while you slept."

Rezkin felt a welling of anxiety in his stomach but stamped it down quickly. It would do no good to dwell on all the things that *could* have happened to him while he slept. He was still alive, and he had important tasks, not the least of which was figuring out who had poisoned him.

As he walked out of the room, Tieran stepped up to stride beside him. The two strikers followed, and Rezkin was uncomfortable with them at his back. He knew that if they had wanted him dead, they would have killed him while he was most vulnerable. Still, he did not know what protocols were in place. There was a chance that they simply had not had the opportunity.

Tieran said, "Rezkin, you cannot believe how relieved I am that you are well."

"You have been granted a temporary reprieve from having to lead."

"No, not just because of that, Rez. I was really worried about you. You are my cousin and, more importantly, my friend." Rezkin said nothing, but Tieran was not deterred. "Your mother and grandfather wanted to see you, but we decided it was best for them to wait until you woke."

"Good," said Rezkin. "I do not trust either of them."

"I know," said Tieran. "I kept it to just the strikers and healers and, um, Frisha—"

"You allowed Frisha into my room while I slept?"

"Yes, well, I know she is not a threat, and she would not be deterred. She was beside herself when we found you. I think she blames herself."

Rezkin abruptly stopped and turned to him. "Why? Did she poison me?"

Tieran's eyes widened. "No, of course not!"

"No," Rezkin said, turning back down the corridor. "She does not have skills with a blow tube, nor knowledge of poisons or venoms."

"No, but why would she *want* to?"

Rezkin stopped again. He nodded for the strikers to fall back and then stared into Tieran's eyes. "What has she told you about me?"

"What do you mean?" said Tieran, suddenly appearing anxious.

Rezkin closed the distance between them and held Tieran's gaze as he watched the man's pupils contract. "What has she confided in you?"

Tieran shook his head. "I know not what you are expecting to hear, but I assure you she has said nothing disparaging about you." Rezkin narrowed his eyes, and Tieran said, "I mean, she did say she had learned things about you that had made her reconsider marrying you, but she did not tell me what those things were. I swear, she kept your secrets. I know nothing more than I did before; and, I admit, it is a source of some distress for me."

Shifting away, Rezkin said, "I have forbidden her from speaking of it, so do not press her."

Tieran swallowed hard, "I understand, but I do hope that you will eventually feel comfortable enough to confide in *me*."

"I did not *confide* in her," Rezkin said. "She stumbled upon something dangerous, and I would sooner keep you from it."

"Dangerous? How dangerous? More dangerous than *you*?" Rezkin looked down the corridor to see that others had begun to gather in the hall at its end. Tieran said, "Does this have to do with Lus following her around all the time?"

"He is now her guard."

"Is she in immediate danger? For how long?"

Frisha appeared at the end of the corridor, her reluctant shadow not far behind.

Rezkin looked back at Tieran as the woman closed the distance and said, "Forever."

2

R ezkin met Frisha with open arms. He knew that she, like Tieran, would wish to embrace him and had prepared himself for it. She wrapped herself around him and cried into his chest. When she backed up, wiping her tears, her accompanying smile could have lit the corridor.

"I don't know what to say. I'm so happy you're alive."

"I am well," he replied.

She nodded and patted his chest as though she were making sure he was real. Then she glanced at Tieran and abruptly pulled away. She took a step to the side, then another to place herself beside his cousin. Tieran awkwardly took her hand but did not hesitate to meet Rezkin's gaze.

Rezkin once again felt the pain in his chest, the one he had come to know as loss, and he did not know why. He was glad Frisha was with Tieran. No matter what happened, she would be cared for, and Tieran would make sure that everyone treated her with the utmost respect. Still, Rezkin could not shake the feeling that he was also personally affected by that turn of events—something that went beyond the failure to fulfill the expectation of a marital contract. He stretched, attempting to relieve some of the tension from the pain in his chest, then pushed the issue aside.

The man he sought was only a few feet away, hovering at the edge of the group. He tilted his head. "Lus, I would speak with you privately." Xa, known as Lus to most of the others, glanced toward Frisha and then back to Rezkin with a silent question. "She will be fine," said Rezkin. "Lead the way to my office."

Xa tilted his head and turned toward the gathered crowd at the end of the corridor. He wore the uniform of a royal guardsman, and the onlookers parted as he passed through their midst. Kai and Farson flanked Rezkin to keep people away, their gazes constantly roving over potential threats just as Rezkin's did. Rezkin, however, donned a pleasant smile and nodded toward his people, who showed signs of elation at seeing him well. He noticed Mage Nanessy Threll standing anxiously at the back of the crowd. She looked as if she needed to speak with him, so he nodded for her to join Frisha and Tieran in the rear. Her face lit up and she scurried over to join their group.

Once past the crowd, Rezkin turned a corner and came to an abrupt stop. At his feet and surrounding Xa were half a dozen of the little white creatures known as *ictali*. They grinned up at him with their sharp little teeth exposed beneath overlarge blue eyes. Two of them struggled forward with *Kingslayer* in their tiny little grips. The ictali were abnormally strong for their size, but even so, the sword was much too long for one of them to carry without it dragging on the ground. Rezkin took the longsword from them, then a second set of ictali came forward with *Bladesunder*. A final two handed him his belt and favorite belt knife. Rezkin glanced at Kai who only shrugged. He seemed just as surprised as anyone else. The ictali, on the other hand, took to celebrating as Rezkin strapped the swords around his hips. They hopped up and down chittering with glee before running down the corridor.

"Those things unnerve me," said Tieran.

"I think they're darling," said Nanessy. He gave her a scornful look, and she added, "Since they're not trying to kill us, I mean."

Rezkin said, "They were some of the original inhabitants of this

KEL KADE

citadel and were servants to the Eihelvanan. It pleases them to serve us in their stead."

"I suppose they are good at that," said Tieran begrudgingly. "They never complain and when they tire, there are plenty more to replace them."

When they reached Rezkin's office, he turned to survey the group. He said, "I will speak with Frisha, Farson, and Lus first." He looked to Kai. "Then, I will get an update from Tieran. You decide who should speak with me next."

Kai frowned. "You just awoke from a week-long coma not twenty minutes ago. You should be resting, not conducting business or holding court."

"I do not intend to hold court, but I am sure there are urgent matters that need to be addressed."

"We *are* capable of running this place without you for a few days," protested Kai.

"Speak for yourself," said Tieran. "Some of these people have me at my wit's end."

"I will help with what I can," said Rezkin, "but I leave tomorrow."

"*What?*" said Tieran. "Where do you intend to go on such short notice."

Rezkin glanced between Tieran and Frisha. "I have not forgotten that, before I was taken ill, I was *ordered* to retrieve Tam."

Frisha flushed. "It wasn't an order—"

"Was it not?" Rezkin said with a pointed look. He turned to Kai. "Make preparations on one of the ships. Unless you have new information, we leave for the Isle of Sand in the morning."

Frisha and Farson followed him into his office where Xa awaited them. Rezkin told them to sit before he rounded the desk and took his own high-backed chair. He liked this particular chair because the interior was lined with iron to his specifications to make it more difficult for someone to stab him in the back.

He looked to Xa. "What happened?"

Xa appeared genuinely surprised. "How could I know?"

"You were there, watching Frisha. I left and only seconds later, I was attacked. It was either *by* you or you should have seen who did it."

The jeng'ri shook his head. "I did not. I was keeping an eye on *her*" —he pointed to Frisha—"and you had rounded the bend. I saw nothing."

Rezkin looked to Frisha. "Was he there? Was he with you?"

She appeared uncomfortable as she glanced from Xa to him. "I think so. I didn't see him move from the tree he was in until we started down the path. It was at least five minutes after you walked away."

Rezkin clenched his fist then opened it. He did not feel ill or weak. Actually, he felt no different than if he had woken from a night's sleep. He considered asking the assassin more questions, but he knew Xa would stick to his story of knowing nothing. He waved at the two of them and said, "You may go."

Frisha started to rise then paused. "Um, Rezkin, there is something else. It is quite concerning."

"What is it?"

"Well, as you know, Brandt went with us on the voyage." He nodded. "It seems, he was also *here*."

His brow furrowed. "What are you saying?"

"There are now *two* Brandts. We discovered them after you fell ill. They look identical, speak the same, and seem to have the same memories—at least, up until we left the island. Even the healers cannot tell the difference between them."

This was strange news indeed and yet it sparked a memory. It was not the first time there had been *two* of his companions. In fact, it had happened more than once. That information was not known by the others, though. "Where are these Brandts?" he said.

"We created some holding cells for them."

"Very well. Tell Tieran to wait a minute before he enters."

Frisha nodded and followed Xa into the hallway.

Once they were gone, Rezkin turned to Farson. He said, "I was unconscious for a week, and you were one of my guards?" Farson nodded once. "Why did you not kill me?"

Farson leaned forward and put his elbows on his knees. "Believe it or not, Rez, I am not out to kill you."

"Since when?"

The man took a deep breath. "Since I realized what chaos would ensue across the Souelian if you were to die suddenly. You have made yourself the keystone of an empire, and there are now perhaps millions of people dependent on you."

Rezkin frowned. "There are a few thousand on Cael at this point. My association with the other kingdoms—"

"Your *kingship*."

"—is new and weak. If I were to fall, things could go back to how they were with little trouble."

Farson shook his head. "I do not believe that. Queen Erisial and Moldovan both upset their courts—what is left of them. Without you, Erisial will be killed and Moldovan no longer has an heir. King Regent Coledon will be overthrown. I still do not understand why you appointed *him*. You barely know the man."

"It was convenient."

Farson grumbled under his breath but said, "There are other problems you have caused as well."

"What now?"

"The unrest in Serret has spread. Channería is now officially at war with Jerea, and both countries are enduring internal struggles between factions."

"That has little to do with me," Rezkin said. "I did not even go to Jerea."

"It has everything to do with you. King Ionius gave Dark Tidings— that is *you*—Prince Nyan's intended bride. Nyan was angered when his father King Vargos would not go to war with Ionius, so he instigated a coup that has caused Jerea to fall into civil unrest. Meanwhile, the *Fishers* in Channería have finally acquired enough power with the *support* of the Raven—also *you*—and Channería is now *also* enduring a civil war."

Rezkin waved his hand. "Those kettles were already simmering. I was merely the catalyst that caused them to boil over."

"Which might not have happened had *you* not been involved. There are rumors, now, that Vargos desires a meeting with Dark Tidings, and the Fishers are calling on the Raven. On top of that, several representatives from Gendishen are here. They arrived a few days ago but refuse to state their business to anyone but you."

Rezkin tapped his finger on the desk, then said, "Fine. Set a meeting with the Gendishen for tomorrow morning. Actually, we will have court."

Farson stood to leave. He stopped but did not turn back as he said, "I am relieved that you are not dead." As the striker left the room, Rezkin thought he might even believe him.

Tieran slipped through the doorway after avoiding the brooding striker. He sauntered over to the side table and poured himself a glass of something dark that had not been in the room the last time Rezkin had been there. His cousin sat on the sofa and crossed his legs as he sipped the amber-brown liquor. Upon noticing Rezkin staring at him, he said, "Oh, did you want one?"

"No," said Rezkin, eyeing the vessel that was easily accessible to anyone desiring to tamper with it. Tieran did not seem concerned, but he had not been in a coma for a week due to poisoning. "What news?" Rezkin said. He quickly raised a hand to forestall Tieran's response and said, "Only the pertinent things." Although he had been unconscious for merely a week, Rezkin had been journeying for two months prior to that, and he was sure there was much Tieran would discuss.

"Well, um, where do I start? There is an issue with Brandt—"

"Frisha has informed me. I am heading to the cells after this."

"Great. Moving on. We have worked out some trade deals—"

"Are they profitable?"

"Yes—"

"Then let's move on."

"Very well, Channería and Jerea—"

"Farson has already informed me."

"Right, well, food production is high."

"There is enough for everyone?"

"And then some."

19

"Very good. Next?"

Tieran pursed his lips. "There were problems with some of the nobles, but—"

"But what?"

"I have taken care of them already."

"Good, then it sounds like you have everything in hand. Is there anything else?"

"No, I suppose not," said Tieran looking a bit discomfited. "Except for this thing between you and me. I think we need to talk about it."

Rezkin furrowed his brow. "What thing?"

"About Frisha. It was never my intention to betray you."

"Betray me? How so?"

"It is just that, well, *you* were with Frisha and then *I* claimed her."

Rezkin sat back in his chair but resisted rubbing his chest where the pain started to tug at him again. "I was not *with* her, and you did not *claim* her. She is a grown woman capable of making her own decisions. I understand why she did not wish to be with me, and her reasons were well considered and appropriate. I did not realize she had developed feelings for you, but if she is to be with anyone, I am glad it is you. You will make a good husband for her. You will be capable of giving her things I cannot."

"Like *what*? You are the emperor. You can give her *everything*."

"Love, Tieran. That is all she really wants. I do not love her."

"And I do not believe you," said Tieran suddenly pushing to his feet. He turned to pace the carpet in front of the desk and said, "I know you say that, and I think you even believe it, but *I* do not believe it to be true. You have feelings for her. No one would act the way you do toward her without feeling *something*."

"Are you trying to convince me or yourself?"

"Why would I want to convince myself of *your* love for *my* woman?"

"Why would you want to convince *me* of it?"

Tieran ran a hand through his hair and blew out a breath. "Because I do not want this to cause a rift between us. I do not want you secretly harboring ill feelings toward me or especially Frisha. You are my cousin and my friend … and I care about you."

Rezkin stood from his seat and rounded the desk. He stood before Tieran holding out his hand. "I hold no ill feelings toward you *or* Frisha. I will endeavor to always honor and protect you both, as per *Rule 1*."

"Right, the famous *Rule 1*," Tieran muttered as he took Rezkin's hand. He met Rezkin's gaze and said, "But, Rez, I feel so guilty."

With a tightening in his chest, Rezkin said, "Your guilt is unfounded. Let that go, Tieran. Be happy."

"Is that another rule?"

Rezkin paused, then said, "No, it is antithetical to the *Rules*, but it is right for you, I think, since *you* are not bound by them."

Tieran took a deep breath then nodded in acceptance. Before he stepped out of the office, he turned back and said, "You know, Rez, you are not bound by your rules either. No one is keeping track. You have free will. You can be happy too."

Before Rezkin could issue a response, Mage Threll entered the room, and Tieran was gone. Farson slipped through the door behind the mage. She curtsied formally and said, "Your Majesty."

"Mage Threll."

A small smile crossed her lips. "You may call me Nanessy, if you like."

Rezkin tilted his head. "Nanessy. What may I do for you?"

"The mages have been meeting. They elected me to liaise with you since they seem to think we have some rapport—since I have traveled with you, I mean."

"You are speaking on behalf of the mages, then?"

"Yes, Your Majesty. It is a matter of communication. We desperately need a mage relay. No one here knows how to make one, but since you acquired all of the necessary items, it was concluded that perhaps *you* know how to make one."

He nodded. "I know how to construct the device, but I obviously do not know the spells involved, nor could I use them if I did since I am not a mage."

Her brow furrowed. "May I speak plainly?"

"Please do."

She bit her lip, then said, "No one here believes you are not a mage. You obviously wield power. We have all seen it used for one purpose or another. If you could put aside your denial for just a little while, we could really use your help."

Rezkin frowned and glanced at Farson who watched him curiously. He looked back to Nanessy. "I am not in denial. I truly am not a mage. Two master readers in Gendishen confirmed it. But I do seem to possess some kind of power, so I will heed your request. Allow me to think on the problem."

She smiled. "Thank you, Your Majesty."

He held up a hand. "You may drop the honorifics in private, Nanessy."

She dipped her head and said, "There is one more thing. It has been apparent for some time that you have chosen Journeyman Wesson to be the king's mage."

"Yes, is that a problem?" he said, giving her a look that said it had better not be.

"No, not at all," she replied hastily. She then seemed to think better of her answer. "Well, yes, it is, but only in that he is still a journeyman. It is apparent that he has a firm grasp of his power and can certainly hold his own. He should be raised to full mage status."

"What is the problem?"

"Well, without the Mage Academy, there is no one to do that."

"And you want *me* to do it?"

"Oh, not just *me*. The others have all agreed that it should be you."

"Except that, as we have discussed, I am not a mage. It would not be appropriate for *me* to raise him. If it is to be official and recognized within the mage community, he should be raised by a council of mages. Perhaps you all should create one."

"Yes, I would normally agree with you, but the problem is, as the king's mage, he is our superior. Without the archmage, Wesson would be the head of the council; in which case, he would be raising *himself*."

"What you are saying is that by choosing the journeyman as my mage, I have put a kink in your chain of command."

"More like you have unraveled it altogether."

"If I may," said Farson. "We could send him to Lon Lerésh or Ferélle to have one of their councils raise him."

Rezkin nodded. "That is a good idea. It has been some time since I left Coledon in charge of Ferélle. I should send a contingent to check on him anyway. Perhaps Moldovan will go back and do the job he so graciously dumped in my lap. It would be much more convenient if he remained king." A thought occurred to him, and he said, "Send Yserria as my emissary. She is the leader of two Leréshi echelons bordering Ferélle. For her to be sent into the king's court, *my* court, it will be a great show of strength. Erisial may think twice before replacing her. Of course, Malcius will need to go with her."

"Why?" said Farson, eyeing Rezkin with suspicion. "You care nothing for the sentiments of marriage."

"I have my reasons. Suffice it to say that it is necessary for him to stay near her." He looked back to Nanessy. "In the matter of Wesson, will this solution serve?"

She blinked at him as though surprised he had asked. "Yes, of course."

"Good, then you should prepare yourself. You will be going with me to retrieve Tam."

"*Me?*"

"Yes, I may have need of an assistant."

"No," said Farson. After meeting Rezkin's challenging gaze, he said, "You need no assistance. You are capable of retrieving him on your own if he still lives."

"*If* he still lives, which we both know is unlikely, he will be in dire need of healing. Healer Jespia is too old for such a journey. I will require Reaylin, and she will require someone who can guide her. Journeyman Wesson will not be there, and I am already familiar with Mage Threll."

"How *familiar*?" gritted Farson.

Rezkin ignored him and said, "Besides, having two women along will satisfy the requirements of propriety."

"Two women, and who else?" said Farson.

Rezkin decided not to tell Farson he intended to take *no one* because the fewer people he had with him, the smaller the chance of betrayal. He knew it sounded paranoid, and it probably was, so the sentiment would not go over well at that moment. Instead, he said, "I have not yet decided. Right now, I must visit the cells." He looked back to Nanessy and said, "You and Reaylin should be prepared to leave in the morning."

He rounded his desk and motioned for Nanessy to depart. Then he followed Farson to the cells with a detour through the kitchen to grab enough sustenance to quiet his grumbling stomach. He figured that randomly stopping in for food, himself, would reduce the chances of being poisoned *again*. Although he had just eaten enough for an entire meal and then some, he was still hungry as he strode through the winding corridors.

It was unclear if he was ascending or descending without peering through the windows since the entire structure contained no stairs or ramps. Somehow, the design of the building and its enchantments defied basic engineering principles. On the way, he spied Journeyman Wesson and bade him to join them.

"I heard you were awake," said Wesson. "I am very glad to see it. You had us all worried." Rezkin nodded, and the journeyman said, "Where are we going?"

"To the cells. I understand there is an issue with Brandt."

"Um, yes, I have studied them quite closely and have not been able to discern which is the real one—if either."

"We shall see," said Rezkin.

As Farson guided him toward where they had established the cells, Rezkin surveyed the number of guards in the corridors. It seemed that either quite a few more trained soldiers had immigrated to Cael or the Eastern Mountains men's training efforts had been successful. He stopped in front of two of the new guards who seemed to be doing nothing more than standing around and socializing. He did not recognize them, which meant it was unlikely he had ever seen them.

Without bothering with introductions, he said, "I need your swords."

Both guards' eyes widened, and they quickly saluted with fists across their hearts. Then they both fell into line beside Farson with swords drawn. Rezkin frowned at them. "No," he said. "*I* need your swords. Give them to me."

One of the guards hesitated, and Rezkin could not decide if this frustrated him or if he approved. On the one hand, he was the king, and his guards should do his bidding without question. On the other, anyone living by the *Rules* would balk at handing over his weapon. Rezkin decided to let Farson figure it out. He took the two men's swords and continued down the corridor with the soldiers in tow.

The corridor with the cells looked to have once been a small residential wing. The two cells were on opposite sides of the corridor and were secured by identical doors. Only the glowing crystals embedded in the walls permitted light as this corridor had no outside windows.

Rezkin peered through the small, barred window into the cell on his right. Brandt lay on a cot staring at the ceiling. When he turned his head and saw who watched him, he jumped to his feet and hurried to the door. Brandt gripped the bars and said, "Rezkin, I am so glad to see you. They said you might die. I swear, I had nothing to do with your poisoning. I have done nothing wrong. Please help me!"

Without a word, Rezkin turned toward the other door across the corridor where another Brandt already stood watching him through the window. "Rezkin, *I* am the real Brandt. Please believe me. I cannot say what *he* has done, but I would never betray you."

Rezkin glanced at Farson and said, "You have the keys?"

"I do."

"Open the cells." Then, to Brandt-on-the-left, he said, "Stand back. We are going to let you out. You will exit your cell and stand against the corridor wall. The striker, the journeyman, and *I* are watching you. Do you understand?"

"Yes, of course!"

As Farson unlocked the first cell, Rezkin turned to Brandt-on-the-right and repeated the command. Once both Brandts were out of their cells and standing against the walls, Rezkin perused their persons with a critical eye. He looked for any inconsistencies or defects. He watched the way they held themselves, the most minute of mannerisms, and the way they watched him in return. They were, in all regards, identical.

Rezkin handed each of the Brandts a sword then drew *Kingslayer*. Both Brandts' eyes bulged, and they each took a few steps, placing them closer together but farther from him. Rezkin followed.

"Uh, Rez. What are you doing?" said Brandt-on-the-left who was staring at *Kingslayer*. His eyes shifted to Rezkin's face just as the other Brandt's gaze dropped to Rezkin's sword.

"You had best raise your swords," said Rezkin.

"B-but there's no way I can defeat you," said Brandt-on-the-right, a sentiment that was echoed in similar words by the other Brandt.

Rezkin said, "This is your only chance to defend yourselves. On guard." Then he swung at Brandt-on-the-right before twisting and striking out at Brandt-on-the-left. Both Brandts blocked his attacks but were hesitant to issue their own. After a few additional swings increasing in both force and speed, they seemed to realize that he was serious. Rezkin continuously switched fighting styles between several he knew Brandt had been practicing. His attacks progressed in intensity until both Brandt's were pushed to their limits. By the time he disarmed them, Brandt-on-the-right had received several scores to his forearms while Brandt-on-the-left lay on his side bleeding from his cheek and neck. Rezkin motioned to the two guardsmen to retrieve their fallen swords, then dismissed them.

"Bilior!" Rezkin called as he sheathed his swords. The others glanced at each other anxiously. After a minute, he repeated the call to the Ancient, a shape-shifting forest nymph. "Bilior! Show yourself."

After another minute, an orange-eyed tortoise-shell cat lazily rounded a bend in the corridor and came to sit at Rezkin's feet. It blinked up at him, then blinked at the two Brandts. Rezkin looked down at the cat and pointed to the twins.

"Explain."

Brandt-on-the-left eyed Rezkin and said, "Thank you for not killing me." Then he looked to Farson and Wesson as he gained his feet. He breathed heavily as he said, "Are you sure he is well? He is talking to a cat."

The cat abruptly began to elongate. Its back stretched upward, its limbs dangled at its sides, and its head sprouted twiggy vines from which swayed feather-like leaves. The creature's eyes enlarged, and the catlike visage was replaced by that of an animated tree. The sound of rain rattled throughout the corridor.

Farson jumped back and drew his sword as Wesson erected a shield ward across the corridor. Unfortunately, the Brandts were on the other side of the ward with the Ancient, and both looked as if they might run away.

"Stay!" Rezkin snapped, gaining the attention of both.

"What fiend is this?" said Farson, stepping to Rezkin's side.

The fiend in question said, "The Shattered One calls, the we do answer."

Ignoring Farson's query for the moment, Rezkin pointed to the Brandts and said, "What is this? Why are there two of them?"

"Thee thinks 'tis known by the we. Should it be? Two of them we see."

Although his words had the sound of denial, the creature's large, blinking gaze suggested the hint of unshared knowledge. Rezkin took a step toward the fae being, causing its leaves to rattle and limbs to shake. He said, "You know what this is. Tell me. Is either of these men really Brandt? Has something happened to him? Do not forget our deal. You were to provide my people with safety in exchange for an army."

Bilior's twiggy hands turned up toward the ceiling, and he seemed to shrug. "No harm befalls the friend of thee. He be safe within the we." Bilior's gaze slid toward the Brandts, then his body followed. He slinked toward them, bouncing and lurching with an unnatural gait. Tendrils of vines snaked out from his hands to caress the Brandts' faces. Both Brandts flinched as the vines slipped across their skin, and they each looked to Rezkin as though pleading for him to save them.

"What *is* that?" hissed Farson.

"*That* is an ancient," said Rezkin.

"The one with whom you made the deal?" said Wesson.

"The same."

Wesson said, "You think he has something to do with this?"

"We shall know shortly."

Bilior's form abruptly began to shift again, this time taking on a decidedly feminine human physique. Blond hair sprouted from its head, and its eyes turned pale and bright. Soon enough, Farson, the Brandts, and Rezkin were staring at Mage Nanessy Threll.

Farson's hand quickly went to his hilt. "No!" he growled, "Not her."

Rezkin stayed the man's hand. "Be calm, Striker. She is elsewhere, unharmed. Bilior takes on the form of a man—or woman—to make communication easier."

"So," said the false Nanessy, rubbing her hands together as the real Nanessy sometimes did when she was anxious. "This is a little embarrassing, actually. You see"—she paused, looking at Farson. "You are upset." She patted her torso and said, "I apologize. This form is easier to hold because it bears the power." She pointed at Brandt-on-the-right and said, "He is the real Brandt." Then she pointed at Brandt-on-the-left. "*And* he is the real Brandt."

"How is that possible?" said Rezkin.

"Well, one of the lesser—one like *me*—"

"A katerghen, or wood nymph," said Wesson.

"Yes, exactly, but a young one. He took on the aura of your Brandt, and, well, he forgot himself. Brandt does not hold the power of a human mage, and the lesser held the form for too long. He forgot who he is."

"How long will he stay like this?" said Wesson.

Nanessy looked sad as she peered between the two Brandts. "He is like this now, permanently, with all the experiences, thoughts, and memories of your friend. There is no difference between them now. My lesser is gone. They are both Brandt."

"*What?*" said both Brandts at the same time. They began to rail, first against Nanessy, then against each other.

"Silence!" called Rezkin. Only the sound of rain and leaves could be heard in the corridor.

Rezkin looked back to Nanessy-that-was-Bilior and said, "What threat is this?"

Nanessy shook her head. "They are the same. The threat he held before is the threat he holds after." Her skin began to shrivel, and it looked as though she were melting into a furry, black and brown puddle on the floor. The cat looked up at them then scurried away.

Rezkin's sharp gaze passed between the two Brandts who were staring at each other in shock. Part of him wanted to end them both just to rid himself and his island of the possible threat, but Bilior had said neither was any more of a threat than Brandt had ever been. Rezkin had no reason to believe the katerghen lied, especially since such a lie could lead to the ancients failing to uphold their part of the bargain. Besides that, Malcius would be furious if he killed Brandt. Malcius had already lost his brother Palis. Rezkin doubted Malcius's mental state could handle losing his best friend as well.

Rezkin's gaze slid to Farson. "Have either of them done anything to warrant confinement?"

"Besides being a duplicate? No."

"Very well. They are free to go, then."

Both Brandts breathed heavy sighs of relief before looking at each other and then to Rezkin. Then, they both began to argue again.

"Wait, Rezkin, you cannot let him go—"

"—no, he needs to stay in there."

"People will think he's *me*—"

"—and *I* am Brandt."

"This cannot be!" they both said in unison.

Rezkin looked between them.

Farson said, "You believe that creature? He is *fae*." This last he spat as if it left a terrible taste in his mouth.

Rezkin nodded toward the Brandts. "They fight the same—*exactly* the same. Their training and skill until this point is identical. They look the same, they speak the same … their *auras* are the same—"

"You can see that?" said Wesson.

Rezkin frowned. "Sometimes, ever since Bilior gave me a fruit—"

Farson's voice was incensed as he said, "You *ate* something from the fae? Did we neglect you in your education? You *never* eat from the fae!"

Rezkin shrugged and said, "The Brandt's are the same. They will be useful. We need more skilled fighters."

"You cannot be serious," said Brandt-on-the-left. "How is this going to work? We cannot both be *me*."

"Perhaps you could begin thinking of yourselves as twins," Rezkin replied.

Wesson said, "I am not sure that will work. Twins lead different lives. They have different experiences and memories. They may look similar, but they are not the same person."

"These two began living different lives as soon as the katerghen forgot who he was," said Rezkin. "They will have to learn to be different people from here on. They will need to be marked in some way so we can tell them apart. And they will need different names."

"I am not giving up my name," said Brandt-on-the-right.

"Nor am I," said Brandt-on-the-left.

"Do you have a middle name?" said Wesson.

"*He* can go by it," said Brandt-on-the-right.

"No, then people will think *I'm* not the real Brandt," said Brandt-on-the-left.

"You are both right," said Rezkin. "If either of you keep your name, people will consider the other to be an imposter. You will both get new names." When they opened their mouths to argue, Rezkin said, "*Or* you can remain in the cells."

They both shut their mouths.

"What will we call them?" said Farson.

"And how will we mark them?" said Wesson.

As Rezkin stared at the identical men, an idea began to form. "Journeyman, please place marks on their wrists—something that cannot be removed. One will be called Blue and the other Red." To the Brandts, he said, "You will remain together. You will eat together, sleep together, and work together. Most importantly, you will train together. You are identical in skill, ability, strength, and thought. Together, you will become a fearsome duo."

Wesson looked at Rezkin curiously, then strode forward and took one Brandt's left hand and the other's right. Gripping their wrists, Wesson muttered a spell. The two men gasped and growled as their skin was seared. When Wesson took his hands away, each man bore the image of a lightning bolt facing opposite directions. On one, the bolt was blue. On the other, the bolt was red.

Farson looked over Wesson's shoulder and huffed. "Fitting."

The two Brandts eyed each other. Rezkin knew it would take some time for them to grow to trust each other; but he felt it inevitable that, if forced, they would eventually realize they were the same person. He looked at them and said, "If you cannot trust yourself, then who can you trust?"

Both men scowled at him.

Rezkin motioned to Farson to escort the Brandts out of the corridor and gave him the hand signal to keep watch over them. Then he turned to the journeyman and said, "I need to speak with you."

Wesson looked at him curiously and nodded. They waited until the Brandts and Farson had disappeared before they spoke.

"I'm sending you to Ferélle," said Rezkin. "The mages have brought it to my attention that you must be raised from journeyman to the position of mage if you are to serve as the king's mage."

Wesson anxiously tugged a curly lock of hair. "But I am not ready. I have been a journeyman for less than a year, and there is no way I can pass the mage exam using constructive power."

"Then use destructive—or a combination. You are good at that."

"But that would make me a battle mage."

Rezkin paused and looked at the mage. "It will make you exactly who you are now except with the title required of your position."

Wesson huffed and shook his head. "Does our agreement still stand?"

"If you are referring to your refusal to kill, I have never required it of you. We both know that has not stopped you when it became necessary. I am confident that you will continue to perform your duties as required."

Thinking of taking *another* mage exam so soon had Wesson suddenly longing for home—not the home he had shared with his mother, but the one where he had learned to wield vimara. His best friend, Tica, had been his rock when his future had been at greatest risk, and his master had always been able to put things into perspective. He dearly wished Tica and his master were with him now.

His master's estate was very far from where he was at that moment, and he wondered what his master was doing. Ikestrius was a former *trained* battle mage, which meant he was not a *natural* battle mage like Wesson. He had learned to use his constructive power in destructive ways. He wondered if Ikestrius had gotten caught up in King Caydean's mage draft. Then he worried about what might have happened to his other mage friends. A sudden icy chill consumed his core as he considered that he might have to go to war against his friends and former master. Tica would never have fought him. Wesson knew that. Tica would have betrayed Caydean before he would betray his best friend. Wesson felt a sudden urgency to find his friends and master and bring them to safety.

"No," he said. The word had escaped his lips before he realized what he was doing. It was difficult to tell with his liege's ever stoic expression, but he thought he had surprised Rezkin, too. "I mean, I understand what you are saying, and if I am to serve as the king's mage, then I agree; but I cannot go to Ferélle. If I am to be raised to full-mage status, then I should do so in Ashai."

Rezkin's icy gaze appeared contemplative as he watched Wesson. He said, "You do realize Ashai is in the caustic grip of Caydean? Your former colleagues are under *his* rule and will therefore be your enemies."

"I know. That is why I need to go. I need to convince them they are on the wrong side. I know the archmage—or, at least, I have met her a few times. She knows the kind of power I wield, as does the battle master at the Battle Mage Academy. If I can convince them to follow you, we may not have to fight a war at all."

"And you think *you* have the ability to make this happen?"

"I do not know, but I am willing to try." Fear wrapped around Wesson's trembling heart. "My friends are deep in this mess. I will not fight them if there is any chance I may save them."

"Your concerns are admirable, Journeyman, but you are more likely to be captured or worse if you go there alone." Rezkin considered for a moment before he continued. "You will go in quietly. Use stealth and subterfuge. Bring as many to our side as you can. Start with your friends."

"There are few," Wesson said shamefully.

"Be that as it may, they are more likely to trust you. Once I have collected Tam, I will join you in Ashai. Together, we will take on the mage academies and seek out the archmage and battle master."

Wesson nodded, still reeling from the task he had just insisted upon undertaking. He had managed to convince the emperor of the Souelian to send him into the viper's nest.

3

Tam glanced up to Uthey, then hefted the boulder just as his partner did the same on the other side of the cart. They moved in unison to place their stones into the container, then turned back to the pile. After weeks of working in the mine chained together at their necks, they had gained a rhythm. They had to. If the slave masters thought they were slacking in their tasks, they were beaten. If either of them was beaten badly enough, they would both be thrown into the pit with the dead. Most of the slaves in the quarry were no longer chained, but those that survived his transport from the Isle of Sand were out of luck. The key to their shackles had been lost in the vurole attack. So had most of the men.

Tam lifted another rock and moved with Uthey while the chain stretched taut between them.

"What did Answon say?" Uthey muttered in Gendishen too quietly for the slave master at the end of the passage to hear.

"He isn't convinced, but he's willing to talk," said Tam pausing as his vision went black. He dropped the rock into the container and held up a hand. He knew Uthey would watch for the guards, while he waited for his eyesight to return. After a couple of minutes, he began to see stars, then his vision slowly came back into focus.

"They are getting more frequent," said Uthey.

Tam had no need to ask how Uthey knew he was enduring another migraine. His sleeve was stained brown from wiping the blood from his nose just as he was at that moment. *"But no worse,"* he said. *"We are lucky to be in the tunnels. The light kills me."*

"Only you would find luck in the black halls of the Hells."

"I should be dead by now."

"The Maker won't have you," said Uthey with a husky laugh.

The slave master glanced their way, and they both turned to grab another stone. After the man turned away, Tam said, *"I overheard Probart talking to Mecca about separating us."* Probart was the master in charge of the clutch of slaves to which Tam and Uthey belonged. Mecca, on the other hand, was a slave, but one favored by the masters. He was a skilled smith and, therefore, more useful, with higher value.

"What did Mecca say?"

"He said he couldn't do it. There are enchantments on the chains."

As Tam lifted another rock, he noticed its wetness. He eyed the dark liquid in the vague light of the single torch that lit their section of the mine. Then he wiped his nose on his sleeve again.

"Why don't they get one of those Ashaiian mages to do it?" said Uthey.

"You know the Ashaiians won't come down here. They've only done so once since they took the quarry."

"It has been nearly three weeks. I cannot believe the Verrilians haven't tried to take it back yet. They will need the resources."

"I think they have bigger problems than this quarry. Once their stockpiles start to run out, then we'll see—if we live that long."

Uthey eyed him in the dark. He nodded toward Tam's bleeding face and said, *"I am not sure you will make it through the day without bleeding out."*

Tam snagged his sleeve on a sharp piece of metal on the edge of the mining cart. He looked down at his torn sleeve, then wrapped his fingers around it and tore it the rest of the way. He wadded the small strip into a ball and shoved it up his nose. As he breathed through his mouth, dust settled in the back of his throat causing him to cough. Uthey shook his head and grabbed another rock.

"So, when do we meet with Answon and the others?"

"We don't, for now. I think he's waiting for us to prove ourselves."

"I can't say as I blame him," said Uthey as he dropped another large stone into the cart. "Even I think you are crazy."

"He will come, and we must be ready when he does."

"You speak of your king? The one who comes to rescue you? Because that is what kings do. They go running off to foreign countries to save crazy, bloody nobodies from quarries."

"I'm not a nobody."

"Right, and what position of value do you hold in this new kingdom of yours?"

"I'm his best friend. At least, I think I am." Tam pressed his palm to his forehead. "Yes, I know it. I am Tam, and I am his best friend."

Uthey pointed to the wad of cloth stuffed up Tam's nose. "Now that you have plugged that hole in your head, have you figured out what to do about the one you say you have in your mind?"

Tam shook his head. "I don't know. When we are down here in the dark, and it's quiet, things become so clear. I think sometimes I can even hear voices coming from the rocks themselves. I wonder if maybe they have the answers."

"If you are looking for answers in the rocks, then you are worse off than I thought."

A piercing sound suddenly filled the small shaft. The knell resounded in time with the pounding in Tam's head. With each ring, he could see a pulse of light behind his shut lids. The chain connected to the shackle around his neck pulled tight as Uthey moved behind the cart. Tam joined him, and together they began pushing the over-burdened load through the shaft toward the entrance to the mine. The rocks around them shuddered, and Tam was almost certain they were speaking to him. The blood pounding in his ears made it hard to concentrate, though; and, as they neared the entrance, the light got brighter and more painful.

When they exited the mine, the waning sunlight nearly brought him to his knees. Uthey grabbed his arm roughly and pulled him up before the slave master saw him lagging. He rallied his mental and physical strength to help Uthey push the cart over with the other carts before they were finally herded toward the pen, which wasn't unlike the kind built to house animals. Within the pen, they were free to walk around, chat quietly, rest, or get into fights. Sometimes the slavers bet on the outcomes of those fights. Tam and Uthey stayed clear of them and generally used the time to recover from their many injuries and ailments. Uthey's arm and leg were mending well enough since the vurole attack they endured during their failed escape, but Tam's problems had only gotten worse. He knew it was only a matter of time before he succumbed to the damage and debilitating effects of the magically induced hole in his mind, and he dreaded taking Uthey with him. The man was rough and a bit crass, but he was jovial for a slave, and Tam knew the pairing could have been much worse.

After waiting in a long line of downtrodden workers, most of whom had forgotten that life existed outside the quarry, Tam and Uthey obtained their meager rations of slop. The so-called *food* was grey with a lumpy consistency, but there was nothing identifiable about it. Still, it took the edge off the pit in Tam's stomach, so he scarfed it down before someone got the idea to take it from him. They rinsed their bowls in a barrel of dingy water and placed them in the stack to be reused.

In the short time they had been eating, a fight had broken out in the middle of the yard between a brawler from the Isle of Sand and a Ferélli former slave master who had managed to get swept up in his own net after falling afoul of some bookies. The Ferélli threw a right hook into the Sandman's jaw causing him to stumble, but the sandman only came back angrier. The sandman crouched, ducked his head and ran straight for the Ferélli, ramming him like a bull. With the Ferélli draped over him, the sandman plowed through the crowd aiming for the side of the barracks. Unfortunately, he had aimed for the building just as Tam and Uthey were skirting the crowd. Both fighters became tangled in the chain that stretched between Tam and Uthey, and all four of them went down in a jumble of limbs.

The sandman freed himself first and stood with a roar as he randomly punched the first face he saw. Uthey took a fist to the temple.

It was not a direct hit, though, as the sandman started to tip when Tam shoved the Ferélli off him, stretching the chain that still entangled them. The Ferélli sent his elbow into Tam's solar plexus, forcing the air from his lungs. Tam blamed himself for not having tightened his core as he had been taught. With the sudden influx of what Rezkin referred to as *battle energy*, Tam's mind cleared of its perpetual fog. He grabbed the Ferélli by the back of the neck, pulling him in tight as he kneed him in the kidney. Then he shoved the man forward causing him to fall into the back of the sandman's legs. The sandman lost his footing and dropped Uthey who was struggling to breathe through the man's tight grip around his neck. Uthey fell on top of the sandman and socked him in the throat. Then he sat up and started pummeling the man's face.

Tam worked quickly to free the rest of the chain from the tangle. Just as it came loose, he felt a warning on the wind that something was about to strike him. He dodged just as a foot sliced through the air where his head had been. He fell into the crowd that had shifted to surround them, but a few of the onlookers pushed him back into the fray. As Tam stumbled forward, he caught sight of the Ferélli tugging something from his boot. The man spun and plunged the bone shiv straight toward Tam's abdomen. Tam twisted to the side, grabbed the man's arm, and bent it backward causing him to lose hold of the weapon. The shiv fell into the dirt, but Tam kicked it upward and snatched it out of the air before shoving it back toward the man in one fluid motion. When Tam pulled the shiv back, his hand came away covered in blood.

The chain that linked him to Uthey abruptly pulled him toward the other man. The sandman had managed to gain the upper hand and was back on his feet. With a giant roar, the man lifted Uthey over his head and threw him, yanking Tam over by the neck. Tam and Uthey both hugged the ground struggling for air as they clutched their necks. The sandman stomped toward them, reaching Tam first. The man bent and grabbed Tam by the shirt pulling him off the ground. With the shiv still firmly in his grip, Tam shoved it into the side of the man's neck then pulled it out to release the flow of blood. Liquid life gushed from the wound showering the onlookers in a spray of red. The sandman dropped Tam and grabbed for his neck in a hopeless attempt to stem the flow.

As the sandman crashed to his knees, Tam scanned for the Ferélli. That man had already succumbed to his gut wound, which must have been worse than Tam realized. He grabbed Uthey's shoulder, helping him to sit and then pulled him up with him as he stood.

"*Come on,*" he growled. "*We need to disappear before the guards realize we've killed them.*"

"*We?*" Uthey choked out. "*You did all the killing.*"

"*What I did, you did,*" Tam said as they stumbled toward the barracks. The crowd was dispersing just as quickly, so they were able to blend with the others fleeing the scene. The slavers might have enjoyed a fight, but they did not put up with their workers killing each other. Tam did not worry that the other slaves would out him. People steered clear of other people's secrets in this place, especially when those people were killers.

He and Uthey paused beside a water barrel at the entrance to the barracks. Uthey shoved a man out of the way as Tam lifted the ladle to pour water over his bloody hands. He quickly splashed his face washing away more blood, then threw a ladleful in Uthey's before they both stumbled into the shadowed space. The barracks were nothing but a barren shelter. They contained no furniture, mattresses, or blankets, and the gaping holes in the walls held no doors or windowpanes. The space along the walls was in high demand since the walls provided the only support for sitting and protection on at least one side, but they were already full. Tam and Uthey made for an empty spot toward the center of the room that was just large enough to fit the two of them. On his way there, Tam inadvertently made eye-contact with a scarred man leaning against the wall. The man's eyes widened, and he nudged his friend, pushing him to the side to make room.

Tam tugged on the chain to get Uthey's attention, then redirected him to the now empty space beside the wall. As they sat, Tam's gaze slid to the side where the scarred man was doing his best to give Tam space.

"*What's wrong with you?*" Tam said in Gendishen.

The man looked at him as though he would rather be anywhere else. Then, in the Ashaiian trade dialect, he said, "I don't understand."

Tam switched languages fluidly and whispered, "What's wrong with you? Why did you move?"

The man swallowed anxiously and said, "I saw what you did out there. I don't want any part of that."

Tam was torn. On the one hand, he had just killed two people without giving it a second thought. On the other—

"I was just protecting myself and Uthey," he said, motioning to his partner.

The scarred man nodded. "I know." He held out his hand. "I'm Milo. I'm from Channería. This is my friend Yin. We were captured together on our fishing boat." Taking his hand, Tam introduced himself and Uthey. Milo looked skeptical as he said, "You are not criminals, then?"

Uthey growled, "Mercenaries." Uthey's trade dialect was not good, but he knew enough to get by. Otherwise, Tam had to translate.

Milo nodded. "That makes sense. You are good fighters, and you fight well together."

"We've been stuck with each other for some time," Tam said dryly.

"Why are you still chained?" said Yin.

"They lost the key," said Tam, running a finger around the inside of the collar. He knew his neck would be severely bruised from the fight. "The chains are enchanted, so they can't cut them."

Milo and Yin shared a look, then Milo said, "Answon will want to speak with you."

"Not likely," said Tam.

"What do you know of Answon?" said Uthey in halting trade dialect.

Milo shrugged. "Sometimes he is interested in what I have to say."

Tam said, "You are his eyes and ears."

"Some of them."

"We have tried to speak with Answon," said Tam. "He has agreed but doesn't seem eager to meet."

"That was before you killed two people in the pen," said Milo. "If you were not on his watchlist before, you will be now. What is it you wish to speak with him about?"

"That's between us and Answon."

"Fair enough. I will warn you, though. Do not waste his time. He is not a patient man."

"Waste his *time?*" said Uthey. "Time is all we have in this glorious dung hole."

"Perhaps, but"—Milo leaned in so that only Tam and Uthey could hear—"he can help you."

"How's that?" Tam said just as quietly.

"I hear he has some small power over enchantments. If he thinks you are worth it, he may be able to separate you." The man leaned back. "But maybe not. If his power was strong, he would not be *here.*"

Tam's head tilted back to rest on the boards that made up the wall. He could hear the wind whisper between them; and, as he began to doze, he thought for the faintest moment that he could understand it. He strained to hear the voice of the wind again, and again it was just beyond his comprehension. Whatever it had to say, though, it was important.

It was just before dawn when Tam was jostled awake. Uthey elbowed his arm then whispered in his ear, *"I need to relieve myself. Come."*

Before he was taken prisoner, Tam might have complained about being woken ahead of schedule for a trivial problem belonging to someone else, but he had come to accept that Uthey was, essentially, an extension of himself. As such, Uthey's needs were *his* needs; and Uthey seemed to have come to the same conclusion. Trifling things like an extra thirty minutes of sleep meant little in the big scheme of things. Misery was misery whether awake or asleep.

They slinked through the darkness toward the refuse pit. Few people moved about, and those that did were usually up to no good or were simply unlucky bastards like themselves. As they both relieved themselves, Tam got the feeling they were being watched. A whisper on the air had him turning toward the shadows of a supply building. The moon shone brightly, but the figure he was sure existed remained shrouded in darkness. Tam stared long enough to let the person know he was aware of his presence even though Tam could not see him. His gaze slid to another shadow just as it moved beneath the eave of the barracks. Tam elbowed Uthey as the person moved toward them. Together, they took several steps to the side so that their backs were not to the pit.

A man who was slightly taller than Tam at about Uthey's height stopped a few paces from them. "Answon wants a word," said the shadowed figure.

Tam's gaze slid to the first shadow he had inspected and knew that was where Answon stood. He tugged Uthey in that direction, and the one who had spoken followed. Tam stopped a pace from the darkness and said, "You called."

Answon stepped forward into the moonlight. He was a few inches taller than Tam and had the mocha-colored skin of someone of mixed Pruari descent. His hair was tied in numerous dark braids that were gathered at his nape; and, although Tam could not see them in the dark, he knew Answon's eyes to be amber with the glimmer of intelligence.

"*I understand you have been wanting to meet with me,*" Answon said in Verrili.

"*That's right,*" said Tam. "*I won't waste your time. I want to escape.*"

Answon laughed. "*Everyone wants to escape. No one does. You cannot escape the quarry.*"

"*I will,*" said Tam. "*The question is, how many will I take with me?*"

Answon laughed again and looked at his comrade that still guarded Tam and Uthey from behind. "*Do you hear this? He wishes to help us escape.*" Then he looked back to Tam. "*I had heard you were mad. I am disappointed to find it is true. You have a lot of potential.*"

"*Potential for what?*"

"*Fighting, of course.*"

"*I am good for many things,*" said Tam. "*Fighting is just one of them.*"

42

"*It is the only thing worth doing well in this place,*" said Answon. He nodded toward Uthey, who stood quietly at Tam's side at an angle so he could keep an eye on the man at their backs. "*He does not say much.*"

"*He doesn't speak Verrili.*"

"*How is it you do, Ashaiian?*"

"*I'm a fast learner,*" said Tam. "*How do you know I am Ashaiian?*"

"*I've heard of you. They say that you escaped once—before coming to the quarry. I also heard that on the isle, you killed a man with a single punch, and the guards didn't even know it was you.*"

Tam narrowed his eyes, not that it made a difference as they were in the dark. "*Who says this?*"

The man shrugged. "*It is common knowledge.*"

Tam turned to Uthey and spoke in Gendishen since Uthey's grasp of the trade dialect was meager. "*These people have been keeping tabs on us. Why? There are many here.*"

"*We are dangerous men, perhaps you more than I. You know sects have formed, even between slave clutches. The leaders of those sects will watch the dangerous men the closest. Answon is one of those leaders.*"

Tam turned back to Answon. "*If you are so opposed to trying to escape, what do you want with us?*"

"*I thought to make you an offer. If you prove yourself, I will make the two of you my men.*"

"*Why would we want that?*"

"*My men are privileged. You would have protection and be first in line for food. We make deals with the slavers for the best work details, and we can get things that others cannot.*"

"*Is that how they do it, then?*" said Tam with a curl of his lip. "*They make you subservient by making you feel special? So long as you keep the rest of us down, you will be treated better? A special slave is still a slave.*"

Tam could feel the air shift around Answon. The man had just gone from dangerous to deadly. "*Are you calling me a coward?*"

"*I'm saying you have been here too long. You have grown accustomed to this life. They put you in chains, and you roll over so they can scratch your belly.*"

Answon lurched toward him. "*You know nothing of what I do. You may fight them and try to escape, but you will end up dead just like all the others. I am a survivor. I make the best of the worst situation. If you do not get yourself killed first, you will come to understand this."*

"You have been cowed. You might as well have been born a slave."

"I was never just a slave. My father was the leader of our clan—the Stormbrew clan of the Drahgfir Mountains. Although we are Verrilians by birth, the northern flatlanders think they are superior. We are at constant war with them. When we lose, they take us prisoner, turn us into slaves. When we win, we take their heads and mount them on poles at the base of the foothills. It has always been this way."

"So, you just accept your fate."

"I accept what cannot be changed and build upon that which can become great. I run my sect with an iron fist, and the others fear me. You would do well to please me."

"If you are pleased with being a slave, then it must not be difficult to do." Tam knew he was pushing, but something in the air—something about *this* man—told him it was necessary.

After a tense moment, Answon laughed. *"You remind me of me when I first came here, so I will not kill you—for now. Once you have accepted your fate and proven yourself, you will come to me."*

Answon and his shadow walked away just as the bell rang for everyone to wake and report for duty.

Uthey said, *"What was that all about? It looked like you were intentionally angering him."*

"I was," said Tam, watching the man walk away. *"He needs to awaken from his sleep."*

4

S linking down the corridor, Rezkin rapidly yet silently padded through the shadows. The sun, still slumbering below the horizon, had yet to light the way. After a week-long fevered sleep, Rezkin had been busy throughout the night with tasks he felt should not or *could* not be delegated. A good portion of the night had been spent working on the relay requested by the mages via Mage Threll. Having produced the best working prototype possible under such time constraints, he had moved on to important matters of the crown. He did not imagine the Gendishen contingent of councilors would be awake at this early hour. They would be securely snoozing in the quarters they had been assigned upon arriving on the island, so he at least knew where they all would be. Unfortunately, it was also where he needed to be.

Rezkin had no desire to meet with the contingent without knowing their intent, and he wondered why the strikers had not taken it upon themselves to discover why the councilors had come to his island. It would have been a more productive use of their time than standing over his bedside watching him sleep, a notion that still caused a chill to run up his spine. For an entire week he had been completely vulnerable. An entire week during which none of the strikers, including his former trainer, nor either of the assassins on the island had successfully ended his life. It was disconcerting to realize that whatever they wanted from him was of greater import than his termination.

His guards that had been posted at the end of the corridor were easy enough to bypass. Upon seeing him, they stood erect and saluted with a fist across the chest. It was what happened after passing them that required the *Skill* he had long ago mastered yet still did not understand. With his intent clear in his mind, Rezkin focused his *will* and enveloped himself in a shroud of confusion. As soon as he was past the guards, they forgot his presence altogether. He knew the *Skill* only worked as well as it did because his own people did not see him as a threat. The Gendishen guards would require a different approach.

The corridor was dark, lit only by a broken trail of glowing crystals that emanated just enough light to cast unusual shadows across the wide space. Rezkin moved within these shadows toward the single guard posted outside the entrance to the chambers of the visiting dignitaries. Rezkin had checked that only five of the foreign guards had been permitted to disembark in Cael, one for each councilor. He figured three of them would be sleeping so as to be alert during day when the councilors were permitted to leave their chambers. That left one more guard on duty inside the chambers.

On swift yet silent feet, Rezkin sidled up to the lone guard beside the door and stuck him in the arm with a thin pin. The man barely registered the prick as he absently rubbed the spot without moving his gaze from the wall across the corridor from him. The man leaned back against the wall and released a heavy yawn before sliding down to fall unconscious onto the floor. Rezkin stepped over the downed man and quickly searched his pockets, finding nothing of interest. Then, pressing his ear to the freshly planed wood of the door, Rezkin held his breath and listened. He could hear no voices nor movement on the other side. He gripped the door handle and pressed the lever to release the latch only to find that it was locked. The guard at his feet had no keys on him, so the door must have been locked from the inside. It was no matter. He reached for the pouch at his waist. He would have the locked picked in a matter of seconds. As soon as the bolt slid to the side and the door swung inward, Rezkin slipped through the opening. It was dark in the antechamber. A single candle glowed on the small table across the room. A guard sat awkwardly perched on a chair with one leg propped on the table. He leaned to the side so that the light of the candle illuminated the pages of the book he was reading. The preoccupied guardsman had not noticed Rezkin's entrance.

Rezkin removed a small tube from a fold in his vambrace and quickly rendered the second guard unconscious with the aid of a blow dart and a bit of *hashtahan venom*. After making sure the man would not fall from his chair, Rezkin checked the servants' quarters to make sure the remaining guards and retainers were indeed asleep. Then he turned back to the antechamber, gripping a glow stone so that its cool light suffused the room with the faintest luminescence.

The antechamber was baren compared to those he had seen in other kingdoms, but Caellurum was young, and furnishings were sparse. The short table surrounded by a mismatch of chairs and stools was in the corner, but it was the large armoire made of reeds and thatch that dominated the room. He opened the doors and riffled through the drawers but found little of interest besides a list of supplies required for the councilors' journey. One item piqued his curiosity, and he wondered if they had truly brought it with them. He settled the papers back into the top drawer and turned toward the first of the three sleeping chambers in the suite.

Placing the glow stone back into his pocket, Rezkin slipped into the room to the soft snores of a slumbering woman. Without the slightest scuff, he rounded the bed to kneel before the two trunks the councilor had brought with her. He did not like having his back exposed to the woman, but he could not otherwise inspect the trunks' contents. The lid released a slight squeak as he raised it, and he paused to oil the hinges before opening it further. He pushed aside petticoats, stockings, garter belts, and other undergarments to find that nothing else was contained within the trunk. Once again, he considered that the number of items worn by women yet never seen was absurd and impractical. He closed the lid and moved on to the next trunk.

Rezkin finished searching the first two rooms by the meager light that spilled in through the open windows and moved on to the third in the suite. He had just finished searching that room, to no avail, and was turning toward the door when he spied something sticking out from beneath the man's sleeping pallet. Rezkin reached for the item and tugged it from beneath the mattress. As he pulled, another item slipped from beneath the mattress to clatter on the floor. Rezkin ducked with both items clutched to his chest as he waited for the man to wake due to his folly. He had broken *Rule 12—Do not make sound,* and for that, he deserved to be caught. He frowned when the councilor did not even stir. Obviously, the man had poor survival instincts.

Rezkin examined both items as best he could in the darkness of the room. The second item was easily identified. It was a dagger—the kind one would hide up one's sleeve. The second device in his hand was a mystery to him. It looked a bit like a thin baton with a couple of ribbons dangling from one end. Rezkin might have dismissed it altogether except that he could feel the enchantment buzzing around it. He considered taking it with him to research what it might be, but he did not want the councilor suspecting someone had been spying on him. With a final perusal of the mysterious item, Rezkin shoved both back beneath the mattress and moved on to the next target. By the time Rezkin had searched the second suite, the sun was near to breaching the horizon.

The guard outside the councilors' antechamber was just beginning to stir when Rezkin hurried past him. Rezkin quickly made his way toward a chamber in the mages' wing and slipped in just as easily. This one was not a suite. It was smaller with only a single bed and a desk along one wall. A few books were stacked atop it along with a wooden box. A trunk was in one corner, and several partially empty travel packs lay beside it. It was not long before the inhabitant woke with a start.

Wesson nearly fell from his bed as he jerked awake. *"What?"* He brushed his hair from his eyes and sat up. The light from the window was just enough to illuminate the figure that stood before him. "Rezkin? Wha-what are you doing in my room? How did you get in here?"

Rezkin hooked a thumb over his shoulder. "Through the door."

Wesson's expression fell. "But I warded it—*strongly*—several times."

With a shrug, Rezkin said, "I slipped around the edge."

"The ward is a dome, Rezkin. It has no edge."

"Well, I found an edge. That is not what is important, though. I need information."

"Now?" Wesson rubbed the sleep from his eyes and blinked at Rezkin again. "I am barely awake. Can it not wait?"

"I am afraid not," said Rezkin.

Wesson scooted back to lean against the wall. "Well, go ahead then. What do you need?"

"I found a device—an enchanted device. I need to know what it is."

"All right. Show it to me."

"I do not have it in my possession," said Rezkin before going on to describe what he had found.

Wesson shook his head. "It could be many things, but it is mostly likely an umbral thwart. It is a device used to nullify any mage power within a certain vicinity. I encountered one once."

"How large is the vicinity?"

"That depends on the quality of the enchantment. It is usually no more than a couple dozen feet in diameter."

"How do we stop it?"

"That part is not hard if you can find it. They are usually hidden or placed somewhere out of reach. If you can get ahold of it, you just need to break it."

"Interesting," muttered Rezkin. "Why would one of the Gendishen councilors have one?"

Wesson's eyes widened. "The Gendishen are wary of any mage power. I imagine he or she would find comfort in the fact that spells cannot exist within their vicinity, but it does not really make sense. The umbral thwart is a mage tool—created by a mage. I cannot imagine a Gendishen councilor knowingly using such a thing."

Rezkin tilted his head in thought. "No, not unless they were truly desperate—possibly unhinged."

"Desperate for what?" said Wesson.

Rezkin considered the dagger he had found with the thwart and wondered if he did not already know its purpose. After all, a dagger was generally not a preferred cutting tool. A dagger was meant to stab, and inside the citadel there was only one thing worth stabbing— a person. It was in the final chamber, that of High Councilor Timbol Urquin, that he had the most damning evidence for such treachery. It seemed not everyone on the council was in agreement on their reasons for coming to the island. Those who protested may have been silenced by the majority, but it seemed they would not sit idly by. From the evidence at hand, it was not obvious whether High Councilor Urquin was part of the dissent.

With a word of thanks, Rezkin quickly vacated the room before Wesson had even left his bed. Rezkin had other matters to which he must attend. One of which involved the two ladies that fell into line with him as he stalked the halls.

"So, it is to be just the three of us?" said Reaylin as she hurried to keep up with Rezkin's longer strides.

"Yes," he said as they entered a large, darkened hall that had yet to be put to use.

"I thought for sure the shielreyah had been mistaken when he said we were going to the Isle of Sand."

"There was no mistake."

Nanessy, who kept pace on his other side, said, "Will there be no guards or ... chaperones?"

He paused and turned to the mage. Meeting her gaze in the soft light of the enchanted crystals, he said, "Have you need of a chaperone?"

Even in the faint illumination, he could see the way her cheeks turned pink. She said, "Um, no, I think maybe I don't."

Reaylin was suddenly between them looking up at Rezkin. "Can't Jimson come?"

Rezkin looked at her quizzically. "Jimson?"

Her cheeks flushed this time. "Well, he and I have, um, been getting to know each other. I don't think he will be happy with me going off alone, especially with *you*."

Rezkin frowned at her. "You will not be alone with me. Mage Threll will be there, too."

Reaylin shared a doubtful look with Nanessy, and Rezkin wondered what the two women were thinking. Then he realized it did not truly matter. All that mattered was that Reaylin did not feel comfortable with going alone and making her uncomfortable was not his goal. He turned to Reaylin and said, "Very well. Go tell the captain to prepare for the trip. We leave in one hour."

Reaylin grinned as she bounced on her toes and then took off across the hall.

Rezkin turned back toward Nanessy. "Are you sure you are okay with this, Mage Threll?"

"Call me Nanessy, please." She seemed to sway toward him. "Yes, I will be fine. We are both professionals."

"This is not a matter of professionalism, Nanessy. It is a matter of desperation. If Tam lives, he will be in dire need of our help."

Nanessy cleared her throat. "Of course, and I intend to be there for him in whatever way I can."

Rezkin heard the slightest shuffle of footsteps across the smooth floor. He turned to find Kai stalking toward him. It was not the striker he had heard, though, but Tieran who walked behind him. Before he could greet them, Kai said, "Absolutely not." Rezkin looked at him curiously but said nothing. "Do not look at me like that," said Kai. "You know exactly what I am talking about. There is no way you are leaving this island with only an apprentice healer and a mage. Two of us and a guard contingent will come with you."

Rezkin knew by *us* Kai was referring to the strikers. He shook his head. "This is a simple extraction. If not for Tam's medical status, I could complete it on my own."

"I have no doubt you are capable, *Your Majesty*, but your station demands security. For the past week, we thought we were going to lose you, and now you want to run off on your own. For the stability of this kingdom—this *empire*—you *need* to allow someone else to complete this task."

What Kai said was true *if* the empire had been Rezkin's first priority, which it was not. Tam was his best friend, and it was his responsibility to protect him. Frisha had been right when she had called him out on it. If Rezkin did not go personally, he would not be worthy of any of the crowns he had claimed. Those crowns were heavy, though, and they were preventing him from completing his own tasks. Rezkin stared at Tieran with unspoken words teetering on the edge of his lips. In that instant, Rezkin considered abdicating all of his royal duties to Tieran so he could be free to do as he thought necessary.

Tieran shifted uncomfortably under Rezkin's gaze and said, "What? I have said nothing."

"But you want to say something," replied Rezkin.

"Yes, I do," said Tieran straightening with resolve. "You cannot leave me here in charge of this chaos you have created while you go off to find Tam, who we both know is probably already dead. I am sorry, but I disagree with Frisha on this. You need to stay here and wage your war while someone else goes. Send the strikers or Connovan, if you must. If they cannot rescue him, then send them with enough money to *buy* him back."

Rezkin closed the distance between himself and his cousin causing Tieran to take a step backward. He said, "I live by a set of *Rules*. No matter the source of these *Rules*, they *must* be obeyed. Even emperors should have rules. If not, then I will be no better than the demons against whom we are fighting."

Tieran scowled at him. "I have heard some of your rules, and they are not the kind of rules a man—and especially an emperor—should live by. They speak of ways to spy and steal and kill, and they insist you form no bonds to *anyone*. Your *rules* prevent you from being *human*, Rezkin. *They* will make you into a demon."

Rezkin understood Tieran's apprehension toward the *Rules*, but he knew what Tieran did not. The *Rules* applied to *him* as Rezkin. They did not necessarily apply to the roles he played. As king, for example, he had to trust in his strikers to carry out their duties. As Rezkin, however, he knew that trust was misplaced.

He said, "When it comes to Tam, I am not acting as king or emperor. I am Rezkin, and he is my friend and apprentice. I will retrieve him myself."

Turning toward the hall's exit, Rezkin called over his shoulder. "Kai, organize whoever you wish to attend, but we leave in one hour. Anyone not on the ship will not be going with us."

"Where are you going?" said Kai.

"I must meet with these emissaries from Gendishen."

Rezkin heard Tieran's clomping steps hurry to catch up with him. "I will go with you," said his cousin. "I have been curious about what they want, but they refused to give even a hint. Perhaps they are here to declare war. From what I hear, Privoth was not in the best of moods when you left, considering that you left a flaming sword buried in his throne."

"Speaking of flaming swords," said Rezkin, "perhaps Journeyman Wesson should join us. They may have brought a purifier with them."

"Should I send for him?"

"There is no need. I have informed the shielreyah."

Tieran visibly shivered. "I think they do not listen to my thoughts the way they do yours; although, they do sometimes appear when I think of them but only when you are not here. They were *agitated* while you were unconscious. I worried about what might happen to us if you died. I think they would not have taken it well."

Rezkin rubbed his chest where his stone was supposed to hang. It had gone missing, and he sorely wanted it returned. The feelings of comfort, peace, and serenity that came with the citadel had been suffusing him ever since he awoke, and he worried it would cause him to lose focus. It was another reason he wanted to leave the island as soon as possible.

He said, "The spells on the citadel have somehow bonded with me. I believe it happened when I first opened the door from the dock. It must have been a test of sorts—to determine whether I was worthy, or possibly if I had the power—to bond with it. The shielreyah are part of those spells. I do not know what will happen if that bond is broken."

"All the more reason for you to stay here and allow someone else to go after Tam."

"I have told you; I must go."

Rezkin saw Tieran's jaw clench. He stopped and turned to Tieran. Using his connection with the shielreyah, he confirmed that no one was around to hear him before he spoke. He said, "You know I am unlikely to survive this war."

Tieran's eyes widened, and he shook his head. "No, you cannot say that."

"You do not know the depths of the turmoil in which I wade. Eventually, it will rise up to consume me. I have been moving pieces all over the Souelian at every level of society and within every tier of power. One day, I shall expose you to them all, and you will finally understand. When this is all over, *you* must be ready to claim the crown or chaos will truly reign."

Tieran's voice was quiet as he spoke. "You cannot put that kind of burden on my shoulders, Rez. It is more than one man can carry."

"I have been carrying it all. So can you."

"Forgive me for saying so, Cousin, but you are not a *man*. You are … you are a tempest."

Rezkin turned back down the corridor and said, "Be ready, Tieran."

They entered the throne room from the rear. Rezkin nodded toward Wesson who stood beside the throne then slid into the seat as Striker Shezar brought him his golden crown resting on a decorative pillow. The crown had been modified to include four separate bands of gold intertwined. They represented the four kingdoms over which he claimed rule: Ashai, Cael, Lon Lerésh, and Ferélle. Moldovan, Rezkin's maternal grandfather and the former king of Ferélle, stood to one side of the room amongst the small crowd of courtiers. Next to him was Lecillia, the queen dowager of Ashai and Rezkin's estranged mother, who looked upon him with a pleading gaze. He knew she wanted to speak with him, but he had not had time to accommodate the woman.

A group of Eastern Mountains men, several mages, and two of the ships' captains stood on one side of the aisle with Frisha, Ilanet, and Xa who was known to most as Lus. These had all sworn fealty to Rezkin in one way or another. Other courtiers of note included a couple of Yserria's Leréshi guards; Shiela Jebai and her newest friend Lady Hilith Gadderand, who seemed to be nipping at everyone with even the slightest personal connection to Rezkin; and Tresq Abertine, a viscount from Sandea who had escaped Skutton with them and still had not managed to find his way home. None of these people held enough status to be considered of note at court except that Rezkin knew each of them to be plotting against him. Two others, whose roles had yet to be revealed, included Minder Thoran and Minder Barkal's assistant Minder Finwy, the latter of whom seemed intent on witnessing everything Rezkin did since he had joined them.

Without fanfare, Rezkin's royal guards Yserria, Malcius, Lieutenant Drascon, and Striker Akris, who had been hidden amongst the Channerían diplomatic entourage to Lon Lerésh, escorted the five Gendishen representatives to the foot of the dais then stood guard over the three men and two women.

Rezkin said, "Welcome to Cael. I am Rezkin. I trust your stay has been pleasant?"

The eldest of the five, High Councilor Urquin, stepped forward and bowed deeply. "Thank you, Emperor Rezkin. Your hospitality has been most gracious, especially considering the unfortunate way things were left when last you visited our court." The man glanced back at his comrades then added, "We had concerns upon coming that you might throw us in the dungeon." From the way the man worried his lip, it did not appear that he was joking.

Rezkin inclined his head and said, "Who are you, and what brings you to *my* island?"

The old man said, "I am Timbol Urquin, High Councilor of the King's Council." He motioned toward two of the men and one woman and said,

"They are Henin Vaugh, Mandis Bent, and Liza Rend, the three highest representatives of the majority party"—he pointed to the final woman—"and she is Asha Candin, leader of the minority party. The five of us are here to swear fealty to you, Emperor Rezkin, on behalf of Gendishen."

As the onlookers gasped and muttered amongst themselves, Rezkin watched the councilors for signs of subterfuge. He detected nothing outwardly hostile or deceptive in these representatives, and he was once again reminded that the place over his chest where his stone should have sat felt empty. He worried that its absence was preventing him from seeing things clearly. As he stared, the councilors began to shift uncomfortably.

Finally, he said, "What of King Privoth?"

High Councilor Urquin offered a slight smile and said, "King Privoth has been removed from the throne and … terminated."

"Why?"

"The council was unhappy with his deception regarding the awarding of Cael to you in exchange for the Sword of Eyre; but it was the satisfaction of the prophecy that prompted his removal. *You* are the Emperor of the Souelian kingdoms, and *you* set the sword aflame. To this day it burns. The purifiers have found no deceit in it, nor do they sense the power of the afflicted—"

"*Talented*," Wesson interjected with an uncharacteristic edge to his voice.

Urquin gave a slight bow and looked back to Rezkin. "The council has agreed that *you* are the emperor of Gendishen described in the prophecy. We have come to request that you return to Drovsk to be crowned king."

"I have no time to return to Gendishen."

Urquin smiled placidly again. "We thought you might say that. It is the reason the five of us were required to attend. We came prepared to crown you here."

Rezkin glanced at Shezar who appeared unconvinced. Then his gaze went to Wesson on his other side. The mage's stare was intense as he looked at Rezkin, no doubt considering the changes he would make regarding the *talent* in Gendishen. Wesson tilted his head curiously and made a flicking motion with his hand, but nothing happened. He nodded toward Rezkin indicating the umbral thwart was definitely in use. He knew that so long as the thwart was active, none of his mages would be effective. He figured the councilor would not have had the time nor access to hide the thwart in the room, so it must still be on his person.

Rezkin completed a final survey of the crowd, noting that Moldovan was grinning from ear to ear, and then settled his gaze on Councilor Urquin.

"I did not seek the throne of Gendishen—only Cael."

"We understand," said the high councilor, "but the prophecy must be satisfied. We fear that, if you are not crowned king of Gendishen—especially after the way things were left, then our kingdom will be one of those foretold in the prophecy to be decimated by your empire. We would rather you be our king than our conqueror."

Rezkin's gaze shifted to the man who likely held the umbral thwart somewhere on his person. "*If* I accept this crown, do you have a regent in mind?"

In his peripheral vision, Rezkin could see that High Councilor Urquin appeared shaken for the first time since his entrance. "Your Majesty, you *must* accept. We have nothing more to give. We are at your mercy."

Rezkin leaned forward and caught Urquin's gaze just to make sure he was paying attention. He said firmly, "I have made no threats on Gendishen."

"As of yet," said the high councilor. "We would make peace before that becomes necessary."

Rezkin sat back. "I was under the impression that Gendishen was a kingdom of soldiers and warmongers. Am I to believe you would roll over and beg without the slightest hint of confrontation?"

"Of course not, Your Majesty. You will be pleased with our mighty forces. Our army may not be the largest, but they are seasoned fighters."

"In case you have forgotten, I have seen your soldiers in action."

The man swallowed, no doubt considering how Rezkin and his

entourage had decimated a double patrol upon first visiting Gendishen. Urquin said, "Yes, that was an unfortunate incident."

"One that could have been avoided had your people not insisted on wearing blinders. Drauglics are consuming your kingdom, yet you continue to live in denial. Now you want *me* to fix your problems." He paused for effect then said, "You have not answered me regarding a regent."

Urquin anxiously spread his hands. "We are prepared to accept anyone of your choosing."

Rezkin pointed to Wesson. "If I were to choose a mage?" Then he pointed to Yserria. "Or how about a Leréshi—a *woman* even?"

The councilor eyed Wesson and nodded. "Some would be more difficult to accept than others, but I am certain we could come to an understanding."

"No!" Rezkin barked, pounding his fist on the arm of the throne to punctuate his protest. The councilors all jumped, so he knew he had gotten their attention. He leaned forward again, and Urquin unconsciously stepped backward. "There will be no *understandings.* If Gendishen is part of *my* empire, then it is under *my* rule. Whether the orders come from me or my chosen regent, *your* job is to bow and say, 'How else may we serve you?' The *council's* job is to see that my *will* is done, not to second guess or question or rule in my stead. Do you understand?"

All five councilors bowed, and Urquin said, "Yes, Emperor, as you wish."

Rezkin leaned back in his throne and flicked his hand. "Very well, I accept. We must get on with this. You have ten minutes."

Urquin's eyes widened, "Your Majesty, only ten minutes to crown a king?"

"I am leaving. If not now, you will have to await my return. I do not know how long that will be."

"No, this has waited long enough," Urquin said, turning toward Councilor Asha Candin. "Our people need a strong rule."

Councilor Candin lifted a dark purple, velvet bag from where it hung at her side and withdrew Ionius's crown while Councilor Bent retrieved a scroll tube from a similar bag tied to his belt. Urquin took the crown and looked to Shezar for direction. One of the ictali brought Shezar the pillow that was intended to hold the crown Rezkin already wore. The councilor eyed the small, white creature with distrust, perhaps even disgust. Once Rezkin's own crown had been removed, Shezar stepped back to allow Urquin to come forward.

Rezkin was ready for an attack. This would be the only time one of the foreign councilors would get close enough to possibly do damage. Although Urquin was old, Rezkin would not underestimate him. Gendishen was known for brutality and deceit. Before Urquin could begin, Shezar took the crown from him and examined it thoroughly. Rezkin would have preferred to examine it himself, but this was one of those situations in which he was required to act in the role of king, rather than follow the *Rules*.

Once Shezar was satisfied with the physical safety of the crown, he handed it back to Urquin. The man blinked at the striker as though he had not even considered tampering with it. Then he turned to Rezkin. After droning on for a few minutes about the figurative weight of the crown and all Rezkin's responsibilities as king, Urquin laid the head-piece on Rezkin's head. Then he bade Minders Thoran and Finwy to come forward as Councilor Bent stepped forward to present the scroll. It was already signed by every member of the King's Council and only awaited Rezkin's own signature.

Rezkin braced himself as Councilor Bent reached into his tunic and withdrew a quill and bottle of ink. Rezkin cautiously took the quill and dipped it in the ink. Just as he was laying the nib to the parchment, he saw the flash of metal. The ink bottle crashed to the floor as the dagger was thrust toward his chest. In one fluid motion, he released the parchment, blocked the strike of the dagger, and plunged the pen into Councilor Bent's throat. He quickly yanked the pen away which left a gaping hole gushing warm blood over himself and the throne. Meanwhile, Shezar grabbed the councilor's dying body and dragged him away.

Minder Finwy, who had moved to the foot of the dais to certify the binding agreement retrieved the parchment with shaking hands.

Rezkin casually took the parchment from the wide-eyed minder and elegantly scrolled his name across the page in Councilor Bent's blood.

As he signed, Urquin and the other councilors bumbled over their shock about the attack that had just happened, assuring Rezkin that they had nothing to do with it and that, unbeknownst to them, Councilor Bent had been a traitor. Rezkin ignored them all as he handed the parchment back to Minder Finwy. Their faces still pale with shock, the minders certified that, in their roles as representatives of the Maker, they recognized Rezkin's claim to Gendishen and, therefore, Cael.

As soon as the last, shaky words of the benediction were spoken, Rezkin rose and handed the crown of Gendishen back to Shezar. He looked at the remaining Gendishen councilors and said, "I will send your regent once I have selected him or her." He nodded toward a man who stood with his son farther back in the crowd. "Until then, Baron Drom Nasque will fill the role."

"A baron?" said Urquin with obvious displeasure.

Rezkin gave the man an icy stare. "Is that a problem?"

Urquin's gaze appeared to follow a dribble of blood that slipped off Rezkin's chin and swallowed hard. He bowed and said, "No, Emperor. As you wish."

Without pause, Rezkin descended the dais and left the throne room. He had wanted to go straight to the docks after the ceremony, but it seemed he was first in need of a bath and a fresh change of clothes. Farson and Wesson were hot on his trail, though.

"Ah, Rezkin ..."

"Yes, Journeyman?"

"Now that you are King of Gendishen, you *must* dissolve the purifiers."

"Of course, Journeyman, but I cannot do it alone. The Gendishen are filled with deep-seated distrust and hatred for the *talent*. Even if we killed all the purifiers in the kingdom, the people would still persecute those with vimaral power. It will take time and work to change their ways. I am placing you in charge of those efforts."

"*Me?*"

"Who better? You do not have to do it on your own, and I think you may even benefit from the undertaking."

"How so?"

"I have not met a person who persecutes *himself* more than you. Perhaps in teaching others to accept the differences between them, you will learn to accept your own."

Hurrying to keep up, Wesson said, "Does this change your plans for me, then?"

"No, you must still be raised to the status of mage. The purifiers can wait."

"Every day that the purifiers exist is another day that the *talented* and their families are burned at the stake."

"We must choose our battles. The *talented* of Gendishen are practiced in escape and hiding. They will have to depend on their own devices for a while longer. Once you claim the loyalties of the Ashaiian mages, you will have enough people at your call to make a difference in Gendishen."

Wesson sighed. "I know you are right, but it makes my blood boil thinking about all those innocents suffering for the hatred of others."

"We cannot make all the wrongs of the world right; but, with time, we may cure many of them. Have patience, Journeyman."

Wesson closed his mouth and nodded, although Rezkin could still see the uncertainty in the mage's gaze. He said, "I found that I had slept enough for the past week, so last night I addressed the issue of the mage relay." Wesson's eyebrows reached for the ceiling as Rezkin continued. "I was able to recreate the construction of the device from my previous observations and study of the schematics. Since I am unfamiliar with spellcraft, I manipulated the *potential*—at least, that is how I was taught to refer to it." His gaze slid toward Farson who scowled in return.

"Do not look at me," said the striker. "I had nothing to do with that."

"Were you actually able to make it work?" said Wesson.

Rezkin tilted his head. "I do not know if it works the way the others do, and we cannot know if it works with existing relays

61

without testing it against one or more of them. However,"—he pulled a palm-sized device from his pocket—"I created six of these in addition to the primary relay."

Wesson took the device. It was a round disk carved from wood. The center of the disk was inscribed with the word Cael and the numbers one through six in an array. Each of the labels was associated with a crystal onto which was inscribed a unique rune. "What does it do?"

"These smaller devices are all linked to the main relay. They are, in effect, smaller relays. They can communicate with each other. I do not know if they are capable of communicating with other existing relays."

Wesson lifted the device in his hand. "*This* is a mage relay? This tiny device? How far can it reach?"

"I do not know. If I understand the way the relays work, they should work independent of distance so long as the relay here in Caellurum is functioning."

"Where is the relay?"

"In a room near the docks. I have already shown some of the other mages, and they are presently exploring it. This device is for you. I have a similar one. If you notice, there is a number inscribed on the back of yours. It is number two, see? Mine is number one. If you need to relay a message to me, you will activate this rune," he said, pointing to the rune labeled with a one. "The rest is rather self-explanatory. Yserria and Malcius will take the third for Coledon's use as King Regent of Ferélle. The others will be issued to teams as they are required to leave the island. Perhaps when you return from your trip to Ashai, you can attempt to make more of them."

"I would not even know where to begin," said Wesson.

Rezkin frowned down at the small device. It had not been difficult to devise, and he wondered why no one had created something similar before now. "Perhaps it has something to do with my seemingly unique power," he muttered. Then to the mage, he said, "Good luck and farewell, for now."

Wesson nodded and then stood staring at the device as Rezkin strode toward his chambers to wash the blood from his body. Rezkin had known his response to the attack would be messy, but the shower of blood had been a great show of power and ruthlessness for those witnessing the event. It was worth the trouble of bathing. After he was once again clean, he made his way toward the docks. Farson joined him keeping pace beside him so as to voice his issues.

"What are you doing, Rez? You are *king* of Gendishen now! You cannot sit for ten minutes to be crowned the monarch of a kingdom and then toss the crown aside as you run off to save a commoner."

"I am not saving a commoner. I am saving Tam, and I do not see what Gendishen has to do with it. I did not ask for the kingdom."

"No, but you took it, regardless, with that theatrical display of the flaming sword in Privoth's throne room. You knew what would happen when you set that sword alight."

"I knew it would sow discord. I did not know it would gain me the crown."

"It was their holy prophecy. Of course, they will yield to it."

"I did not set out to satisfy their prophecy. I care nothing for such things. If they see me as the protagonist in their fantasy, then perhaps it is for the best. It works in my favor."

"But does it work in *theirs*? You care nothing for Gendishen or its people, just as you do not care for the Leréshi or Ferélli. They have placed their faith and hope in you, yet you play with them like they are toys."

Rezkin frowned at the striker who knew better. "I cannot say I understand your meaning since I was never engaged with *toys* or *play*."

Farson looked as though he had been punched in the gut. He clenched his fist then said, "You do not take this seriously because all of this is meaningless to you. You do not engage with the people, you have no feelings for anyone, and *you* will continue to survive and thrive no matter the chaos you sow. Meanwhile, everyone else will suffer."

"You taught me well, yet you speak as though these are problems."

As they entered the dock area, Farson said, "You know I am going with you."

"Yes, since I know you will follow Mage Threll."

"If I did not know better, I would say you chose her just to spite me."

Nanessy stepped around a stack of crates with her arms crossed. She looked at her uncle with narrowed eyes and said, "I think he chooses me to keep *you* with him."

Farson huffed. "Why would he do that?"

"For the same reason you stay with him. You care about each other."

Rezkin and Farson both looked at her like she was mad. Then Farson stalked off without another word. Nanessy met Rezkin's gaze and flushed. "I did not mean to be impertinent, Your Majesty."

Rezkin shook his head. "I disagree with your assessment, but I do not take offense. Even so, I chose you for your skills and *talent*. It has nothing to do with your uncle."

"Are those the only reasons?" she said as she peered up at him through her lashes.

He tilted his head curiously and said, "What other reason would there be?"

Her eyes dropped and her coy expression evaporated. "I had better get aboard," she said. "I would not want to miss the ship."

Rezkin nodded and followed her aboard.

5

Rezkin steadily exhaled into the cool air then adjusted his feet on the rocking deck. The Souelian Sea was calm during the winter months with the exception of the occasional winter storm. Although the breeze blew cold, the air temperature that far south never dropped so low as to freeze one to the bones. A decent coat or cloak was more than enough to keep one warm, even standing exposed on the open deck of a ship. Rezkin's cloak was not keeping him warm at that moment, though. It was a weapon, and he had just used it to wrap his opponent's head before he jerked the man to the wooden planks at his feet.

He deftly unwound the cloak and snapped it around the second man's legs. Rather than fall, the striker threw himself into an aerial spin, unwinding the cloak in the process. He hit the deck in a crouch, ready to attack once again. Rezkin was dodging the quick succession of kicks and thrusts sent his way by the first man. Shezar was wily and fast, faster than Farson. Farson had the benefit of experience, though. He knew how to fight Rezkin, even if he could not beat him. The two, together, made a decent team, though. Rezkin ducked under Shezar's left punch, but before he stood in recovery, he hooked the man's ankle. Then he arched himself backward slamming his elbow into Shezar's face as he yanked his foot off the deck. Shezar struck with a thud on his back, placed his feet in Rezkin's middle and tossed him over his head.

Rezkin rolled over the deck, caught his feet and turned just in time to stymie Farson's next attack. They caught each other's arms and spun in a deadly dance until Farson pulled Rezkin into him. Rezkin dropped his shoulder and twisted until Farson's feet left the deck. He tossed Farson into Shezar just as the second striker recovered. A strange pulsing sound reached Rezkin's ears beneath his shroud of concentration. After a breath, he realized it was not his pulse he was hearing, but a summons.

He raised his voice and said, "Halt!"

The two strikers stalled in their advance as Rezkin turned toward Nanessy Threll, who was holding the small satchel he had handed her while she watched the skirmish. Rezkin wiped his face on his cloak and reached out for the satchel.

"Um, would it not be easier to fight *without* the cloak?"

"That is the point," he said as he dumped the satchel's contents into his hand. "If one intends to wear an item, one should be capable of fighting in it. A cloak, especially, is a hindrance when fighting; but with proper training, one can use it as a weapon."

Rezkin held the portable relay in one hand as Nanessy stared in fascination. Reaylin and Jimson walked over to hover over it as well. He activated the rune to accept the summons from the main relay in Caellurum. It blinked twice before the link was established.

"Ah, h-hello? This is the mage relay in Caellurum," said a shaky voice.

"This is Rezkin. Confirm this is a test of the link. We are now a week out at sea. We are in sight of the city of Esk in Ferélle."

"Your Majesty, this is Kai," said a second voice, gruffer than the first. "We hear you clearly. The test is a success, and your progress is noted. You have made good time."

"Yes, Mage Threll has been of great value in speeding our voyage." The woman smiled up at him and dipped her head.

"That is excellent news. We have also heard from Regent Nasque in Drovsk, who is using relay four, by the way. The link was clear. Journeyman Wesson is nearly ready to embark and will be taking relay two."

"Good," said Rezkin, "group three will be separating today upon landing and will head for the capital in Bromivah."

"Very good. I will make note of it in the log."

"Thank you, Striker. Relay one out."

"Fascinating," said Jimson who was peering over Reaylin's shoulder. "This device could change the way the army functions."

"It could change the way the *world* functions," said Reaylin. "Can I have one?"

Reaylin gave a slight pout as Rezkin wrapped the relay in its soft pouch and pocketed it. He said, "These are not easy to make, and I do not know how I would have done so without the crystals at the citadel."

"The crystals hold power in a unique way," said Nanessy from his other side. "So far, you are the only one who has managed to imbue them with instructions like this."

Rezkin furrowed his brow as he thought. "I should have had Journeyman Wesson attempt to use them for enchantments. It would be an interesting experiment. He could use various ratios of power—"

Nanessy said, "It still amazes me that he can do that—use both constructive and destructive the way he does."

"That's not normal?" said Reaylin, still being new to her power.

Nanessy's eyes were wide as she said, "As far as I know, only Wesson can do it. It was unanimously considered to be impossible, but he has proven otherwise."

Reaylin rolled her eyes. "He's such an over-achiever. I'm glad he's on *our* side."

"Let's hope it stays that way," said Farson as he walked up to them.

"What makes you say that?" said Nanessy.

"He's going to Ashai where he will be surrounded by the enemy, and all of his family and friends will be in danger. I can think of numerous ways to force a mage to switch sides. Besides that"—he gave Rezkin a disparaging look—"our emperor never required him to swear fealty."

The others looked at Rezkin in surprise, and he narrowed his eyes at the striker. "That is not for public discussion."

"It should be," said Farson. "They should know what they are getting themselves into. The next time they see Journeyman Wesson, he may be more foe than friend."

"You would know all about that," said Reaylin practically snarling at the striker.

Farson merely chuckled at the petite warrior-healer, but it was a mirthless laugh.

Rezkin said, "While it would be remiss to excuse the notion completely, I have confidence the journeyman will remain steadfast. He may not have sworn fealty, but he has been an avid supporter since we met, and he has no love for Caydean."

"Fear can shine brighter than love," said Farson. Then he nodded toward where their Ferélli captain was speaking with the dock master who had boarded from a smaller Ferélli escort ship to perform the inspection. "The captain says we will be docking soon. Yserria and her entourage are ready to disembark."

"Very well. We will stay the night here to exercise the horses, then move on to the Isle of Sand."

"The dock master has already sent word ahead to secure room and board. He says there is trouble on the Souelian, though. Apparently, Ashaiian troops have been seen in Verril. Rumor has it that they have entrenched themselves along the northern coast, and some skirmishes have broken out on the sea between here and the isle."

"Is that so? Caydean is finally moving his troops. I did not expect him to go after Verril."

"Perhaps you have sown enough chaos in the other kingdoms that he just wanted to even it out."

Rezkin looked at Farson askance. "Was that a joke?"

The man huffed. "Half a joke, maybe. I still would not bet on which of you will cause the most destruction before this is over."

Something about Farson's comment did not sit well with Rezkin.

The striker had previously made his feelings about Rezkin's activities clear; but, in this moment, the truth behind the sentiment seemed more real to him. Without another word, he left the striker to tend to Pride who would be flustered by his removal from the ship. As Rezkin walked, he caught sight of Reaylin and Jimson who were chatting near the entrance to the cabin. The two had grown closer—literally. The space between them seemed to be shrinking by the day. Rezkin had been watching them carefully. He knew the two were interested in each other romantically—or, at least, that the captain had been pursuing Reaylin. Having had the opportunity to watch their relationship grow since they had met, Rezkin was beginning to understand more about the way genuine *feelings* of attraction between two people presented themselves. Theirs was a romance uncontrived, and it had taken much longer than Rezkin would have thought for them to finally fall into sync.

The way women had pursued *him* had been overt and full of promises and inuendo, much of which he knew he had missed at the time. Women like Hilith Gadderand, Shiela and even Reaylin had used their femininity and sexual prowess—or in Erisial's case, her power—to rouse his interest. Had he been less discerning, those relationships would have proceeded quickly and without the merit of the deeper *feelings* Reaylin seemed to have developed for Jimson. Rezkin had known at the time, even if he had not fully understood it, that those women were not truly interested in having a relationship with him. They each had other motives for desiring his attention. The one woman that still confounded him was Frisha.

Being honest with himself, he knew he had developed some concern for her well-being. It was in the nature of *Rule 1* that he should. He had even, at times, found himself physically affected by her womanly attributes. He had been mistaken in the nature of his relationship with her since the very beginning, and he supposed that had confused her in kind. He knew that she would never be happy with him, and he would not feel secure with her. There would never be a time when she would not look upon him with judgment and even abhorrence. He could not understand why, despite that, she still fawned over him regardless of her apparent interest in his cousin.

After securing the blindfold over Pride's eyes, Rezkin led the horse toward the hoist that would lift him from the ship and deposit him on the pier. The battle charger seemed just as eager for some action as he was. After spending a week in a coma and another playing emperor on a ship at sea, Rezkin felt his energy pushing him to escape the confines of his station.

Once they finally docked and secured their feet to land, Rezkin and his entourage slowly but steadily made their way to the inn whose name translated to mean Crystal Swan. It was the primary establishment visited by dignitaries and ambassadors but never an emperor. It would have been more appropriate for him and his entourage to be hosted by the Duke of Regidae, but the man had been one of many killed during the battle at Moldovan's court, and his house was still in disarray. That was the *official* reason for not imposing on the new lord. In truth, Rezkin did not want the bother of travel and fanfare. He wanted only to rest and leave again and would have stayed on the ship if not for Pride's need for exercise.

At six stories, the Crystal Swan was the tallest building on the street. The interior was full of beautifully carved furniture and statuary, and drapes, pillows, and cushions woven from luxurious fabrics were plentiful. Each room had a large chandelier that illuminated painted walls and furnishings of different colors. Rezkin did not speak to the proprietor as he was the emperor now, and those kinds of things were done *for* him. He and his entourage followed Jimson to a small room called a *lift* that transported people and goods from one level to the next like a very large dumbwaiter. It was operated by a young journeyman mage who seemed nearly too anxious to sustain his vimara in Rezkin's presence.

Rezkin's suite was on the top floor, which he appreciated since it gave him roof access. The fact that it was higher than all the other buildings in the area meant it would be slightly more difficult for someone intending harm to reach him. The suite contained a large master bedroom and a smaller bedroom, presumably for a manservant. It also had a washroom, study, and sitting room, each with furnishings, carpets, and linens of the highest quality. Everything was polished, plumped, and tucked so that not a single piece was out of place. The theme that tied all the rooms together seemed to be the colors red and gold.

The thought briefly crossed his mind that he did not care for the red as it reminded him of all the blood he spilled. He preferred the more peaceful blues and greens that invited feelings of earth and nature. His brow furrowed as he considered these odd thoughts. It seemed pointless to prefer one color over another, but he could not deny the truth of it.

Several servants slogged into the room under the weight of the bags and trunks with which Rezkin was expected to travel. He watched them as they settled the items then exited the rooms with haste. Rezkin turned to Jimson who had just finished a search of the rooms.

"Captain, please have Mage Threll and Reaylin tend me in my sitting room when they are settled. We have much to discuss."

Rezkin removed his cloak and settled it and the nameless black blade on the nearest table. Then he went about his usual task of searching the rooms for traps and poisons. Although he had learned that it was far less likely to find any in the outworld than it had been at the northern fortress, he always sought for them. It would take only one missed trigger or poisoned pin to kill him.

"Yes, Emperor," Jimson said as he started to leave. If he was offended by Rezkin's insistence on searching the rooms again, he did not show it.

Rezkin said, "You know, Captain, we have traveled and endured much together. You need not call me emperor when in private quarters."

Jimson appeared uncomfortable, but a small smile ghosted the corners of his lips. "Perhaps I will cease to use your title when you cease to use mine."

"Point noted … Jimson."

Jimson dipped his chin in a nod and said, "Rezkin." Before he could leave, though, Shezar and Farson appeared in the doorway.

Rezkin rose from the floor where he had been searching to find that Nanessy had also joined the waiting party.

"And Reaylin?" he said, noting her absence.

"She left our room ahead of me," said Nanessy. "I had thought maybe she was already here."

"I have not seen her yet," he said as he stepped over to the seating area. "We need to discuss—"

He turned as something began to tickle his senses. He felt that someone else was present—no, not present but coming, and he wondered if it was merely his paranoia taking hold again. "Do you feel that?" he said, not truly expecting an answer.

"Feel what?" said Nanessy as the others looked at him quizzically.

When he turned back, two people were standing just inside the door behind the strikers. A man and a woman—or, rather, a male and a female, for they were not human—stood there, and they were as solid as he. The male was taller than he by several inches. His broad shoulders topped a torso that narrowed at the hips in fit form. He wore a pale green shirt under a highly embroidered, sleeveless tunic. It was cinched at the waist with a brown leather belt from which hung a sword gripped in a brown leather-covered scabbard. The ends of the man's loose trousers were tucked into short leather boots. His chiseled features were smoothed by pale, flawless skin, and his straight, black hair appeared as dark and smooth as Rezkin's own. The male's eyes were a brilliant green, almost as though lit from within by mage light. What caught Rezkin's attention, though, were the male's ears, the pointed tips of which peeked out from beneath his hair.

Rezkin had merely a second to take all this in before the strikers sensed the intruders' presence. Rezkin's gaze quickly shifted to the female. She was only slightly shorter than he, her skin so pale it seemed to have a silvery sheen. Her lithe body was covered in the hardened leather armor of a warrior, the kind designed for ease of movement and stealth. On either hip were identical short swords also housed in leather scabbards. The female's hair hung nearly to her hips in strands of the purest white snow, and she stared at him with silver eyes. He knew in an instant that this was the woman from his dreams —the woman whose face he could never remember. Hers was striking. Her soft jawline defined a heart-shaped face, and her sharp cheekbones and thin nose and lips made her eyes stand out all the more.

Neither of these people had their weapons drawn when he first laid eyes on them, yet they met the strikers' reactionary attacks with ease. As the clash of metal and shouts of alarm resounded around the room, Rezkin felt as though he were merely a witness to the fray and not its focal point. Something about the way these newcomers stood, poised and ready, made him think they could both become deadly as quickly as he. Their swift, fluid movements as they easily subdued his strikers proved he was right. Shezar was swiftly rendered unconscious, and Farson had taken a hard strike to his temple with the pommel of the male's sword. On his knees, Farson blinked up at Rezkin with dazed eyes that were attempting to focus through the blood and obvious pain.

A side table suddenly lurched across the room toward the strangers. Pieces of wooden debris were sprayed throughout the room as the table struck an invisible shield ward surrounding the two. Nanessy yelped and ducked as splinters peppered her. Meanwhile, Rezkin had drawn *Kingslayer* and *Bladesunder* and was already moving forward to meet the newcomers. He propelled himself over their heads with a step and leap off a footstool. As he descended upon the closest of the strangers, the male, *Kingslayer* sliced through the ward. The male appeared briefly surprised but recovered faster than Rezkin would have thought possible. Their blades clashed, and with a swipe of *Bladesunder*, they clashed again. Rezkin's opponent moved too fast for notice, swiping his single blade more effectively against Rezkin's two swords than anyone he had ever fought against.

After a spin, dip, and jump, Rezkin lashed out with a thrust at the male's neck. The male stepped backward, opening enough space that Rezkin could take a half breath to capture his surroundings once again. He noted with irritation that Jimson was also down, and the female was not engaged at all. She merely stood back with a smirk as she held her two short swords in suspense. Every once in a while, Mage Threll would cast a spell their way, but nothing seemed to penetrate the shield ward. The male was somehow able to overcome Nanessy's own shields with ease. Rezkin leaned into the clash of swords, this time pushing against his opponent until the man pushed back. Then he slipped beneath the man's guard and rounded on him to attack from behind. Before the attack could land, the male was facing him again, ready to block anything Rezkin threw his way with the slightest lift of his lip.

"You will lose (*earnest*)," said the male, blandly, as though commenting on the weather.

"I know," said Rezkin, and it struck him that, for the first time in more than a year, he truly *did* know it. According to the *Rules*, he should retreat in the face of failure and possible capture; but he found that he cared about the people in the room and worried what might happen to them should he abandon them. With that revelation, he realized that not only was he about to break *Rules 41, 42, 47, 117,* and *245,* he was also neglecting *Rules 37* and *257.* This gave him pause, but he ultimately decided it did not matter. *Rule 1* was his priority; and, therefore, he would stay to protect his friends.

As Rezkin faced them, the male's gaze slid toward Nanessy. He tipped his chin in her direction and said, "Take her," before he looked back to Rezkin.

Nanessy squeaked and released another spell as the female moved toward her. Rezkin did not know what the spell was supposed to do, but he was pretty sure it was not intended to rebound off the woman's shield back at her. Nanessy ducked as the spell struck the wall and showered her with splinters. Before she could fully recover, the female had grabbed Nanessy and had somehow rendered her immobile as evidenced by her lack of struggle.

"We intend her no harm," said the male, his green gaze unwavering, "but you must come with us. She will release the mage if you agree (*earnest*)."

Rezkin shifted his grip on his swords and glanced between the male and Nanessy whose expression had become determined as if she were resisting an unseen force. Rezkin understood the reasoning behind the *Rules* more bitterly now. If he had been following them, Nanessy would not have been a target. If he had no care for her welfare, her safety could not be used against him. It would be advantageous to call their bluff or perhaps even cut her down himself to show them that he was not a man with whom they should trifle. The male had moved closer now, so whether Nanessy lived or died no longer made any difference. Rezkin would not be able to flee before they caught him, and he could not win against them. The best he could do would be to ensure her safety.

With a nod, he lowered his swords and sheathed them at his hips. As soon as he did so, the female released Nanessy who came stumbling toward him. He waited for the strangers to speak, but they simply stared at him as much as he did them. Nanessy shifted next to him, and the male's gaze flicked to her. Rezkin noticed the shock move through her in the way her body tensed, in her sharp inhale, and in the way she had suddenly reached over and grabbed his wrist with her nails. The strange female's gaze dropped to where Nanessy held him, and he had the sudden urge to distance himself from the mage. He maintained his stillness, though, determined not to be the first to react.

Rezkin watched the male like a hawk as he gripped something that hung from his neck and held it out for Rezkin. When he focused on the object, he realized it was the stone he usually wore around his own neck—the one that had gone missing when he was nearly killed by the unidentified poison. He cautiously held out a hand, and the stone dropped into his palm. As Rezkin placed the cord around his neck so that the stone rested against his skin, the male's brow furrowed ever so slightly. The male turned to look at the female, and she frowned as well—at least, the slight downturn of her eyebrows appeared somewhat like a frown.

After a long pause, during which the slightest movement of air sounded like a raging gale, the male spoke. "You must come with us (*determined*)."

Rezkin said nothing, and the man glanced at the female beside him.

"Azeria, I have said this correctly, yes (*uncertain*)?" A slight tilt of the female's head seemed answer enough for the male, and he repeated himself. "You must come with us (*determined*)."

Rezkin's entire being was prepared to do battle with the slightest hint of aggression. Although these two were strange and had invaded his personal space and essentially defeated him with ease, he did not feel that either of them was a threat, and that concerned him. He knew he was outmatched, if not by the male's skill, then certainly by his speed.

Rezkin had noted the strange inflection the male had added to the end of the statement. The final word was spoken in Fersheya, the language of the Eihelvanan that Rezkin had been learning from the shielreyah; and it seemed to communicate the male's feelings.

With another pass of his gaze over the two, he said, "Why?"

"You are the danger (*irritated*)," said the male who was otherwise unmoving.

"To whom?"

"Everyone (*determined*)."

The male's expression did not change as he spoke, despite the words of emotion he added at the ends of his sentences. Although older texts mentioned the Eihelvanan on occasion, it was largely accepted by modern scholars that they were nothing but myth. Considering that he and his people were residing in an Eihelvanan citadel, he had known them to be real—or, at least, to *have been* real in the past. This was the first encounter of humans and Eihelvanan that he knew of for more than a thousand years. If they were to communicate effectively, he needed clarity. Rezkin said, "Why do you speak your emotions?"

"You speak our language (*curious*)?" said the male.

"The shielreyah have been teaching me."

He looked at Rezkin, his face betraying nothing of his thoughts, then answered. "We are not human (*irritated*). Our faces do not show emotions like the humans', just as yours does not. It is rude to conceal them with your words as you do (*offended*)."

Rezkin said, "To reveal your emotions is to be vulnerable."

"To hide them shows deceit (*anger*)," said the male.

Rezkin glanced to the female the male had called Azeria. She was watching Mage Threll. Her gaze flicked to where Nanessy still held his wrist before refocusing on him. Nanessy's grip tightened, and she leaned into him as she whispered, "Ask them who they *are*."

"That is not pertinent at the moment," Rezkin said.

Her eyes widened. "How can it not be pertinent?"

Rezkin looked back to the two who had so easily defied his guards and defenses. "Because they intend to make us go with them regardless of who they are."

The male blinked. Then he tilted his head in affirmation. "You may come by or against your will. The human mage may remain (*determined*)."

Nanessy's grip tightened again on his wrist, and she said, "Where he goes, I go."

"So be it," said the male.

With that, Rezkin was suddenly wrapped in a powerful binding. His heart raced with battle energy as he struggled against the power that secured him. To his eyes, the bindings looked like swirly colors of light. To his skin, they felt like frozen rope. He struggled both physically and mentally as he strained to impose his own will upon them. His will seemed to catch on the bindings every so often but would then slide off as if the rope had been oiled. The male tilted his head and looked at Rezkin with a curious glint in his eyes. Then he nodded to Azeria whose entire being started to glow. Her hair began to float around her in a halo of white as a giant streak of light broke the air between them like a jagged, frozen lightning bolt. The bolt widened enough for a person to pass through, then the female drew her swords as though running into battle and launched herself through the rent in the air.

The male closed the distance between himself and Rezkin then pushed Rezkin through the tear. Sizzling streaks of static snapped between the currents of a tumultuous wind that whipped Rezkin's hair from its binding so that it slapped furiously against his skin. His clothes thrashed punishingly against him as though they might be ripped from his body at any second, and he could feel, if not hear, the crunch of his boots across what felt like broken glass beneath his feet. He squinted against the torrential currents to observe a plane of grey crystal shards that blended seamlessly in the near distance with the equally grey haze that surrounded them.

Rezkin felt the clutch of another binding, this one softer yet just as firm about his waist. He looked back to see Nanessy pressed against him as she struggled to remain upright, her robes threatening to yank her from her feet. Lightning crackled as another rent opened in the air to his right. As its light refracted off the crystalline faces of the ground shards, something in the grey haze shifted. It reared up, its shadowy form broad and imposing, its white glowing eyes standing out from its near formless figure. The silhouette grew larger, and Rezkin realized it was closing on them.

Azeria moved to stand between them and the shadow monster, her short swords raised in challenge. She yelled something over her shoulder, and the male shoved Rezkin through the illuminated tear. Unable to move so much as a finger, Rezkin abruptly fell into a dirt path, barely managing to avoid his face colliding with a stone. Nanessy, equally bound by ropes made of light, tumbled on top of him a moment later pushing the air from Rezkin's lungs. He inhaled sharply drawing dirt into his mouth and nose, which caused him to cough. The male stepped through the rift just as Rezkin rolled to his side to survey his surroundings.

He first noted the relative silence. After the gale-force winds and crackling thunder that had inundated his senses only seconds before, the soft sounds of the forest went almost unnoticed. Rezkin focused on readjusting and sharpening his battered senses as he took in the lush, green forest of towering trees and dense foliage. The well-traveled path on which he was sprawled led away from them in either direction. Part of his view was blocked by Nanessy who squirmed against him as she tried to right herself. Her long, blonde hair hung in front of her face and after several seconds of trying to toss it from her eyes, she seemed to give up. Her head dropped to Rezkin's chest, and she lay atop him breathing heavily.

"Are you okay?" he said.

"Um, yes, I think. I just … can't move."

"Relax. I am sure they will move us shortly."

Before Nanessy could reply, the male gripped the luminescent ropes around Rezkin's middle and helped to draw him to his feet. When the ropes around his legs disappeared, Rezkin immediately spread his feet for more stable footing. The male helped Nanessy to stand and even brushed her hair from her face for her. He said, "You may run, but you will be caught, and you have nowhere to go. You are very far from your home (*earnest*)."

"I have no intention of running," said Rezkin, glancing at the silver-eyed woman who stood poised with her swords drawn. She breathed heavily as if whatever they had just endured had taxed her. "The restraints are unnecessary," he said. The male shook his head and turned from him. Rezkin lifted his chin toward Nanessy and said, "At least release the woman. She has no martial skills and no desire to run into the forest alone. She is only here for me."

"Why does this human female believe you require her?" said Azeria, speaking for the first time since she appeared.

Rezkin started to answer then realized he did not really know why Nanessy had insisted on coming with them. He turned to look at her with the same question.

Nanessy squeaked as the bindings disappeared from around her. She straightened her spine and lifted her chin as she said, "He is my king and emperor. I will not leave him to be taken alone. It is my duty to protect him if he cannot protect himself."

Azeria glanced to the male and said, "*Confused.*"

The male tilted his head as if in agreement then looked at Rezkin.

Rather than address the unspoken question, Rezkin said, "Where are we and where are you taking us?"

"We are in the *Freth Adwyn*," said Azeria. "We are taking you to the *Syek-lyé.*" She motioned down the path and said, "Walk."

"Well, that cleared things up," muttered Nanessy as she began down the path.

With his upper body still bound by an immovable force, Rezkin's steps felt awkward. He followed Nanessy, who led the way, while Azeria walked beside him and the male brought up the rear. Neither seemed concerned about potential threats from the forest, nor did they seem to consider Nanessy to be a danger. In fact, he doubted they would care if she ran away.

Although he was cognizant of the threats these two strangers posed, his desire to know more about them and his role in their plans overwhelmed his concerns.

"What is the *Freth Adwyn*?" he said.

"A forest to the southeast of the Drahgfir Mountains."

"*What?*" said Nanessy, rounding on them. "That is impossible. We were just in Esk. How could we possibly have traveled so far in only a few steps?"

The male said, "Azeria is a pathmaker. She opened the pathways between the two places to bring us here quickly." He met Nanessy's gaze and said, "You are lucky she is capable of bringing others through the pathways or *you* would have been lost (*concerned*). You do not possess the necessary power to travel the pathways."

Nanessy opened her mouth as if to protest but something else seemed to have caught her attention. "*I* would have been lost, but not *he*." She said this last with a wave toward Rezkin. "He could have traveled these pathways without trouble?"

"Yes," said the male.

Nanessy crossed her arms. "Why?"

Azeria said, "You are a human mage. He is not. He has the power to travel the pathways, if not to open them (*earnest*)."

Nanessy's eyes widened, and Rezkin could see the excitement that filled them. "You know what he is! If he is not a mage, what is he?"

Azeria looked toward Rezkin and narrowed her eyes. "You do not know (*suspicious*)?"

Rezkin considered lying. He could pretend he knew and simply had not told anyone. Admitting to such a significant lack of information would show vulnerability. If he did lie, however, then he could not ask questions; and he dearly wanted answers.

"No, I do not know," he said, holding Azeria's gaze. Then he added, "*Earnest.*"

Azeria's eyes widened only slightly, and she glanced toward the male. Rezkin turned as well. The male seemed to ponder something before he waved his hand back toward the path. "Keep walking," he said.

Rezkin turned toward the path, as did Nanessy. He said, "Her name is Azeria. What do we call you?"

The male said, "My name is Entris."

With a nod toward Nanessy, Rezkin said, "Her name is Nanessy. I am Rezkin."

"Are you?" said the woman. "I heard that is not your name. It was said that you do not have a name (*curious*)."

"You hear much," said Rezkin.

"We have been watching you for some time (*thoughtful*). Why do you not have a name?"

"What am I?"

She glanced over her shoulder again and then said nothing. Rezkin decided that Entris must be in charge; or at least that he made the decisions on how much information to share. Thus far, they had been more open and accommodating than he would have expected kidnappers to be. Neither did they show signs of aggression, although he had yet to attempt to defy them since agreeing to come with them. He did not have to wonder how quickly they could react if he chose to fight them. Entris's speed at the inn had been unmatched. Rezkin still wanted answers, though, so he followed Nanessy as ordered.

The forest itself was beautiful and, besides the path, appeared untouched. Tall pines and oaks were interspersed with maples, alders, and even a few aspens. Sunlight breached the canopy to flit between shadows across the forest floor. Bright green moss covered the scattered grey boulders, and pine needles, and brightly colored leaves created a soft carpet for their feet. The underbrush was minimal and traversing the forest would not have been difficult even without the path.

To their left, the land sloped upward. As the trees swayed, brief breaks in the canopy revealed tall, rugged, mountainous peaks. Somewhere nearby, Rezkin could hear the rush of what was likely a cold mountain stream. The rushing current was accompanied by other forest sounds, those of creaking branches, singing birds, and shuffling burrowers. A jay flitted between branches overhead, and a fresh breeze rustled Rezkin's hair that had come loose from its tie.

Rezkin hoped that if he kept walking, the two strangers would continue to be accommodating with their answers. Although his breathing was partially constricted by the vice of the insubstantial binding, he still had enough breath to walk and talk. "You said we were going to see the *Syek-lyé*." The term had been used by the shiel-reyah at the citadel to refer to him. He said, "What does that mean?"

Entris said, "*Syek* is what you would call a king. *Syek-lyé* is best translated to high king."

"Why do the shielreyah call me that?"

Out of the corner of his eye, he saw the muscles of Azeria's jaw clench. It was possibly the greatest expression of emotion he had seen on either of their faces.

Entris said, "We are aware that the shielreyah call you this (*angry*). What did you do to bond them to you (*disgusted*)?"

"I did nothing." Rezkin was surprised by the sudden expression of negative emotion in Entris's words. It was then that he realized just how unreliable their outward demeanors were. Although they had not treated him with aversion, it seemed they were far from accepting him.

"You must have (*frustrated*)," said Entris. "What happened when you opened the door? How were you able to do it (*inquisitive*)?"

"Apparently, I died," Rezkin replied.

Azeria's gaze slid over him. "The door killed you (*incredulous*)?"

"Not exactly." Rezkin wondered if he should say anything at all, but he figured that if he stopped answering questions completely, they would as well. "When I laid my hand upon the door, it seemed to attack me with overwhelming power. Something inside me responded. I struggled against the citadel's power, during which time my heart stopped. The power was still surging through me, though, keeping my blood moving. I ultimately overcame the power of the citadel, and the door opened. Also, I lived."

Nanessy glanced back at him, a look of horror etched across her face. She had not been one of his close friends or retainers at the time and likely knew nothing of what had happened.

"I see," said Entris. "How did you overcome the power of the citadel? From what I have seen, your power is too weak (*earnest*)."

"Weak?" said Nanessy. "He can probably overpower any of the mages, perhaps even Journeyman Wesson."

Entris scoffed. "Of course, he can. Even a weak *Spirétua* can overcome a human mage (*scornful*)."

Ignoring Entris's tone—or, rather, his statement of emotion—Rezkin said, "What is this *Spirétua*?" He had assumed that the term used by the shielreyah had something to do with the nature of his power. The shielreyah, though, refused to tell him what it meant, as though he should already know.

Entris shoved Rezkin's shoulder and pointed up the hill to their left. "Here we leave the path."

It had become obvious that Entris did not like Rezkin questioning them about the nature of his power, and yet he was certain the male had the answers he sought. He began thinking of ways he could get those answers from the Eihelvanan male. But first, he would have to get out of the bindings. Since the male seemed to know much about Rezkin's power, he wondered if, perhaps, he had the same kind of power. It was likely the same kind of power that surged throughout the citadel, the power of the Eihelvanan. If he was capable of overcoming the power of the citadel, he surely should be able to defeat these simple bindings.

Rezkin reached for the power that dwelled within him. He could feel *something* deep inside. It was like hearing the echo of his voice in the depths of a well—like the resonant drip of water into a larger pool. He could almost hear the ripples as the surface was disrupted. Try as he might, though, he could not grasp it. It was simply too deep, too far away. As he continued to climb the hill, huffing through the constriction on his chest, he studied the colorful swirl of light that wrapped around his torso. He thought that if he could somehow dive into it, like he had with the crystals when he had fought against the demon, he could possibly disrupt the flow of power. As he mentally prodded at the bonds, his will skipped off them like a stone over a frozen lake. He felt tiny shards of ice chip away, but they sealed back just as quickly.

He felt a shove from behind.

"Stop fighting them," said Entris, "or I will render you unconscious (*irritated*). I do not want to carry you up this hill, and you *will* go up it no matter the method (*earnest*)."

Rezkin had not managed to break the bindings, but he *had* gotten Entris's attention. That meant he was doing something right. His gaze shifted up the hill. The trees grew thicker there, and he could not see where they were going. He did not care for the idea of being unconscious and completely at these people's mercy for the trip. Plus, he needed to keep an eye on Nanessy. Although he did not know her well, she had stood by him on numerous occasions, even defying her only living relative to do so. Besides being his subject, he had begun to think of her as a friend; and, as a friend, she was due his protection.

Rezkin's gaze shifted from Nanessy to Azeria. The wind tousled her pure white locks, and the brief flecks of direct sunlight glinted off her silver irises. He thought back to his many dreams in which she had appeared. How had he dreamt of her before ever seeing her? *Why* had he dreamt of her? What was their connection, and did it go only one way?

She must have felt him watching her because her gaze slid to him. She pursed her lips, and although the expression was slight, he thought she looked angry. She said, "Stop looking at me (*irritated*)."

"I have many questions," he said, his body struggling against the lack of oxygen due to the tight bindings.

"(*Frustrated*) I do not have to answer them," she replied, and her fingers graced the hilt of one of her swords.

The motion reminded him that his own swords were inaccessible at his hips, so close yet so far. It was no matter. He had other weapons; and, besides those, he *was* a weapon. Despite the swords they carried, he doubted those were the kinds of weapons he would need against these people. He needed to access his power. He needed to understand it. Whatever these people knew about him probably held the key to granting him that access and understanding.

They traversed the apex of the foothill then continued upward. The slope increased, and Rezkin's chest ached with his struggle for air. He was not sure if the bindings were getting tighter or if his lungs could no longer handle the constriction. His efforts to hide his struggles finally failed when, for the first time in memory, he was forced to stop to catch his breath.

"Keep going," said Entris.

"Remove my bindings," Rezkin replied. "It is difficult to breathe."

Entris growled and stepped forward. He jerked Rezkin's shirt and grasped the stone that hung from the cord beneath it. He started to lift it over Rezkin's head, but Rezkin lurched backward. "Leave it," he snapped.

Entris dropped his hand. "(*Frustrated*) I should take it back; or, better yet, discard it. It keeps you weak (*disgusted*)."

Azeria said, "Let him keep it. It is better for us. You should be glad he embraces his weakness (*disgusted*)."

"How is it keeping me weak? What is it?" said Rezkin.

It was Entris's turn to show the slightest hint of emotion. "(*Surprised*) You do not know? You wear this against your skin, willingly, and you do not know what it does to you (*disbelief*)?"

Rezkin had been required to accept many things that he did not understand since leaving the northern fortress, and especially since that fateful day in the forest when he met the Ahn'an named Bilior. It was his ability to accept and adjust to the unknown that had kept him and his people alive. He did not know why, but it grated on him the way these two looked at him with such condescending judgment. They thought him inferior and, apparently, inept. Azeria refused to meet his gaze, but by the twitch of her lip and the clench of her jaw, he could tell that she was as disgusted as she had said. For some reason, that bothered him.

"I am not ignorant of the danger," he said, "but trust me when I say I have my reasons."

"Do you know the danger?" said Entris, and it sounded like an accusation. "Do you know that it could result in your death?"

"Rezkin!" gasped Nanessy from a few paces up slope. "Please, take it off, whatever it is."

"I need it," he said, and it disconcerted him to hear those words in his voice.

Detritus skittered down the slope as Nanessy slid closer to him. She hesitantly placed her hands on his shoulders and said, "Since when do you *need* anything? My uncle told me something of your training, and I know that you would never make yourself dependent on anything, especially some rock that could easily be taken or lost."

Rezkin knew her words to be true, and yet he was still unwilling to part with the stone. He took the deepest breath he could manage, stepped around her, then began ascending the hill.

Behind him, Entris called, "It will never amount to anything. It will never quicken."

Rezkin did not know what that meant, but he knew that even if he asked, Entris would not explain.

6

By the time the first building came into view, the sun was dipping behind the mountains. The first stars glistened in the small patches of open space in the canopy, and the sounds of day were surrendering to those of night. More than once, Rezkin spotted a deer or elk deftly maneuvering between the trees toward some unseen grassy patch or another.

As they neared the building, Rezkin studied its design and architecture. He noted the concave curve of the roof that came to a point in the center and whose wooden shingles flayed outward toward the edges. The logs and stone that made up its walls were of the same that he had seen in the forest. It had a double door at the front and several pane-less windows along the sides. Through the open doorway, Rezkin could see that it was mostly empty. Although the building looked old, it was obviously well kept. He thought perhaps it was a temple.

Beyond the temple, the slope flattened somewhat, and other buildings began to appear. The first were small and looked to be uninhabited, perhaps used for storage. Rezkin could see that more buildings lay ahead, and he could hear people. Some sounded as if they were talking, others laughing, and he thought one voice was even singing.

Before they could get close, though, Entris tugged Rezkin to a stop. He stood in front of him and stared into Rezkin's eyes resolutely.

"We have arrived at the village. I am torn as to whether I should release you. It will be unnerving and, frankly, embarrassing for the people to see a *Spirétua* bound as you are (*earnest*)."

"Leave him bound," grumbled Azeria with a flick of her gaze. She did not add an emotional inflection, and he wondered at the implication.

Entris huffed at her as he shook his head. Then, to Rezkin, he continued. "The people would think disparagingly of you hence forth. Since you have not yet been judged, I see this as unfair and potentially disastrous."

Azeria sniffed as though she disagreed—or perhaps she did not care.

Entris said, "However, you are a great risk to yourself and to our people. If I am to release your binding, I require your oath that you will not attempt to escape or cause harm to our people (*cautious*)."

"He is human. You cannot trust his oath (*disgusted*)," said Azeria.

Although Entris's expression hardly wavered, the subtle motions of his lips and eyes led Rezkin to believe he was conflicted.

Rezkin said, "It is true that I need to leave as quickly as possible." His gaze slid to Azeria. "At this point, I require your assistance in opening the paths if I am to complete my task." He looked back toward Entris. "I also need answers, however, and your people seem to have them. I give you my oath that I will not run *today* or fight you so long as neither I nor Mage Threll are threatened." Then he added, "*Earnest*" in their language to make his point clear in a manner they would understand.

Entris studied him for a moment before finally making a decision. The bindings abruptly disappeared, and Rezkin immediately took the opportunity to stretch his arms and back. Azeria scoffed and strutted into the village, apparently expecting them to follow. Nanessy and Rezkin turned to join her with Entris at the rear.

The village was an odd hodgepodge of buildings, some of which looked very old and had a consistent design with their simplicity of shape and subtle scrollwork. Other more ornate buildings had been erected around them, all appearing to be of different ages and styles. Some were painted in pale pastels in varying hues, while others were bare presentations of the natural clay, wood, and stone from which they were constructed. Most of the buildings had sharply pointed roofs of clay or wood shingles, and those nearest the mountainside seemed to have been built such that the stone edifice made up one wall. These were stacked atop each other, many only accessible by tall ladders leading to platforms between the roofs and to wooden walkways that led from building to building. Most of these appeared to be residences, and men, women, and children went about their business peaceably.

"Oh, look at that," said Nanessy from beside him. She was pointing toward an area where water spilled off the side of a cliff at least a hundred feet above them into a pool. Platforms had been built within the pool at varying levels to allow people to bathe, swim, and play in the cool, clear water; and there were many people laughing and lounging about the area. A massive water wheel churned beneath the fall to deliver a stream into a stone aqueduct that traversed the village over their heads delivering water, presumably, to its farthest extents.

They crossed a wooden bridge that spanned the stream, passing several others going in the opposite direction. A female and male walking together stopped to gawk at the two humans in their midst, whispering to each other about their strange appearance and dress. Rezkin did not think they were dressed oddly in comparison. The clothes and armor he wore were not completely unlike those of Entris and Azeria, but when he glanced toward the onlookers, they appeared shocked. Nanessy's mage robes were more likely the source of their interest, though. None of the people he had seen thus far were wearing robes of any sort. The majority of the people were wearing shirts and pants that would be acceptable in any human city, although he had only seen a few women in dresses. It seemed most Eihelvanan women preferred form-fitting pants and short tunics.

On the other side of the river, the number of buildings dramatically dropped, and trees and trimmed hedges occupied the spaces between them. These buildings looked to be of the official sort as they were sparsely decorated and identified by signs written in Fersheya. Fewer children were about, and people came and went with baskets and parcels, some full, others empty. The path curved to the left, and there was a long stretch with no buildings. Their destination became apparent when they approached the side of the mountain. An entryway had been built across the rockface, and two bored guards stood leaning against the stone pillars that held it.

Azeria and Entris nodded toward the guards. No words were exchanged, but both guards fisted their hands to their chests and ducked their heads, apparently recognizing Rezkin and Nanessy's escorts on sight. Beyond the open doorway were steps carved directly into the stone. The steps wound back and forth up the cliff face with a short wall on the exposed side to prevent people from falling. After four such switchbacks, they came to the broad expanse of a platform. Atop it was built what looked to be a temple similar to the one they had encountered upon reaching the town. The front façade was built of wood, and the carving on the double doors depicted a massive tree. Azeria pulled one of the doors open, and Rezkin could see that the rest of the temple had been carved directly from the mountain.

Rezkin made to enter the building, but Entris's hand gripped his shoulder. Rezkin tensed, prepared to do battle, although he felt it unlikely that these two would go to the trouble of bringing him this far just to kill him.

Entris said, "This is the Temple of Rheina. It is a place of peace. Do not draw your weapons in here (*cautious*)."

Rezkin had been a little stunned that he had been permitted to keep his weapons. It would not have surprised him to be divested of them, but it only emphasized their perceived superiority. He said, "I will keep my oath."

Entris nodded and released Rezkin who turned to see Nanessy staring at them with wide eyes. She gave Rezkin a commiserating look then followed Azeria into the temple. Rezkin followed her down a short corridor lit by torches with a white-blue flame that did not flicker or smell of pitch. The corridor opened into an enormous cathedral. Similar torches dotted the walls all the way to the ceiling far above their heads. While the room was no doubt a cave at one time, it had been completely chiseled and finished to create a smooth, shining, circular hall that would do any palace justice. Rows of benches curved around the room facing the far end. Smaller, blue-flamed torches were interspersed throughout the benches along with small placards addressed with arcane writing. The front two rows of benches were occupied to nearly full by stiff-backed men and women who appeared to be waiting for something to begin.

At the front of the hall was a raised dais upon which was a long, semicircular table. At the table sat seven men and women, each wearing a well-made albeit plain green tunic, and none appeared to hold a position greater than the others save for the man in the center who wore a golden laurel leaf coronet.

Azeria motioned for Nanessy to take a seat at the end of the third row of otherwise empty benches along the aisle, but Entris tugged Rezkin toward the front. It was then that Rezkin realized all these people were gathered to see *him*. He tried to get a feel for the room, but as he scanned the faces of those present, he realized it was nearly impossible. They each held themselves with the same stone-faced stoicism to which he had become accustomed to with Entris and Azeria.

Rezkin stood before the group at the table, which he assumed to be a council. He examined each of the counselors starting at the ends and working his way toward the center. When his gaze finally rested on the man with the crown, the man spoke. His words were foreign to Rezkin's ears, in the Fersheyan language; but, thanks to the teachings of the shielreyah, Rezkin was able to understand about half of what he was saying.

Entris stepped to Rezkin's side and said, "*Syek-lyé*, should we not conduct ourselves in the Ashaiian trade language so that the accused may address the council with full understanding of the proceedings (*respectful*)?"

Several of the counselors, but not all, nodded their agreement. The crowned man, the *Syek-lyé*, or high king, dipped his chin and said, "Of course, *Spirétua-lyé*, you are correct (*agreeable*). You have spoken on his behalf. Do you, *Spirétua-lyé*, intend to represent the accused?"

Entris looked as though he had been caught off-guard. He glanced at Rezkin then back toward the syek-lyé. "I am uncertain of my feelings on the matter at hand. I do not feel that I can represent the accused with conviction (*earnest*). However, if no others are willing to represent him, then, with your permission, I will provide him counsel."

The lithe, brunette female counselor second from the right raised her hand and said, "He cannot stand trial without representation (*determined*). He is unfamiliar with our laws and customs. Does he even know that for which he is accused?"

"No, Counselor Iraguwey, we have told him nothing," said Entris.

Another female, third from the left, said, "He stands here before us unbound and willing, and you have not yet told him why? How did you get him to agree? Was he too weak to defend himself?" This woman had more curves than the first who had spoken, but the muscles of her arms were well-defined as, Rezkin was sure, was the rest of her body. She looked to be a warrior, herself.

"Counselor Rythia," said Entris with a slight bow. "He came bound, but willingly, to the village. He desires answers and believes we can provide them. I released him upon arrival so as not to unjustly poison the people against him (*earnest*)."

The first on the left, a male with short, white hair, said, "That was well-considered but unnecessary. We all know what he is. He will be dealt with accordingly (*determined*)."

Counselor Rythia hissed under her breath. "That is enough, Shohtu. That has yet to be decided (*irritated*)."

Shohtu pursed his lips, but his expression did not otherwise change. Rezkin thought that even that small amount of expression relayed the strength of his anger. He did not know *why* the male should be angry with him. He had only just met these people, and he was certain he had done nothing to them. He could only think that perhaps it had something to do with his taking control of the citadel.

Entris glanced at Rezkin again before saying, "Counselor Shohtu, we have observed this one for several weeks, following him in his travels." This was a surprise to Rezkin. Despite his constant vigilance, he had never noticed them. "He has not demonstrated the traits we normally would expect with one of his kind. In fact, besides knowing what he is, I have had no reason to detain him (*earnest*)."

A ripple of whispers went through the onlookers and even between some of the counselors. The syek-lyé leaned forward.

"This is true, *Spirétua-lyé*? He does not show the madness (*cautious*)?"

"Besides a slight paranoia at times, none that I have seen (*earnest*).

The syek-lyé's gaze slipped over Rezkin to land on Azeria. "You have observed this as well, General?"

Azeria pursed her lips. Rezkin had come to recognize this slight expression as significant amongst the Eihelvanan. He could tell the female did not like him. The fact that she was a general had been a surprise, not because she was a woman but because she seemed to defer to Entris more often than not. She said, "The *Spirétua-lyé* speaks truth, of course, but I still would not trust him. He hides much, and he is deceitful (*angry*)."

The syek-lyé looked back to Entris who said, "What the general says is true, but it is not a deceit born of evil or madness (*cautious*). He is a trained warrior, one who is skilled in the art of deceit for use against his enemies. From what I have gathered, most of his lies and omissions are designed to protect others (*earnest*)."

"You said you would not represent him, yet you speak freely in his favor (*curious*)," said the syek-lyé.

Entris bowed and said, "I speak only the truth of my observations (*earnest*)."

Finally, the syek-lyé's gaze landed on Rezkin. His attention seemed to focus on every part of him as he assessed and judged. He said, "What is your name?"

Under the syek-lyé's hard green gaze, Rezkin felt that if he were to lie, this male would know. He felt it in his best interest to hedge with the truth as much as possible. "I do not have a name, but many call me Rezkin."

"Why do you not have a name?" said Counselor Shohtu. "Were you unwanted (*disgusted*)?"

Rezkin met the man's judgmental gaze and said, "On the contrary, I was wanted for a very specific purpose and thus was never given one."

"What purpose was it that you should not need a name?" said Shohtu.

"It is none of your business," said Rezkin, which earned him a definitive scowl from the male. For some reason, this gave Rezkin some satisfaction. He turned back to the syek-lyé and said, "Why am I here? Of what am I being accused?"

He did not receive an answer, but rather another question from the counselor second from the left. "Is it true that you have claimed many kingdoms on the Souelian?"

Rezkin did not like the way the male posed the question, nor did he care for the accusatory glint in his eyes. The male's hollow cheeks and knobby fingers gave the man an almost emaciated appearance, but it was his calculating gaze that gave Rezkin pause. He said, "I have claimed only one standing kingdom."

The male glanced toward Azeria then leaned back in his chair and crossed his fingers. He appeared satisfied, as though he had just caught Rezkin in a lie. He said, "You think we are without resources or knowledge. We know several kingdoms on the Souelian now bow to you."

"This is true," said Rezkin, and he could see the confused blinks of the other counselors. "In addition to the Kingdom of Ashai, which I claim by right of birth and destiny, I have formed another kingdom, which resides on the island of Cael where the once-great city of Cael-lurum has stood uninhabited for over a millennium. In addition, the responsibility for several other kingdoms along the Souelian has been thrust upon me, and I now bear the crowns of Gendishen, Lon Lerésh, and Ferélle."

The same male pointed a craggy finger and said, "He freely admits it. He is a destroyer of kingdoms, a usurper, a conquering emperor (*repulsed*). Does this not demonstrate madness?"

"Or greatness," said the female third from the right.

Shohtu said, "There is a fine line between madness and greatness (*resolute*)."

The female said, "But on which side of the line he stands is demonstrated by intent and method (*apprehensive*)." She looked to Entris. "How terrible have these wars been such that he lays claim to these kingdoms?"

"Counselor Leyin," Entris said as he bowed, "from what we have uncovered, he has not yet engaged in any war, although there has been some bloodshed (*cautious*)."

"Did he shed this blood himself or send others to do it?" said Counselor Leyin.

"Much of this blood was spilled by his own hand, although he has many who serve him willingly. One such individual, a human mage, is present. She insisted on attending him (*amused*)."

Counselor Leyin's gaze darkened, but Rezkin could not tell if she was satisfied or unnerved by the news. Without knowing the culture of these people, it was difficult to tell what they might think of his actions. These people seemed to be judging him for madness, yet he still did not know why they thought it an issue, nor had any of his own questions been answered.

"I have many questions," said Rezkin. "You all seem to know what I am, yet I do not. If I am to represent myself in this court, should I not understand *why* I am being accused of anything?"

A rustle of shifting seats and whispers went through the crowd, and the counselors all stiffened before looking toward the syek-lyé at the center. The male was tall even when seated, and he was lean yet muscular like a warrior. His long black hair hung to his waist, and his emerald-green eyes stared at Rezkin over a sharp nose set into a chiseled face. His skin was as pale as white alabaster, the same tone as Rezkin's own, and it occurred to Rezkin that if it were not for the male's pointed ears, they might appear to be related.

The syek-lyé leaned back and crossed his long fingers over the table in front of him. He said, "This is a reasonable request, and it is not surprising that you do not know what you are. I am quite stunned, however, that you are capable of standing here before us with such collected calm and that you are able to make sense of the proceedings (*astounded*)."

Rezkin frowned as he looked at the male. "I am not addled. My mind is sharp, and my bearing honed. Why do you all assume I am mad?"

"Such is the way of your kind. By the time you reached puberty, you would have begun your descent into madness, if not sooner. It is the way of it—*always* (*earnest*)."

"What kind is that?" said Rezkin.

"You are a *Spirétua*, a *human Spirétua*."

Rezkin glanced at the counselors, all of whom seemed to think that declaration explained everything. It did not. Rezkin said, "The shielreyah at the citadel have said as much, but I do not know what that is."

The syek-lyé waved toward Entris. "*Spirétua-lyé*, I do not believe this male to be an immediate threat."

"He is a highly skilled fighter (*cautious*)—for a human."

With a nod, the syek-lyé said, "Perhaps, but he has no reason to cause us harm at the moment. Now that I know he maintains his faculties, I believe he needs to understand what is happening here before we proceed. You will take him to the *accomodis*. You will explain to him what he is and why it is significant. You will evaluate his performance in battle, his mental capacity, and his disposition. We will *all* be watching him. As the *Spirétua-lyé*, he is in your care until such time that this council rules otherwise."

Rezkin would have been thrilled by the opportunity to get such answers, but he had more important things to do than sit around waiting for the council to rule on something that seemed to be out of his hands. He stepped forward and said, "Syek-lyé, I have an important task that I *must* see to immediately. My friend's life is in danger, and every moment spent here or in trying to reach him is a moment in which he may die. It is my responsibility, my life's purpose to honor and protect my friends, and he is the highest among them. I do not have time to spend playing your games. I *must* get to him as quickly as possible."

The syek-lyé stared at him for a moment then looked to Entris. "Is this true?"

Entris bowed his head and said, "Yes, he speaks truth. One of his subjects, the one he calls friend, was taken by slavers. It seems he has some medical condition that, if left untreated, will be the death of him. We intercepted Rezkin on his way to retrieve this friend (*earnest*)."

"I will think on this, and the council will discuss what we shall do," said the syek-lyé. "We will reconvene tomorrow at this time." Then, to Rezkin, he said, "Until the council has ruled, you and your companion will be treated as honored guests during your stay, so long as you remain peaceful and do as you are told (*cautious*)."

"I understand," said Rezkin, and he did. So long as he was a *guest*, he was not a prisoner; and, according to the *Rules* he could not be taken prisoner. He would fight to the death before he allowed that to happen. Only, he was no longer just the king's assassin—the Rez. He was an emperor, and his people needed him. They could not afford for him to die for the sake of avoiding becoming a prisoner. He could possibly find a way to escape. He did not think they would hurt Nanessy, but he still felt as though he could not leave her behind. Escape would not grant him what he wanted most, though—answers —and it seemed he was about to get some.

Rezkin and Nanessy followed Entris and Azeria back down the cliffside and a short way down the path. At one point, the path split, and Rezkin was surprised that he had not seen the second path on the way to the council. They took the second path which led into the forest farther from the village. As they walked, Rezkin noted that Entris appeared to be struggling with some internal conflict. Eventually, the male heaved a sigh and spoke.

"You should know that I did not wish to bind you on the journey here. I was only concerned that you would attempt to fight me, and I did not want to have to kill you."

"Are you certain that you could?" said Rezkin.

"Yes. You are a skilled fighter, but you are slow."

Nanessy looked at Entris, shock written across her face. "You are saying that *Rezkin* is slow? I have never seen anyone as fast as he, at least, not until today."

Entris did not appear to take the questioning as a challenge but merely a statement of facts. He said, "I have seen him fight. He is quick for a human, but we are much faster. He is young, though, and may improve with time."

Nanessy huffed. "I do not see how. He is already too fast to follow, and most people get slower as they age."

"That may be true for humans, but the Eihelvanan live much longer than humans. He would still be considered a child by our standards. We are not considered grown adults until we reach the age of forty, and we do not reach the age of majority until eighty."

"What is the difference between adulthood and the age of majority?" said Nanessy.

"Adulthood is when the body ceases to grow and mature. The age of majority is when we are permitted to participate in government and hold positions of authority. He nodded toward Azeria. "She is the youngest to hold her position. She is eighty-seven."

Nanessy looked at him wide-eyed. "That is amazing. She does not look to be over twenty-two. And you? How old are you?"

"One hundred and fifty-seven, and I am also very young for my position."

"By the Maker, how long do your people live?"

"We do not know. None have died of old age."

"Then, your people could live forever! You should have millions of people, yet your village is so small."

"This is only one village of many. Still, old age is not what tends to finish us. We are still susceptible to disease and violence. Those who live very long are eventually overcome with the *yelishila*."

"What is yelishila?"

"The old ones become overwhelmed with nostalgia and ennui. They are overcome with time. They become tired of living; their minds can no longer be sustained. They often kill themselves or request a friend or family member to end them. It is a sad but honorable way to go. There are other ways for some to end their suffering, but we shall not get into that right now. We are here."

He motioned toward the imposing building that occupied the majority of the clearing they had entered. It stood four stories tall and was built of wood and stone that had been left natural in appearance. Like many of the other buildings they had seen, the rooftop curved from flat along the outer edges to a peak in the center, and the walls had many open windows along each level. Wooden balconies encircled the structure at every level, as well, each with several open entrances leading inside. A short log wall extended from the sides of the building around some unseen amount of land behind it. No one guarded the entrance or manned the walls, but Rezkin could hear the clash of weapons and shouts emanating from somewhere in the yard behind the building.

As they approached the entrance, they passed a well set within a small garden of shrubs and flowers. With a quick perusal, Rezkin realized most of the plants were herbs useful in cooking or medicine. The interior of the building was sparsely decorated with scrolls and torches dotting the walls. The bottom level appeared to be one large room, the floor of which was covered in an extensive woven mat several inches thick. A small walkway extended around the perimeter of the mat, and they were careful to keep to this walkway as they skirted the edge. A wide stairwell extended off to one side. It curved around to take them to the second level, but it spilled them onto the balcony rather than the interior of the building. Rezkin realized that the second level consisted of rooms that were each accessible from the balcony.

Entris stopped at the first room and said, "The human mage may stay here."

As Nanessy stepped up to the door, Entris moved to the next doorway. He looked at Rezkin and said, "You will stay here." He pointed toward the backside of the building. "The rooms each have a bowl with running water for relieving yourselves and a second for washing. A larger washroom is around the other side if you wish to bathe. You are free to walk about and explore the grounds (*cautious*)." He looked toward Nanessy. "Be careful in the yard. Our trainees are skilled, but accidents may happen (*concerned*). Someone will retrieve you in a few minutes for a meal. Food is always available in the kitchen."

Nanessy cautiously stepped through the doorway to her room, and Rezkin turned to do the same. It was not a large room. It contained a simple bed made for one and a small wash area in one corner. The only decorations were the scrolls that hung along the walls. Although Rezkin could not read them, he noted that they held the same script that was inscribed on the plaques in the council chamber. He decided it must be a kind of prayer or mantra, and since it seemed to be so common, he doubted any of the Eihelvanan actually needed to read them to know what they said.

He had barely had time to survey the room when a large shadow filled the doorway. "Hello," greeted the newcomer with a cheerful tone. "I am honored to serve you, *Spirétua*," he said with a deep bow. The male was about Rezkins' height and build. He had shoulder-length black hair and brilliant violet eyes. The man glanced to his right and grinned before tilting is head in a slight bow. "Human mage, greetings." He stepped back as Nanessy approached the doorway. Then he said, "I am Brelle, a windwalker. It is my duty to serve you while you are here." He grinned broadly, and his face lit with childlike glee. "I volunteered for the honor (*pleased*)."

"Oh, thank you," said Nanessy. "That was kind of you."

He shook his head and glanced at Rezkin. "No, it will be kind if the *Spirétua* accepts. It is not often that one of my station is blessed with such an honor."

Rezkin glanced between them, noting Nanessy's pleased smile and Brelle's eagerness. He said, "It is pleasure to meet you, Brelle. Your face is expressive by comparison with the others."

Brelle's cheeks flushed, and he dipped his head. "I was raised by humans. Some of my people are put off by this, but it was one of the reasons I was accepted for this honor. Spirétua-lyé Entris thought you would be more receptive to someone with similar tendencies (*uncertain*)."

Nanessy smiled. "That was thoughtful of him. And thank you for volunteering."

Brelle's grin was broad and genuine as he said, "Spirétua-lyé Entris is a good man. He cares greatly for the Spirétua—all of them. I know he hopes that—" He looked back to Rezkin and snapped his mouth shut. "Ah, I should take you to the kitchen. Entris said that it has been some time since you have eaten."

The kitchen was located in a separate building and consisted of a grand cooking area with stoves enchanted for heat, several ovens, and even a small room kept to near freezing temperature. A long counter stretched around two sides of a large room filled with empty tables and benches. Upon the counter was a feast of fruits, vegetables, meats and cheeses, both fresh and in various prepared dishes. Diners were expected to fill their plates with whatever and however much they wanted. Rezkin appreciated the fact that everyone ate from the same fare and that he could choose his own dishes since it was less likely that community foods would be poisoned. He deduced that the dishes themselves must have been enchanted since hot foods were somehow kept hot and cold foods were chilled.

Once at the table, Nanessy sat next to Brelle with Rezkin across from them. As she had approached, Brelle patted the seat next to him and gave Nanessy a wink, which made her smile and blush. It turned out Brelle was not just expressive but playful and flirtatious, which made Rezkin think the male was perhaps very young by Eihelvanan standards.

Brelle said, "I am really excited you are here. I have not been around humans for a while. I miss my human family. My parents died years ago, and my siblings moved to the human city of Dask. Are you familiar with it?"

Rezkin frowned and said, "That is the capital city of Galathia, is it not?"

Brelle nodded. "That is right. They were tired of living in the forest. My brother and two sisters thought they could make better lives for themselves in the city, so they moved together. Of course, I could not go with them." He meaningfully flicked the tip of one of his pointed ears. "I came here instead. It was better for me anyway. I needed training (*embarrassed*)."

"Why does that embarrass you?" said Nanessy.

"Oh, well, I sort of made a mess of things at my parents' home. You are a mage, so I am sure you can understand. My power, I did not know how to use it properly."

Nanessy cringed. "I hope you did not cause too much damage when you came into your power."

Brelle shook his head. "Humans come into their power. The Eihelvanan are born with it. My control was okay when I was younger, but when I started trying to actually use it, I encountered more problems (*frustrated*)."

"I did not know that," said Nanessy. "How did you come to live with humans?"

"I was found as a baby by a human man hunting in the forest. Many humans hate the Eihelvanan—those who know about us, anyway. Some hunt us for sport. Others gather us for slaves or for other terrible purposes. The human who found me assumed something must have happened to my Eihelvanan parents because when I was found, I was alone. He and his wife adopted me. My parents—my human ones—said they loved me since they first set eyes on me." A soft smile graced his lips as he thought about them. "They were good parents."

"Since you live so long, they must have been very old by the time you were grown."

Brelle shook his head. "We age quickly when we are young, about the same as humans, until we are about twenty-five. Then our aging slows to nearly nothing. I assume that if anyone lasted long enough, they would *eventually* die of old age, since we *do* age. I am twenty-two, so I am not yet done growing (*excited*)."

The young Eihelvanan glanced at Rezkin's plate, and his eyes widened. "Oh, no. You can get as much food as you need. Here, let me." Then he bounded from the table over to the counter and began loading food into a giant mound atop a plate. He quickly returned with the plate piled high and slid it in front of Rezkin.

Rezkin looked at the plate, then glanced up to Brelle. "Are you not eating?"

"It is late—or early—for a meal," he said with a nod of his head to indicate the empty dining hall. "I will eat at dinner time with the others."

"This is too much food. I cannot eat all this."

Brelle's eyes widened. "But you are *Spirétua*. You must."

Rezkin said, "I have never eaten so much."

"Do you not feel the hunger?" said Brelle. "*Spirétua* must eat *a lot* if they are to replenish their energy." Then a look of understanding crossed his face. "Oooh, I get it. Entris said you keep yourself weak. You are starving yourself. Why would you do that?"

"I am not starving. I have always eaten this way."

Brelle nodded and picked up his drink. "That is one of the reasons you barely have any power. I bet you do not sleep enough, either."

"I sleep for a few hours every few days. I meditate in between."

Brelle nearly choked on his drink. "Every few days for a few hours! How can you be *alive*? No, *Spirétua* can go days without sleep, but they use their energy to sustain themselves. If you are to be at full strength, you must sleep at least six hours per night."

Rezkin scoffed. "I have never slept that long in my life." A small voice inside his mind said, *Except when you were unconscious.*

Brelle tilted his head and narrowed his eyes at Rezkin. His searching gaze seemed to settle on his ear, and Brelle muttered, "It is probably for the best."

"Why do you say that?" said Rezkin.

Brelle dipped his head and said, "I should probably leave that to Entris to discuss. It is not my place." Then he turned to Nanessy with a smile. "So, what kind of mage are you?"

"My affinities are for fire and water," she said.

"Oh, that is an unusual combination. Did I mention I am a wind-walker? We could make some great magic together (*charmed*)," he said with a waggle of his eyebrows.

Nanessy flushed and covered her face with her hand. Then she cleared her throat and said, "What, exactly, is a windwalker?"

"It is the power over wind. I think you call it tropestrian (*uncertain*)."

"Oh? Perhaps we could share spells? I bet the Eihelvanan have so many we do not have."

Brelle shook his head. "The Eihelvanan do not use *spells*. Only human mages use those. Our power flows freely. We direct it with our will. It requires a kind of intense concentration and focus that humans do not possess."

Nanessy's eyes were wide again. "That is amazing. I would love to see you cast." Brelle stared at her intently as a light breeze began to circle around them ruffling her blonde hair. "Oh, wow," she said, "it is so subtle yet controlled. I did not even feel any power emanating from you."

With another shake of his head, Brelle said, "Humans pull power into themselves and force it into the form of spells. The power bleeds away, as you call it, causing others to feel it. *Our* wells are connected to everything around us. We use the power where it resides and will it to flow freely. There is no bleed (*earnest*)." He lifted his chin to Rezkin. "His well runs dry because he does not eat or sleep enough. From what I can see of his physical form, he burns off whatever energy he might recover."

Rezkin did not like Brelle assessing him aloud, but he was appreciative of the revelations regarding his power. The solution to his apparent power drain seemed so simple. He was only slightly concerned about the safety of the food on the second plate, but he forced himself to eat all of it anyway. To his surprise, he did not feel overfull when he was finished, and the constant gnawing hunger he had been feeling for months was somewhat abated.

"How do you know so much about human *talent*?" said Nanessy.

"My adopted mother was a human earth mage (*nostalgic*). She helped me to learn to focus and control my power when I was young but not in the way of the Eihelvanan. I had to relearn that once I came here." He turned to Rezkin. "You do not speak much, do you?"

Rezkin tilted his head. "I speak only when necessary."

Brelle furrowed his brow. "You are not expressive, yet you do not speak your feelings. I cannot tell how you feel about that, and it makes me uncomfortable (*earnest*)."

Rezkin picked up the last piece of bread on his plate, tearing some off with his fingers. He said, "I was trained not to have feelings. There is nothing to express."

Nanessy gave him an inscrutable look, and Brelle shook his head as if he did not understand. He was about to say something when Azeria was suddenly looming over the end of their table. Brelle abruptly stood and bowed toward her. "General."

Azeria nodded then looked toward Rezkin. "You are summoned."

Rezkin stood and looked down at his plate.

Brelle waved him on saying, "Go. I will take care of it."

Then Rezkin looked toward Nanessy who glanced back at Brelle.

Brelle grinned and said, "I will take care of her, too (*intent*)."

Nanessy flushed again but did not protest as Rezkin followed Azeria. They left through the back of the building and walked past a practice yard filled with a couple of dozen males and females practicing martial skills. Then they proceeded down some steps that descended between rows of flower beds. After rounding a short retainer wall, they came to a small stream next to which sat a circle of logs around a campfire. Entris sat on one of the logs. He indicated that Rezkin should sit on the log to his right while Azeria sat across the circle from them. It was difficult to tell from her bland expression, but the way she moved gave Rezkin the impression that she did not want to be there.

Entris stirred the fire with a long stick and shifted on his seat several times before finally speaking. "To completely understand the nature of our power, you must know the history starting at the beginning, the beginning of everything." Rezkin could tell this was going to be a long story, so he stretched his feet out in front of him and waited. "At first, there was nothing. Not emptiness, not darkness—for those are something. There was no existence. The nothing then split into time and space, and those were the first to exist. The result of that existence was *awareness*. This awareness is not like that of an animal. It is more basic, more primitive. It is the intrinsic knowledge that energy must have—knowledge of its state of being, knowledge of what it *is*. This awareness emerged as three states of existence—we call them *gods*. These gods do not bear a consciousness, not in our sense of the word, but they are *aware*, in their own way. These states are called Mikayal, Rheina, and Nihko."

Rezkin said, "I have heard of these gods but never described in this way."

Entris nodded. "Mikayal is the existence of time, and Rheina is the existence of space. Although these two gods existed together, they did not possess the same type of consciousness, and within this infinite time, they both became, for lack of a better word, lonely. Rheina began creating that which exists within space, what we call *matter*, hoping to share herself with something. She created stars, worlds, earth, water, and air. During this time, Mikayal was also busy seeking companionship. He tore pieces of himself away hoping to replicate himself. From these pieces, he created *souls*.

"The very existence of Rheina and Mikayal's new creations generated a new state of existence. *Memory*. You see, time and space do not exist in one plane, and therefore, they are not organized into any sense of order on their own. They are independent of each other. *Memory* became a map of what has been and what will be, what exists in one place and what exists in another during specific times. This memory is called Nihko. Nihko, however, possesses a different consciousness than both Mikayal and Rheina. Therefore, neither Mikayal nor Rheina had accomplished their goal. Although they each had created something, their products individually, were still only pieces of themselves. Therefore, they were still lonely.

"Mikayal and Rheina were aware of each other, though, and eventually they found a way to work together. They hoped to create something new—something that would be different from themselves to keep them company. Out of this partnership, they created the ahn'an —beings possessing the powers of both Mikayal *and* Rheina. Humans call them fae.

"These beings possess the consciousness of both gods and so they are able to relate with each of them. Their relation was too basic, though. The ahn'an were conscious, but they were not gods. So Mikayal and Rheina tried over and over to create something as great as themselves but different enough to keep them company. The ahn'an, however, could not change with time because they existed as they were in the past, present, and future. They were incapable of becoming more than they already were, and they never ceased to exist. If their physical bodies became too damaged to contain their souls, their souls returned to Mikayal and became one with him again. Their bodies likewise returned to Rheina, unchanged."

Rezkin said, "They were never truly separate from the gods that had created them."

Entris nodded. "Yes. Rheina began to wonder if Mikayal did not have the answer to her problem. It should be noted that at this point, Nihko was also becoming lonely. Rheina decided to work with Nihko, who could imbue her creations with memory. Together, they created the daem'ahn. It quickly became apparent, though, that Nihko's existence was very different from that of Rheina. Where Rheina was order, Nihko was chaos. The daem'ahn were beings of chaos that existed within an organized world. They began destroying all that existed within the world, including their cousins, the ahn'an. So, Rheina and Nihko created a new world for them."

"H'khajnak."

"That is right. The daem'ahn were banished from this world."

"Did Mikayal and Nihko attempt to make beings together?" said Rezkin.

Entris tilted his head. "It is believed that they must have. How could we know, though? If they did, these beings do not exist in this realm, because the realm of life exists within Rheina. Perhaps the Sen know more."

Rezkin accepted that he might never know, although he once again wondered at his former masters and the secrets they had held.

Entris cleared his throat and continued. "The three gods, having failed otherwise, decided they should work together if they were to create a new being to keep them company. From this union, they created the ahn'tep. The ahn'tep are beings that are composed of the power of all three of the gods. Therefore, they have, in some way, a consciousness that can relate to all three gods. The first ahn'tep were the plants and animals. With physical bodies that were capable of memory, these beings were able to die. *Death* has a very specific meaning. It means that when their souls left their bodies, they went to the realm of Nihko where they stayed separate from Mikayal. There-fore, they were able to maintain a separate consciousness in death—they remained separate from Mikayal. For this reason, Nihko is often called the goddess of death, but she is also the goddess of rebirth. Nihko could hold these souls within her or allow them to reenter the world of the living in new physical form.

"The first ahn'tep, however, were very basic and did nothing to alleviate the loneliness of the gods. But because their physical forms had memory, the gods were able to manipulate them over time. The plants and animals *evolved*. The first animal to become truly self-aware was a birdlike creature, an ancient ancestor to the modern-day raven. That is why the raven is often used to symbolize Mikayal. Eventually, the Ahn'tep evolved into humans. The human's greatest connection was to Mikayal because their consciousness was the same as his, the consciousness of the soul. It was difficult, if not impossible, for most of them to make a connection with the other two gods."

"So they could not access the powers of Rheina and Nihko."

Entris nodded. "I should add here, that during this time, the ahn'an became intrigued with the ahn'tep. The ahn'an even went so far as to breed with them. From these unions between ahn'an and ahn'tep came many great and terrible beings, as well as new races of people such as the darwaven and argonts."

"The dwarves and giants," said Rezkin.

With a nod, Entris said, "And the Eihelvanan. The ahn'an, called fairie, also sometimes called the angelae, bred with humans to create the race of Eihelvanan. It is because we have a greater connection to Rheina that we possess more control over vimara, the power of Rheina, than do humans.

"At first, all of the Eihelvanan were Spirétua. Eventually, the Eihelvanan and humans interbred creating human mages and diluting the bloodline of Eihelvanan so that fewer and fewer Spirétua were born. Like the darwaven and argonts, though, the Eihelvanan possess much longer lifespans than humans because we have less connection to Nihko. It is for this reason that we are incapable of bearing the power of Nihko without the aid of the daem'ahn."

Rezkin said, "You make it sound like the ahn'an are plentiful. If there are so many, why do we not know them?"

"The gods became frustrated with the ahn'an. With their interbreeding, they were disrupting the evolution of the ahn'tep, and many ahn'an took to killing the ahn'tep. The first wars were between ahn'an and ahn'tep, and although few records exist from that time, we know that they were devastating. The gods feared their new creations would be destroyed, so Mikayal and Rheina created another realm for the ahn'tep called Ahgre'an. Most of the ahn'tep were forced to go there and leave this realm. Those who stayed must follow a set of rules. One of those rules is that they cannot interfere in ahn'tep affairs directly. The only exception to this is if the daem'ahn are involved."

Rezkin considered all that Entris had told him. While some parts had been known to him, most of it was new information. "I hear what you are saying, and I will deliberate on the meaning of all of this later. What I do not see is how this relates to why I am here or of what, exactly, I am being accused."

Entris tilted his head up as his gaze sought the first stars of the evening.

"Just tell him," said Azeria. "There is no point in delaying."

Entris sighed and said, "Very well. We should begin with what you are, I suppose (*uncomfortable*). You are familiar with the concept of vimara?" Rezkin nodded, and Entris continued. "You have likely been told that vimara fills a well inside a person and that each person has access to only so much and some none at all. This is true in some ways. Vimara actually fills everything—plants, the air, the water, animals, rocks, *people*. Some plants, animals, and people can use this vimara to affect things outside of themselves. Others can only affect things internally, within themselves. This power is like light passing through a prism. It is separated into different colors, and each person can only access certain parts of the spectrum. This is the reason for the different affinities of most of the Eihelvanan and human mages.

"You and I, however, are *Spirétua*. We are able to access *all* the colors of the spectrum but for us, they are not split. They are all combined into one power. To others who can feel it, this power feels cold—freezing, actually. Amongst the Eihelvanan, Spirétua is the position of the highest authority below the Syek-lyé and council. I am the Spirétua-lyé, the leader of the Spirétua here."

"That is why I am not a mage," said Rezkin. "My power is like yours."

Entris tilted his head. "Yes, but this is a power that does not occur in humans. It is only amongst the Eihelvanan."

"Then how is it that I have it? I know who my parents were. They are both human."

"Yes, sometimes an Eihelvanan is born to humans."

Azeria hissed and scowled at Entris. She obviously disagreed strongly for the statement to have elicited such a discernable expression of emotion.

Rezkin looked back to Entris. "I am not Eihelvanan. I am human. You have said as much."

Entris winced. "Yes, you are both, in a way. The power runs in the blood, so-to-speak, and Eihelvanan blood is stronger than that of humans. It is dominant. Sometimes, when humans intentionally breed for strength of power, the blood concentrates such that the strength of the Eihelvanan component outweighs that of the human."

Rezkin was immediately reminded of the Ashaiian breeding requirements for royalty. "Matches for the Ashaiian royalty are highly regulated. Each groom and bride are selected for the power they wield. My parents were the king and queen."

Entris nodded. "This phenomenon most often occurs amongst human royalty or religious groups since such adherence to breeding standards is otherwise unusual. Most often, it goes unnoticed because the vimara is split into affinities and unrecognizable to humans as anything but seemingly erratic mage power. But, once in perhaps a million times, the blood may become so concentrated that the resulting offspring is almost purely Eihelvanan. Even more rarely, this offspring may bear the power of the Spirétua. Your build, your stature, your sleek, black hair, the brightness of your eyes—they are all traits of the Eihelvanan; but more importantly, so is your power. You were born to human parents; but you are, with the exception of a few small differences, Eihelvanan."

Rezkin was rocked by the revelation that he instinctually knew to be true. Not only was the nature of his power inhuman, but so was *he*. He finally had some answers, though. This explained why his power was so different from the mages and also, at least in part, why the Eihelvanan were interested in him.

He said, "I take it this power of the Spirétua works differently than that of the mages."

"Yes, but we shall get to that.

Entris's gaze was so intense, it seemed to burn a hole into him. He said, "You are not what I expected (*earnest*)." The male met Azeria's gaze across the fire. Rezkin felt as though some unspoken message had been exchanged.

Azeria said, "The problem is you are just human enough to be dangerous (*revolted*)."

"What does that mean?" said Rezkin.

Entris said, "The power of the Spirétua was not meant to be contained in a human vessel. The human mind does not possess the intense focus and strength of will necessary to control it. Every Spirétua who has ever been born to humans has gone completely mad by the time they reach human adulthood. They become volatile, destructive, and cruel. If they are not stopped, the chaos and madness they rain upon the world could obliterate it. It is my job as the Spiré-tua-lyé to seek out these human Spirétua and end them before their madness infects the world (*wary*)."

Rezkin felt a chill suffuse him, and it was not from the air. Was he mad? He did not feel mad. Would he know if he was going mad? He thought of the flights of paranoia that had begun to afflict him on the island. Were they the first signs of the madness?

He said, "I am not mad."

Entris shook his head slowly. "No, I do not believe you are—not yet (*cautious*). It is only a matter of time, though. I believe your madness has been delayed because of the way you were trained."

"How do you know how I was trained?"

Entris raised a finger and pointed at Rezkin's hands. "I see the marks on your skin. You may hide them from others, but you cannot hide them from me. You were trained by Sen."

Azeria gasped and looked at Rezkin as though seeing some beast risen from the dead.

Rezkin nodded. "SenGoka. I did not know what they were at the time."

"That is not possible (*alarmed*)," said Azeria. "He cannot wield the power of Nihko."

"No," said Entris, "but they wielded it on *him* (*appalled*)."

Rezkin's gaze flicked from Entris to Azeria and back. What knowledge he could gain from Entris was worth sharing a bit of his own, he decided. "From what I have been told, the SenGoka were sent to the king, my father, by a Knight of Mikayal. They claimed me as a babe and together with the strikers trained me to become a warrior unlike any other. I was told that I was not a mage—that I had no power. I did not know that I wielded any power until recently."

Entris nodded slowly. "Yes, that is probably what saved you from the madness thus far. They taught you to suppress your power, using only a trickle for minor tasks such as hiding those markings. How do you suppress it?"

Rezkin shook his head. "I do not know. I know not how the power works."

"He has no feelings," said Azeria. "He said as much. He must have been taught to repress those as well (*revolted*)."

Entris nodded slowly. "As I mentioned before, we do not use spells as human mages do. The power of the Spirétua, of *all* of the Eihelvanan, is fueled and guided by our emotions. If you are repressing your emotions, then you may wield little or no power (*concerned*)."

"I do not see how that is possible," said Rezkin. "I have seen few enough emotions from any of you."

Azeria said, "Just because we do not *show* them, does not mean we do not *have* them (*irritated*). We feel quite deeply, more so than humans, I am sure."

Rezkin looked from Azeria to Entris. Entris said, "She speaks truth. Our emotions are the soul of our culture. All that we are and do is guided by them. Our faces do not show our feelings as with humans, but we share them through our actions and our words. I had thought that you were like us—you hide your emotions well. But if what you say is true, and you truly do not feel them, then you will never be capable of wielding your power. If you wish to truly be Spirétua, you must learn to not only *feel* but to harness those feelings and focus them to your *will* (*earnest*)."

"It is better this way," said Azeria. "If he does not wield the power, then he may not go mad (*cautious*)."

"You would deny him the very soul of his existence (*appalled*)?" said Entris.

"If it means preventing him from becoming that which we must fight (*determined*)."

The two of them began arguing in earnest but in a language Rezkin could barely comprehend. As they did so, he began revisiting all that had happened since he left the fortress. No, it did not start with leaving the fortress. It began with finding his *friends*. At first, he felt nothing, as was consistent with his training. Over time, though, he had become closer to them. He had developed feelings of concern, of protectiveness. Then he remembered the short outbursts of anger and hurt that he felt in his chest and the deeper pains to his heart that he had come to identify as loss. There were times when he had been confused by the way he felt around Frisha and his frustration with her constant ability to find trouble. He had even claimed a cat—or had she claimed him?—and he had been overwhelmed with anger when he thought Bilior had eaten Cat.

Rezkin realized that he had not been the emotionless warrior he was supposed to be. He had been feeling emotions for far longer and more frequently than he had realized. The most disturbing to him had been at the citadel. He had been suffused with a sense of calm and serenity ever since stepping foot within its doors, and only the stone he wore around his neck had kept him from becoming overwhelmed by it.

Rezkin abruptly noticed the two Eihelvanan in his presence had stopped arguing and were both staring at him. He said, "I have realized that I *have* been having some feelings, especially since entering the citadel of Caellurum."

Entris nodded. "You have bonded with the citadel. No doubt you have noticed the crystals that fuel its power. The crystals can only hold power for so long. They must be recharged. They are enchanted to absorb the energy of the Spirétua who live there. You will have felt the shift of power through you."

"The citadel is syphoning power from me?"

"Yes, but it also helps to refuel you. A Spirétua has access to unlimited power. Our wells recharge constantly. With many Spirétua living in the citadel, it would be continually fed to overcapacity, at which point, it would begin to fuel the Spirétua when they are low. *You* have been drained of power at all times due to your lifestyle of deprivation. You do not eat or sleep nearly enough, and you function physically and mentally at a level that does not allow you to replenish your energy. I believe the SenGoka taught you this way intentionally. Once you entered the citadel, though, it sensed your depletion and began feeding you power. You would have felt revitalized, calm, and peaceful, except that you are wearing *that* (*repulsed*)." He nodded toward where the stone rested against Rezkin's chest beneath his shirt.

Rezkin pulled the stone from its hiding place and held it up so that he could see it clearly. "I did not care for the feelings the citadel impressed upon me. With them came paranoia. I, at times, felt as if I was truly going mad. I realized that this stone took away those feelings."

"As your well was replenished, the madness began to seize you."

Entris nodded toward the stone. "The *vagri* has also bonded with you. It drains your energy for its own use. You should dispose of it. It will never quicken, and it keeps you weak (*cautious*)."

"No, he should keep it," said Azeria. "Keeping him weak means preventing the madness (*earnest*)."

"Without his energy, without his emotions, he is not a whole person (*despondent*)."

"He does not need to be a whole person—just a sane one (*guarded*)."

"I agree with Azeria," said Rezkin. The woman looked surprised for the briefest moment before her face was shrouded in apathy once again. "I have no use for emotions, and I do not need them. Weakness, however, cannot be tolerated. Now, more than ever, I need strength. The demons are upon us."

"Daem'ahn?" said Entris with alarm. "Then you are aware they are in your midst."

Rezkin nodded. "We have encountered several. I believe they are being summoned in Ashai, my home. I am not the only offspring of my parents. I have two brothers. One is missing, presumed dead, but the oldest is king of Ashai. He has been wreaking havoc on the kingdom and its neighbors for several months. It is rumored that he killed our father and brother. I believe he may be the source of the demons. Everyone says he is mad. What if he is also Spirétua?"

Entris glanced at Azeria then said, "If this is true, then it is my responsibility to find and destroy him."

"That is ultimately my goal," said Rezkin. "It is my mantle to bear. My brother has surrounded himself with an army and all the mages of the kingdom, and even as he works to tear down that kingdom, they do his bidding. So, you see, I cannot stay here. I must find my friend and save him if I can, I must fight the daem'ahn, and I must unseat and kill the mad king." Rezkin considered not saying the last part, but if he wanted their help, they would need to know. "There is also the matter of the deal I made with the ahn'an."

"You made a deal with the ahn'an (*shocked*)?" said Entris.

Azeria scoffed. "He is already mad. We should kill him now (*fearful*)."

Rezkin told them of the deal he had made with Bilior to provide an army in exchange for the safe haven that was Cael. Even Entris could not hide his disapproval over hearing of the deal, but he seemed intrigued that it was Bilior who had led Rezkin to the citadel.

"The ahn'an recognized your power for what it was," said Entris. "From what you have said, I believe you made a deal for something other than what you believe."

Something in Rezkin's stomach curled tightly at the implication. "What is it you think I have done?"

"A human army, even one with mages, will not be enough to fight the daem'ahn should they be summoned in force as you believe they are. The ancients made this deal with *you* (*disgruntled*). They defined you by your power, believing you to be Eihelvanan. When they demand an army, they do not seek a human army."

The tightness in his stomach clenched into a knot. "You mean they expect I will bring them an army of the Eihelvanan?"

Entris nodded. "They know that we are sworn to fight the daem'ahn any time they appear (*determined*)."

Things suddenly made sense. Bilior had told Rezkin on more than one occasion that *they* were coming. He now believed that the ahn'an knew the Eihelvanan would respond once he had bonded with the citadel, intentionally setting things into motion by sending him to Caellurum in the first place. Bilior knew he would trigger the enchantments that would alert the Eihelvanan to his presence. Whether he and his people had lived or died made little difference to the ahn'an. The Eihelvanan would be forced into the battle by the sheer existence of demons in their midst.

Rezkin had thought he had the upper hand in his deal with the ahn'an. It seemed so much simpler for him to build the army that he was already intending to create than for the ahn'an to keep his people safe as he attempted to claim the enchanted island. As it turned out, he had not been betting on the game with full knowledge of the players and consequences. The many warnings of lore against making deals with the ahn'an echoed in his mind, and for the first time, he felt the fool. Still, all that he had done had led him to this point, and he had more answers now than he ever would have been able to obtain otherwise. If he had it to do over again, he would make the same choice. He thought perhaps he was the fool twice over.

"This changes things (*anxious*)," said Entris. "I must speak with the syek-lyé before the morrow. Azeria will see to you in the meantime."

Azeria scowled at Entris as the man moved away from the fire, and she and Rezkin were left alone. The woman held out her hand and clenched it into a fist. As she did so, the flame in the pit extinguished. She said, "Come. If I must spend time with you, we shall do something useful (*frustrated*)."

7

Rezkin followed Azeria around the side of the building and into the training yard. Eihelvanan of varying ages occupied the open space. They appeared to be as young as ten and as old as fifty, although Rezkin could not presume to know their true ages. Entris looked to be no older than his late twenties, yet he claimed to be nearly a hundred and sixty years old. Rezkin could only imagine how old someone appearing to be in their fifties truly was and how long they had worked to perfect their *Skills*. He could not afford to under-estimate them. All of those in the yard were practicing their martial skills, some with weapons, some without. They were all very fast, though. In fact, he was having trouble observing their *Skills*, despite his training. He wondered briefly if these people were using their power to bolster their speed, and he posed the question to Azeria.

"That is a skill that we occasionally use in battle, but it drains our wells sometimes too quickly to recover." She flicked a hand toward some of those who were sparring. "Here we are not using our power. This is practice for physical endurance and skill alone. Entris will work with you to use your power if he decides to do so. I think that would be a bad idea (*wary*)."

"You do not like me much," Rezkin observed.

"No, I do not (*earnest*)."

"Why?"

"Besides the fact that you will go mad and destroy anyone and anything with which you come into contact?"

Rezkin gave her a reproachful look. "Yes, besides that."

Azeria strode to the weapons rack and picked up two staves. She tossed one to him and walked to an empty space, expecting him to follow. She set her stance, waiting for him to do the same. Rezkin examined the stave. It was slightly heavier than those used by humans, and even this practice stave had metal caps on the ends. He spun it, testing the balance, then nodded toward her.

Azeria did not delay. She stepped forward and swung directly at his head. She said, "First of all, I do not like humans."

Rezkin dodged and swung his stave toward her legs. She jumped over it with ease then twisted hers toward his shoulder before shifting her grip and thrusting the opposite end toward his sternum. Rezkin blocked the attempted strike at the same time as he spun, bringing the stave around toward the back of her head. He said, "Entris says I am not human."

Azeria ducked and swept her stave backward as she turned. Rezkin rolled under the swipe but before he could recover, her stave smacked him in the back of the head. He blocked the next strike, but her stave moved faster than he could anticipate straight into his abdomen. He doubled over but dropped to the ground before the other end connected with his back. He rolled and recovered his feet just in time to avoid another attempt at his head. He swung his own weapon, striking one of Azeria's feet. She easily recovered, dancing over the stave as if the moves were choreographed. Her movements became more rapid, spinning in a blur, and before Rezkin knew it, he was on his back with the metal cap of the stave pressed into his throat.

"You are human enough," she spat as she looked down on him.

Rezkin was surprised but not shocked. It had been a long time since he had been beaten, but before he had only human opponents to fight. The Eihelvanan were much faster than anyone he had ever fought, including the SenGoka. As she stepped back, he got to his feet.

"I bet you three *saboli* that he can be faster," said a male who approached from behind Azeria.

Azeria turned and bowed. "Elder Jao'hwin," she said respectfully. She glanced at Rezkin, the scorn evident in her fiery gaze if nothing else. "I respectfully disagree," she said through clenched teeth.

Jao'hwin nodded once and said, "Then you take the bet?"

"I do (*skeptical*)."

Jao'hwin held out his hand for her stave. As she handed over the weapon, he looked at Rezkin. "It is only obvious by your ears," the man said thoughtfully. "In all other respects, you look to be one of us (*earnest*)."

Rezkin said, "I have never before been told I was slow—not since I was a small-man. You believe I can be faster?"

"Your problem is you have not been challenged," said Jao'hwin. "You will only become fast enough to defeat your opponents, and your opponents have been human (*reassuring*). I will teach you a sequence of moves. Then we will do them together."

The elder's stave slapped against Rezkin's indicating that he should set himself. The man swung the stave over and around, forward and in reverse. It was a dance filled with smooth shifts and abrupt stops. When he was finished, Rezkin nodded and performed the same series of moves. Jao'hwin gave him a nod of approval then moved to stand across from Rezkin. They then began the dance together with Rezkin performing the assigned moves and Jao'hwin answering them. Their staves clacked together and slid off each other every so often. When they had completed the moves, they moved seamlessly into the pattern again. Round after round they performed the same sequence, each time getting faster.

It was not long before Rezkin felt himself pushing to meet the man's next move. He began to breathe heavier, and his muscles strained to keep pace. There was no time for talk or question, no time for thought or doubt. Jao'hwin's movements accelerated to nearly a blur, and Rezkin met each one with extreme effort. At the very instant that Rezkin felt overwhelmed, the butt of the elder's stave smashed

into his sternum thrusting him several feet be
ground.

Jao'hwin and Azeria kept their distance
Although the pain lancing through his chest wa
not show his discomfort. It was not difficult to
the *Skills* necessary to defeat him. It had not beer
completed his training. He was used to the mas
him suffer. Only now, Rezkin had little to no o
instructor's intentions. There was no agree
between himself and any of the Eihelvanan, and
so far was for the strict purpose of testing his san

The elder looked to Azeria and held out h
took something out of a pouch at her belt be
"He was not *that* much faster," she said, and it
the lie in her words.

Jao'hwin barked a laugh that jarred Rezkin.
sound the Eihelvanan were familiar with, bu
have some sense of humor. "If you push him, I
He is more Eihelvanan than you think, Azeria

The elder inhaled deeply, then he and ev
abruptly began replacing their weapons in
toward the building. Rezkin had not seen
something had alerted them of the time. T
sweet and smokey tickled his senses.

Azeria smirked. "It is sweetwood. The kitch
is time for dinner. Come."

"I ate only a couple of hours ago," said Rezk

She shook her head. "You can eat again. E
weakness unacceptable. Until I am told othe
strengthening you (*irritated*)."

As they walked toward the dining hall, R
general, yes?"

"I am."

"But you answer to Entris?"

and no. He is Spirétua. I am not. Therefore, he is of a higher

d *I* am Spirétua."

gaze flicked to him, and by the way her jaw clenched, he could
did not like being reminded of the fact. "Yes, but you are
. Human Spirétua must be killed (*determined*)." He could tell by
t in her gaze that she meant what she said. He noted her intent
continued. "Entris is the Spirétua-lyé. He is responsible for the
ing and actions of all of the Spirétua, including you. Until the
é orders your death, Entris will insist on assisting you in
ing the greatest you can be.

n the other hand, have a different task. I am a pathmaker. It is a
ility, and the few pathbuilders are all generals. We lead our
through the paths between realms. These paths are dangerous,
angry beings, some of which are lost between realms and
that live within the paths themselves."

e monster in the mist," Rezkin said, remembering the shadowy
that had targeted them in the paths after Entris and Azeria had
im.

ery traverse has the potential to become a battle, a war even.
we are in the paths, *I* am the leader."

the time Azeria had finished her explanation, she and Rezkin
ched the front of the line along the counter that held the feast.
shes from earlier had been exchanged with different ones, and
was actually looking forward to trying some of the new
. He filled his plate, but every so often Azeria would glance his
d say *more*, encouraging him to claim more food. She did not
own plate so full, however.

kin found a seat at a table with his back toward the wall so that
ld not be surrounded on *all* sides. To his surprise, Azeria sat
across from him, and after a few minutes, Nanessy and Brelle
them. Brelle sat close to Nanessy so that their shoulders were
ng, and Nanessy seemed to be trying to find a way to put space
n them. He smiled at her and said, "Are you enjoying your visit
s?"

She looked at him, so close, and flushed then glanced toward Rezkin. "Um, it is difficult to *enjoy* my time here knowing that my emperor's life is in jeopardy."

Brelle's brow rose, and he said, "Who is your emperor and why is his life in jeopardy?"

Nanessy frowned at him, then pointed to Rezkin. "*He* is my emperor, and his life is in jeopardy because *your* people want to *kill* him."

Brelle's eyes were wide as he looked toward Rezkin. "*You're* an emperor? Of what empire?"

Nanessy said, "He named it the Cimmerian Empire, but most people just call it the Souelian Empire."

With his brow furrowed, Brelle said, "*Souelian?*" His eyes lit up. "That's the sea to the northwest on the other side of the Drahgfir Mountains." He grinned at Azeria and said, "See, General, I was paying attention to my lessons (*earnest*)." Then his brow furrowed again, and he said, "I don't remember an emperor ruling over it, though."

Azeria said, "That is because one did not." She poked her fork pointedly toward Rezkin. "Until now."

Brelle's eyes were wide as he said, "And you've stolen him?"

Azeria glanced toward Entris who had just entered the dining hall and was heading their way. "He has been raining terror on every kingdom along the sea for months, consuming all that he can into his empire. If that does not show madness, I do not know what does (*frustrated*)."

Rezkin continued eating his food as the others talked around him *about* him. He pretended to ignore them, but everything they said could have some bearing on the case against him. Entris gave Azeria a warning look before going to fill his plates.

Brelle said, "You think he's one of *those* Spirétua? Like the humans?"

Azeria scoffed. "He *is* human. Do you not see his ugly, stunted ears?"

Brelle shrugged. "I thought maybe he was just deformed."

"Hey!" said Nanessy with a brush of her fingers over her ears. "We are not ugly *or* deformed. These are how human ears are supposed to look."

Brelle grinned back at Nanessy. "I did not think *you* were deformed. You are obviously human, and I think your small ears are cute (*interested*)." This last he said with a wink.

"Of course, you would think so," said Azeria. "You were raised by *humans*. You may as well have been raised by livestock."

"Azeria, do not antagonize the boy," said Entris as he came to sit beside her.

"Boy?" said Nanessy. She looked at Brelle. "How old *are* you?"

He grinned around a mouthful of vegetables. "I thought I told you. I'm twenty-two."

"Right," said Nanessy, looking at him doubtfully. "I forgot. You look older."

Entris said, "That is still a youth to the Eihelvanan."

Rezkin said, "I recently turned twenty."

"You had a birthday?" said Nanessy with alarm. "We should have celebrated!"

Rezkin frowned at her then turned back to Entris and continued. "I am not a youth or a small-man."

"No," said Entris. "You likely matured at a human rate, perhaps faster due to your power. It is difficult to say what will happen with your aging process since most Spirétua like you will have been killed by your age or close enough. It is presumed that your aging process will soon slow as it does with the Eihelvanan. No one knows how long you will live, but it could be hundreds or thousands of years. You may not age at all beyond your middle years if you are very much like us (*doubtful*)."

Nanessy, her eyes gone wide, "Wait, why is he going to live forever? This is because of his power?"

"No, it is because he his Eihelvanan," said Entris.

"He is *human*," growled Azeria.

"He could live forever?" said Nanessy, glancing between them.

Entris shrugged. "It is possible if he does not succumb to *yelishila*."

124

"You said *yelishila* is basically when your people become tired of living?"

"More or less. We do not speak of this (*cautious*)."

"Oh, I am sorry."

Entris tilted his head then gave her the slightest smile. Nanessy appeared pleased with the expression, which caused Brelle's expression to fall. He quickly drew her attention back to himself as he began talking about his accomplishments in his lessons. Nanessy nodded politely and maintained the conversation, but Rezkin could tell she did not feel the same enthusiasm as the boy.

He felt another gaze on him as he drew his own attention from the mage. He met Azeria's gaze, apparently startling her before she quickly turned her attention back to her food. Rezkin glanced down at his own plate and was surprised to find that he had consumed every morsel. He had eaten more over the past few hours than he ever had at one time, yet he did not feel overfull.

He looked up at Entris. "You spoke with the syek-lyé?"

"I did."

"Will he reconsider this *trial?*"

Entris glanced at him then dropped his gaze back to his plate. "We will reconvene tomorrow as planned. He will reveal to us then what he has decided. Until then, you must rest. I have watched you. You do not get enough sleep."

"Besides the time he was out from the *mirandra* (*amused*)," said Azeria.

"Mirandra?" said Rezkin. "Was that the poison with which I was shot?"

Azeria smirked, but Entris said, "It was not a poison, not exactly. It was a test. Your energy was so depleted we could not tell if you were truly Spirétua. If you had not been Spirétua, though, the mirandra would not have affected you."

"So your *test* nearly killed me because I *am* Spirétua?"

"No, it nearly killed you because you were so depleted (*repulsed*). If you had been at full capacity, it would have made you mildly sick for a few days. This shows how deeply weakened you are. It is why I took the vagri from you." Rezkin patted the stone that rested against his chest. "It would have killed you had you continued wearing it during the ailment. I did not like wearing it for you, but since you insist on powering it, I could not in good conscience allow it to suffer your temporary loss (*irritated*)."

"It can suffer? What is it?" said Rezkin.

"You truly do not know (*surprised*)? Yet you wear it anyway." Entris shook his head but whether it was in disapproval or disbelief, Rezkin could not tell. "Long ago, the Eihelvanan were many, as were our enemies. The ahn'tep descendants of the ahn'an and daem'ahn battled for land, for resources, for the very right to exist. Some formed alliances. One such alliance was between the Eihelvanan and drahg'ahn."

"Did you say dragon?" replied Nanessy. "But dragons are not real."

"They are real (*earnest*)," said Entris. "Their race was spawned from daem'ahn and ahn'tep during the time before the daem'ahn were cast out of this realm. Our race and theirs were allied not just against other ahn'tep but against certain ahn'an who would see us eradicated as well."

"What does this have to do with the vagri?" said Rezkin.

"The alliance between Eihelvanan and drahg'ahn was formed by virtue of the bonds between individuals of the two species. A member of the Eihelvanan, a rhai warrior, would initiate a bond with a drahg'ahn by feeding it power during its formation within the egg, the vagri, and throughout its youth. This bond joined the rhai and drahg'ahn in a way that could not be broken, even in death. It was said that should one die before the other, the soul of the deceased would join with that of the living."

Rezkin held the small stone, no larger than his thumb, up between them. "You are saying *this* is a dragon egg?"

Entris nodded. "Yes, at least, it once was. This one was likely preserved by the waning power of the citadel, but after twelve-hundred years there was not enough vimara to sustain it. They are usually at least ten times as big when they are laid. They grow larger with an influx of vimara either from their mother or a rhai warrior.

This one is small and starved. It will never quicken. You have been bonding with it since you acquired it, yet it is merely a parasite feeding off your vimara and providing nothing in return. You should allow it to die."

Rezkin stared at the vagri in wonder. He would never have guessed that this small stone contained the life of a dragon. Entris claimed the vagri gave him nothing in return, but Rezkin did not think that to be true. He had found much comfort in the relief it had given him from the soothing sensation at the citadel.

Entris stood from the table and collected his plate. "We shall discuss this more another time. For now, you should rest (*earnest*). I warn you, do not skulk about tonight searching for an escape. You will not succeed, and you need the sleep if you are to regain any strength in spite of the vagri (*irritated*)."

Entris and Azeria both abandoned the table leaving Rezkin, Nanessy, and Brelle alone. Nanessy looked at Rezkin and said, "It is so hard to read them. Almost no one here shows facial expressions."

Rezkin was reminded that Nanessy could not understand the Fersheyan words of emotion the Eihelvanan peppered within their conversations. He glanced to Brelle and abruptly realized that was probably the reason the youth was so expressive. Brelle was considering Nanessy's needs. Just as Entris and even, at times, Azeria had been concerned with his own. The Eihelvanan often had a strange way of showing it, but he thought their actions demonstrated a true desire to help others. The question that concerned him was *why?*

When Brelle collected their empty plates and left the table to dispose of them, Nanessy scooted over on the bench toward Rezkin. He stiffened at her close proximity. She said, "I am glad I am here with you. You cannot imagine how worried I was when it became clear they intended to take you."

"There are things in this world that I cannot defeat," he said, turning to meet her worried gaze. "I do not believe they are one of them. I may not presently have the *Skills*, but I will."

"But that is just it, is it not? If they truly wanted you dead, you would be. Do you think you could escape?"

"Perhaps, perhaps not. But rest assured that I will not leave without you."

She shifted, but he did not sense that she intended him harm. Her warm hand covered his own. "Maybe it would have been better if I had not come, but I am still glad I did." Her cheeks turned pink as she said, "I feel better when I am near you."

"It's his power."

Nanessy jumped and snatched her hand back as she turned to see a disgruntled Brelle staring down at them. "W-what?"

Brelle frowned as his gaze shifted to Rezkin, then his expression softened again as he looked back at Nanessy. "Human mages and other Eihelvanan are often drawn by the power of Spirétua. They inspire loyalty in us"—his expression soured again—"sometimes even attraction."

Nanessy's eyes widened as her blush deepened. "You think I am loyal to him because of his power?" She shook her head vigorously. "No, there are so many more reasons that I accept him as my emperor."

Brelle crossed his arms. "Are you sure about that? Maybe you have found other reasons to justify your attraction."

"I am not—You know what? It does not matter." She stood from the bench appearing flustered. "I am going to bed." Then she turned and left the dining hall without a backward glance.

Rezkin frowned and looked at Brelle. "She is *attracted* to me?"

Brelle looked at him dumbfounded. "With all due respect, Spirétua, are you blind?"

Rezkin stood from his seat. "I can see that *you* are attracted to *her*."

Brelle shed his irritation like it was water as a huge smile crossed his face. "I have made no attempt to hide it. She is a beautiful woman, and I enjoy her company. I am eager to experience her power."

"Her power?"

Brelle scratched the back of his head, appearing suddenly bashful. "That is a way of saying I'm interested in her. We, um, share power when we are intimate."

It occurred to Rezkin that he did not know much of how vimara suffused Eihelvanan culture. He said, "Do all Eihelvanan possess power?"

With surprise, Brelle said, "Of course. It is who we are."

Rezkin pondered this as he left the dining hall heading for his room. Life amongst a people steeped in power had to be very different from what he was used to, especially since he had been trained with the understanding that he possessed no power. The truth, though, was presently threatening his existence, and he was tempted to do exactly what he had been warned against. Although he was not necessarily interested in finding an escape, he was hopeful to discover anything that might be pertinent for his self-defense before the council the following day.

Rezkin had no change of clothes or armor, and he could not easily skulk about with his swords slapping at his hips. The Eihelvanan were faster and more agile than humans, but they did not pose an immediate threat to him since they currently wanted him alive. Therefore, he elected for stealth over armament. Once back in his room, he removed his sword belt, armor, and tunic leaving him with only his shirt, pants, and boots plus a plethora of knives hidden about his person. He would have preferred to have been dressed in darker colors for the night, but the green and brown he wore would still blend in with the forest.

He did not bother to hide his passage as he left the entry to the stairs that led to his room and rounded the building. Surveilling the area, he saw that most of the outbuildings were dark, and few people were out and about. It was odd to him that an entire training compound would sleep so early in the evening. Apparently, few stayed awake after the evening meal, or, at least, that was what he was intended to believe. He had not ventured into their rooms to confirm that they were truly abed after all.

Through a break in the trees, Rezkin could see the flickering of small lights. He silently stalked down a narrow woodland path while maintaining his surveillance of the forest. A rustling in the bushes a few paces to his right sounded like a small forest creature. A deer grazed in the underbrush to his left. Rezkin was satisfied that she did not take notice of his passage. Several dozen yards down the pathway, Rezkin came to a small pond. Tiny little rafts containing illuminated candles enveloped in leaves shaped to look like flowers sailed placidly across its smooth surface. The dark water reflected the tiny flames doubling their effect.

A squat building no larger than his assigned room in the *accomodis* sat at the edge of the pond. From inside, Rezkin could hear voices. He surrounded himself in stealth as he approached, and the voices became louder—one male and one female. He recognized those voices. Edging closer to the window, Rezkin took refuge behind an overgrown holly, peering through its prickly branches to spot his quarry. Entris and Azeria stood in the center of a small room sparsely furnished with a simple rug and a few benches along the walls. It was brightly illuminated by several lanterns that hung from loops in the rafters. Although they spoke in Fersheya, they spoke slowly, and Rezkin found that he could understand much of what they were saying.

Azeria was speaking, and her voice held more than a hint of frustration. *"I told you, I do not wish to speak of this now, (determined)."*

"They have been waiting for an answer for five years, Azeria," said Entris. *"They have waited long enough. I have waited long enough (impatient)."*

"You can all wait another five years—fifty years, as far as I am concerned (irritated)." She held her hands near the hilts of her swords as if she thought she might need to defend herself, although it did not appear to Rezkin as though she was in any physical danger. Entris seemed frustrated, even angry, but his tone was pleading.

"Why do you reject me? I am Spirétua-lyé. Any other woman would eagerly accept me."

"I have not rejected you. I only have not accepted you."

"If you have not accepted me by now, you may as well have rejected me (angry)."

Rezkin could not understand her next words, but they were followed by, *"If that is how you feel, then so be it (annoyed)."*

"That is not what I meant—"

"*Do you think I care what you meant? I had no say in this arrangement.*"

"*It is for the good of our people (earnest).*"

"*That is a lie, and you know it. When has this kind of arrangement ever done our people any good. The results are—*" Rezkin could not catch the remainder of what she said.

"*Is this about him?*" said Entris.

"*Him who?*"

"*You know who. He is the one, is he not? The one from your dreams (disappointed)?*"

Azeria crossed her arms over her chest and leaned toward Entris. "*Is that why you bring this up now? You are jealous? I have no interest in the human (disgusted).*"

"*Now, I think you are the liar. You feel a connection to him.*"

Azeria silently clenched her teeth as she fumed at Entris. "*So what if I do. It makes no difference in how I feel about him. I think you should kill him and be done with this.*"

"*You know I cannot do that. He is Spirétua. He is my responsibility, as is his brother if what he says is true (frustrated).*"

"*Then you will speak on his behalf tomorrow?*"

"*I already have. I spoke with the syek-lyé this afternoon.*"

Azeria growled. "*He is not to be killed then?*"

"*The syek-lyé has not given me his decision yet. I am ashamed to admit that part of me wishes he will order him killed. I think you would not so easily reject me if he were gone (sad).*"

She huffed and dropped her arms. Then she seemed to cave in on herself as she leaned forward and rested her forehead on Entris's chest. He ran his hands over the bare skin of her upper arms and rested his chin on her head. "*I have not rejected you, Entris (lost). I only need more time. Since we set out on this journey, things have been shifting inside me (confused).*"

"*You mean since the dreams began.*"

She nodded her head but did not back away.

"*Will you share power with me tonight?*"

"*You know I will not. We have never before. Why would that change now?*"

"You cannot blame me for trying."

A genuine smile crept across Entris's face, and Azeria lifted her head to look at him. He brushed his thumbs over her cheeks, and Rezkin had the feeling this was a moment that should not be witnessed by others. He was not just any other, though. He was the Rez and the Raven, and these moments were often worth more than gold. One never knew when this kind of information would be useful.

Azeria reached up and pulled Entris's hands from her face then turned toward the door. Rezkin watched as Entris's face fell, and the male hung his head to stare at the floor. Azeria rounded the building, stepping into the light that spilled from the window just as a pulse of energy struck. It was followed by another, and the source was clear. It was Entris. Azeria turned back toward the window, and sadness was etched across her face as she looked almost longingly at him.

Rezkin's discomfort with the whole situation grew as he watched Azeria disappear into the darkness of the path. It was a surprise to him that his involvement with these two went beyond the issue of his power and their duty toward their people. With this knowledge, Azeria's antipathy toward him made more sense. She, too, had been having dreams. There was some kind of connection between them, and it seemed she resented him for it. In spite of the mysterious connection, or perhaps because of it, she wanted Rezkin dead.

Entris, on the other hand, had placed his duty before his own self-interest it seemed, or so he had said. At least this was a sentiment Rezkin could understand. It was the sentiment of a leader. Entris doused the light of the lanterns and left the building to follow the same path as Azeria. Neither had shown any sign that they had noticed Rezkin, and he felt reasonably confident that they would have outed him if they had. He uncurled himself from the shadows and, rather than follow them down the well-worn path, he traversed the game trail the deer had taken earlier. Although Entris had not detected him, he was sure the male would be in a foul mood should they encounter each other. It was better to take a separate route.

Despite what Entris had said, Rezkin intended to use the many available hours of the night to inspect other buildings and visit the village. A nearly overwhelming curiosity had been piqued since learning of his supposed power. If he continued to eat ridiculous amounts of food and sleep more often, would he gain greater power? Rezkin knew that, for a warrior, he ate little. Especially robust warriors often consumed great amounts to keep up their strength. Rezkin had never needed to, though. He realized now that he had found another reserve of strength—his vimara. And, it seemed, that his masters had taught him to deprive himself intentionally.

It was difficult to believe that his masters, who prized strength, had deliberately kept him weak, but not if they had known he would go mad with exposure to his own power. The question that plagued him, though, was if he did replenish his well, would he go mad like his brother? Suddenly, the small weight of the vagri on his chest meant not just a reprieve from the uncomfortable sensations of the citadel. It could possibly mean the preservation of his sanity. Rezkin appreciated the vagri even more, although he still did not know what it was.

Rezkin silently padded through the forest circling the *accomodis* and traipsed through the underbrush until he came to the river at the edge of the village. He paused and stared into the narrow gap between two trees as he looked across the small stretch of open ground that preceded the entrance to the cliffside temple. No one was guarding the doors at this time, which told Rezkin that the guards who had been stationed there earlier were not meant to protect the building or its contents but rather to prevent people from interrupting the day's proceedings. The glare of the moonlight was unavoidable as he crossed the open space, and he could only hope no one was watching.

A wooden block held the doors secure, but they were not locked. Rezkin removed the block and pressed his hand to the door. It swung open freely, but as it did so, a frigid power like icy water slid across his palm and then began climbing his arm. With a gathering of his focus, Rezkin pressed against the liquidlike power in an attempt to force it back down his arm. Its momentum stalled, yet he could not force it to retreat. He tried to shake some warmth back into his arm, but the limb would not wake from the numbing cold. Rezkin glanced up the stairwell then back into the night as he considered retreating until he had dealt with the power that would not release him. His need for knowledge ultimately won out, though, and he proceeded up the stairs, ducking behind the short wall when he would have been visible to those outside.

The council chamber looked just as it had earlier that day except that it was devoid of life. The flameless sconces illuminated the recesses, and the stillness of their light created stagnant shadows, few large enough to conceal a person. As Rezkin moved toward the councilors' table, he had the sense that he was being watched. He surveyed his surroundings with heightened vigilance as he continued moving forward but detected no one. After rounding the table, he slipped through the open doorway from which the councilors had emerged. A long hallway that looked to have been carved from a natural fissure stretched before him. It was lit with the same flameless sconces, and every so often an alcove decorated with statuary or a doorway broke the monotony of the dark passage. The first three doorways led to offices that held nothing of interest besides a few papers and parchments filled with script he could not read. The fourth and fifth doorways led to new passages that branched in opposite directions, and the sixth doorway led to vacant sleeping quarters. The room was baren save for the bed, and the door was fitted with a heavy lock, so Rezkin presumed it to be a prison cell.

As Rezkin turned from the room, he again had the sense that he was being watched. Out of the corner of his eye, he caught the briefest flash of light, as if from a blade, and he launched himself into the room. Behind him, he heard the telltale *schling* of a weapon slicing the air. When he turned, though, no one was present. He lurched to his feet and swiftly caught the door just before it closed him into the cell. A heavy weight pressing on the door from the other side threatened to overcome him, but Rezkin pushed with all his might. Just when he thought his opponent might succeed in capturing him, the weight was lifted and Rezkin stumbled back into the corridor. His head swiveled as he searched each direction, but again he found no one.

Rezkin drew his belt knife and proceeded down the corridor toward a pale green light he had not previously seen. As he tried to close the distance, he realized the light appeared to be moving away from him. He hurried his steps while still maintaining his awareness of his surroundings. It would be all too easy to become distracted by the mysterious light and fall prey to another attack. Rezkin paused before passing another corridor and noticed another green light, this one appearing to move toward him. He glanced back toward the waning light that he pursued and wondered if he should continue seeking one light while avoiding the other. It would be easier to wait for the light to come to him. That, however, would not provide him with an answer as to who had attacked him.

He hurried after the first green light, following it around a bend, then noticed a third green light coming toward him from another corridor. A spike of alarm sizzled against his nerves, and Rezkin glanced back to see that yet another light was indeed pursuing him. It occurred to him that whoever he was chasing had probably led him into a trap. Rezkin broke into a run, closing the distance between himself and the first light. The dank scent of musty earth gave way to the fresh aroma of evergreens and water. A cool gust struck him in the face just as the corridor abruptly ended at the entrance to a huge natural cavern that lacked a ceiling, leaving it open to the stars. The silvery light of a gibbous moon shined down into the cavern to spill over the dark pool at its center. A shadowed idol stood upon a pedestal surrounded by the placid water, but even had it been properly illuminated, Rezkin presumed he would not be able to recognize the likeness of the effigy for it had been worn away by time and exposure.

Rezkin spied the green light moving on the other side of the pond. He had taken only a few steps toward it when something struck him from behind. He was launched several paces forward into the dark water. His hands absorbed the impact of his fall into the pool as they slid across the sharp edges of the crystals that lined the bottom. Rezkin pushed against the bottom with his knees and then stood, gasping to collect the air he had lost during the initial impact. He pivoted in the water that reached only to his upper thighs as he sought his assailant. A green light zipped past his head, and he realized the lights were not torches or mage lights and they were not carried by people.

Another of the lights surged toward Rezkin. He attempted to dodge it, but it abruptly changed directions in a way unlike any flying thing he had ever seen. It struck him in the shoulder, knocking him backward and causing him to spin and lose his footing. Rezkin caught himself again on the sharp crystals of the base of the pool, this time scoring himself deep enough to draw a rivulet of blood. As his blood ran into the pool, it gathered into a stream that crawled toward the faceless statue in the center of the pond. Rezkin tried to stifle the blood streaming from his cut, but he was too late. Enough blood had gathered in the dark stream to reach the idol, where it began its ascent. As the blood slid over the statue's surface, the effigy changed. Its features twisted and morphed until they became recognizable, and they bore an eerie likeness to *him*.

Rezkin slowly backed out of the water as he glanced around him. More of the green lights had gathered in the cavern, some almost near enough to touch him, others barely visible within the recesses of the walls. Rezkin had counted about fifty of them when they suddenly became agitated. A droning sound began to warble around the cavern, and then they started to move toward him. At first, they approached slowly, and he attempted to swat them away. They deftly dodged his attacks as they pattered against him. With each of their strikes he felt like he was being pelted with rocks and sliced with razors. Then they picked up speed as they darted at him from farther away. These faster strikes caused him to stumble, and as they struck him more frequently and with greater strength, Rezkin decided these things wanted to kill him. He was not sure if he would bleed out from the many lacerations or if they would bludgeon him to death first.

With barely a thought, Rezkin raised a ward, surrounding himself in a protective shield of power. As he did so, the vagri that hung around his neck heated almost painfully. A few of the lights abruptly collided with the ward, and something dropped to the ground directly in front of him. The lights suddenly ceased their attack, and Rezkin knelt to examine his attacker. A tiny creature lay on the stone floor. It was smaller than his hand and grey like the rock. Humanoid in its appearance, it had long, pointed ears and a sharp nose, overlarge silver eyes, and filmy wings that glowed green as they vibrated. The creature looked up at him with a vehemence so fierce that Rezkin wondered what could possibly have engendered the powerful feeling in such a tiny being.

Rezkin reached out and plucked the angry creature from the ground by one of its long horns that curved over its head. It kicked and clawed at the air and snapped its jaws to no avail. Its wings vibrated harder, creating a buzz that was echoed by its brethren around the cavern as the drone began to rise in volume. The green lights began to attack his shield in force, and it wavered as they pounded against it with fury.

Rezkin held the little creature up in front of him and said, "Can you speak?"

The little beast stopped struggling for the briefest second then started anew.

"Why do you attack me?" he said, but the little beast did not respond.

The drone and the beating against his shield ward became so loud that he could not have heard a response from the creature even if it had deigned to reply. Rezkin shook his head then set the creature on a rock outside his shield. It squirmed furiously then took flight and joined its brethren in attacking his shield. With each collision, he could feel a ripple of power skirt the surface of his shield, and once in a while he could almost feel a sting as though his ward had been punctured. The cacophony continued for several minutes before the shield began to crackle and fracture like a broken eggshell. Rezkin knew it would not be long before his protection collapsed, and he did not think he would be able to outrun the horde.

After considering his predicament for a moment, Rezkin decided that swords and daggers would be of limited use against such tiny and numerous foes. He would have to use the power that he knew he should spurn if he were to retain his sanity. Surely these little creatures occupying the caverns were not a threat to the Eihelvanan who inhabited them. He needed to convince these little flying beasts that he, too, was Eihelvanan—or, at least, that his power was.

He sought his well of power, that sense of calm that had suffused him upon igniting his power. It did not feel calm at that moment, though. It felt as though it was wriggling beneath his skin, already prepared to heed his will. Something was missing, though, and he knew what it was. His emotions. Entris had said the power of the Eihelvanan was fed by emotion, and Rezkin presently felt little but irritation. It would have to do. He fed the squirming force inside him with as much of his frustration as he could muster. As he did so, it grew, and Rezkin realized that those feelings went much deeper than he had realized. He *was* frustrated. He was frustrated with the Eihelvanan for taking him from his mission. He was frustrated with himself for putting Tam in such a terrible predicament in the first place. He was frustrated with the outworlders for being so weak that so many should need his help. He was frustrated with Frisha for— well, he was still not sure why he was frustrated with her, but he knew that he was. He was frustrated with all the lies and deceit and secrets and betrayals and for so many things that he could not wrap his mind around the extent of his frustration.

Just as Rezkin thought he might become overwhelmed with the feelings he had allowed himself to experience, he heard a calm, clear voice. *"Release it."* And he did.

The power surged out of him in a wave of energy that shattered his own shield ward and sent the horde of tiny, vicious creatures hurtling toward the walls of the cavern. Most of the little fiends recovered quickly, but they did not resume their attack. Instead, they scattered and hid amongst the cracks and fissures or flitted out of the open ceiling.

Rezkin stood panting in shock over the magnitude of his own power. Then he realized he could see another color of light beyond the retreating green glow. A pale blue lantern moved toward him as the green lights subsided. Although they vacated his space alto- gether, and presumably no longer posed a threat, the beasts had created a distraction and enough noise for him to get caught.

Rezkin squinted past the blue-white light to see who held the lantern. He was surprised to find the syek-lyé himself casually standing before him unarmed and appearing unconcerned. He belatedly recognized the voice he had heard a moment ago to be that of the syek-lyé.

The syek-lyé looked Rezkin up and down, seeming to take note of the numerous cuts that crossed his arms and neck. He said, "The pixies will no longer try to harm you now that you have shown your power."

"If I had not?"

"You would be dead. You are not used to your power. Raising a ward should have been instinctual. It would have been had you been raised by the Eihelvanan."

"Had I been raised by the Eihelvanan, I would have been killed long ago."

The syek-lyé tilted his head in acquiescence. "Perhaps, but the loss would have been mourned. Every death is one too many, especially among the Spirétua. We are so few now." He paused and then said, "I am glad you came."

"You are not angry?"

"Why would I be?"

"I was warned not to go exploring."

"Likely for your own good. Entris wants the council to see you as amiable and compliant. He is protective of you."

"He seems to hate me nearly as much as Azeria does."

"Perhaps he does, but he takes his position very seriously. It is why he was chosen. He will not allow his personal feelings to intrude on his duty." A small, uncharacteristic smile graced his lips as he said, "Still, you should not presume to know the feelings of others, especially of Azeria. She is complex."

Rezkin huffed. "She seems pretty straightforward to me."

"Do the feelings of others toward you concern you so much?"

"I only care for the feelings of outworlders because they allow their emotions to control their actions, particularly if those actions are taken against *me*."

The syek-lyé raised his lantern so that more of Rezkin was illuminated. "What do you do to those who act against you?"

Rezkin thoroughly considered the question before answering. He did many things to people who acted against him—most of them resulting in death. That was not always the case, though. He knew that some people had good reason to take actions that were not in his interest and that it was not right for him to hold it against them, particularly when those people were his friends. Such was the source of many of his frustrations.

"Every case is different," Rezkin said. "Sometimes their actions demand death. Other times, I must accept that not everyone will agree with me."

"On the surface, that seems to be a reasonable response. However, who is it that decides which times are which?"

"Obviously, *I* must choose."

The syek-lyé nodded. "That is what concerns me. If or *when* you lose your mind, what kinds of decisions will you make? How many will suffer unnecessarily?"

"I will not lose my mind. So long as I do not use my power—"

"As you just did."

"It was necessary."

"I think you will find that on your chosen path there will be many more times where it becomes necessary to use your power. I have fought such a war before. The daem'ahn you seek will become stronger the closer you get to their source. Your swords and daggers will not be sufficient."

"The ahn'an tasked me with bringing to them an army, apparently one comprised of *your* people."

"Entris told me of your bargain. The fact that you made one with the ahn'an is cause enough to doubt your sanity. The ahn'an always get what they want. Since the moment you made that deal, we were destined to meet. The Eihelvanan are sworn to rid this realm of the daem'ahn with or without you. You need no longer involve yourself. You may go. Abdicate your thrones, find yourself a lover, and live in peace somewhere far from battle. Perhaps in this way you *will* retain your sanity."

"Is it so easy? I walk away from my quest, and you allow me to live?"

The syek-lyé chuckled. "I doubt you see that as the easy option."

The syek-lyé was right. Rezkin could not fathom walking away from the path on which King Bordran, his father, had set him. The *Rules*, *his* rules, were all that made him who he was, and his rules required him to protect and honor his friends. He could not walk away.

"No," he said, "I have a purpose, and that purpose must be fulfilled. No matter what you decide, I *will* save my friend, Tam. Then, I will gather whatever forces I have available to me and begin my assault on Caydean and his demons."

"You think you will be able to leave this place without my blessing?"

"I think you need me. You and your people have avoided the outworld for too long. Without me you will find resistance from those who would otherwise be your allies."

"What you say is only partially true. We have our ways. We do not need you as much as you might think. Still, you are a boon so long as you retain your wits. I will take this under consideration when I decide your fate."

"My fate was chosen long before you, and I doubt it will change now."

"That may be true. I heard the SenGoka who trained you were sent by a Knight of Mikayal."

"So I have been told."

"The Knights of Mikayal are few. I have not seen one since the last time the daem'ahn threatened this world."

Rezkin was surprised to see the great sadness that seized the syek-lyé's visage as he seemed to be lost in his memories. He said, "You knew him well—the knight?"

The syek-lyé's gaze cleared and he nodded. "He was a friend, as was *she*."

"She who?"

"It matters not now. They are both long dead, and our problems reside in the present, not the past." He turned to leave and said, "You had best leave this place quickly before the shielreyah decide you are an intruder."

"There are shielreyah here?"

"Yes, and these do not recognize you as their syek-lyé."

The syek-lyé backed away then disappeared through a passage to one side that Rezkin had not previously noticed. Rezkin took one last perusal of the open cavern. The effigy in the center of the pond no longer held his likeness, and the glowing green pixies kept their distance as they hovered near the fissures that parted the walls. Rezkin turned and abruptly stopped as he nearly collided with a wispy wraith. The shielreyah stared at him with vacant eyes as Rezkin sidestepped it. It did not follow as he retraced his steps through the long passage, and it was not difficult to decide which direction he should go as similar wraiths occupied the other passages. He wondered if they were actively guarding those passages from him or if they were simply *encouraging* him on his way.

Having already been caught skulking about, and by the syek-lyé no less, Rezkin quickly made his way back to his room. After checking for traps and poisons, Rezkin set a few traps of his own with the meager supplies he had collected. That night, when he settled his head on his pillow, he slept deeply.

8

Frisha glanced back to see that the corridor was unoccupied, then hurried into the room, shutting and locking the door behind her. The room was empty save for the strange columns that depicted scenes in bas-relief of fires destroying cities and a few thick mats woven of reeds covering the floor in the center of the space. She had taken only two steps forward when Xa stepped from behind one of the columns.

She jumped with a shout, then holding her hand over her racing heart, said, "How did you get here before me? I just left you in the great hall." A moment later she wanted to slap the grin off his face.

"You are slow, and I have my ways," he said. He made a show of looking behind her toward the door and said, "You have locked us in a room together ... *alone*; yet I do not think you are looking to make me happy."

Frisha growled and balled her fist. "You know I'm not. I figured that whatever you have to say is best said in private."

"Ah, you *are* capable of observation."

Crossing her arms, Frisha said, "What do you want?"

"I must go to Channería. I have business with the Order."

"So?"

"You must go with me."

"What? *Me* go to Channería? Haven't you heard? Channería is in the middle of a civil war. Why would *I* need to go anyway?"

"I am do'riel'und for you. I must keep you safe. I cannot do that from afar. Therefore, you must go with me."

She raised a finger. "First, I did not *ask* for you to be do'riel-*whatever*. That was decided between Rezkin and you. Second, do not *want* to go to Channería. And third, there is no way Rezkin *or* Tieran would allow it."

"That is too bad," said Xa, taking a step toward her. "Because none of you have a choice. You are going."

Frisha stepped backward until she bumped into the door. As she worked the handle ineffectually, she wished she had not stopped to lock it earlier. She turned back to Xa who had closed the distance between them. Her voice shook as she said, "You are sworn to protect me. You cannot hurt me."

"I do not need to harm you to take you."

She looked up into the assassin's hard eyes and tried a different tactic. "You serve Rezkin. He's like your god or something, right? You cannot take me against his wishes."

"What I do, I do to advance his cause. My methods are none of his concern."

"They will search for me. He will come for you."

"He is busy. Besides, I have already come up with a cover. You're going to be sick of the heart for a few weeks. You will be back before they know you are gone."

"How will you manage that? They will realize I'm missing."

"No, they won't. I've taken care of it. Now hold still. I do not wish for you to hurt yourself when you fall."

"Fall?"

There was an abrupt pain in her neck, and Frisha heard no response as her world went dark.

Not only were the tunnels dark, but now they were wet. Tam's boot scuffed a rock as he tried to dislodge the thick cake of mud from its sole. It had been raining for three days, and it did not look as if it would stop any time soon. Tam wiped his forehead then hefted the pickax once again. The loud *clink* of Uthey's pickax against the stone resonated through Tam's brain. His mind felt like mush—mush that was being stabbed repeatedly. As he brought his own pickax down on the rockface, stars danced behind his eyes. When his vision cleared, he saw the rock shifting, and not in a way fractured rock should move. He paused to stare at the rock, willing it to move again. When it remained still, he swung his ax again. The rock groaned. Somehow, within the crunch and stutter of shifting stone, Tam understood its meaning. It was a warning. Someone was coming.

Tam reached for Uthey, forcing him to pause in his hacking at the mine shaft. Uthey looked at him with fatigue and only a faint hint of curiosity. Once again, they were alone in their shaft, but this time the slaver only spied them every so often when he walked by on his rounds.

"What is it?" Uthey whispered so as not to gain the attention of the slave masters.

"Someone is coming."

For a few seconds, they both listened to the incessant whacking of rocks by slaves in other tunnels, then Uthey said, "I hear nothing unusual. It is probably the guard coming by on his rounds."

"No, this is different. This is a threat."

"How do you know?"

"The rocks told me."

Uthey released a heaving breath and shook his head. "We must get back to work. If the guard sees us standing here, we will be punished."

Just as Uthey lifted his pickax, a clutch of shadows slinked across the barely illuminated walls. Tam and Uthey moved to stand at what they had deduced was the ideal distance from each other and squared their feet. A second later, three men came around the corner, and Tam easily recognized them despite the dimness.

"Montag," he said.

The man, who looked to be about ten years his senior, smirked and cracked his knuckles. The scars of long-faded ink gave nearly all of his exposed skin a dingy, puckered appearance. If not for that, Montag might have been a decent-looking man. His two lackeys, both missing a few teeth, grinned sadistically, no doubt imagining themselves committing some horrors against him and Uthey.

Montag spoke in Gendishen. *"I hear you've been speaking with Answon."*

"What of it?" said Uthey.

Montag's smirk fell, and the gleam in his eye spoke of violence. *"If you're working for Answon, then you're working against me."*

"We don't work for Answon," said Tam. *"But he has tried to recruit us."*

"If you're not working for him yet, then you don't have his protection. Give me a reason why I shouldn't end the threat now."

Tam glanced behind Montag looking for more shadows. None appeared and the crackle of the rock next to him told him that they were alone. He lowered his voice anyway. *"We have plans, and they are not limited to one sect. You may be included as well if you want."*

Montag narrowed his eyes. *"What kind of plans?"*

"We're going to get out of here one way or another."

Montag laughed. *"Escape? You're nuts."*

"You have no idea," muttered Uthey.

Tam said, *"The guards are fewer than us."*

"They have mages," replied Montag. *"Besides, they control the lift, and that's the only way outta this quarry. If they think there will be a revolt, they'll cut the cable and we'll all starve down here."*

"Look," said Tam, *"we're not working for Answon, and we're not working for you. We're working to get out of here, and we'll take anyone with us who'll help."*

Montag shook his head, the motion barely visible in the meager light. *"I'd heard rumors that you were mad. I can see now that they're true. You're gonna get yourself and him"*—he nodded toward Uthey—*"killed, and I don't wanna be around when it goes down. Stay away from us and stay away from Answon—that is, unless you're taking him down with you."*

"Take him down? We're slaves. We've all been taken down. How much farther down are you willing to go? You can die a slave if you want. I am the master of my destiny, not these guards. I'll not die in this hole. I serve someone greater, and he will come for me."

"That's right. I've heard of this king of yours. One of the new arrivals says there's an emperor now—Emperor of the Souelian, he says. This wouldn't happen to be the same king, eh?"

Tam glanced at Uthey. *"I'd bet on it. If anyone could become emperor, it'd be him."*

"So, you're saying this emperor—the man himself—is gonna come down here and save the likes of you."

A tendril of doubt threatened to wrap around Tam's heart, but he pushed it away. Rezkin had not been training him to be a victim in need of saving. *"I'm saying I won't need saving by the time he gets here."*

Montag took a few steps backward, shrouding himself in the shadows, and his lackeys shifted ahead of him. He said, *"No, you won't, because you'll be dead."*

The two toothless men moved toward Tam at the same time, each drawing a weapon they should not have been able to obtain in the quarry. The daggers glinted in the flame-light of the lone torch as they flashed toward him. Tam twisted just as he heard a loud smack from behind him. One of the henchmen toppled backward. Tam glanced at Uthey who had lobbed a heavy rock at the other man's head, and he was once again glad his partner had his back. Uthey jumped on the downed man just as the other henchman launched himself at Tam. Tam's back hit the wall, and his arm snaked out to block the knife attack. The blade struck the stone with a *chink* creating a spark that snapped beside Tam's ear. The toothless man didn't wait a second before he swung his fist into Tam's side, and Tam kneed him in the groin. The man doubled over, dropping the knife, and Tam's foot connected with his chin.

The unconscious henchman fell atop Uthey where he struggled against his bloodied opponent on the ground, and the chain linking Tam with Uthey yanked Tam forward. Tam looked over in time to witness Uthey's opponent sinking a knife into Uthey's side. He shouted, "No!" as he grabbed the other dagger from the cave floor and stabbed it into the man's neck. Without thinking, Tam yanked the other man off Uthey and smashed his head into the wall. Then he smashed it again and again until the man was unrecognizable and Uthey pulled him away. Tam looked around for more opponents, but Montag had disappeared.

When it was apparent the men were no longer a threat—and never would be—Uthey said, *"That went well."* He held his injured side where dark blood seeped between his fingers. *"Tell me, do you really think this emperor of yours will come?"*

Tam leaned against the wall as a wave of dizziness consumed him. He crouched with his head between his knees and breathed deeply. The rock beneath his fingers seemed to vibrate. It pulsed in rhythm with his pounding heart, and it whispered to him. Not for the first time, he thought he understood its meaning. He pressed his flushed face to the cool stone and listened to the thrumming. Then he straightened and said, *"He'll come, and I intend to prove myself to him. When he does arrive, I will greet him with an army."*

Uthey's wheezing laugh broke the stillness of the air. *"Ha! What army?"*

"These men," said Tam. A glance toward the corpses hardened his voice. *"I will make them mine."*

Uthey gave him a look that spoke volumes, but he eventually sighed and said, *"If you intend to create an army out of slaves, then you will need more than a promise of protection from some mysterious emperor."*

"I'm working on it," he said as he pushed Uthey's hand away from his wound. Then he bent to inspect the damage.

"You had best work faster," grunted the other man as Tam prodded the wound. It appeared as though the dagger, having glanced off a rib, had not struck too deep.

"What is this?" said a new voice, this one speaking Verrili.

Tam froze and Uthey groaned. The guard rushed forward eyeing the two dead slaves. The sting of a whip lashed Tam's side as the guard ordered him to back away. He had turned to avoid meeting the slash head on but was not quick enough. The whip cracked again, this time striking Uthey. The third snap bit into Tam's back as his chest struck the wall, and a fourth scored Uthey as he ducked to avoid its sting.

"You keep working while I retrieve some more guards to deal with this," said the guard as several more slaves shuffled into their tunnel. They silently eyed the two dead men then took up their pickaxes. *"We will deal with your punishments once I have returned. That work will become much more difficult while you bleed."*

"They attacked us," said Tam.

"Did I say to speak?" shouted the guard as he whipped Tam again. The guard pointed at their pickaxes and said, *"Pick them up. Now!"*

Tam retrieved his ax as instructed, as did Uthey. Then, as Tam started to swing his ax, he lost his balance in a wave of dizziness and stumbled against the wall. The guard growled and lashed him again and again as Tam tried to recover. Something primal welled within him, and as the whip swept toward him again, Tam threw out his arm and grabbed hold of it. Before the guard knew what was happening, Tam had yanked the whip from his hands.

"You will not strike me again," growled Tam.

The guard withdrew a baton from a loop at his belt and stepped toward him. Tam squared his shoulders as the guard took another step.

Uthey grabbed Tam's shoulder attempting to pull him back, but Tam shook him off. Through gritted teeth, Tam said to the guard, *"Back away. Leave us be."*

The guard did not listen. As he took another step and raised his baton, a rumble shook the cave. A loud *crack* echoed through the rough-hewn halls. The ceiling began to collapse. Chunks of rubble and dust crashed to the floor crushing the guard beneath a tumble of jagged boulders. The other slaves, Tam, and Uthey scrambled over and around the falling debris to vacate the tunnel as those who occupied different passages likewise ran from the cave. Tam was nearly to the sun-filled entrance when the ground seemed to come up and bite him. He did not remember becoming disoriented *or* tripping. His chain was yanking at his throat as he tried to re-establish his footing. He turned to gain his bearings and saw the image of Uthey hovering over him saying something that was not discernable beyond the rumbling in his ears. Another figure was perched behind Uthey. It shifted just as Tam opened his mouth in warning. A fisted rock struck Uthey in the back of the head, and then Tam could see nothing as his partner's still body covered his face.

The rumbling stopped as Tam pushed at the heavy weight that was Uthey. He knew Uthey lived because the man's chest rose and fell with every breath. Once he finally managed to free himself, Tam realized the mine had not fully collapsed as everyone seemed to think it would. The rumbling he had heard must have been predominantly in his head because most of the cave stood unaffected. Within the cave, only the small pile that buried the guard had been displaced. The mouth of the cave, however, had also collapsed, which left light streaming in through only the smallest hole, barely large enough to fit a rat.

Tam shook Uthey eliciting a groan from his partner. From the corner of his eye, he saw something shift in the dark. He turned his attention toward it but could see nothing unusual. He refocused using his other senses as Rezkin had trained him to do. He sniffed the air and listened intently but could not mentally separate anything odd from the rubble.

Realizing they had been spared by whatever spirits inhabited the cave, and not knowing if they were alone, Tam considered the man who had attacked them. He had not needed ample light to recognize *that* face. It had belonged to Demetrus, himself. With whitened, crisscrossing scars, the man's face looked as though it had been used to smash a window. After Answon and Montag, Demetrus was the final sect leader at the quarry, and the one about whom Tam knew the least. Demetrus was a quiet man with an angry visage that promised violence with every glance. While Answon and Montag each played an intelligent game in their own ways, Demetrus ruled through fear—not by threats, but by actualization. The fact that Demetrus had taken the rock into his own hands was not surprising. The fact that Tam and Uthey had garnered his interest *was*.

Tam surveyed the darkness for any motion, and although he saw nothing that appeared human, his eyes seemed to be playing tricks on him. The minimal light that glinted off the crystalline surfaces of the walls gave them the appearance of movement, as though they were flowing like water. He squinted his eyes trying to focus his overactive senses. His ears picked up a subtle rumbling, more like crunching on a miniscule scale, and the sounds seemed to coincide with the motions of the walls. The pain in Tam's head receded for the first time in weeks, and the relief of it nearly brought him to his knees. Then something in the dark moved for certain, and Tam knew he was not seeing things.

A large figure shifted toward him as it separated from the cave wall with a groan. The sound of shifting gravel echoed through the chamber as the figure took one step and then another. Its bulbous head and shoulders were poorly defined in the meager light, but Tam knew that what he saw was not human.

"Who are you? What do you want?" he shouted.

The ground shook with the reverberation of a growl, and Tam bent to pull Uthey away from the cave creature. He knew it was a futile task, though. The creature moved toward them steadily as Tam struggled with Uthey's weight. When it was only a few feet from them, it stopped and became silent. Tam could hear only his own heavy breathing as he stared at the figure that stood several feet taller than him and blocked his entire view of the cave behind it. In the silent seconds that passed, Tam began to question his sanity once again. Was there truly a mysterious figure standing before him or was he seeing things in his broken mind?

The figure abruptly released a grinding sound, and to his shock, Tam understood its meaning, as though the grating noise were words. *"Our shifting brings the oathsworn to you, Tamarin Blackwater of the human tribe."*

Tam held his breath wondering if what he had heard was real. When it did not speak again, he ventured a word. "H-hello."

The figured groaned, *"We are Goragana, Ancient of the Ahn'an."*

"The ahn'an?" said Tam. The term had a familiar ring to it, but he could not place it. Just then, several boulders separated from the walls in every direction and rolled toward him. When they stopped in a ring around him and Uthey, they unfolded into beings about the size of human toddlers. They looked to have a head, torso, two arms, and two legs, but that was where the likeness ended.

Goragana's form crunched and rattled as it moved its stoney hand to hover over one of the smaller figures. It said, *"These are the lessers. We are the leyaghens."*

"Leyaghens?" Tam understood the grinding sounds but still did not know what the being meant. There was only one thing he had ever heard of that might explain these so-called ancient beings, though. He said, "Are you fae?"

"This is the grumble the humans make. We are the leyaghens."

"No!" shouted Tam backing up until he nearly tripped over Uthey. "No, no, no. I can't talk to you. You're never supposed to speak to the fae."

"The deal is made."

Tam's heart thudded in his chest. "But I made no deal!"

"We are oathsworn to the other oathsworn."

It took Tam a moment to process what the rock creature meant. He posited, "Someone else made a deal with you? Then why have you come to me, and why can I understand you?"

"Humans cannot grumble with the leyaghens, but your mind is open."

Tam smacked his forehead with his palm. "It's the hole in my mind, isn't it? That's why I can understand you. But why are you here?"

"We are the ancient of the oathsworn. Tamarin Blackwater must be safe."

Tam's hand fell to his side as he stared at the creature in shock. "Someone made a deal with you for my safety? Who?"

"The shattered one."

"Who is that?" Tam shouted. He could not think of anyone who would be so foolish as to make a deal with the fae, and certainly not for *his* safety. Then again, he did know a person who might be *brazen* enough to do it. "Was it Rezkin?"

"The humans grumble this name for the shattered one."

Tam froze as one of the smaller rock people rolled toward him. It brushed against his pant leg then seemed to lean into him as it wrapped its stoney arms around his calf. His first instinct was to shake it off, but he held himself still as it began to vibrate. The vibration flowed in steady waves, and Tam realized the small rock creature was purring. He looked back at the larger fae being.

"What do you want with me?"

"Tamarin Blackwater is safe in the caves. We will shift and fracture the strata. You will be free."

This time when Tam's heart thudded in his chest, it was an echo of the joy he felt. "You're going to get me out of here? Out of the quarry?"

"*We are the oathsworn,*" said Goragana. "*We go now.*"

Without thinking, Tam said, "No!"

Goragana bent forward until its head was level with Tam's and it was looking into his eyes through dark black crystals set into its face. "*You do not wish to be free?*"

"I do," Tam said hurriedly. "I just can't go yet. There's something I need to do. Can you wait a little while?"

Goragana straightened and pointed toward the rocks blocking the cave entrance. As one, the lesser leyaghens rolled toward the pile of boulders and began shifting them out of the way. Goragana said, "*Time is not our concern. You will grumble to us when you are ready.*"

Goragana's head spun on its bulky body until it faced the rear. The ancient leyaghen lumbered back into the cave before melding its body with the cave wall, and the lesser leyaghens followed. Although the entrance was still blocked, the pile of rocks had decreased considerably.

Tam shook Uthey and patted his face. Uthey moaned and winced as his hand rose to rub the back of his head. His fingers came away dark with blood. He muttered, "*Why is it I am always the one being injured, and you are the one doing the killing?*"

"*My own body does enough damage to itself,*" Tam said as he wiped his nose on his sleeve for the hundredth time. With the retreat of the leyaghens, his headache had returned with a vengeance. "*And you are welcome to do the killing. I always thought becoming a deadly warrior would be exciting. Now that I understand the result, I have changed my mind.*"

"*It is better than being dead, no?*"

"*Touché.*"

Tam helped Uthey to stand. With Uthey's arm draped over his shoulders, he practically dragged his partner toward the entrance to the mine. It was not unusual for one of them to be helping the other, but Tam begrudgingly admitted to himself that the circumstances were usually the other way around. Between his incessant nose bleeds, migraines, and dizzy spells, Tam was practically an invalid, especially outside of the cave where the influx of information overwhelmed his senses as it surged through the hole in his mind.

Tam began digging through the remaining rubble blocking the cave entrance as Uthey hung his head trying not to lose what little sustenance they had consumed that morning. They could hear slaves digging from the other side, and Tam was thankful that they would not be left to die of thirst in the cave. He did not disillusion himself into thinking the slavers cared for their lives. The entrance that had collapsed was the only entrance to the mine shaft, and so long as it remained blocked, their production suffered. Tam did not think it would be long before the hole was large enough for them to fit through, and he hoped the guards would be satisfied with their work for the day once they were freed.

"*I have plan,*" Tam said as he grabbed another rock and chucked it over his shoulder. "*I have a way out.*"

"*A way out of what?*"

"*This quarry.*"

"*And that just came to you, did it? Was I unconscious for so long?*" said Uthey, wincing as he attempted to straighten. "*You suddenly have an escape route? If that is true, then let us be gone.*"

"*It's not that easy,*" said, Tam, wiping his bloody nose on his sleeve.

"*Of course, it's not.*"

"*I still need my army.*"

"*If you miraculously find us a way out of here, then I will gladly join your army even if it's just an army of two.*" Uthey bent, grabbing his injured side and damaged head at the same time. "*I may need a few days to rest, though.*"

By the time they reached the light of the waning sun, the other slaves were already being herded toward the pen. They dragged their feet toward the barracks, and Tam's stomach churned both with hunger and the queasiness brought on by the onslaught of sensations. Tam was helping Uthey rinse the cut on his scalp at the rain barrel when he realized they were being watched.

"*Who is it?*" said Uthey.

Tam surveyed the curious glances of their fellow slaves. Some were gathered in small groups muttering amongst each other while others went about their business snatching furtive glances as they kept their distance. *"No one ... and everyone."*

"Do I look that bad?" Uthey said with a miserable chuckle.

"We're both bloodied but not enough to garner interest. You're fine. It's just a small cut."

"That's good. One of us needs to keep his head intact."

"What does that mean?"

Motioning toward Tam's face, Uthey said, *"It means you're bleeding more than I am."*

Tam had felt the hot liquid running over his lips but had ignored it while he tended to his partner. Now he rinsed his face with water from the barrel and pinched the bridge of his nose. It probably would not help, but it made him feel like he was doing something useful.

"It was Demetrus," he said.

"Demetrus attacked me?" Uthey replied.

"You're surprised?"

Uthey grunted. *"Only that I still live."*

"I think he was expecting the cave-in to finish us off."

"I didn't think a man like him would leave it to chance."

"He was probably just taking advantage of an opportunity. I doubt he really has it in for us—at least, not yet."

"We've got Answon and Montag on us. Why not Demetrus?"

"That's what I don't get. We haven't done anything. So what if we killed a few slaves?"

"You killed a few slaves."

Tam shrugged. *"That's not a big deal here. Slaves die every day. What do they care?"*

Tam took Uthey's elbow and guided him into the dimly lit barracks. Most of the other slaves were already lining up for food in hopes that it might be served earlier than usual given the prompt evacuation. Tam knew better. They were more likely to miss the meal altogether or to be sent back into the cave to make up for time lost. As they moved toward the back of the barracks, a group of worn slaves abruptly scattered leaving the coveted spot in the corner open. Tam and Uthey both glanced around to see who had elicited such a response and saw no one.

They took their seats and gently leaned back against the corner walls, ever cognizant of their wounds, and Milo and Yin sidled up to sit next to them.

"Is it true?" said Milo.

Tam shifted to keep his wounded side from pressing against the wall. The lashes of the slaver's whip had cut deep, and he was only just beginning to feel them now that things were calm. "Is what true?"

Milo nodded toward a group of slaves that were glancing their way and whispering furtively. Tam recognized two of them as those who had joined them in the tunnel before the cave-in. "They're saying you used the rocks to crush the guard who was beating you. Are you a mage?"

Tam looked toward the others who quickly diverted their gazes. "I didn't crush the guard. The rocks crushed the guard. They didn't like that he was beating us."

"The *rocks* didn't like it?" said Milo, leaning back as if he was suddenly unsure.

Tam rubbed the scraggly hair along his jaw. "No, I suppose it wasn't the rocks exactly." Milo seemed to relax—until he finished his thought. "It was the spirit in the rocks."

"The rocks have a spirit?" said Milo skeptically. "And you can speak to it? It heeds your call?"

Tam laid his head back on the wall and closed his eyes against the throbbing pain. "Something like that."

In broken Ashaiian, Uthey said to Milo, "What do you want?"

Tam opened his eyes again as Milo said, "They want to know if you will accept them as your men."

"Who wants to know this?" said Uthey.

Milo nodded toward the group of five. "Them."

"What does that have to do with *you?*" said Tam.

"They assumed Yin and me are your men because they saw us speaking earlier. I did not correct them."

"Why?"

Milo grinned. "Because I have not yet decided whether you are too mad to follow."

Tam rubbed his temples. He had intended to gain the confidence of the other slaves, but this made no sense. He had not yet done anything worthy of a leader. "Why would they want to follow me?"

"You have garnered the attention of all three sect leaders. One of them allowed you to live, and the other two failed to kill you. You have already proven that you are capable of killing to protect yourself and yours"—he nodded toward Uthey—"and you obviously have some power if you can control the rocks. You killed a guard, and it looks like you will get away with it. It is obvious that you are the newest sect leader, and they want to get in early to get the best positions."

Uthey grunted a laugh. "The madness is catching. So it begins."

9

She came toward him, her hips swaying with sultry purpose, her eyes shining with silver light, and her long, white hair blowing loosely around her shoulders. The supple strands trailed across her face with the softest caress. She reached out her hand and grasped the stone that hung from around his neck with elegant fingers.

"You do not need it," she said. "I will share your power."

He pulled her close, and his mouth crashed down atop hers. They fell onto the soft grass, and she sprawled across him, her small, lithe body supported by his strength and bulk. She pulled away only to gaze down at him. Eyes that swam with liquid silver reflected the cool blue ice of his own as he stared back at her. One of his hands was buried in her snowy locks as the other brushed against her cheek and across her soft lips.

He said, "I will share everything with you."

The smile that graced her face and danced in her eyes was brighter than the sun that shined down on their entangled bodies. She laughed and kissed him again.

Rezkin jolted awake. He abruptly tugged the vagri away from his burning skin. It had heated to a degree that was far beyond comfortable. Then he jumped up from his bed and threw himself to the floor. He did a few floor exercises to steady his overactive nerves. The sense of calm and pleasure and *rightness* that had suffused him in his sleep was quickly replaced by alertness. The dream disconcerted him. He rarely dreamt, but when he did, they were the one part of his life he had never been able to control. His dreams never seemed to have meaning, though. Today, he could not help but feel that this one was different. He could not fathom how he had felt such *contentment* in the arms of a woman who wanted to murder him. Nearly every action and word of hers since they met had been filled with vehemence, yet, in his dreams, she seemed a different person. It was evidence enough that the dream was not real.

His disquiet abruptly settled. His realization was exactly the problem. The woman of his dreams may look like Azeria, but she was decidedly a different person—a person that did not exist. Rezkin wondered at the *reason* for the dream, then quickly decided there was no reason. Even as his mind said it, though, he knew it to be lie.

Rezkin opened his door to find Nanessy standing on the other side with her hand raised to knock.

"Oh!" she said, "I did not realize you were awake. I suppose I should have known. Since I have known you, you have never slept so late."

Rezkin glanced past the roofline at the sky. The sun had risen at least two hours past, a truth that did not sit well with him. He *had* slept late.

"I was just coming to see if you were going to eat breakfast. I am heading down there now."

Rezkin nodded and closed the door behind him as he stepped onto the walkway. Backing away, Nanessy said, "I was a little worried about you."

They turned toward the stairs, and Rezkin indicated for her to go first. He said, "Why?"

"Well, I heard strange noises coming from your room. I thought maybe …" As her voice trailed off, her cheeks darkened to nearly red.

"You thought I was with a woman?" he said.

"Well, yes, actually."

"And who, exactly, would I have been with?"

"I, ah, I do not know."

"I can think of no one," he said, and again he could hear the lie in his own words. "I was exercising."

"Oh, that makes sense. Um, the others were exercising down in the yard. I am surprised you did not join them."

"Perhaps I should," he said. "Last night, during practice, I moved faster than I have ever moved. It would do me good to train with them. Hopefully, though, we will not be here that long."

"You are worried about Tam."

"I fear he is already dead."

"I admit that I think so, too. I am not a healer, but I do have some understanding of what was done to him. Even if he *is* alive, it will have changed him in unimaginable ways. He will not be the same person."

"I know, and it is my fault. I should not have allowed it."

"Why *did* you?"

Rezkin considered the question carefully. All the reasons he had told himself in the beginning seemed to be lacking with the aid of hindsight. No reason seemed good enough to have risked Tam's life; but Rezkin knew he would not have done so without fully considering the consequences. He wondered if the power infusing him from the citadel had induced a madness in him just long enough to ruin Tam's life. Even now, though, he felt that his decision had been justified.

As they neared the dining hall, Azeria fell into step behind them. Rezkin did not acknowledge her presence just as she did not acknowledge his.

Rezkin said, "Tam wanted things—he wanted to *be* things—that would not have been possible given his level of knowledge and skill, especially at his age. I had thought that opening his mind, just for a few weeks, would somehow provide him with what he was lacking."

"You hoped to give him his dream."

Rezkin thought about it then nodded. "Yes, I suppose I did."

Before they got to the feast counter, Nanessy stopped him with a brush of her hand against his. She looked up at him with bright hazel eyes and said, "You are very kind."

Rezkin's brow reached toward the ceiling as he said, "*Me*? I have never been accused of such. I also fail to see how risking my friend's life is a kindness."

She shook her head. "You did not do it for yourself. You did it for him. In fact, everything I have ever seen you do—good or bad—was for someone else." She took a step closer. "Do you never have the desire to do something—to have something—just for yourself?"

Rezkin's gaze slipped from Nanessy to Azeria. The general held his gaze for a second before glancing away. Rezkin wondered if she had dreamt about him again as he had her. If so, did she have the *same* dream, and if she had, were they truly in it together? He looked back to Nanessy and said, "Pleasing myself is not my purpose." With a slight bow, he said, "*Rule 1* is to *protect and honor* my friends."

"I heard my uncle. That is not the rule."

"It is *my Rule*."

Nanessy nodded, then turned toward the feast.

Azeria stepped up next to him and said, "She pines for you (*amused*)."

"She is confused," said Rezkin. "Brelle says it is my power."

Azeria looked at him and pursed her lips. Then she nodded. "It happens."

"But not with you?"

Azeria followed his gaze to see Entris already sitting at a table. She looked back to Rezkin and narrowed her eyes. "You know nothing of me. Stop trying (*vexed*)." Then she pushed past him to find her own food.

When it was Rezkin's turn to gather sustenance, he piled his plate higher than usual. Although he wanted to find a seat alone, he knew it would not sit well with the others. Instead, he took the only empty seat at the table between Nanessy and Azeria. Entris sat across from him, and Brelle sat across from Nanessy. The young windwalker seemed quite pleased to be in the presence of the mage.

Entris glanced at Azeria then cleared his throat. "Mage Threll."

"Nanessy, please," she said.

He nodded once. "Mage Nanessy, this morning we will be assessing Rezkin's power."

"*And* his mental state," grumbled Azeria.

Entris shook his head and looked back toward Nanessy. "You are welcome to join us for the exercises (*inviting*)."

"That would be great!" she said. "I am interested to see how your power works."

"I am afraid there will not be much for you to see. Casting by the Eihelvanan is an internal process. You will not be able to see the process itself, only the results."

"Still, it is an amazing opportunity. I am honored that you are willing to share your power with me."

Brelle suddenly choked on his food as everyone turned to stare at Nanessy. She looked around startled then peered up at Rezkin. "What did I say?"

"She didn't mean it (*earnest*)," snapped Brelle.

Entris shifted uncomfortably. "I know what she meant. It was just..." He trailed off as he looked at her like he was seeing her for the first time.

Nanessy blinked at them, her face turning rosy as she said, "What did I say wrong?"

"It was not what you said, exactly, but your phrasing," said Rezkin. "I believe you just invited Entris to be intimate with you."

Nanessy's eyes widened, and heat crept up her neck to color her face red. Then she laughed. It was an anxious, boisterous laugh that tugged at the attentions of others in the room. It occurred to Rezkin that Nanessy looked lovely with those bemused sparkles in her eyes. A motion from Azeria on his other side caught his attention, and guilt suddenly washed over him. He was perplexed as to why any of these thoughts had crossed his mind, but he was certain that guilt had no place in them.

The rest of the meal passed in relative silence, with Nanessy surreptitiously glancing around. Entris's gaze traveled to Azeria a few times. Although his face was impassive, Rezkin thought he saw a note of sadness in his eyes. Azeria sat silently and kept her gaze on her food. At one point, she brushed against him, seemingly inadvertently; but Rezkin thought that for someone with such control of her own body, the motion had to be intentional.

Rezkin finally turned to her and said, "Did you sleep well last night?"

She startled like a deer caught in the torchlight. The silver orbs of her irises were on full display as her eyes widened, and she darted a glance at Entris. "Um, yes, why do you ask (*anxious*)?"

"Why are you anxious?" he said, turning toward her.

"What? I am not," she replied with a shake of her head.

"You just said you were."

"No, I mean, why do you ask?"

He tilted his head curiously. "You are quiet today."

She stared at him as though a cornucopia of thoughts were flitting through her mind. Her startled expression abruptly gave way to anger, and she snapped, "I am fine. I have many things to think about, and none of them relate to *you* (*frustrated*)." Azeria grabbed her plate and stalked away from the table. When Rezkin turned his gaze back toward the others, he found Entris glaring at him.

"Well, that was an … interesting … meal," said Nanessy as she too got up from the table.

Still looking at Entris, Rezkin said, "Shall we get on with this?"

Rezkin and Nanessy followed Entris and Azeria back to the fire pit where Entris had first explained Rezkin's powers to him. Brelle had skipped ahead and was already lighting the fire as they approached. This time, Entris sat across the fire from Nanessy with Rezkin standing to his right, his back to the water. Azeria took the seat next to Nanessy, then Brelle sat down on Nanessy's other side. Everyone looked at Rezkin expectantly.

"What, exactly, do you intend for me to do?" he said.

Entris stood and held out his hand. "I will carry the vagri for you. It would be best if you are not in contact with it while casting. It continues to drain you." Rezkin did not like parting with the vagri, but Entris's reasoning made sense. After Rezkin handed it over, Entris said, "Now, show us your power."

For the first time in a long while, Rezkin did not know what to do. Everything he had done in the past had been with purpose and generated by *need*, and he had been figuring it out as he went. Now, he was being tasked with casting for the sake of casting, and he was at a loss.

Nanessy seemed to pick up on his concern, though. She said, "Show them how you walk through wards." Then she cast a glowing shield ward between him and the others.

Almost without thought and without issue, Rezkin stepped through it. Entris tilted his head as though examining him but appeared unimpressed. Nanessy stood and turned toward him. "How about I lob a few spells at you to show them what happens?"

"Very well."

Nanessy launched a whirling fireball about the size of his head at him. Rezkin did not need to move. It splashed against him and dissipated. Small droplets dripped onto the leaves at his feet causing them to smoke, and he casually stamped out the tiny fires. Next, Nanessy tried to attach a sleeping spell to him, but it slid off without eliciting so much as a yawn. After a few more attempts to attack him with spells, Entris called a halt.

He said, "What are you doing when these spells strike you?"

"Doing? I am doing nothing. Most spells simply do not affect me."

Entris shook his head. "That is not what is happening (*impatient*). Is your only experience with passive casting?"

"I have been able to do a few things actively. I did not know at the time that I was using vimara."

"Show me."

Nanessy picked up a large stone and tossed it to Rezkin. She said, "How about you show them that thing you call a *potential* ward. You can break the stone apart with it."

Rezkin caught the stone and nodded. Then he focused his mind and will and pinched his fingers together, slowly stretching them out to the width of the rock. The potential ward he held between them was stable and strong, and he pushed it into the rock with his *will*. A fracture formed in the rock with a *pop*, then he forced the potential ward into the fissure prying the rock open with force. The two halves of the rock landed on the ground at his feet with a thud.

He said, "I also managed to draw power into the crystals at the citadel. I used them to syphon off the energy being used during a demonic ritual." He glanced at Nanessy before saying, "I think I may have inadvertently trapped a part of the victims' souls in the crystals during the process."

Nanessy's eyes widened. "You did *what*? Why was I not told of this?"

"You are not the king's mage."

Nanessy pursed her lips but quickly looked away.

Entris looked at him with suspicion. "The chiandre is the link between a soul and its vessel or body." Rezkin nodded, already versed in the subject. "You created a new chiandre attachment to the crystal? The Spirétua do not possess this power (*cautious*)."

Rezkin shook his head. "No, I did not create the attachment. The link was already made by the demon. I did not wish to sever the link made by the demon in case it killed the victims, so instead, I drew the ritual's power into the crystals, effectively snuffing out the ritual. Unfortunately, I believe it also drew in a part of the soul connected by the chiandre."

Entris stood but maintained his gaze on the fire in the pit as he thought. Eventually, he said, "I begrudgingly admit I am impressed that you were able to interrupt a demonic ritual in progress without killing the victims. How did you know to do this?"

"The mages had some knowledge of ritual magic, but the solution came to me from Liti and Itli."

Entris looked at him aghast, for once exposing his feelings. "The *fire ancients*?"

Rezkin felt uncomfortable with sharing so much information, but once again, he felt the promise of answers was of greater value than his secrets. "I told you of the deal I made with the ahn'an. They were trying to uphold their end of the bargain. I found Liti and Itli in a crystal—or, perhaps, they found me. They spoke, in a way, and it was almost as if I could understand them. I knew what I needed to do."

Entris sighed before motioning for him to have a seat. Then Entris retook his own seat and said, "From almost all that I have seen, I can say that you are not actively casting. Your protections against mage attack, the way their wards do not affect you, even the way you hide the markings on your skin, are all passive. These are skills and techniques you learned as a youngling and continue to maintain without conscious thought."

Nanessy said, "How is it possible that he does these things without knowing the spells?"

"Only humans use spells," said Azeria. "Your *spells* provide a method of focusing your vimara that Eihelvanan are capable of doing on our own."

Entris said, "Eihelvanan casting, and that of other creatures that use vimara, is focused almost entirely by our emotions."

Nanessy's eyes widened. "I mean no offense, but as far as I can tell, you all *have* no emotions."

Brelle took Nanessy's hand and said, "Most Eihelvanan do not *show* their emotions on the outside, but that does not mean we do not have them. We are a *very* passionate people. We feel an emotional depth and range much greater than any human ever could. I learned from my adoptive parents to show my emotions more openly. I would be happy to show you more of them."

Nanessy's face flamed, and she quickly averted her gaze. Entris shook his head and turned back to Rezkin. "You, like us, do not show your emotions. Unlike us, however, you claim to have none."

"*Rule 37* is to *separate from one's emotions*," said Rezkin. "Emotions are a weakness that a warrior cannot afford."

Entris nodded. "The SenGoka intentionally taught you to reject your emotions. I believe they did this to minimize the risk that you would go mad."

"How so?"

"Without emotions, the Spirétua are without power (*cautious*). Our emotions are the way in which we focus our vimara."

Rezkin's gaze dropped to where Entris held the vagri in his hand. "That is why the vagri heats when I *feel* things. It is responding to a surge in my vimara."

Entris nodded. "So long as you refuse to embrace your emotions, you will never truly be Spirétua."

Rezkin faced a conundrum. In order to be the warrior he was trained to be, he was required to dissociate from his emotions; but in order to capitalize on his innate power, he would need to embrace them. He swallowed hard as he took the vagri from Entris. For the first time in many, many years, Rezkin felt true fear. The prospect of *feeling* things was more than he could abide.

After leaving the riverside campfire, they all went to the training yard. Nanessy seemed to be satisfied with watching the proceedings while Rezkin trained with the Eihelvanan. Jao'hwin volunteered, again, to train with Rezkin, pushing him to move in a way that defied even his elite training. Although the weapons and moves were familiar to him, they felt completely new at the unnaturally fast pace. The speed at which the Eihelvanan moved was only unnatural for *humans*, though, and the trials were more proof that Rezkin was not like other humans. He was, perhaps, barely human at all.

Azeria took the opportunity to land Rezkin on his back, and his side, and his rear, and his head over and again. Jao'hwin would merely laugh and then tell Rezkin to move *faster*. Rezkin had worked up quite a sweat by the time the lunch aroma reached his nose. Like many others, Rezkin had removed his shirt during the exercise to prevent it from becoming soaked. He strode over to where a few outside showers stood between the training yard and the armory. He bent over beneath its spray rinsing his torso but keeping his pants dry for the most part. Then he dried with one of the many towels stacked along a shelf and pulled on his shirt. The chance to clear his head had been much appreciated, but as he made his way toward the dining hall and collected his food, turbulent thoughts invaded his mind.

Rezkin had been taught to decry weakness—any weakness. His masters had insisted that all emotions were weaknesses he could not afford, and thus far, that sentiment had aided him in his time as a warrior. On the other hand, he was a weak Spirétua, and he would forever remain weak so long as he failed to embrace those very emotions. Although Rezkin had always believed he had no mage power, he had thought that if he had, he would have mastered that as well. Now, in order to master his power, he would need to break the *Rules*, and breaking the *Rules* would render him a lesser warrior, not to mention a potentially *insane* warrior.

The others must have sensed his inner turmoil for they did not press him to speak during the meal. In fact, they all ate in silence until they were finished. At that point, Brelle invited Nanessy to go for a long walk with him along the river.

"Is the trial not coming up soon?" she said.

Brelle nodded, his expression troubled. "Yes, but"—he sighed—"it may not go well, and I do not want you to have to see … *it*."

Nanessy stiffened, and her brow furrowed in anger. "*It?* You mean the death of my emperor?"

Brelle shifted uncomfortably. "Well, um, yes."

Nanessy opened her mouth but never got the chance to speak. Entris said, "Mage Threll is a grown woman and dedicated to her liege. She is perfectly capable of comporting herself with dignity at the trial."

Nanessy appeared surprised as she looked at Entris. She closed her mouth and lifted her chin proudly. "Yes, thank you, Spirétua-lyé."

He tilted his head and said, "You may call me Entris."

Nanessy started to smile, but her face fell before the expression was fully formed. She looked over at Rezkin but said nothing more.

Rezkin, however, was not thinking about the trial. He doubted they would execute him, but even if they did decide such was his fate, he had already decided not to let them. He would fight until he died fighting and perhaps even longer if history had anything to say about it. His masters, the Sen, were no longer around to draw him back from the Gates of the Afterlife, though. Once his last breath passed his lips, there would be no more.

Rezkin followed Entris out of the building toward the path that would take them back to the cliffside council chamber. A tug on his sleeve brought him to a halt. He turned, expecting to find Nanessy, but instead he was met with the silver gaze of Azeria. Before she spoke, her face scrunched in consternation and she huffed. Then she said, "For what it is worth, I have changed my mind. I do not believe you to be mad—*yet*, and I do not think you should die."

"Thank you," he said, because he could think of nothing else to say.

Her expression became blank as ever. "I still do not like you." Then she motioned for him to continue walking as she took up the rear behind Nanessy.

When they finally made it up the cliffside to the council chamber, they found it to be empty. With the councilors not yet arrived, Rezkin had the opportunity to survey the details of his surroundings from his seat in the front row of benches. There were scenes in bas-relief on the stone walls that looked to be of the same artistry as those at the citadel in Cael. Most of the scenes were fairly domestic, showing people gathered around an orator or hunting or building things. It was the one on the ceiling that captivated Rezkin's imagination, though. In the center was a ring of Eihelvanan men and women who appeared to be worshipping a giant tree. To their left was a group of humans looking over the Eihelvanan, each of them holding an infant in his or her arms. To the right of the Eihelvanan was a group of winged people who were larger than the others and surrounded by glowing crystals. These seemed to be looking down on the Eihelvanan as though they were inferior.

Rezkin drew his gaze away from the scene at the sound of a door opening. A line of people entered through the open doorway at the other end of the room. They filed into their respective council seats, with the syek-lyé at the center. Rezkin stood and took his place on a small, elevated platform before the councilors. He examined each of the men and women with a critical eye hoping to ascertain the slightest hint of what they might be thinking. Unfortunately, their expressions were as stoic as ever so that he could not tell a friendly face from a deadly one. It put his nerves on edge that he could be so bereft of insight in this moment between life and death. He had already run through a number of scenarios in his mind in which he might attempt escape should things not go his way. None of them were particularly promising, considering the power wielded by these people.

Again, Rezkin was on edge as he considered his vulnerability. He was used to having the upper hand in any situation, but those were all scenarios involving humans. As his muscles clenched, the stone resting against his chest began to heat. It was a reminder that he was becoming emotional. He took a few steadying breaths and reassessed himself once he was relaxed enough to move fluidly. It occurred to him that he would not be in this situation if he was not so weak in power. If he had been trained to *use* his power rather than suppress it, he might have a chance against these people. *But* he might also be as mad as Caydean.

The syek-lyé broke the silence. "I understand that there are time-sensitive matters at play, so I will not delay with unnecessary formality." He met Rezkin's gaze, but his expression lacked any familiarity he might have gained the previous night. "Do you now understand the charges against you?"

Rezkin donned the persona of a politician and said, "If you are referring to the unfounded accusation that I may be mad, then yes."

"How do you plead?"

"Not guilty."

"And how do you justify your actions of the past few months (*curious*)? I am told that you have conquered multiple kingdoms and wreaked havoc in others. You have made deals with the ahn'an. And you maintain the presence of a daem'ahn in close company—"

Rezkin's muscles clenched at the last proclamation. He said, "I am aware of no such demon. If this is true, then identify it, and I will root it out."

The syek-lyé tapped the table. "Perhaps you are unaware of its presence (*skeptical*), but these creatures cannot hide themselves for long. You have surely seen the consequences of its power, yet you continue to embrace it (*disapproving*). Like daem'ahn, madness often craves chaos."

"I do not crave chaos. I have only endeavored to create order. I established an entire kingdom on Cael for the sole purpose of protecting and honoring my people. Everything that I have done since has been in service to those people. I did not ask for the other kingdoms. I did not set out to claim them."

"Yet it happened anyway." The syek-lyé held up a hand to forestall any additional argument and continued. "The Spirétua-lyé has informed me that you have two older brothers. One purported to be mad, and the other is said to have been killed by the first. Is this correct?"

"Yes."

"He also claims that your training dictates that you remain weak in power."

"So he says."

"He believes it is for this reason you retain your mental faculties. I am inclined to agree with him." The male leaned over the table and placed his hands flat on the surface. "This establishes a problem. You are now aware of your power and have been for some months. You have begun using it in increasing amounts and, as such, your mind is at risk. Since you are still sane, however, this court does not have the authority to take your life."

Rezkin heard Nanessy release a heavy breath, and to his surprise, he felt inclined to do the same. He kept his thoughts to himself, however, and continued to stare at the syek-lyé.

"Your brother is another matter, however. If he also possesses the power of the Spirétua and is already mad, then it is our responsibility to seek him out and dispose of the problem. It seems you share this goal. As such, I have a solution that will satisfy us both."

The syek-lyé looked to Entris and gave a curt nod. Then the leader looked back to Rezkin. "Spirétua-lyé Entris has agreed to join you on your quest. He will remain at your side for its duration. This will enable him to monitor your mental state and confirm that any further actions you take are those of the leader of your people and not of a madman." The male's emerald gaze bore into Rezkin as he said, "Should you lose your mind, it is his prerogative, his duty, to end the threat. Upon completion of the mission, you and he will return here."

"Why should I allow this?" said Rezkin. "You have no authority over me."

"I *do* because you are Spirétua, and you and your actions are my responsibility … and his. You will allow it because you have no choice. To help make you more amenable, though, I have agreed to allow him to train you. Perhaps with proper training in the way of the Eihelvanan, you may retain some of your sanity. He tells me you possess remarkable focus for a human born."

"You said that I will need to return here. For how long?"

"Indefinitely."

Rezkin decided that the conditions the syek-lyé were placing on him were temporary and could be dealt with later. He was glad they had decided not to try to kill him, and he was even looking forward to learning how to use his power from a master of the art. Rezkin nodded and said, "Agreed."

Nanessy abruptly stood and said, "Wait! He cannot come back here. He is our emperor. We need him."

The syek-lyé turned his steely gaze on Nanessy. "Mage, this is not a punishment, nor is it up for debate. In all likelihood, with time, this man will go mad. He has already accumulated much power and influence. It is for the safety of your people, for the safety of the world, that he is trained properly, subdued, or—if necessary—terminated (*earnest*)."

Nanessy appeared shaken as she looked at Rezkin with wide, terrified eyes. She blinked several times, and she scanned the council as though looking for a lifeline. "But … but we need him."

"Emperors can be replaced," said the syek-lyé. "That is my ruling."

Azeria abruptly appeared beside Rezkin. She bowed and said, "Councilors, if I may?"

Rezkin was suddenly concerned about what Azeria could possibly add to make things worse. She was quite open in her hostility toward him, although she *had* confessed that she did not want him dead.

The syek-lyé nodded, "Yes, General?"

"This mission may take some time. If Entris is to risk the human world, he should not go alone. I volunteer to accompany him. Since he will be so far from home, my skills as a pathmaker will be invaluable."

Entris met her gaze and tilted his head curiously. "I am glad you feel that way, Azeria. I had intended to recruit you regardless."

A smirk started to form at the corner of the syek-lyé's mouth. "Approved," he said before he stood. The council followed his lead, and then they made to exit. The syek-lyé paused and looked at Entris. "You should find Gizahl. If anyone knows a way to stave off the madness, it is he." Then he and the councilors all left the chamber.

Rezkin turned to Azeria. "Why would you volunteer? Your aversion for me has been obvious. Why would you wish to spend *more* time in my presence?"

She lifted her chin and said, "I am not going for *you*. I am going for Entris."

Entris rocked back on his heals as his own lips turned upward. "Is that so? Have you come around to me, then?"

Azeria scowled at him. "Not in that way," she snapped. "I volunteered *as your general*—nothing more (*irritated*)."

Entris seemed to deflate. "That is disappointing. Perhaps, though, this will give us the time together to come to terms (*hopeful*)."

Rezkin already knew the answer to his question, but he posed it anyway. "What, exactly, are you coming to terms over?"

Entris dropped his chin and tore his gaze from Azeria. He seemed to consider whether to answer then blew out a breath and said, "She was supposed to be my bride, but she has rejected me."

Rezkin noted Nanessy's quick inhale as she covered her mouth. For once, Rezkin was surprised to hear himself say, "I can relate."

The vagri around his neck heated, and he felt a tight pain in his chest.

"Yes," said Entris. "We noted that your bride-to-be rejected you for your kin."

"No," said Rezkin, "Frisha rejected me because of *me*. She chose him because he can give her what I could not. I do not disparage her choice."

"She does not deserve Rezkin anyway," muttered Nanessy, who

glanced up with wide eyes, seemingly surprised that she had spoken aloud. Her cheeks flushed and she looked away as though she had said nothing.

"Truly?" said Azeria. "You are content with your love choosing someone else (*skeptical*)?"

"She was not my love. I care for her well-being, but I do not believe I could ever *love* her."

She shifted her stance, and her shoulders loosened. "So, you let her go."

Rezkin was genuinely surprised by her skepticism. He said, "Of course. I could not honor her by making her miserable."

Azeria's lashes fluttered over her silver irises as she glanced at Entris, but she could not seem to meet his gaze. Entris swallowed hard, and it was as though some unspoken message had passed between them. Without another word, Azeria turned and headed toward the exit. Entris, Rezkin, and Nanessy followed her out of the council chamber and down the cliffside. When they neared the accomodis, Entris spoke up so that Azeria could hear him from where she strode ahead of them.

"We will leave in an hour."

She raised a hand in acknowledgement but did not look back as she disappeared around the corner. An hour later, they all stood back in the same spot staring at each other. Azeria and Entris each carried a pack on their backs and a smaller satchel at their hips. Rezkin and Nanessy had no supplies when they had been kidnapped, so they had none for the return trip.

"I will create a pathway back to the place where we acquired you," said Azeria.

Rezkin said, "Can you take us to the Isle of Sand?"

"No, I can only create paths to places I have been. It is too dangerous to try to create them otherwise."

Nanessy said, "Rezkin, we need to go back to the inn. Everybody will be looking for us."

"Of course," he replied. "I was only hoping to get to Tam faster."

A look of concern crossed Nanessy's face, and she said, "I

understand."

Azeria looked to Entris. At his nod, she began creating the pathway. She held her hands before her, her fingers entwined. Then she slid them past each other and abruptly pulled them apart. Her whole body seemed to glow with silvery light, and her hair began to float around her head as if she were under water. A rent formed in the air in front of them, and it grew until it was large enough to step through. Azeria entered the illuminated fissure first. Then Nanessy approached it slowly, her eyes wide and her mouth agape with awe. Rezkin then slipped into the stream of light. As he did so, power slid over his skin, and his nerves buzzed with delight.

Inside the pathway, the air swirled turbulently around them, and it crackled with power. The mist parted in one direction, and Rezkin saw something large shift toward them. He drew his swords as he surveyed the creature. Its body was about the size of a house, and its long neck stretched high into the tumultuous sky. Its attention shifted and its head lowered nearly to the ground where Rezkin could see a smaller version of the being running to hide behind the legs of the larger one.

Azeria's hand landed on his shoulder, and she shook her head. Her voice was nearly lost in the storm as she said, "It is only a uruptee. It is not aggressive. It is a plant eater." Then she motioned toward a second tear in reality that she had just created and told him to follow Entris through. As soon as his foot struck the ground, he was standing in the room from which he had been stolen the previous day.

The sturdy floorboards gave only the slightest creak, and the smell of sustenance drifted up from the kitchen somewhere below. More alarming, though, were the multiple bared blades that surrounded them. Rezkin quickly surveyed the bearers of those blades and found them to be worthy but unlikely threats. Farson, Shezar, Jimson, Reaylin, and Marlis Tomwell surrounded them with swords bared, their primary focus on Entris. Rezkin stepped forward so that Nanessy and Azeria would not collide with him upon arrival, which occurred a breath later just before the pathway disappeared.

Shezar's voice held a hard edge as he said, "Emperor, are these people a threat?"

Rezkin replied, "Of course they are, but you may sheath your weapons." His gaze shifted about the room quickly before he said, "Why are you all in my suite?"

Farson scowled as he roughly seated his sword in its scabbard. "You disappeared. When you did not return this morning, we became concerned. We were just having a meeting about where to look for you."

"Ah, you would not have found me," said Rezkin closing the distance between them.

Shezar's gaze slid to the side. "Reaylin suggested there was little reason to worry since you were with Mage Threll."

Rezkin furrowed his brow at Reaylin. "You think she is so powerful that she could protect me from any threat?"

Reaylin chuckled. "No, I just thought maybe you two wanted some *alone* time."

Farson growled, "I thought, perhaps, I would need to try to kill you after all."

Azeria raised an eyebrow as she glanced between Nanessy's heated face and Rezkin. For some reason, Rezkin did not want Azeria to think he and the mage were intimate. He flicked his hand toward the newcomers. "This is General Azeria and that is Spirétua-lyé Entris. Obviously, they are Eihelvanan." With a smirk, he said, "They graciously invited us to visit their home. We have just returned."

"Returned from where?" said Farson.

"Freth Adwyn," said Entris.

"Where is that?"

"It is a forest to the southeast of the Drahgfir Mountains," replied Rezkin.

"Impossible."

Rezkin shook his head. "I will explain all once we are aboard the ship. We have lost an entire day of travel. Tam can wait no longer. We must go."

"Regarding that," said Jimson, glancing uncomfortably at the Eihelvanan as he unfolded a slip of paper. He held it out for Rezkin. "We received this information from an unnamed informant. It claims that several weeks ago a number of slaves were transferred from the isle to a quarry in Verril. The informant believes Tam was one of them."

Rezkin examined the missive and turned it over to see if there was any more information. "This was all that was delivered?"

"Yes, Your Majesty."

Rezkin had spread word to the various thieves and assassins' guilds that he was looking for information on Tam, but he had not truly expected to find anything. Without knowing the identity of the informant, he could not confirm the information provided in the missive. If he wasted time going to the isle, Tam could die in the quarry or vice versa.

"I can take you to Southern Verril," said Azeria. All eyes turned to her. At his questioning glance, she said, "I went there once many decades ago. I can open the pathway."

Rezkin handed her the slip of paper that had a roughly drawn map of the location of the quarry. "Will it get us close to this place?"

Azeria tapped her lower lip as she studied the diagram. Finally, she nodded. "Perhaps. It has been long since I was there, and this is not an accurate map. With horses, though, we may be at the quarry within a few days."

"But we will be much, much farther from the isle if it turns out Tam is not there."

"We could split up," suggested Shezar.

"It will be necessary anyway," said Azeria. "I cannot bring this many mundane humans through the paths."

"Why?" said Rezkin.

"The more people, the longer the route. The route for those without access to vimara is even longer. The paths are dangerous. They would not survive."

"But the travel from the Freth Adwyn to here was nearly instantaneous."

"Yes, that is because I traveled it recently, we all possessed power, and two of you are Spirétua. This makes the paths shorter."

"Emperor, my I speak with you privately?" said Farson, eyeing the

Eihelvanan.

Rezkin glanced back at Entris, who had remained relatively silent, and then to Azeria. If they took offense to Farson's tone, they did not show it. Rezkin motioned for Farson to step into the other room.

"What is it?" said Rezkin.

"Who are these people, and why do they seem to think they will be traveling with us?"

"It is a long story and not one I necessarily care to share with you."

Farson's jaw clenched. He said, "I know we taught you to trust no one, but I am asking you to put some trust in me. I can help you with whatever is going on."

Rezkin tilted his head and looked at Farson with skepticism. "You no longer wish to kill me?"

"We have discussed this. Truth be told, I never wanted you dead. I just wanted you to … to *not be* what we made you. But you are different than I anticipated. Since you left that fortress, you have become something else. You are not the monster we thought we created."

Rezkin felt an icy shard invade his tongue as he said, "I am *exactly* what you thought you created; and *they* are here to make sure I do not threaten the world. Between that which was bred into me and that for which I trained, it would be impossible for me to become like these outworlders. It is clear to me now more than ever that I cannot and *will not* ever be one of them—one of *you*."

Farson failed to hide the sadness that haunted his gaze. "Maybe not, but you care about them."

"*Care* is an emotion, Farson, and I cannot afford those."

"You can no longer deny them either."

"I must until these Eihelvanan train me to control them."

"Is that why they are here? To train you?"

"No, they are here to *kill* me should I go mad like Caydean."

Farson's eyes widened. "They think you will?"

"It seems it is inevitable, but I intend to destroy my brother and put the world to rights before I do. Now, we need to split up, and you are not going to like my proposal."

10

Neither Farson nor Shezar had liked Rezkin's plan and had protested adamantly; but, in the end, he was the emperor, and they conceded to his will. Wherever they found Tam, he would surely require a healer's care. Reaylin was their only mage healer, so he assigned her to the group going to the Isle of Sand, along with Yerlin Tomwell. As a life mage, Yerlin could potentially aid Reaylin in helping Tam should they find him. Rezkin was hoping the Eihelvanan would be able to treat Tam if they found him in Verril, but he did not want to depend wholly on his unlikely companions, so he claimed Nanessy as part of his group. Although she was not a healer, she was well-trained as a mage and would hopefully have some insight. What aggravated the strikers was that he refused to take either of them since neither possessed the *talent*, and mundanes would make the route through the paths longer.

After reclaiming Pride and acquiring three more horses in Esk, Rezkin, Nanessy, Azeria, and Entris had crossed through one of Azeria's rifts, leaving Esk and quickly landing themselves in southern Verril on the northern edge of the Drahgfir Mountains. The path had released them onto a steep mountain path atop a cliffside that over-looked the forested hills that made up most of the kingdom. This far south and at such an altitude, winter's bite was severe. The frosty wind whipped their exposed flesh until it was red and tender, and the dry air wicked the moisture from their lips until they were cracked. Along with the others, Rezkin gathered Pride's reins and led the horse on foot down the rocky slope as snow drifts obscured the mountain's treacherous hazards.

It was not long before the snow had soaked his lower pantlegs, and although he wore good-quality boots, his feet were becoming numb. Rezkin focused his mind on his body as he had been trained and *willed* it to warm his frozen extremities. As they heated, so too did the vagri that hung against his skin under his shirt. It was Rezkin's only indication that he was actually using his vimara, and it so disturbed him that he nearly stopped. Encouragement from the frigid chill of the wind, though, kept him going. Once they had rounded a turn where they were protected from the worst of the wind, they paused to regroup.

Nanessy shivered tremulously beneath her wool sweater and even the horses stamped and quivered. Although they had known southern Verril would be cooler than the lands nearer the Souelian, they had not expected to be cast into a blizzard. Rezkin removed his cloak and wrapped it around Nanessy.

"No, please, you need it."

"I will be fine. I have other ways of warming myself."

Nanessy's eyes were wide and not just from the cold. "You cannot use your power to keep yourself warm for too long. Your well will run dry quickly."

"It has never been a problem," Rezkin said.

Entris looked at Rezkin before addressing Nanessy. "Spirétua can regulate body temperature for much longer than a human mage or other Eihelvanan." Turning back to Rezkin, he said, "Still, you are already weakened. You should not depend on your power."

Rezkin ignored Entris's warning and looked at Azeria. "You did not warn us that we would be atop a mountain."

Azeria shrugged. "It has been a long time since I was here. I could not remember exactly where the path led. You are lucky I remembered it at all."

Rezkin shook his head and said, "Let us get as far down this mountain as we can before nightfall. We will look for shelter on the way."

With Azeria in the lead, they made their way down the mountain with great effort. If a trail had ever existed there, it had long been decimated by the natural effects of time, weathering, and erosion. More than a few times, the horses stumbled, and Rezkin was cautious in guiding Pride so that he would not break a leg. After a couple of hours, a new sound reached them on the wind. The insufferable howl of a wounded animal, a wolf, was abruptly truncated. The silence that followed was more concerning than the noise itself.

Rezkin paused, listening intently, his mind filtering out as much of the wind as possible. Beneath its incessant rush was another tone. The low rumble was barely audible to his ears. The horses began to shift nervously, and even Pride tugged at his reins as his teeth gnashed at the air. The tumble of feet against the snow, the crackling of limbs in the underbrush, and the soft whine of frightened beasts grew louder with each passing moment. Seconds later, a pack of wolves, thin with hunger, came rushing out of the dark forest heading straight for them. Rezkin reached over and grabbed the reins of Nanessy's horse as it balked, but he knew he would not be able to fight the wolves and hold the horses in check at the same time. The wolves did not gather or circle as was typical of such hunting parties, though. Instead, they ran with abandon, tripping over each other and yelping as they skidded over the snow and slick, loose rocks. They rushed past Rezkin and his companions without slowing and disappeared around the bend.

From the forest came a blistering screech, like a whet stone sliding across a blade but greater by a thousand-fold. It split the air with concussive force. Every muscle and nerve in Rezkin's body thrummed with anticipation as his gaze roved the dark wood for its source.

Entris's voice was a hushed shout. "Drahg'ahn!"

"*Dragon?*" exclaimed Nanessy. With wide eyes, she looked at Rezkin. "Did he say *dragon?*" Rezkin turned back to look at Entris, as did Nanessy. "But, no!" she said, "I thought they were extinct."

"No," said Entris, "but they are extremely rare. "Their numbers are few, but some dwell here in the Drahgfir Mountains. They tend to hibernate in the winter, but something has awoken this one."

"We should find another way," said Azeria.

"Can you open another pathway?" replied Entris.

"Not so soon, and not here. It took much to get us this far."

A rush of wind shook the trees and then there was a second followed by a third. Thick puffs of snow drifted dizzily over the forest as the cracking of splintered wood accented the thrum of flapping wings.

"It is taking to the air," said Entris. "We must take refuge in the trees. Hopefully it will not see us. Hurry."

The horses protested as they rushed toward the tree line drawing closer to the infernal beast that had not yet come into view. As soon as they were beneath the blanket of the thick canopy, a shadow fell over the snowdrifts that still held the evidence of their passage. The beast swooped from the air, landing on the craggy slope with enough force to dislodge a slurry of boulders and ice that tumbled over the path. The beast's body alone was nearly the size of a galleon, and its long neck and sinuous tail stretched the creature to thrice the length of its body. Its head was large enough to encapsulate an entire horse within its maw, even filled as it was with sharp teeth like giant shards of obsidian. The ridges and horns that gave shape to its face continued gracefully carving out curves and edges down its entire length, and the pale yellow of its underside gave way first to brilliant orange then darkened to burnt embers across its back.

The dragon's long neck arched downward so that its muzzle raked through the snow where Rezkin and his companions had passed, then it turned its head curiously peering into the shadows through a slitted gold-green eye. It nuzzled the ground again, inhaling great whiffs of scent; then it began crawling forward in a tumble of debris.

"It *smells* us," whispered Nanessy.

The beast paused, tilting its head to the side as if listening. Rezkin was still as he gripped the handle of the black blade that was sheathed across his back. Nothing moved, not even the horses, and Rezkin wondered if Entris had done something to them to keep them calm.

The dragon swung its head to and fro as if trying to catch a hint of sound in any direction. It suddenly reared backward, raising its head high and looking into the distance. In a rush, it flapped its wings, once again sending snow and debris into the air, and lifted into the sky. It quickly swooped into the distance as if homing in on prey.

"We must move quietly," whispered Entris, "and we should stick to the trees."

"Agreed," said Azeria. "We should be safe once we reach flatland. They do not like to leave the mountains."

"Truly?" said Nanessy. "It will not follow us?"

Azeria shrugged. "I do not really know. It was meant to sound encouraging."

Nanessy frowned. "That is not helpful."

Entris led his horse down the slope, and then mounted upon reaching less steep ground. As everyone else followed his lead, he spoke quietly. "The drahg'ahn have excellent senses of sight, smell, and hearing, but they have short attention spans. They are easily distracted and will not work hard for what can readily be gotten elsewhere."

"Hence him flying off so quickly," said Nanessy from where she rode beside Entris.

"Yes, but I believe that one was a female. The females are larger than the males."

"You seem to be very familiar with them. Do you encounter them often?"

"No, this is the closest I have ever come to one," said Entris. "They are best avoided."

"No kidding," muttered Nanessy.

"They are not uncommon in the pathways," said Azeria. "My warriors and I have had to fight one on three different occasions. We were eventually able to kill one of them but at a heavy cost (*distressed*)."

"And the other two?"

"We escaped the pathway before they ate us—*most* of us (*agitated*)."

"I am sorry for your loss," said Nanessy, turning around in her saddle to meet the other woman's gaze.

Azeria gave a curt nod. "It was a long time ago."

Although her face gave away nothing, Rezkin could see the pain behind her eyes. He had found that the longer he looked at her, the more he could see the heavy, hidden emotions she had claimed were a trait of the Eihelvanan. He told himself that he only looked so long and hard for the sake of knowing his potential enemy, but he knew that was not the full truth. He wanted to understand what drove her, what made her who she was. He wanted to know *her*, and that sentiment confused him. He did not comprehend why he should care except for the strange connection between them. He wanted to ask her about it; but he sensed she would not be forthcoming.

Nanessy's next question broke through his thoughts. "How many warriors did you have when you killed the dragon?"

"We were fifty-seven strong at the time," said Azeria.

"And how many lived?"

"That is not important."

"Not important? There are only four of us!" said Nanessy. "But"—she pointed toward Entris—"they are Spirétua. That means we're stronger, right?"

Entris said, "Vimara will do us little good against them. The drahg'ahn are strong with power. They can counter anything we throw at them. Our best chance would be to defeat it in physical combat."

Pride abruptly tensed beneath Rezkin, and he suddenly felt warmth at his back. Alarmed, he turned in his saddle to find an inferno barreling toward them. The flame was so hot that the air became heated to a scalding vapor, and trees and leaves were incinerated in a flash as their sparkling embers whipped around on turbulent currents. "Shields!" Rezkin shouted just as the flames singed the long hairs of Pride's tail.

Without question, four layered and interlocking shield wards manifested around the riders and horses. Azeria turned her attention toward the dragon that was licking the air like a snake as it turned its head and spied them with one giant yellow-green eye. She jumped from her saddle and quickly secured her horse to a tree. It balked and squealed as its large eyes rolled around in its head. Even if the dragon did not kill the beast, it was likely to damage itself attempting to escape. Rezkin followed Azeria's example, and even Pride was becoming more difficult than usual. Entris had already secured his horse and was standing in the middle of the scorched path with his sword drawn.

Another burst of flame barreled their way. The horses jerked at their reins and bucked, threatening to break through the wards as they tried to escape the conflagration. Azeria patted her horse's neck and laid her forehead against its face as she whispered something that caused it to settle down until it appeared to be sleeping. Although the fiery assault lasted only a few seconds, it felt like an eternity to Rezkin as he was surrounded by the flames battering his shield. Although it was not the first shield he had created, it was the first one he had erected out of pure instinct. His place at the rear of the party placed him directly in the flames' path, and he was not certain his shield could withstand the brunt of the onslaught. Just as its surface began to break into glimmering fractures, the flames disappeared.

Rezkin's eyes burned with hot tears as he peered through the dry, heated air. Every tree, rock, and speck of dirt was reduced to black powder or melted into a black, glassy puddle in the singed path of destruction. At its terminus was the towering orange and red monstrosity he had hoped to never see again. It stretched its wings amongst the timbers behind it that had been spared its infernal wrath. Even the largest branches were not safe as it thrashed against them, and its victorious screech echoed off the mountain loud enough to elicit a rumble in response.

"I cannot yet open another path!" said Azeria. "There is nowhere to run. Our only hope is to defeat it."

"What?" shouted Nanessy in dismay.

Nanessy's eyes widened with fear then abruptly filled with resolve. She darted over to a young tree and snapped a spell through the air that separated one of its larger branches from the trunk. After clearing it of limbs and shearing the end until it came to a point, she raised it like a spear. Rezkin glanced at the dragon that was shaking its head as it rumbled a warning. Then he looked back at Nanessy. Entris and Azeria were also staring at her.

Nanessy looked between them and said, "What?"

Azeria cocked her head curiously. "Do you know how to wield a spear?"

Nanessy frowned. "No, but I have no sword and would not know how to use one anyway. If I'm going to die, though, I will at least die fighting." She hefted the spear as if to draw their attention toward the dragon and said, "Should you not be focusing on *her?*"

"Just ... hide," said Rezkin as they all turned.

The dragon coiled its long neck and crouched as if preparing to attack. Rezkin did not take his eyes from the beast as he said, "Do we have a plan? What are its weaknesses?"

"I do not know," said Azeria. "Last time we got lucky. One of our spears found a soft spot at the base of the wing. When the dragon fell upon it, the spear was thrust through its heart. At least, that is what we assumed happened. We did not stick around to find out. The fight had attracted *other* things in the paths."

There was no more time. The dragon flapped its wings and surged forward faster than a beast that large should have been able to move. Rezkin hefted his black blade and ran to meet it. The dragon seemed to become confused by his motion and snapped her jaws early. Rezkin's blade rebounded off her hardened jaw with a flash of green lightning. Entris ducked beneath the dragon's head and attempted to impale her from below, but his sword did little damage as it clashed against her scales with a spark. They both rolled out of the way as her neck and then head swung their way. Meanwhile, Azeria was struggling to flank her to no avail as the dragon's long, scaley tail whipped back and forth hindering her progress.

Entris dodged the beast's next attempt to bite his head off only to fall prey to the wicked talons protruding from its dexterous fingers. He fell to the ground with two grievous trenches gouged into his back through his clothing and armor as if he had none. As Azeria attacked from the other side, Rezkin pivoted to grab hold of Entris and drag him from beneath the beast's bulk. Entris pushed away Rezkin's hands as soon as he had gained his feet. Although his eyes were wide with pain, and his jaw was set against his torment, Entris raised his sword and prepared to attack the beast again. Rezkin nodded in approval, then turned to meet the dragon.

They both dodged a swipe of the tail as the beast turned away from them in pursuit of Azeria. The general continued her assault on the beast's left flank as she searched futilely for a weakness. A shadow fell over them, and Rezkin looked up in time to see the beast's leathery wing descending. He flattened himself to the ground as the heavy bone-lined wing beat against his back, pressing the air from his lungs. It swiped once as it ascended pushing him to forcefully roll into a tree trunk. His armor took the brunt of the hit, but Rezkin felt something crack in his back causing a sharp spike of pain to run down his leg. Soft hands gripped his arm, and he looked up to see Nanessy trying to pull him to his feet.

"Get up!" she shouted, and her eyes widened as she looked over his head. Then she darted away from him gripping her spear with white knuckles.

Rezkin steadied himself on his knees and blinked up through wet tears just as the dragon's maw descended upon him. He felt the strong tug of air as it inhaled deeply. Raising the black blade, he prepared to slice the beast from the inside if necessary. Just as the dragon's jaws began to close around him and he could see pieces of flesh, fur, and bone between its razor-sharp teeth, the dragon paused. Rezkin could hear shouts from the others as they attacked her from behind, but she ignored them. She backed inches away and snapped her jaw shut in his face, disregarding the ping of his sword off her impenetrable scales. She pressed her face into his chest, knocking him over and pinning him against the tree as she took several sharp breaths through her nose. When she was finished sniffing him, she turned her massive head so that her yellow-green eye peered at him from within arm's reach. Her slitted pupil narrowed as it roved his person. Rezkin's grip on his sword tightened as he considered thrusting it into the vulnerable tissue. She seemed to read his motions, because the eye abruptly focused on his sword. She glanced back at him as if in warning, huffed, then whipped her head away in a dizzying motion that sent snow flurries exploding into the air.

Entris had somehow made it onto the beast's back in the time she was preoccupied with Rezkin. The dragon was ignoring them both, though, as she snapped repeatedly at Azeria who was flipping gracefully through the air like an acrobat. Azeria's sword lashed out during one such aerial maneuver, scoring the dragon's tongue and drawing first blood from the beast. The dragon hissed and chomped at Azeria as Entris attempted to wedge his blade between two scales on the dragon's neck. Rezkin thought he must have been successful because the beast suddenly roared and reared backward launching Entris into the air. Just as her underside became exposed, a wooden spear flew past Rezkin to lodge itself in the soft tissue at the base of the dragon's wing. The dragon twisted her head to spy the spear then ducked to yank it out with her teeth.

Rezkin took a deep breath and sheathed the black blade that had been ineffectual against the dragon's hard scales. Hoping the enchantments on his Sheyalin blades would fare better, he drew *Kingslayer* and *Bladesunder* and shot forward with a speed to match the Eihelvanan. He ducked and dodged heavy footfalls as the beast stomped and reared in her efforts to dislodge Entris and Azeria from her back. A snowy gust propelled him forward as a wing nearly clipped him, then Rezkin's blades collided with her underside. Deep rents were gouged into her scales near the injury Nanessy had already inflicted. Rezkin jumped over a flailing tail and rolled to avoid a clawed foot before bounding to his feet. He thrust his swords upward with an accuracy born of years of training. *Kingslayer* and *Bladesunder* found the gouges in the beast's armor, slicing deeply into the tissue beneath and spilling blood over Rezkin's face and torso. The dragoness released a bellow louder and more penetrating than all her previous screeches.

A phenomenal crack echoed through the air, and the ground began to vibrate. The shifting became a rumbling, and Rezkin glanced behind him toward the source of the cacophony. Massive pilings of ice and snow were tumbling down the side of the mountain gaining momentum and mass as they accelerated toward the lower land where they stood. The dragon's head swooped upward as she thrust out her wings and stood on her hind legs. She spied the oncoming avalanche and roared once again before taking to the air. The beast had abandoned them to their plight as the ground shook and trees began to topple. Azeria and Entris came rushing toward Rezkin shouting something he could not hear, but he did not need to know what they said to understand the urgency.

Rezkin gathered Nanessy and pushed her toward her own horse as he closed the distance with his battle charger. As the first boulders of snow surged into the scorched clearing, Rezkin kicked his steed into a frenzied gallop down the forested slope. He did not look back to see that Entris and Azeria followed. Instead, he urged his horse onward with the expectation that the others were doing the same. Just as Pride's hooves left the edge of an embankment over a rocky craig, the avalanche overcame them. Rezkin tumbled and turned as he tried to tuck his limbs and head into his body. It was only seconds before he came to a stop and the rumbling subsided.

Surrounding Rezkin was frigid ice and snow, dark in the depths yet subtly illuminated toward the surface. He shifted and squirmed to gain breathing space, but the snow was packed tightly around him. Without concern for the energy drain, Rezkin began accelerating the heating effect on his body, the vagri at his chest becoming particularly hot, until the snow around him began to drip with moisture. It crackled and shifted as it turned to icy slush, and then he was able to push his way toward the surface. It had been his luck that he had been buried only a few feet deep. As soon as he was free of his frigid prison, Rezkin began searching for his companions. Entris was already free and digging through the snow toward what Rezkin hoped was a person. Rezkin spied Nanessy's horse, which was only half buried and was thrashing to be free. He rushed to its side and began sifting through snow to find the mage.

The snow pulsed as if a bubble was popping beneath it, and Rezkin knew it had to be Nanessy attempting to use her power to break herself free. He knelt beside the spot and tossed mounds of snow to the side. Eventually, he found a frozen hand and grabbed for it. A startled squeak emanated from the snow before he managed to pull her free. Nanessy's lips were already turning blue as she shivered in his grasp. Rezkin placed his hands on either side of her face and shared the warmth of his vimara with her just long enough to stop her shivering. He noted that Entris had found Azeria relatively unharmed, then turned to search for the horses.

Pride had managed to free himself with his thrashing and flailing and had, luckily, been uninjured. Azeria's horse, on the other hand, had suffered a broken neck and was deceased. Entris's horse had come up lame but was still able to walk. After finding most of their supplies still secured to their saddles, they trudged down the snowy slope. When they came to the cover of forest at the edge of the debris flow, they stopped to see to their wounds.

Nanessy ordered Entris to sit on a fallen trunk, and he did so without argument. She leaned over him as she pulled at the tatters of his shirt. "You are severely injured," she said.

"Yes, the dragon's claws scored my back."

She swallowed and nodded. "I saw that. I thought it had killed you."

He hissed as she set to removing debris from the wound. "I am not so easily defeated," he growled.

Azeria dropped her pack at Entris's side, and Rezkin noted that she was favoring her left shoulder. She turned to him with a sharp command. "Heal him."

Rezkin nodded and reached for his pack. "I can suture the wounds, plus I have some herbs that should prevent infection and stimulate healing."

"No, *heal* him," she said. "I have little ability, but all Spirétua possess some amount of healing ability."

"Not *all*," growled Entris.

Azeria shrugged, which caused her to wince. "He has many abilities. He surely has this one. Show him how so that he may repair you."

Entris released a heavy breath and waved Rezkin toward him He said, "Those who are in tune with their own bodies are most successful in healing. With your physical training, you should do well; however, it requires compassion to guide the power."

"Compassion?"

"Yes, the more you *feel* for the plight of the patient, the stronger your healing ability."

Rezkin's hand began to hurt, and he realized he was gripping *Bladesunder*'s pommel too tightly. He released his grip and relaxed his hand. His teeth then began to hurt, and he noticed he was clenching his jaw. He inhaled a deep breath and relaxed his muscles. He wondered why he was so tense. The battle was over, and he did not perceive any imminent threats—unless the dragon returned. It was a possibility. But that was not what had him wound tight. He was disconcerted, uncomfortable, and unwilling. He did not want to *feel* anything for Entris, compassion or otherwise. Entris was an ally for now but could easily become an enemy. As an ally, Rezkin wanted Entris in peak form, but Entris was faster and possibly stronger than he was. If the Spirétua-lyé became an enemy, Rezkin would prefer him weakened with injury and pain. Allowing himself to *feel* for Entris was out of the question.

"I cannot help him."

Azeria took a step toward him, her hand resting on her own hilt. She was tense and scowling. It appeared that in her fatigued and disheveled state, she was less able to maintain her composure. "You *can*not or you *will* not?"

Rezkin met her challenging gaze. "I will not."

"Rezkin!" Nanessy gasped in dismay.

Rezkin did not turn to look at the mage and instead maintained his hold on Azeria's gaze while he watched Entris in his peripheral vision. While Azeria's stance had become hostile, the Spirétua-lyé was looking at him contemplatively. Entris said, "It is fine, Azeria (*earnest*). Let him be."

She turned on Entris. "How can you say that? Your wounds are deep, and he refuses to assist you (*incensed*). Perhaps we were wrong in our assessment of him."

"No," said Entris. "He is exactly who he claims to be (*disappointed*). *This* is who he is, and this is why he has not gone mad."

"Then it matters not whether he is mad," she replied. "A ruler without compassion is more dangerous than a madman (*wary*)."

"He does have compassion," said Nanessy. "I have seen him. He cares for his people."

This time Rezkin did look at her, and he did not bother to hide his incredulity. "Logic dictates that I take care of my followers. They are valuable resources that would go to waste should they fail to thrive. It is *Rule 98 – Conserve resources*. Compassion has nothing to do with it."

Her jaw hung open in disbelief. "Resources? Despite what you and my uncle claim, I cannot believe that is all we are to you."

"Then you choose to disillusion yourself even when all evidence points to the contrary."

"No, it is not *all evidence*," she spat. "It is what you were taught to believe about yourself, but I know that you are more than that belief. You are *good*, Rezkin, whether you know it or not. Your actions, if not your words, prove it to be so."

Rezkin shook his head and turned back to Azeria, but she was no longer looking at him. She was staring at Nanessy. She glanced between the two of them as if she did not know who to believe. Entris groaned as he straightened, and Azeria seemed to make up her mind. She scowled at Rezkin and said, "This is your rule? Conserve resources?"

Rezkin gave her a curt nod. "It is."

"Is knowledge not a resource?"

"Yes, sometimes the greatest."

"Then acquire this resource—the knowledge of healing (*determined*)."

Rezkin looked from her to Entris. The ability to heal *was* valuable knowledge. Such had been his reasoning for requiring Reaylin to make use of hers, and it was one of the many reasons he had become a master healer of the mundane. Perhaps the knowledge of healing would be more valuable than keeping Entris weak. Although he felt no compassion for Entris, he could see the value in helping him.

"Very well. I will do this," he said.

Entris was visibly discomfited with having Rezkin at his back, particularly in his vulnerable state, but he endured it regardless as he explained to Rezkin how the healing worked. Rezkin followed the Spirétua-lyé's directions, yet his troubles came when searching for the link between his own vimara and that of Entris. Every time he tried to make the link, it was as if his power recoiled. When it did not work on his fifth attempt, Rezkin took a step back.

"You are not *trying*," hissed Azeria, her breath a puff in the frigid air.

"I have tried five times," replied Rezkin.

Entris's breath hitched as he stood. He removed his tattered shirt and began slicing it into strips using his belt knife. "Leave him be, Azeria," he said. "He cannot do it (*pained*)."

"It should be easy for him," she said. "He has the power (*frustrated*)."

"He was not lying, Azeria. He cannot make the link because he feels nothing (*disturbed*)."

"That is deplorable," she said, stepping into Rezkin's personal space. She pointed to Entris's ravaged back and said, "How can you look at that and feel *nothing* for his suffering? He is a *person*."

"He is a warrior," said Rezkin. "He was injured in battle. He failed to protect his back. It is a consequence of his actions, and with proper treatment for infection, his body will heal on its own."

"You act as though you have never been injured," said Azeria.

"Of course I have been injured. People have had their own reasons for wanting me alive and well. Compassion did not play a role in that either."

"You are disgusting," growled Azeria as she turned and stomped toward Entris. After performing what little healing she could provide, she snatched the strips of cloth from his hands and began winding them around Entris's torso. Rezkin looked back toward Nanessy, but she only crossed her arms in a huff and turned away from him. With both woman angry with him, it occurred to Rezkin that it was not a good idea to alienate his companions. They wanted him to have feelings, yet he had only been following the *Rules*, and the Eihelvanan had already established that his lack of emotion was what kept him from going mad. These outworlders were a contradiction he could not resolve.

After a short rest and the consumption of a few trail rations, the party was ready to move again. Although Entris could not heal himself, he did well in healing Azeria's injury and those of the horses.

Nanessy said, "Since Azeria's horse was killed in the avalanche, I could ride with Entris. I can keep an eye on him in case he develops a fever."

Rezkin did not care where Nanessy rode, although if she did ride with Entris, she could alert them quickly if he passed out and fell from his horse. He said nothing when Entris glanced at him questioningly.

Azeria, on the other hand, said. "You and I should ride together. We are lighter than the men. It will be less strain on the horse (*earnest*)."

Nanessy opened her mouth, but Entris quickly said, "It is fine, Azeria. Nanessy can ride with me."

A crease formed between Azeria's brows as she looked at them, but she said nothing further.

They worked their way down the mountain sticking to the densest forest so that they might not be seen from above. They had survived their first confrontation with the dragon by chance, and they did not want to risk another. When the dragon did not return, it was Nanessy who broke the silence.

"Rezkin, why did the dragon not kill you?"

Rezkin reached up to clutch the stone—no, *egg*—that hung around his neck. "I am uncertain but believe it recognized the vagri."

"I agree," said Entris. "It probably felt the bond. Drahg'ahn are not mindless beasts. They are intelligent creatures. It probably realized that to kill you would mean the death of the vagri as well."

Rezkin noticed the shiver that overtook Nanessy and understood her concern. It was one thing to be hunted by a predatory animal and quite another to be pursued by a calculating intelligence.

"You moved fast," said Entris, "much faster than I have seen you move in the past (*impressed*)."

Rezkin slid him a glance but said nothing.

Entris turned toward Azeria. "You said you did not believe he would improve appreciably. Are you still not convinced?"

Azeria did not spare a look for Rezkin, and by the tone she took, she was still angry with him for not healing Entris. "Yes, he was fast. He should not have been able to improve so quickly. Are you sure you had nothing to do with that (*suspicious*)?"

"I would say if I did (*earnest*)."

Azeria's stern countenance did not change as she kicked her horse to ride ahead. The sun was still high upon the ridge, but once they descended into the shadow of the peak, the wind stirred, and the temperature dropped. Rezkin's stomach was rumbling, and his eyes felt heavy, but he was still alert. Entris looked worn as well, but he and Nanessy were at least able to share some body heat and help shield each other from the wind. Azeria eventually fell back to ride silently beside Rezkin, although she still had not spoken with him. Her cloak was wrapped tightly around her, but her lips were pale and her hair whipped around her head with every gust. Rezkin's brow furrowed as he stared at her. Although she glanced his way, she opted to ignore his attention, and her demeanor did not change. Her eyes seemed darker and deeper set, her mouth turned downward, and she was slumped in her saddle.

Rezkin steered Pride closer to her side and said, "You are fatigued."

She looked at him and nodded with a sigh.

His studious gaze roved her body, and although she had expressed no discomfort, he realized she was miserable. "You are not Spirétua. You are unable to regulate your temperature for long, and you have no winter gear. You also spent much energy in the pathways and attempting to heal Entris."

"Yes," she said, seemingly surprised he had noticed.

Rezkin decided that if he could warm himself, then he should be capable of warming her, too. He said, "I would like to try something, if I may."

She looked at him skeptically but nodded.

He slowly reached over to her, and she quickly ducked away from his grasping hand. He held his hand still as if reassuring a wild animal that he meant no harm, and she eased back within his reach. She stiffened as he lightly gripped her neck just below her ear, his thumb pressed over her pulse, which seemed to quicken the longer he touched her. Then he imagined the warmth of his body growing and spreading into her. He could feel *something* shifting and moving within him as though it was unfurling. Azeria's eyes widened, and then they fluttered shut on a sigh as she relaxed. The color returned to her fingers and lips, and she actually smiled.

Rezkin pulled his hand away, and he felt as though he had lost something. He wanted immediately to touch her again to get it back. Azeria gave him an odd look, which he assumed was her distaste for him warring with her appreciation for the warmth. Rezkin did not wait for her thanks as he dropped back to ride behind her. She shifted in her saddle and glanced back at him a few times but said nothing.

After a few hours' ride, the sky had darkened, and Rezkin raised his voice only enough that Entris and Nanessy, who had taken the lead, might hear. "There," he said. "We can make camp in there."

The place he had indicated was not a cave exactly. A fallen tree leaned against a massive boulder pressed up against the cliff face, and additional branches and talus had accumulated atop the two to create a hovel. Upon further inspection, it was clear that the space could fit them and the three horses, so long as they huddled closely and did not move about.

"This will not hold up against the drahg'ahn," said Entris.

"No, but if we hide and are quiet, it may not detect us," said Rezkin.

"I do not like it," said Azeria. "It has no defenses and only one path of escape. Also, we will not be able to light a fire here (*dissatisfied*)."

"I know it is not ideal, but it is nearly dark. Either we stay here or out in the open. This will at least protect us from the snow and wind."

"I see your point," said Azeria. "We will need to keep watch."

"I will keep first watch," he said.

They secured the horses inside the hovel, and Nanessy used her power to heat enough snow to slake their thirst without having to start a fire. Rezkin sat down beside her and shuffled through his pack to find some dried meat and fresh fruit, and the others did the same. They ate in silence, still shivering from the cold but protected from the wind.

"We should sleep," said Entris as he finished consuming his rations.

Nanessy shivered and pulled Rezkin's cloak more tightly around her. "I do not think I can. I am too cold."

Entris shifted to sit beside her then said, "Come. I will keep you warm. It will be easier if you are closer."

After another shiver wracked her body, she scooted into his embrace. Azeria appeared thoughtful as she watched them. Then she looked at Rezkin and said, "Would you expend less energy if we were close, as well?"

Rezkin considered the question. The answer was *yes*. He had been sharing his energy with her for hours, and he was feeling the drain on what little he had left. At the same time, he was not sure he wanted the general to be any closer. The woman was skilled with a blade and possessed the power of the Eihelvanan, not to mention it was not so long ago that she would have been satisfied to see him dead. As she looked at him with those entrancing silver eyes, though, the thought crossed his mind that it was perhaps worth the risk.

As fatigue gripped him, Rezkin dipped his head and then sat next to the female so that their sides were touching. He did not pull her into him, though, and she did not move toward him. Rather, when they touched, she stiffened, and it was some time before she began to relax.

He said, "Sleep. I will keep watch over the entrance from here and wake you when it is your turn."

Azeria nodded and then lay down beside him with her head on her pack. The curve of her backside pressed against Rezkin's leg, and an unfamiliar thought crossed his mind. He briefly wondered what it would be like to be closer to her, to be intimate, even. Would she try to kill him like the first woman his masters had set upon him? Would she use him for her own gain like Erisial? More importantly, though, what was *his* motivation for wanting such a thing? He was not in a position to be siring offspring, and he could not think of an advantage to such intimacy between them. Although he was aware of the obsessions and cravings that motivated outworlders, he had never thought to succumb to such weaknesses. Could it be that the only driving force behind his thoughts was simple *desire*?

He shook his head at the thought. There was nothing simple about desire. It drove men and women alike to do unspeakable things when it could not be sated. Desire was an enemy in and of itself, one that he intended to vanquish before it had a chance to take hold inside him. He put thoughts of Azeria out of his mind and turned his attention toward the entrance where he could see the last vestiges of day surrendering to the frigid night.

11

Grey met Rezkin and his party that morning. The sky was grey. The snow-covered land was grey. Even the trees appeared grey as the sun seemed incapable of making an appearance. Throughout the day, they forged a path over the forested hills. As they descended, the biting wind gave way to cool currents, and the incessant cloud cover that blocked the sun's soothing rays dissipated. The appearance of wildlife was the first indication that the dragon had not visited the lower altitude, and some of the tension in Rezkin's shoulders released. By the time they broke at midday, they felt reasonably confident they could risk a small fire to cook a fresh kill.

They were seated about the fire awaiting the meal while Rezkin continued to mull over the thoughts that had been plaguing him all morning. Since his inability to heal Entris, a chill had settled between him and the rest of his party that had nothing to do with the weather. Rezkin was considering the conundrum when he broached another topic that had been on his mind. "The syek-lyé spoke of someone named Gizahl. Who is he?"

Entris shifted uncomfortably and glanced at Azeria before answering. "Gizahl is the oldest of the Eihelvanan still alive—we *believe* (*hopeful*). It has been a couple of centuries since anyone has laid eyes upon him. He is thousands upon thousands of years old."

"Where is he?"

"We do not know for certain, but the last person to speak with him said he was going to Pruar."

"That was over two hundred years ago," said Azeria. "If he is still alive, he could be anywhere by now (*doubtful*)."

"But the syek-lyé thinks he can help me. Is there no one else?"

"As I said before, every human-born Spirétua has gone mad. If there is a way to prevent it, no one knows—besides, perhaps, Gizahl (*skeptical*)."

"I cannot imagine possessing the amount of knowledge he must have acquired," said Nanessy. "Thousands of years' worth of information—where would you put it all?"

"You are assuming he remembers it all," said Rezkin. "It is possible that any knowledge beyond that of a few centuries disappears with time."

Entris shook his head. "I do not believe that to be the case. While I cannot presume to know the extent of his memory, it has been reported that he has many memories of ancient times, as do the other elders. The syek-lyé, for example, is nearly two thousand years old, and when he speaks of the time of the Great War, he does so with clarity, as if it were only yesterday."

"When was this great war?" said Nanessy.

"About fifteen hundred years ago."

She said, "I cannot believe that man—the one in the council chamber—was two thousand years old. It seems so impossibly long, and he looks so young."

"I have often pitied humans their short lifespans," said Entris. "You must live quickly—squeezing all of your life into only a few decades (*doleful*)."

Nanessy shifted. "Mages live a little longer than mundanes."

Entris gazed at her steadily as he said, "Yes, but still such a brief time by comparison (*mournful*)."

Nanessy held the male's gaze. "We learn to seize opportunities before they are gone."

An odd energy seemed to hover between the two as Rezkin watched the exchange. It seemed some unspoken message had passed between them. Azeria huffed with disgust as she got to her feet and tromped into the trees.

"Where are you going?" said Entris, as if suddenly realizing he and Nanessy were not alone.

"That is none of your business (*determined*)."

When Nanessy looked at Rezkin, her cheeks turned pink, and she quickly dropped her gaze to the ground. Rezkin had the sudden sense that he should leave the two of them alone, then wondered if it was better that he did not. Although he was not Nanessy's keeper, he did feel some obligation toward her and, oddly enough, toward her uncle Farson. After another glance at the two, though, he decided that Nanessy was not his charge and whatever did or did not happen between them was none of his business.

He stood, collected one of the spits from the fire, and followed Azeria into the trees. Although she had not been attempting to hide her tracks, she had left little by which to follow her. Rezkin did manage to find her, though, sitting beneath the boughs of a rowan tree. She appeared peaceful as she stared up through the boughs, but he knew he had caught her attention.

"I brought you something to eat," he said as he took a seat beside her.

She gave him a sideways glance and said, "I have no desire to speak of it (*irritated*)."

"I did not ask," he replied.

Rezkin began cutting through the meat with his belt knife, and after a few silent seconds, Azeria said, "Do you not care?"

He glanced at her then refocused on butchering the small catch. "Why would I care?"

She did not appear upset but merely thoughtful. "All this time she has wanted you. I have seen it, so obvious. And now she has suddenly turned her attention toward *him* (*bemused*)."

Rezkin shrugged as he handed her some of the hot sustenance. "Perhaps it is his power that attracts her. It makes no difference to me. I do not want her." He paused, then said, "I do not see why it matters to *you*. Entris said you rejected him."

"I-I did not exactly reject him, but neither did I accept him." She shrugged. "But that is not what sickens me. I care not if Entris chooses another. I only do not want it to be *her* (*earnest*)."

"Why? Nanessy is *ro*. She is an innocent, and she is an accomplished mage. I see no reason for you to dislike her."

"I do not *dislike* her. She is *human*. She will grow *old* and die, and he will keep living. It disgusts me."

Rezkin pondered this as he ate. Then he said, "What about me? If I were to choose a lover, who should it be? I am human born, but I may live much longer than a human, perhaps as long as the Eihelvanan. By your reasoning, I should not choose a human, yet you have clearly communicated your disapproval toward me having anything to do with your people."

Her gaze sought the darker shadows of the forest as she ate. Then she said, "You are an anomaly. You do not belong to either race."

The pain Rezkin felt in his chest was difficult to suppress, and the vagri abruptly began to heat. Ignoring the feeling, he said, "Entris believes I belong with the Eihelvanan."

Azeria's sharp gaze snapped to his face. It traced his features as she looked at him inscrutably. "You have our looks. Some might even think you handsome. But you are deformed (*disgusted*)."

He tilted his head curiously. "Deformed? How so?"

"Your ears are stunted. Perhaps you could use your power to make them appear normal."

Rezkin wondered how she had come to that conclusion. He had been born to humans, so he looked human. To him, that was not a deformity. "Why should I?"

She shrugged. "To belong?"

Rezkin felt something unusual bubble up from within him and he laughed—a genuine laugh. Azeria's eyes widened with surprise. He said, "Are my ears all that keeps me from belonging? Would you accept me should I change them? I think not. There is more. Why do you treat me with such disdain?"

"In all the time that I have watched you, I have never seen you laugh," she said.

"Nor I you," he replied, except that he did remember her laughing —in a dream. Something about the look she gave him told him that she knew it as well. He leaned forward. "Are they real?"

She blinked at him. "Are what real?"

"The dreams. Are you truly there, or are they mine alone?"

Her eyes widened again. "What dreams?" she whispered.

"I have been dreaming of you since long before I met you. I already knew you when first I saw your face, and I think you knew me. Do you dream of me?"

Azeria swallowed hard, and for the first time, he saw an expression other than disgust or apathy. It was fear. She abruptly stood and said, "We need to go. We do not have time to sit around chatting like younglings." She stepped around him, and Rezkin followed her back to where their companions waited.

Barely more than an hour later, Pride's hooves trod across level ground. They had left the mountains behind and, hopefully, the dragon. Rezkin had decided that the Drahgfir—which translated to *dragon fire*—Mountains were aptly named and not just the result of bygone legends. Now that he knew the ahn'an, daem'ahn, Eihelvanan, and drahg'ahn truly existed, he wondered what other mysteries the world held. Prior to his adventures, he had thought the worst he might encounter in the wilds would be wolves, drauglics, or vuroles. He knew, now, that he needed to reassess the priorities on his list of potential enemy combatants.

As Pride clomped across the narrow expanse of dry, deserted plain toward the forest that covered most of Verril, Rezkin considered what improvements to his weapons he could make. *Kingslayer* and *Bladesunder* were rife with enchantments, none of which would necessarily improve performance with the blades. The black blade, on the other hand remained pure and mysterious. Master Swordsmith Keskian from Skutton had explained that the sword had been forged with a previously undiscovered mage material, and Journeyman Wesson had mentioned that mage materials more easily held enchantments than did natural materials. Rezkin considered the way he had trapped the fire elementals in the Sword of Eyre in Gendishen, causing it to become eternally enflamed. He thought about the many ways in which he might improve upon the black blade using enchantments and elementals, yet he could not decide what would be most advantageous.

Rezkin swung the blade in lazy circles switching hands and spinning it in front and behind him, enjoying the weight and balance of the unique weapon. Nanessy's gaze was riveted by his motions, and Entris and Azeria both cast glances his way. Eventually, Entris said, "May I examine your blade? I have never seen its like."

Rezkin tipped his head, and Entris drew his horse closer to Rezkin's earning a snort from Pride. After handing over the blade, Rezkin felt a brief but sudden loss. He did not know why he had such a reaction. He still had the two Sheyalins and plenty of other bladed weapons should he need them. Somehow, though, it felt wrong to hand the black blade to another.

Entris said, "The weight of this weapon is deceiving. By its length, it should be much heavier. From what material was this forged?"

"That is a bit of a mystery. It was a previously unknown mage material, and the smith used all that existed in the making of the blade."

"Fascinating. I have seen you fight with this. It glows when struck."

Rezkin nodded. "Yes, it seems to absorb the energy of the strike, preventing it from reaching me. I believe it may be capable of compounding the energy against my opponent, yet I have not been able to make it happen. I have been considering what enchantments I could place upon it."

Entris handed the weapon back to Rezkin. "You have much power of your own, if you would only allow your well to replenish. I suggest you enchant it with power that is not yours to wield already."

Rezkin considered that as he sheathed the sword. "You mean a power against the demons?"

With a nod, Entris said, "Perhaps. It would be advantageous when fighting the daem'ahn and their ahn'tep progeny. It is easier to fight them with their own power."

"But where would I get such enchantments? So far as I know, the only sources of such powers are the Sen, and the only Sen I have known are no longer living."

"Perhaps your companion would accommodate you. Your close partnership has astounded me from the beginning, but it seems he is willing to do your bidding (*appalled*)."

"Of which companion do you speak?"

"The daem'ahn, of course."

Rezkin's blood froze at the thought that one of his companions might be a demon. He remembered, now, that Entris had mentioned a demon amongst his followers once before, but he had been preoccupied with other matters at the time to fully consider it. He said, "Who is this demon?"

Entris and Azeria both looked at him with surprise. Entris said, "Your mage—the one called Wesson."

The shock that rocked Rezkin was only superseded by the knowledge that what Entris said was true. Although he had not known nor considered that Wesson might be a demon, he could not deny that it felt right.

Nanessy exclaimed, "*Wesson* is possessed by a demon? I cannot believe you. He is one of the kindest souls I have ever encountered."

"I did not say he was possessed," said Entris. He looked at Rezkin. "Can you truly not see it (*surprised*)?"

"Wait," said Nanessy. "You just said Wesson is a demon. Now you say he is not?"

Entris shook his head. "This Wesson is not *possessed* by the daem'ahn. He *is* the daem'ahn. I do not know how he resides in this realm, but he is just as much daem'ahn as he is human, perhaps more so."

"You are saying he is some kind of hybrid spawn?" shouted Nanessy.

"No, I cannot explain it. When I look at him, it is as though I am seeing both at the same time. He is both human *and* daem'ahn (*confused*). Can you honestly tell me that you have not seen it in his power? Does he not find sadistic pleasure in his destruction?"

Nanessy shook her head adamantly. "No, he is so sensitive. He hates himself when he hurts people." Then she paused as if remembering, and the memory seemed to shake her. "Well, I do remember once …"

She trailed off, so Rezkin prompted her to continue. She peered at him through unshed tears. "It was when we were fighting the sea monster and the demon that controlled it on the ship. I had struck my head and thought I did not remember it correctly. Wesson was casting, and as he released his destruction, he laughed. His eyes were full of glee. But it was only moments later that he was huddled on the deck sobbing in grief."

Entris said, "I have never heard of a daem'ahn existing in this realm in such a way. It is possible that, unlike a possession where the daem'ahn controls the body, Wesson's humanity and strength of will allows him to maintain control over his destructive tendencies (*skeptical*)."

"Yes!" said Nanessy, as if grasping for any reason to uphold Wesson's good name. "Wesson is capable of wielding both destructive *and* constructive power. Surely that shows that he has been able to overcome his, um, *demonic* nature."

"Although it is an interesting study," said Entris, "the daem'ahn cannot be permitted to remain in this realm (*adamant*). All daem'ahn must be eradicated."

"Just as you would eradicate me?" Rezkin said, his voice carrying with it the frigidness he felt inside. Although these Eihelvanan seemed to want to help people, they were quick to judge and even more eager to destroy anything they thought to be a threat. Rezkin did not like that they considered him to be one of those things, nor did he care that they thought so of Wesson. The mage had been a dedicated and loyal follower even though Rezkin had never required an oath of fealty from him.

"Wesson has proven himself time and again to be both capable and trustworthy," he said in a tone that would brook no argument. "There will be no more talk of ending him from *anyone*. If and when he should need to be dealt with, *I* will be the one to do it."

Entris began, "You may not be capable—"

"I said I will do it," Rezkin growled. "He is to be left alone, and anything relating to him and demons is to be kept between us. Am I understood?"

Entris stiffened and pulled his horse to a stop blocking Pride's passage. Pride stomped and gnashed his teeth at the other horse, which shied away to Entris's frustration. With his mount under control again, Entris said, "You are in no position to be issuing orders."

"I am the Emperor of the Souelian. It is my duty to issue orders."

"And it is my duty as Spirétua-lyé to see that no daem'ahn treads in the Realm of Life (*determined*)."

"Just as you take your duties seriously, so do I mine. Wesson rides beneath *my* banner. He is my responsibility."

Entris's heated gaze might have burned through him had he not met it with the frigid ice of his own. After several tense breaths, Entris said, "Very well, but should you fail, I will not hesitate to exorcise the daem'ahn from this world."

12

As Wesson stepped onto the deck, his wavy, caramel-colored hair was snagged by the wind, tossing the curls into his face. He looked back into the dark interior of the cabin and said, "You may want to grab a shawl if you plan on coming out."

Celise was full of energy as she pranced up to him and took his hand. Wesson immediately found it necessary to brush his hair from his eyes with the same hand, using the wind as an excuse to extricate himself from the woman who claimed to be his matria. Celise did not seem to take offense as she pulled her bright orange shawl around her bare shoulders. She slid past him and stood beneath the sun, bathing in its light with her face tilted toward the sky. Her loose, orange pants rustled in the wind, and her shawl billowed behind her, exposing the tanned expanse of midriff that was not covered by the feeble wrap of her top. The beads woven into her chestnut locks glimmered gold in the sunlight, and when she turned to smile at him, Wesson was sure she was secretly fae. Nothing less would have the power to grip him like she did.

His cheeks flamed, and he quickly drew his gaze from the young woman. Although she was beautiful, she was not Diyah. The deck-hand upon which his gaze landed next was decidedly less intriguing than Celise, and Wesson quickly turned to searching for the striker with whom he needed to speak. He found Kai lounging in a net that was stretched like a hammock to hold his weight.

"Journeyman, so good to see you out in the fresh air. I take it your, ah, *friend*, there, is feeling better?"

Wesson glanced behind him to see that Celise had followed. She kept her distance, though, as she usually did from the other men on the ship. Wesson could tell that she was hesitant around the larger warriors and seafarers, and for some reason that reticence bothered him. He worried that perhaps something untoward had happened to her in the past.

Turning back to Kai, he said, "Have we skirted the isles yet?"

Kai cleared his throat. "We changed course in the night. Ships were seen on the horizon. We thought it best to avoid them. It seems the southern waters are swarming with Caydean's men. Apprentice Mage Manding was up most of the night speeding our voyage. We will be disembarking to the east of the isles. Ashaiian ships will be near."

"East? Then we backtracked."

"Aye, but it will put us closer to Kaibain. We only have to get through the Fendendril Forest to meet the Lorelis Trade Route in Banton."

"I am familiar with the area. The locals do not take kindly to anything unusual coming out of the Fendendril."

"I should think not seeing as how it is haunted."

Wesson gave the striker a reproachful look, but Kai only grinned.

"It seems that after his death, Duke Ytrevius's forces in the south were conscripted by the royal army," said Kai. "They're occupying the Southern Trade Route from Cerrél to Port Manai. It will be extremely difficult to infiltrate the Mage Academy in Kaibain right now." Kai held up the portable mage relay. "We just got word that the army is being sent to subdue the west."

"Caydean is moving against the west? Why?" Wesson's heart raced with alarm as he thought about his mother and Diyah in Benbrick.

"Well, it seems the west is under rebel occupation; *and*, apparently, Torrel and Sandea are on the move. They've been sending troops down the coast by sea as well as by land. I would say Caydean will want to stop any sort of agreement from forming between the two groups. Perhaps we should forget about the Mage Academy and head to the west. We could dock in Port Gull to resupply. From there, we can sail up the Aen to Maylon. The river is large enough to permit a vessel of this size."

"I am familiar with the route," said Wesson.

His gaze sought the placid shifting grey-blue of the sea as he considered all the conditions that had set him on this course toward his home, the home from which he had fled little more than six years ago with a mob on his heels and guilt in his soul. He wanted more than anything to take the striker's suggestion, but he had a responsibility for the Mage Academy and for Rezkin.

"We shall disembark in the east and make our way to Kaibain. I need to at least try to get the Mage and Battle Mage Academies on our side."

Kai rubbed his beard and looked at him thoughtfully. "Very well. This is *your* mission. If you think it has a chance of success ..." He paused then shook his head. "From what I have heard, you are our strongest mage, *and* you are one of the few among us who seems to have Rezkin's trust. We can ill afford to lose you in a hopeless effort."

"It is not completely hopeless. I believe I have a real chance of swaying their opinions."

"If you say so. Will you be taking the little lady?" He nodded toward Celise.

Wesson frowned and glanced back at Celise. She grinned and gave him a small wave. "Ah, she may need to remain on the ship, but it will be difficult to convince her. She does not exactly recognize my authority."

"You are in charge of this mission. I am only here for moral support."

Wesson shook his head. "I am merely a journeyman, Striker Kai. No one would listen to me. They *have* to listen to you."

Kai raised an eyebrow. "I think you would be surprised by how much influence you possess. You may be a journeyman in name, but you are the emperor's mage for a reason."

Wesson nodded and stroked his hand down his plain grey robes devoid of panels, which marked him as a generalist. He knew it was probably wrong of him to continue wearing the drab garb. After all, he was more than a simple generalist, and part of the reason for a mage's uniform was to warn people of what they were up against. Unfortunately, he knew of no other way to define himself, besides that which he refused.

A small, soft hand gripped his own, and Wesson turned to find Celise beside him. In her heavily accented and broken Ashaiian, she said, "Come, my Wesson. We will eat and be happy in the sun."

Wesson sighed and followed Celise to an unoccupied space on the upper deck where they sat with their backs pressed against a couple of barrels secured to the ship. Tipping his head back, Wesson's gaze was drawn to a seagull that had taken up residence on one of the masts. The sails were taut with the power of the wind, and ropes and wood creaked as water lapped against the hull. His attention fell to the horizon where, in the distance, he could see dark clouds releasing their burden over the waves. A bolt of lightning illuminated the shadowed crests, and Wesson inwardly groaned. The storm was moving toward them, albeit slowly. He hoped the storm rained itself out before it reached them.

Celise moved to kneel beside him. She leaned over him as she reached for his hair. Wesson firmly but gently stayed her hands. "What are you doing?"

She held up a thin, red ribbon. "I will braid this into your hair." She reached for his hair again. "Your hair is not long, but it will grow."

Wesson grabbed her wrist and held it so that the ribbon was as far from him as his reach would allow. "No, Celise. I told you. I do not recognize your claim."

Celise extricated her hand and donned a pout. "But you are *my* Wesson. I leave my home. I come here with you. We will be good together."

"I told you already. My heart belongs to another."

"But you say this *other* has claimed someone, and your women claim only one man. It cannot be you."

"No, I said she is *probably* married already. I do not know yet."

Celise's teeth grazed her plump lower lip as she anxiously twirled the ribbon around her finger. Wesson could see the moisture in her eyes as her lashes fluttered, and he hoped she would not start crying. He was not sure he could handle her crying. Eventually, she said, "I will wait for you to see that she claims a man, but you are still *my* Wesson until she challenges me."

Wesson shook his head. "That is not how it works here. Women do not challenge each other, and they do not have champions. Why do you want *me* anyway? You are a beautiful woman, Celise. Any of your men would be proud to be your consort, I am sure."

"I do not want them. *You* are my consort, and I will keep you." Her eyes lit up as though she had just thought of something. She gathered her feet under her and quickly stood as she said, "Coledon is not here. I must find a big man to be my champion. Do not worry, my Wesson. I will find us a strong warrior. No one will take you from me."

Before Wesson could say any more, Celise was gone. He laid back on the deck, and this time he did not stifle his groan. His gaze found the seagull atop the mast, again, only this time it was not alone. The two squawked and yakked at each other, their cacophony echoing the turmoil inside him. Celise was going to end up approaching every man on the ship looking for a champion, and there was no telling what she would agree to in order to keep him. She was a strong woman capable of navigating the intrigues of Leréshi court, and at the same time she was completely oblivious to the way the world worked outside of Lon Lerésh. Here, she did not hold power, and for some reason, he felt obligated to keep her safe.

He rolled to his feet and went to find the young woman who seemed to think she owned him. He was both relieved and frustrated when he found her talking to Kai again. When Kai glanced at him, it was with a mirthful glint in his eye. The striker no doubt found Celise's mission to be highly entertaining. At least he was reasonably sure Kai would not attempt to take advantage of the woman.

213

"You will do this for me?" Celise said. Her arms were crossed, and her spine was straight. She looked down at the lounging striker as if she were the queen, herself, looking down on her vassal.

Kai grinned and looked back at Wesson. "What do you think, Journeyman? Should I aid this kind lady in her efforts to save her love?"

Wesson gritted his teeth. "She does not love me. Perhaps she should claim *you* and force you to comply."

Celise scowled at him, the first such look he had seen directed his way from her, and Kai's grin fell.

The striker said, "There will be no more claimings. We are not in Lon Lerésh. Besides, I am already married—at least, I *was*. I can only assume she still lives. That is beside the point, though." His taxing grin resurfaced, and he nodded to Celise. "I would be honored to fight as your champion against anyone who thinks to take your consort."

Celise beamed and launched herself at Kai, sprawling on top of him as she gave him a hug. When she finally righted herself, she did the same to Wesson. "You see this, Wesson? You are mine. The striker knows this. He is a strong warrior."

Wesson scowled down at the striker who continued grinning as he stretched and placed his hands behind his head. He looked as if he had not a care in the world. Wesson briefly considered setting the man's pants on fire.

Just then, a shout from the crow's nest raised the alarm. Kai leapt to his feet, and deckhands began running every which way. Wesson snagged Celise by the arm and pulled her toward the entrance to the cabin. The ship rocked as it turned, and Wesson glanced up to see several ships on the horizon. His stomach soured as he realized the ships appeared to be coming about in pursuit.

Wesson deposited Celise in the small berth they unfortunately shared since she had attempted to stow away. Although she had been caught, Wesson could not find it in him to turn her away once she had started crying.

He said, "Please, stay below deck. You will be safer in here."

She reached for him, her hands finding purchase on his robe. "You stay. You will be safe here, too."

Shaking his head, he said, "No, my skills are needed above."

She looked at him skeptically, and Wesson realized that Celise did not have faith in his abilities as a mage. He figured it was just as well that she had never been present when he had found it necessary to cause the kind of destruction she might fear.

"Trust me. I will find you when this is finished, okay?"

She nodded and clasped her hands together as she backed toward her bunk. This berth, thankfully, had more than one bed.

When Wesson found the captain, he was speaking with Kai and Waylen Nasque, who had been taken under the striker's wing for his first mission after recently coming of age. Waylen was an excellent swordsman, and what he lacked in body mass, he made up for in speed. At least, that is what the other swordsmen had said. Wesson was not capable of assessing such things since he had never learned to wield mundane weapons. His father had died when he was too young to learn, and since he had come into his power, he had never considered it necessary. Only once had he ever been unable to access his power, and that had been an extreme circumstance.

Wesson turned his attention back to what the captain was saying. There were, apparently, four Ashaiian naval ships on the horizon, but only three had turned to intercept them. The captain hoped that their evasive maneuvers would be enough to outpace the vessels and they could put enough distance between them that the Ashaiians would give up pursuit.

"We are too far for a typical patrol," said Captain Estadd. "I had not expected them to be so far out."

Kai shook his head. "It is not your fault, Captain. It seems they are patrolling all the way to Verril. It was only a matter of time before we encountered someone."

"But we are faster, right?" said Waylen.

Kai did not answer but turned to Wesson instead. "Can you do anything to hide us?"

Wesson's brow stretched toward the sky. "You want me to hide an entire ship?"

"Can you do it?"

Wesson glanced toward the enemy ships off the starboard side, then looked to port toward the incoming storm. Squeezed between the two threats as they were, things were about to get very uncomfortable. Wesson considered his options then decided on something he was not entirely sure he could do.

"Sail into the squall, Captain. I can hide us in the storm."

The captain peered into the dark where the line demarcating the sea from the sky had all but disappeared. The waters were already choppy, and the swells in the distance were worse than imposing. He said, "If we sail in, there is no guarantee we will come out in one piece. We may not even make it into the squall before they catch up to us."

"Do what you can, Captain," said Wesson, raising his voice above the wind. "I would not like to try to take on *three* Ashaiian naval ships at all, much less at the same time."

"No, certainly not," said the captain.

As they sailed toward the squall, Wesson watched their pursuers. It would not be his first sea battle, but he dreaded a repeat of the last one. This one was closer to Ashai, though, and it was likely the ships each contained more mages than usual. He pondered ways in which he might slow them, but each time he thought of something, he also thought of reasons the efforts might come back to haunt him. The ships were still too far away for direct strikes, and Wesson hoped they did not get any closer.

Stargazer managed to stay ahead of the Ashaiian ships, but the presence of mages was apparent in how quickly the enemy ships closed the distance. Just as the ships were coming within range for vimaral attacks, the first raindrops wet Wesson's face. He had barely noticed them before he was suddenly inundated by the sky's angry torrent. He was inclined to go hide in the relatively dry cabin, but he had a job to do.

The ship rose and dove over the waves, and Wesson grabbed onto the railing to keep from tumbling about the deck. He needed to be able to concentrate on what he was doing, though, which would prove difficult if he was being thrown from his feet. He skidded over the wet planks toward the mizzenmast. When he finally grabbed ahold of a loose rope, he tied it around himself, securing himself to the mast. A crew member took one look at him and laughed before he began scaling the mast net.

Wesson turned his attention back to the sea. The grey and black clouds blended with an equally grey and black ocean, and somewhere amidst all that grey and black were ships that appeared grey and black in the shadows. A sudden flare of light caught his eye and then another. Wesson realized the grouped enemy ships required the lights to keep from sailing into each other. It was lucky for him, though, because now he knew where to aim his assault.

As Wesson stared at the ships, he noticed something seemed to be penetrating the air, distorting the rain. With sudden alarm, he quickly composed a shield ward as far from the stern as he could, but he knew it would not be far enough or large enough. Although the majority of the energy was absorbed or deflected by the shield, a powerful blast slammed into the ship thrusting it over a wave crest. The ship shook and cracked as the keel slammed down into the trough.

The rope dug into Wesson's sides, but he tried to ignore the pain as he began erecting additional wards beyond the ship. People were shouting, and although it was difficult to hear them over the raging wind and waves, he could feel their fears and worries compounding in his mind.

Wesson's first instinct was to target the other ships' sails. If he could stall their forward motion or even slow them down, his own ship might have a chance of escaping. He lobbed a few fireballs toward the lead ship, but between the rain and wind, none were able to close the distance. They were still too far, and he was hoping to prevent them from getting any nearer. He needed his incendiaries to go farther faster. A memory stirred within his mind—one of a game played during his youth, a game that set his master's keep aflame. In the game, he had used a club enchanted with a special ward to bat the fireballs over a great distance. Wesson realized he could do the same here except with greater speed and control. Instead of using a club, Wesson constructed a spell in the shape of a sling, like a miniature vimaral trebuchet, and settled within it a small inferno. He targeted the lead ship's main mast using a beacon spell. Upon pulling the trigger, the fireball shot forward with unmatched speed.

The fireball wavered slightly as it was battered by rain, but it struck the mast with enough intensity to set the sail alight. Wesson's internal celebration was cut short when a funnel of water swiftly cascaded over the burning sail, snuffing the flame. Of course, the mages on the other ship were water mages. Most who sailed were *talented* in either air or water or both. Wesson quickly realized fire was not going to be enough. He had no *spells* for a task as large as this one, but that did not mean he was without power. The insipid darkness of his destructive power called to him, and he knew that it would heed his call if only he would release its bindings. As vimaral attacks mounted against his wards, Wesson knew death was inevitable—his or theirs.

With that in mind, it occurred to Wesson that he could combine an innocuous spell with pure nocent energy to accomplish something treacherous. The question was, did he have the constitution to use it?

As the ship careened over another swell, Wesson's wards faltered. His physical distress, the pain of the rope biting into his abdomen, and his anxiety over causing harm to his fellow Ashaiians were causing his focus to waver. When another concussion rocked the ship, he knew he was out of time. He built the familiar spell in his mind and fed his carefully constrained nocent power into it. The power leapt forward almost gleefully, and if vimara could be said to have a spirit, he thought his must be wicked.

The hydrophobic spell surged forward and latched onto the lead ship in the center. The spell quickly spread over the entire vessel, encapsulating it in a vimaral film that repelled water. The ocean water and rain surged away in every direction causing the ship to sink into a depression that continued deepen as walls of water rose around it. The force of the rising water pushed away the other two ships as they slid down watery slopes. Wesson abruptly withdrew the spell, causing tidal waves to collapse over the central ship, crushing it beneath the weight of the sea. As eddies sloshed and spun the other two ships were promptly sucked into the void so that they collided in its center.

Masts were toppled, hulls were breached, and decks listed as the two remaining ships were jostled about like toy boats in a tub of water.

Wesson's guilt for having sunk one ship was enough to nearly cripple him. He hoped the other two ships and what was left of their crew survived. Either way, they were obviously hobbled and would not be capable of continuing the pursuit. Wesson hung his head, hiding his tears in the rain as he waited for *Stargazer* to outpace the squall. He noted that had he been willing to perform his duty in the first place, they would not have needed to enter the squall at all. As he mourned the loss of all those souls aboard the sunken ship, he realized the futility of his resistance. They were at war. If he continued avoiding the conflict, his companions would suffer, and he would be swallowed by the guilt anyway.

The ship turned, although it took them much longer to leave the squall than it had for them to enter it. When the sea was finally calm enough for Wesson to free himself from the mast, he stumbled toward the cabin. Kai and Captain Estadd congratulated him on a job well done. Wesson tried to shake it off, but Kai stopped him with a hand on his shoulder.

"That was good work there."

Wesson shook his head. "No, Striker, there was nothing good about *that*."

"I understand your reticence, and to be truthful, I am glad you feel that way. When you stop caring about the consequences of your actions you have crossed over from being a good man who does bad things to being a bad man."

Wesson considered the elation he felt upon releasing the dark, destructive power, and bile rose in his throat. He said, "Is it possible to be both?"

"I have seen what drives you, Journeyman, and I have seen what these things do to you. You are not a bad man, Wesson. Like Rezkin, you are a young man with the weight of the world on your shoulders. You were not at fault here. This war is Caydean's doing. Let him carry the weight."

Wesson nodded, but his conscience was not appeased. He made his way to his berth and ignored Celise's inquisitive gaze as he sloughed his wet robes and hung them up to dry from a line that stretch across the ceiling. Then he crawled into his bunk and wrapped the blankets tightly around himself. It was not long before he felt Celise crawl into the bed behind him and wrap him in her arms. For once, he did not have the energy to fend off her advances, but she seemed content to merely hold him as he fell asleep.

That night, the ship rocked steadily up and down and side to side as they were tormented by the remnants of the squall that had been moving toward the land. Wesson's nap had refreshed him enough that he could remove his thoughts from the hundreds of people he had killed when he sunk the Ashaiian naval vessel. Celise pressed against his back as he stood huddled in the captain's cabin amongst the others. Corporal Namm, formerly of the Ashaiian army, Waylen Nasque, Baron Nasque's son who had only recently come of age, and the Torreli Fedrin Malto were also present, and Wesson felt the room was getting a bit too stuffy.

"This is the most direct route," said Kai as he leaned over the map stretched out on the desk. Shadows danced across the map as the lantern swung above them.

Wesson pointed to a spot on the map amongst the trees. "There is a small village here. They breed horses as well as donkeys and mules for the surrounding villages. It is not located on any road, and the king's men do not visit it but once every five years or so, during normal times, at least. We should be able to procure horses without trouble."

"That is good," said Kai. "That means we can be in Kaibain within a few weeks, assuming we can avoid the patrols."

"What makes you think there are patrols?" said Namm. "From what we could tell, the king drafted all the able-bodied men to the main army. Do you think the army will bother sending patrols into the Fendendril?"

"You may be right, Corporal, but we had best be cautious," said Kai.

13

The small boat rocked as Xa darted to the other side, and Frisha lifted her head to peer into the mist. Somehow Xa had managed to get them off the island, and once they had left Uthrel, Frisha had had no choice but to cooperate. Not that she could have stopped Xa from taking her anyway. Her helplessness chafed at her. She inhaled the scents of salt and fish and scrunched her nose. She could not see much in the fog, but she could tell by the placid water and pungent scent that they had to be near a fishing pier. Xa stood at the bow of the small fishing vessel as a small crew rowed them toward the distant lights that struggled to escape the mist.

"There," said Xa in a hushed voice that only the crew could have heard.

The boat turned toward a dark dock that was barely visible. Once docked, Xa helped her from the boat then shoved her pack into her arms. Frisha was relieved to finally step onto land, although her legs shook as the ground seemed to sway.

"Come. Stay silent," whispered Xa.

Frisha might have laughed if she had not been so tired. Xa always told her to be silent. He was silent as well. They both sat in silence for days on end. Frisha was tired of the silence, but she had little desire to speak with Xa. He had kidnapped her. She could feel solace only in the fact that he had sworn a mage oath to keep her safe. Despite anything else that might happen to her, she would live if he could help it. And he *was* the Jeng'ri of the Order, after all. He was not without exceptional skill. Still, she was certain that Rezkin would kill the assassin when he found out Xa had taken her for no other reason than to reassert his authority.

After leaving the boat, they walked for hours. It was dark, not yet dawn, and the fog permitted them to see no more than a couple of paces in any direction. Somehow Xa kept them going the right way, or at least kept them from walking in circles. Sometimes the ground was a hardened dirt path, and other times they traversed over rocks and scrub. Every so often, Frisha could hear people and animals moving about in the fog, but Xa kept them at a distance. Eventually, she and Xa came to a wall that looked, to her, like other walls they had passed. It was made of brown stone and partially covered in climbing vines. She and Xa followed the wall to the side of a building and stopped before a wooden door. Frisha tilted her head back and tried to see more of the building, but her efforts were in vain.

Xa turned to her and raised a finger to his lips. She wanted to yell that she had heard him the first time; but while she was reasonably confident that, due to his oath, he would not kill her, she knew he could make her life very uncomfortable if she made trouble for him. Xa did not knock, nor did he open the door. They simply stood outside it waiting. Frisha wondered how anyone would know they were there. She had seen no lookouts and doubted anyone could have seen their approach through the fog anyway. As she stood waiting, she stared down at her feet. The boots she wore, like the pants and shirt, were not her own, and they were a little too loose. Her coat smelled of fish, but it kept away the chill of the wintery air. She did not know if it ever snowed this close to the Souelian, but she figured it would not be long before the first freeze. Still, it felt warmer in the fog than it had over the open water.

The door abruptly opened, and Xa grabbed Frisha's hand. Her instinct was to pull away, but his grip was tight as he dragged her across the threshold. It was dark inside, but Frisha could hear Xa whispering with another person that she could not see. After a moment, a soft golden glow suffused the room. Xa stood over the freshly ignited oil lamp, and when he moved, the light illuminated a cozy space. It held three beds lined up against one wall, a darkened hearth on the adjacent wall, and shelves filled with baskets and trunks on a third wall. In the center of the room was a table and six chairs. The floor was covered in rugs, the beds held blankets and pillows, and fresh wood was stacked beside the hearth, but no one else was present.

"Well, this is comfortable," Frisha muttered.

Xa scowled at her, and she snapped her mouth shut. Then he said, "We will stay here tonight. You may clean up in there." He motioned with his chin toward a doorway she had missed upon her initial survey.

Frisha cautiously peered through the doorway and saw a bathing chamber, but there were no other doors and whoever had greeted Xa was nowhere to be seen. She said, "What is this place?"

"It is a safehouse used by my people."

By *my people*, she knew he meant the Order—the Order of Assassins akin to the Black Hall. The chill that suffused Frisha had nothing to do with the temperature of the air. She shivered then removed her smelly coat, hanging it on a hook by the door.

"Are there fresh clothes in here?" she said, tipping the lid of one of the baskets on the shelf.

"Do not touch those," snapped Xa.

Frisha jumped at his sharp tone and pulled back her hand.

Xa shook his head with frustration and came over to rummage through the trunks. He said, "Some of these contain items that could be dangerous to you. Many of them have traps."

"Hmm … traps and poisons," she mused. "Rezkin is always looking for traps and poisons."

Xa handed her a bundle of fabric and said, "That is because he knows the world, and he is prepared. *You* are *ro*. You do not belong here."

She gave him a pointed look. "*You* brought me here. I didn't ask to come."

He huffed. "I had no choice. You were not safe alone in Cael."

"I wasn't *alone*. There are plenty of guards and mages—"

"And assassins and traitors."

"What traitors?" said Frisha with alarm.

"I do not know, which is the point. Where there are important people, there are traitors." He pointed toward the washroom. "Now, go clean yourself before I change my mind and send you to bed."

Frisha frowned. "I am not a child." At the look he gave her, she abruptly turned and entered the washroom. It had no door, so she had to hope that Xa was honorable enough to let her bathe in private. Once inside, she raised her voice only slightly to say, "I'm hungry. Might we have a hot meal?"

A moment later, a chunk of bread bounced off the wall to land on the floor. "Very funny," she called back, but she worried that he was not kidding. Frisha looked around the small space to find that pipes ran along the ceiling and walls, the same kind that had graced the washroom in Skutton. She smiled, pleased that she would not have to lug in buckets of water to fill the tub. She hoped the water was heated as it had been in Skutton, as well. A hot bath sounded marvelous. She was not disappointed.

After bathing and relaxing until her fingers pruned, she reentered the main room dressed in a fresh pair of black pants and a long black tunic that hung nearly to her knees. Xa pointed to a bed where she sat as she combed out her damp hair. A fire blazed in the hearth, over which hung a small pot filled something savory by the smell of it. Frisha was overjoyed that it did not smell like fish.

"Can you tell me now? What are we doing here?"

"I was called here by the Ong'ri. I have a job. *You* will stay here out of trouble."

Frisha narrowed her eyes. "*You* have a job? I thought you were excommunicated or something."

"I come when the Ong'ri calls. I am needed."

"But why *you*? Aren't there other people who could do it?"

"Do you always argue this much?"

"I'm just wondering why *you* have to do this job. You were away, excommunicated, in another kingdom, but it has to be *you*."

"You should be pleased that it is me. If I am here, I can work to convince my people that Rezkin is the Riel'gesh. Then I will not be *excommunicated*. I will be able to rejoin my people."

Her expression softened. "You miss them."

He scoffed. "I do not *miss* them. I belong with them. It is where I am effective."

"You *do* miss them, and you're tired of babysitting me all the time. I get it. I wouldn't want to babysit me all the time either. It would be so boring." She threw her hands up. "Imagine *being* me."

He gave her a curious look. "You do not like being you?"

Frisha leaned back against the wall. "I don't really know who *I* am. I am surrounded by amazing people, by warriors and mages and weapons masters. Everyone is striving to be better at *something*. What am I doing? I merely *exist* from day to day."

Xa poured some of the savory sustenance into a bowl and handed it to her. Before he turned away, he said, "You are young. You can change. If you do not like who you are, then be different."

Frisha released a growl of frustration. "I do not know *how* to *be* different."

He shrugged as if it did not concern him in the least. "If you do not, then you will always be who you are now."

Something wet dripped onto his face, and Rezkin opened his eyes. Only the smallest slivers of sky were visible between the rocking boughs, but what he could see was the pale lavender of the early morning just before the sky lightened. He reached up to wipe away the moisture, and his fingers came away sticky with sap. He rolled over and used a leaf dampened with morning dew to wipe his fingers and face. It was not enough, though. He smelled of horse and sweat and road dust, and he wanted a bath. *Rule 187* was to *remain unde-tectable to the senses*, and he could not do that if his opponents could *smell* him.

The hairs on the back of his neck began to stand on end, and he glanced over to find Azeria staring at him from where she lay. He held her gaze for a breath before she looked away and got to her feet. As she disappeared into the brush, Rezkin checked his boots for unin-vited guests and then pulled them onto his feet. Nanessy groaned but sat up to gaze drearily around their campsite. Her blonde locks were a disheveled mess around her heart-shaped face, and her pale eyes looked to still be held in dreams. Entris stood from where he was bent over a small campfire holding a steaming mug. He held it out for Nanessy.

"Coffee?"

Her eyes widened. "Oh, thank you. You are amazing."

He tilted his head curiously. "Am I?"

Nanessy seemed oblivious in her groggy state and simply hummed under her breath as she blew across the top of the mug. Entris reached up to tug her hair into more orderly fashion, and Nanessy giggled as she tried to do the same. "Oh, I must be a sight."

"You are," Entris said without mirth, and then they held each other's gaze long enough that even Rezkin became uncomfortable.

"We should be moving," he said as he grabbed Pride's saddle and tack.

Pride was grazing on a small patch of berries when Rezkin approached. The stallion seemed content with the other horses and had even taken a liking to Azeria's mount, a dappled mare with a gentle disposition. Rezkin was saddling the horse when suddenly a blade was at his throat. He ignored it and continued cinching the belt.

"You did not even detect my approach," said Azeria from behind him.

"I felt you."

"Yet you did not try to protect yourself."

"I did not see a need. You are not a threat. Not right now, anyway."

"But you think I will be in the future?"

Rezkin grabbed her wrist and twisted, stepping into her guard and knocking her off balance so that she was wrapped in his embrace. He whispered into her ear, "You did want me dead a few days ago."

Azeria said, "That was before."

She shifted her hips, stepped back and tossed him over her shoulder. Rezkin rolled to his feet as he rounded on her but did not close the distance.

"Before what?" he said.

"Before I came to know you."

Now he did close the distance. He stepped close enough that, although she was taller than most women he knew, she had to look up at him. "And what do you think you know of me?"

Her gaze dropped to his mouth, then quickly shifted back to his eyes. "I know very little about you, and what I do know seems to contradict itself."

"How so?"

"You are cold and empty; yet there are times I see a fire in your eyes."

"A fire?"

She reached up to touch his face as if she could not stop herself. "Tell me," she said. "What is it that makes you burn?"

Rezkin was caught in her mesmerizing gaze, captive to the liquid silver of her eyes. Something pulled him toward her, and he had no desire to fight it. The power that stirred inside him whispered *surrender*, and he did.

A branch cracked behind him, his heart leapt, and the spell was broken. Azeria ducked out of reach and rounded his horse as Nanessy came stumbling through the brush with Entris behind her. Rezkin turned to Pride and finished preparing for the ride and all the while was thrown by the way his body had reacted to whatever had happened—or rather, what did *not* happen—between him and Azeria. His heart was racing, and his blood felt nearly as hot as the vagri that hung from the cord around his neck. He felt like he had just come from a battle, yet he was not sure who was the victor.

Throughout the day, Rezkin tried to push thoughts of Azeria from his mind. Her bravery and prowess in battle had only stirred his interest more, though. Although she had many decades on him, by Eihelvanan standards, she was barely into adulthood. She was hostile and condescending, and yet he could not blame her for her opinions. Every story and experience she had of his kind told her to distrust him, to *kill* him. Despite that, Rezkin wanted to know her, to know the female as he knew her in his dreams, and that not only disturbed but excited him. He had never had such thoughts about a woman, much less one with the ability to defeat him.

"Rezkin?"

He was roused from his thoughts at the sound of his name, and he realized he had been staring at Azeria who was riding slightly ahead of him. He drew his gaze from her snow-white hair to look at Nanessy who was riding with Entris beside him.

"Yes?" he said.

She frowned at him. "It was not a yes or no question."

"What was?"

"I said, 'How long until we reach the quarry?'"

"If all goes well and our map is somewhat to scale, it should be a couple of days at most."

"I hope there is somewhere between here and there where we can acquire another horse."

Entris turned slightly in his saddle to look over his shoulder at her. "Are you uncomfortable? You could try riding in front of me."

Nanessy grimaced as she shifted. "Perhaps when next we break. Though I enjoy your company, it would still be better if I had my own horse."

Entris nodded. "Agreed. This could be particularly dangerous if we must make haste."

After a few hours, they entered the old forest that covered most of Verril. The trees were tall and thin, and the underbrush was sparse. The floor, however, was carpeted with pine needles that hid the hazards of the uneven ground. If there was a road that led through the forest, they had not found it, and they were left to navigate on their own. The thick canopy blocked their view of the sky, and the trees looked similar in all directions such that the potential for walking in circles was real. Rezkin and the Eihelvanan were well-trained in woodcraft, though, and by the time darkness fell, they had covered a significant distance.

Upon selecting a campsite, Rezkin and Azeria excused themselves to scout the area, each taking a different direction. For some time, Rezkin had been wondering if they were being followed, so he took to the south. It was not long before he came upon several individuals in mountain garb ghosting their trail. Their clothes were the colors of the mountainous forest in greys, greens, and browns and mostly consisted of furs and leather. Three men and three women each carried a bow and quarrel as well as a large belt knife and short spear. They chattered and tromped over the detritus with seemingly no intention of hiding their presence. Rezkin followed them for a bit hoping to discern their purpose. Their garbled Verrilian dialect was not one he had heard outside of training, but he understood it nonetheless. By the time he returned to his comrades, Rezkin knew the newcomers were looking for someone.

At the campsite, Nanessy had just placed a cookpot over the fire when a clacking sound reached their ears. Azeria donned her hood, strung her bow, and knocked an arrow in the span of a breath. Meanwhile, Entris disappeared into the trees. The clacking grew louder as it moved closer, and a shield ward suddenly flashed around Rezkin and Nanessy. Rezkin glanced at her, and she grinned.

"I have this."

Before long, the party of six came into view. The man in the lead was banging together two sticks as they approached. When they were close enough to be heard without yelling, they stopped and bowed as one.

"*Hello to the travelers,*" said the man in the lead, speaking Verrili.

Rezkin glanced at Nanessy who shrugged. Then he said, "*Greetings to the travelers.*"

The lead man grinned. "*We mean you no harm. As you could hear, we announced our presence. We seek information and will pay if you have it.*"

"*Information about what?*"

"May we join you?"

"To what end?"

Again, the man smiled. *"To exchange information, of course."*

Rezkin perused their party then considered his own. He decided that these people were likely little threat and obtaining information about the area was worth the risk. Rezkin motioned for the six strangers to join them as Nanessy turned back to the cookpot. The lead man was friendly and open as he approached, but the five people at his back were more cautious. The three immediately behind him carried their short spears at the ready, and the two in the rear were prepared with their bows.

"I am glad you allowed us to join you. There is safety in numbers," said the leader.

"Safety from what?" replied Rezkin.

"There are vuroles in these parts, and they have been traveling in ever greater packs."

Nanessy's face fell as she looked at Rezkin urgently. "Did he say vuroles? Please tell me that word means something else in Verrili."

The lead man looked at Nanessy curiously, although it was apparent that he did not understand her. Then he looked back to Rezkin and said, *"We have seen kythes, as well."*

"Kythes, in Verril?"

The man nodded. *"Those flying monsters are worse than vuroles."* He spit on the ground then raised a fist to his chest. *"I am Brogan."* He nodded toward each of the others as he introduced them. *"We are of the Archebow Clan. Who are you?"*

"I am Rezkin. This is Mage Nanessy Threll. That is Azeria, and"—with a nod toward his companion who seemed to have appeared out of nowhere behind the newcomers—*"that is Entris."* Entris had also donned a hood, presumably to hide his elfish appearance.

Brogan did not seem surprised that one of theirs had flanked him and his party. He nodded and said, *"You sound like a Verrili. She is Ashaiian? And they are?"*

"From nowhere you would know," said Rezkin. *"It does not matter*

anyhow. You said you wanted information. About what? I doubt your interest is in regard to four strangers in the woods."

"No, not really. We are interested in the city of Gauge."

Rezkin had never heard of Gauge, but now he wanted to know what *they* knew. *"What of it?"*

"Have you any news?"

"Where is this city of Gauge?"

Now Brogan did look confused. *"It is the nearest city to the north. You would have come through it on your way here."*

Rezkin shook his head. *"We are going the other way. We have not yet been there."*

"Then you are coming from the mountains? You are not of the clans, though. How is it that you come from the south and you do not know of Gauge?"

"Suffice it to say that we took a different route than the one to which you are accustomed. Why are you interested in Gauge?"

Brogan appeared skeptical and a little concerned but answered anyway. *"One of our trading parties traveled to Gauge a few weeks ago, and they have not yet returned. We have come in search of them. We grew concerned that they may have been attacked by vuroles or captured by lowlanders."*

"You are concerned about being captured by lowlanders, yet you go to their cities to trade?"

With a shrug, Brogan said, *"Some of the closer cities trade with us. Their officials look the other way because our goods bring them profit. The lowlanders may hate us, but they covet our craftsmanship. It is not safe for us to travel farther to the north, though."*

A tug on his sleeve got Rezkin's attention, and he looked toward Nanessy who bore a questioning look. After explaining to her what had been said, she responded, "What happens to their people who are captured by the lowlanders?"

Rezkin posed the question to Brogan who said, *"They are taken as slaves. Many go to the quarry."*

With the mention of the quarry, Rezkin's interest was piqued. *"Do you know where the quarry is?"*

"*No, we do not venture that far north. Those who are sent to the quarry are lost to us. We bury their belongings instead of their bodies.*" Brogan's sad gaze was lost in the fire for a moment before he said, "*My brother was one of those gone to Gauge. I will go there to search for him. If he is not there, I will mourn his loss for many seasons.*"

"*How far is it to Gauge?*"

Brogan eyed the horses, then said, "*A half day's walk to the north, maybe a couple of hours on horseback.*"

Rezkin said, "*Please, excuse us while I have a chat with my companions.*" Brogan nodded as Rezkin indicated for Entris, Azeria, and Nanessy to join him far enough away that Brogan's party could not hear them. He explained the rest of what Brogan had told him, then said, "Tomorrow we will ride for Gauge. I am curious about what has befallen his brother."

Azeria shook her head. "Why do you care what has happened to these people? We have a different purpose (*irritated*)."

"I care because they may have been taken to the quarry. That means there is probably information in Gauge *about* the quarry. It is on our way anyhow."

Nanessy folded her arms and looked at him in disapproval. "And here I thought you were concerned about an injustice."

Rezkin was confused as he looked at her. "What injustice?"

She gasped in frustration and said, "Those people being taken as slaves!"

"The highlanders and lowlanders have been at war since these lands were first settled. I cannot right all the injustices of the world, Nanessy."

She dropped her arms. "Okay, I get it, but you do at least recognize it as an injustice?"

"Of course. Many studies have proven that people are not as efficient when forced to work against their will and in poor health."

"That is not what I meant!" she snapped. "I was talking about slavery being *wrong*, or are you in support of it?"

Rezkin wondered how they had gotten from a proposed visit to Gauge to her thinking he supported slavery. His training had prepared him for a type of slavery. He was meant to be a slave to the crown. Had things gone differently, he would have been serving Caydean. Rezkin abruptly realized that he *liked* the fact that he had chosen his own *Rule 1.* He said, "There are many things about the outworld with which I do not agree, yet I have little or no control over them. For the record, I do not support slavery for a multitude of reasons including the fact that people should be free to choose their own purposes."

"See?" said Nanessy with a broad grin. "I told you that you are a good man, and you will be a superb emperor. You should never doubt yourself."

"I do not recall doubting myself," said Rezkin.

"Okay, maybe you did not, but neither did you recognize your humanity. I just helped point it out."

Rezkin realized he had nothing to say to that. She had, in fact, forced him to consider his personal opinions on slavery. In that moment, he acknowledged that not only did he oppose slavery, but it made him angry. The vagri burning against his chest reaffirmed that feeling. It was an odd sensation to *care* about anything, for good or ill, but he was coming to recognize more often when it occurred.

That night, Brogan's group camped far enough from them to feel separated but close enough to deter most wildlife from attacking their greater numbers. Rezkin and his companions took turns keeping watch as did members of Brogan's group. By the morning, though, everyone seemed fairly rested, at least, more so than they had in the mountains. Rezkin and his party left the Archebow Clan behind and rode for the city of Gauge. With a draught of cool mountain air at their backs, clear skies overhead, and the shade of the forest around them, they found the ride to be pleasant enough. Their first indication that something was wrong was the army sitting between them and the gates. The city of Gauge was under siege.

"Who are they?" said Azeria from her perch in a tree at the crest of a hill located a couple of hundred yards from the city wall.

Rezkin was crouched behind a small thicket next to an outcropping of limestone. His gaze roved over the flags and tabards. For him and Nanessy it was not difficult to identify the invaders. "It's the Ashaiian army."

"This is the army of your brother?" said Entris from beside him.

"Only part of it," replied Rezkin.

"What are they doing here?" said Nanessy from his other side. "How did they get so deep into Verril?"

He doubted she was expecting a response since he obviously did not have an answer. Still, the question plagued him. If Ashai had gotten this far, they surely had possession of the quarry. Aside from its proximity to the Drahgfir Mountains, Gauge was not a strategic military position. He wondered why Ashai would bother with it at all.

"I'm going in there," he said.

"By yourself?" cried Nanessy. "It's surrounded by an army that would love nothing more than to kill you."

"Firstly, they are not expecting me. They have no idea we are even in Verril. Secondly, I am well-trained for a task such as this."

Azeria dropped down from the tree behind him. "I will go with you," she said.

"No, you are too obvious. You could never blend in."

Her expression was placid, but her silver eyes sparked with irritation. "They will not see me. I have no need to *blend* (*annoyed*)."

"And if you are caught?" said Rezkin.

"I will not be."

Nanessy stepped closer. "But if you *are*?"

Azeria's gaze shifted from Nanessy back to Rezkin. "I am a capable warrior, and I am not without power."

Rezkin sighed and then looked to Entris. The male said, "I will remain here on lookout with the mage. We will be your backup should you need it."

Azeria glanced between Entris and Nanessy then smirked. "Do not get distracted."

Nanessy's cheeks blushed, but Entris's eyebrows lowered as though he were offended. "I am the Spirétua-lyé. I do not get *distracted*."

Azeria looked at Rezkin. "Are we infiltrating the army or the city?"

"First we will do a survey of the army. I want to know who is in charge and why they are here. This contingent is a little small for a full siege on a city this size. They are either packing more power than is obvious or they are expecting reinforcements. Then we will go into the city and look for information on the quarry."

Azeria's fingers moved deftly through her long, white locks as she plaited them into a tight braid behind her head. Then she pulled up her soft, grey hood so that her silver eyes practically glowed from within its shadow. Rezkin could not draw his gaze from her. When he finally reacquired his control, he chided himself for his brief loss of attention.

As they moved toward the army encampment, Rezkin marveled at how utterly silent Azeria was beside him. It was as though her feet did not even touch the forest floor. The strikers had not been able to match him in stealth, but Azeria was perhaps even more skilled than he.

The Ashaiian army was camped in the small clearing before the front gates of Gauge. The walls were constructed of timbers and were relatively short. They were likely meant to keep out vuroles and other wildlife rather than an army. Rezkin decided the Ashaiians must not have been there very long or they would have already overrun the city's meager defenses. The encampment was not the most orderly of military installments, either. Sleeping tents were haphazardly constructed between those with an official function, and equipment was stashed seemingly wherever it would fit. The disorder made for easier infiltration but led Rezkin to wonder who could possibly be in charge.

Azeria followed Rezkin as he slipped between the tents, keeping to the shadows cast by the larger trees at the clearing's edge. In a few hours, the sun would be high, and the shadows would disappear for a time, so he was glad they had elected to break camp before dawn that morning. Regardless, most of the soldiers paid no attention to the goings on around them as they reclined lazily around campfires—most of them drinking—or remained in their tents beyond reach of the cool breeze. Rezkin quickly moved toward the largest structure in the camp, a half open tent shaped more like a lean-to that seemed to possess a constant ebb and flow of people, many of them officers and even a few mages. When he and Azeria drew close enough, Rezkin noted that a second tent had been erected at the back of the main tent where they nearly touched. The tent flap was open, and it appeared to be an armory. Rezkin and Azeria moved into the darkness of its shade. It would hide them from prying eyes as they listened to the workings of the command center.

"Do you know where it is yet?" said a harsh voice just as Rezkin settled. Although the man spoke Ashaiian with fluency, he bore a foreign accent with which Rezkin was not familiar.

"No, sir. The Gaugians aren't talking," said an Ashaiian.

"Or they do not know," grumbled the foreigner. "Capture some more."

"Sir, none have ventured out since they sealed the gates. We'll have to take the city before we know more."

"And we will, Colonel Whitner. Just as soon as we are sure they cannot use it against us."

"If I may say, sir, I believe they would have used it by now if they could."

"Perhaps, you may be right. Armas!"

"Yes, Master. What may I do for you, Master?" said a third voice that grew louder as it neared.

"Armas, have you acquired everything we need?"

"Yes, Master. Once we have it, it will be ours."

"*Ours?*"

"Yours, Master. Of course, yours."

"Very well. Colonel, If they have not used it by this eve, we will move on them at dawn."

"Yes, sir. The men will be ready."

Rezkin doubted that. These men would still be deep in their cups or paying the price for it by dawn. Still, it would not take much to overrun the city considering the people of Gauge likely had little more than a city watch to defend them.

"You are dismissed, Colonel." After a pause, the master said, "What of the mages, Armas? Are they causing any problems?"

"No, Master. Mages Lantrik and Olivus are both compliant. Your spell works well."

"Of course it does," the man snapped. "I only wanted to know that they are preparing the vessels properly."

"Yes, there are no problems, Master. Would you like me to bring you one?"

"Not now, Armas," growled the master with irritation.

The foreigner called *master* could be heard moving away as Armas prattled platitudes at him, and before long, all Rezkin could hear were inconsequential orders being issued. Rezkin motioned for Azeria to retreat from the tent. When they were far enough away from the camp not to be heard, she said, "The people of Gauge have a weapon."

"So it would seem, but it sounds like they are incapable of or unwilling to use it."

"Why would they not? They are under siege by a hostile military force."

Rezkin pondered the question, then said, "I do not know. Perhaps they do not know how."

"It could be a vimaral device," she said. "Most humans do not possess power. Perhaps they have no mages."

"It is a possibility. This is a remote city, and any mages worth their spells tend to flock toward more profitable ground."

"Then we go into the city and take the weapon," she said resolutely.

With a curt nod, Rezkin said, "If we cannot acquire it for ourselves, then we must destroy it." He paused in thought. "What concerns me most is why any weapon of significance would be in Gauge."

"How is that what concerns you *most*?" huffed Azeria. "The fact that it is dangerous enough to be of value to an invading army should concern you more."

"That is true. Either way, we will not allow them to have it."

"What about this army. Do you know who the *master* is? He seems to be in charge."

Rezkin shuffled through his memories. A name had caught his

attention. *Armas*. He had heard that name before. "Yes," he said slowly. "Armas was the name of the assistant to Berringish, Caydean's childhood tutor and present-day chief counselor."

"So what of him? Should we be concerned?"

"It is curious. Why would the king's counselor be leading an army contingent against a remote Verrilian town in search of a weapon?"

A crease formed between her eyes as her brow drew downward. "He did not sound like the others."

"No, in fact, he is from your side of the mountains—Galathia, I was told." As his memories reorganized themselves, he recalled something Connovan—the former Rez—had told him more recently. He considered holding the information back but decided it was relevant and important enough to acquire her input. "According to one source, he is Sen."

Azeria's eyes widened. "Another Sen in Ashai?"

"Yes, my source told me that he arrived twenty years ago with the SenGoka who trained me. It was apparent, then, that he was not exactly one of them. At King Bordran's insistence, he was left to teach Caydean while the other two went on to train *me*."

"But he was not SenGoka?"

"Not from what I was told—only Sen."

"This is very disconcerting. Anything in which the Sen might be interested is likely extremely dangerous (*unnerved*)."

Rezkin agreed but said nothing. The Sen had been interested in *him* for two decades, a point that he did not want to revisit with Azeria who was already disturbed by him.

"We should report back to Entris (*cautious*)," she said. "He will want to know of this. From the hilltop, I can see beyond the walls. I will be able to open a pathway directly into the city (*eager*)."

Rezkin shook his head. "No, he will insist on accompanying us, and I would rather go alone."

"If this weapon is of interest to the Sen, it could be related to the daem'ahn. We will need Entris if we are to face it."

"I am capable."

Azeria looked at him coldly and said, "Regardless of what Entris says, you are not truly Spirétua."

"If you disagree with the Spirétua-lyé in matters of the Spirétua, that is between you and him. I have dealt with the demons before, and I can do so again."

She huffed her irritation. "You are an arrogant human."

"No, I am confident in my abilities," he said, taking a step toward her, "and, apparently, I am Eihelvanan." Although Rezkin was hesitant to accept that fact, for some reason, he felt it was important that *she* accept it. Azeria gazed up at him, and he could see the battle within her expressive eyes. He leaned toward her, and she abruptly dropped her gaze. Then she huffed as she began the trek back through the woods to rejoin the others.

Rezkin looked over his shoulder toward Gauge. He considered leaving her to do as she pleased and taking the city on his own. He had *other* reasons for wanting a solo mission. It was time he extended his influence as the Raven in Verril, and he might as well start with Gauge. A glance back at her retreating form had him following after her, though. It seemed Gauge was to be a group mission after all.

14

Frisha paced around the small room. Xa had been gone for a while, and she had no idea when he would return. He had said he had a mission, but he did not say what that mission was or how long it might take to complete it. Frisha wondered what would happen if he *didn't* complete it. What if he had been caught? What if he had been killed? Would someone come for her? Would she have to find her way back to Cael on her own? She tried to tamp down on those thoughts. She was driving herself crazy going in circles. Staying in that room was driving her crazy, but each time she thought about going outside, she imagined Xa's disgruntled expression. While she felt no remorse for irritating him, she knew the things he did were meant to keep her safe. It might not be safe outside. The room she was in had no windows, and she still did not know *where* the room was. She could not have said if she was in a city or the country, only that it had been relatively quiet.

Suddenly the door shook, and Frisha's heart leapt. She turned to stare at it. When the locking latch slid to the side, she felt only relief. Xa had finally returned, and they could be gone from that place—back to Cael, back to Tieran and her friends. When the door opened, though, it was not Xa who stood there. It was a woman backed by two men. The woman stood tall with dark brown hair wound atop her head and brown eyes filled with irritation. Her sour expression did not change as she sauntered into the room. She wore a long, brown skirt and yellow blouse with frills down the center. Her brown cloak with yellow silk lining swished around her as her booted feet quietly slipped over the floorboards.

"Who are you?" exclaimed Frisha when the two men followed the woman into the small room. They were both of average height and weight and had muddy brown hair and several day's growth on their chins. Their clothes were those of workmen and nothing about them stood out. In short, they were completely forgettable.

The woman tisked and glanced around the room. When she finally met Frisha's gaze, she looked at her as if deciding whether she was worthy of her time. Then she tilted her head and said, "I suppose you're doable. You're the right size, anyway."

"Doable? What are you talking about, and who are you? I think you're in the wrong place."

The woman carefully removed her yellow silk gloves and tucked them into her skirt. "You are Frisha Souvain-Marcum, yes?"

Frisha's mouth hung open and her gaze darted to the two men who were moving toward her. "Wait, no!"

Then their hands were on her. She struggled against them, and just as she was about to scream, one of their hands covered her mouth. She tried to bite the hand, but she was jerked roughly toward the bed. She kicked and wailed, her sounds muffled, as they pressed her face down into the mattress. Her face was jerked upward, and a knife appeared next to her eye. One of the men leaned over her and said, "Be quiet and stop struggling, or we'll kill you. We don't need you alive to complete our mission."

Frisha clamped her mouth shut with a whimper. Their rough hands released her, and she was allowed to sit up, but both men remained at her sides. The woman held up a drab sack dress then bundled it up and tossed it to her.

"Put this on and give me your clothes."

Frisha glanced at the two men, but it was obvious she would not be afforded any privacy. Tears streamed down her cheeks as she removed the black tunic and pants and donned the dress. Then one of the men placed a gag in her mouth and secured it tightly behind her head. The woman said, "You will not speak unless spoken to. Then, you will call me mistress. Do you understand?"

Frisha nodded once, too afraid to move with a gleaming dagger so near to her face. The man who held it watched her carefully.

Satisfied, the woman looked at the other man and said, "Bring it in."

The man exited the room and returned several minutes later with a third man, and they were carrying something between them that looked very much like a person wrapped in linen. The person did not move or make a sound, and Frisha wondered if he or she was dead. Alarm shot through her as she considered that it might be Xa. Had he failed his mission *and* led them back to her?

She quickly discovered that the body was not that of Xa when they laid it on the floor and unwrapped it. In fact, it was not a body at all, at least, not in truth. Although it was humanoid in shape, it appeared to be made of clay and lacked any defining features except for a hole in the center of its chest that was a few inches deep.

The mistress snapped her fingers, and Frisha realized the third man had already left and returned with a small box. He opened the box and handed it to the mistress. The man who stood at Frisha's side holding the dagger abruptly grabbed her arm as the first man came around to hold her down once again. Frisha screamed into her gag while the second man dragged the dagger across her forearm. Dark blood welled up from the long gash, but the woman was quick to catch the blood as it poured into the box, which held something that looked very much like a heart. Frisha cried and squirmed as they continued to collect her blood, but strong hands and arms held her still. Finally, the woman laid two fingers upon Frisha's arm. She felt the tingling of healing energy suffuse her and the gash closed. Then the woman wiped a damp cloth over her arm removing any traces of blood.

The mistress hummed under her breath as she moved toward the body-shaped clay. She withdrew a silver spoon from her skirt pocket and used it to baste the heart in Frisha's blood. Then she scooped the heart out of the box and placed it into the hole in the clay.

"This golem would be better if it were *your* heart, but we just don't have time to deal with the mess. This one will have to do."

The woman did not seem to expect a reply as she used the damp cloth to smear blood over the entire surface of the clay, careful not to spill even a single drop on her dress or the floor. When she was finished, she placed the cloth into the box and handed it back to one of the men. The mistress then jabbed what looked like a very large thorn into the palm of her hand and dripped several drops of blood onto the "face" of the clay. She used the blood-covered thorn to trace a slit where the mouth would be then pressed the thorn into the slit. Finally, she stood over the clay form with her hands hovering over it chanting something in an arcane language that Frisha could not identify. It occurred to her that Rezkin would probably know what the woman was saying, but *he* would never have gotten himself caught.

The hairs on Frisha's arms stood on end as the clay began to move. It rippled and flowed, morphing to look more and more like an actual person. Frisha felt sick when, after several moments, the clay was no longer clay. It appeared to have skin and hair and all the tiny nuances that made up a person, and it looked exactly like *her*, and it was nude. The mistress stepped back and wrapped a bandage around her damaged hand then looked at Frisha.

"Speak."

Frisha blinked at the woman. "Um, what do you want me to say?"

The golem inhaled sharply and opened its eyes. It stretched its arms and legs then bounded to its feet. Frisha flushed upon seeing the body, which to all the world looked like hers, bouncing around completely unfettered by clothing or propriety. She glanced at the man next to her who was eyeing the form appreciatively. With a shiver she turned away only to find herself looking into the eyes of another man. This one was looking at *her* as if *she* were the nude form.

The mistress handed the golem the clothes Frisha had been wearing when they entered and instructed it to dress. The Frisha form did so then came to stand in front of Frisha. It peered at her curiously then smiled in a way that Frisha was certain she had never smiled. It was filled with malevolence and dark promises.

"Frisha."

She and the form both looked at the mistress, but the mistress only held the golem's gaze. "You know what you have to do. Stay in character."

The golem smiled then spoke with Frisha's voice. "Yes, Mistress, but can't I have a *little* fun?"

The mistress's lip twitched. "So long as they do not suspect anything, I don't care what you do. Stay close to Tieran Nirius. Do not distance him or the usurper."

The Frisha golem gave Frisha a sultry smirk and said, "I have no intention of *distancing* them. Quite the opposite."

The mistress leaned into the golem's face. "Stay. In. Character. You have no idea what I had to do to get her here. I expect regular reports."

The golem's deceitful expression abruptly dropped, and then it was as if Frisha were looking into a mirror. "Yes, Mistress. Anything I can do to help."

The mistress nodded once, then motioned toward the men. Frisha found herself suddenly bound and gagged and tossed over one of their shoulders. They paused at the door, and the Frisha golem gave her a little wave. Then they were out the door and across the street with no one the wiser. Frisha was thrown into the back of a wagon, and a tarp was thrown over her. One of the men threatened to stick her with his knife if she moved or made a sound. Then they waited.

Frisha's heart pounded against her breastbone while she lay trussed beneath the tarp. The cold seeped into her flesh, and her shivering became quakes. She longed for that fishy smelling jacket Xa had procured for her. After a while, the shivering subsided, and Frisha became drowsy. As she tried to find a way to stay awake, her gaze landed on a space between the boards that made up the side of the wagon. She tried to be subtle while shifting toward it, but her movements earned her a kick from one of the men. The kick pushed her closer to the gap, though, and she was able to see through it to view the street. As she watched, Xa slinked out of the shadows to reenter the room from which she had been stolen. Frisha hoped to the Maker that he would realize the golem was not truly her. Her hopes were dashed when a little while later, Xa exited the room with the false Frisha beside him. As they made their way down the street, it became obvious to Frisha that she had been replaced.

Gauge was dark that night. The city's officials had issued a curfew and had opted to keep the streets dark, probably to hide the movements of their few city guards and militia troops from the Ashaiians outside their gates. It was good for Rezkin and his companions, though. With the streets dark and so few people about, they could easily go undetected. Although he had little to worry about with Entris and Azeria, who could move quickly and silently, Nanessy was not used to moving with stealth.

"What about now?" she said.

Rezkin and Entris both looked at her as if waiting. Entris said, "I can still see you (*earnest*)."

"I, as well," said Rezkin.

"No, it is good (*approving*)," said Azeria. "You can see her because you are Spirétua, but to me, she appears blurry, as if I am looking at her from afar through a fog. She will be nearly invisible in the dark."

"Where did you learn such a spell?" said Entris.

Nanessy smiled. "Wesson taught it to me before we left. He thought, since I was traveling with Rezkin, that it might come in handy."

Rezkin looked to Entris and nodded. "You see? He is an excellent king's mage."

Entris shook his head and muttered, "Daem'ahn are not *excellent* in any form."

Rezkin looked to Azeria. "Let us be going. We have much to do tonight. Not only do we need to contend with this mystery weapon, but we still need the information on the quarry."

With a nod, Azeria initiated her power. The air began to crackle, and a localized breeze fluttered the edges of her cloak. She glowed with power as a rent formed in the air. Rezkin glanced down the hill into the city where he saw a similar tear form in the dark alley between a couple of storehouses and the city wall. Entris suddenly stepped out of the tear into the city, and Rezkin realized it was his turn to go through. The pathway, this time, was instantaneous. He took one step and then he was standing next to a pile of broken crates in Gauge. Nanessy came through next, followed by Azeria.

Rezkin said, "You three go look for the weapon. I am going after information on the quarry." Before anyone could object, he sped down an alley in the opposite direction they had planned. He knew he had frustrated his companions, particularly Azeria who seemed to want to keep constant watch over him. He was the Raven, though, and the Raven defied scrutiny.

The others were looking for a weapon, which would likely be held in some sort of storehouse or presided over by the city watch. The storehouses were usually located near the perimeter where there was room for wagons, supply stores, and training grounds. What he was after, though, was much more important—information, and it was unlikely such a treasure would be housed with the weapons. He was looking for the city offices, most likely those of the magistrate or governor. These would be part of the city government near the city's center, and where there was government, there were those who opposed the government. A place like Gauge was unlikely to house much in the way of an organized underworld, but thieves and cutthroats were everywhere.

Rezkin was unfamiliar with the layout of Gauge, but most cities were about the same. He headed for the largest building he could find and let himself in through an upper floor window. As he had guessed, it was secured with a basic latch and had no warding of any kind. The room was of moderate size and full of chairs with one table toward the front. It looked like a meeting room. He stalked across the room and into the hall, all the whilel keeping an ear out for guards. After he had circled the top floor and then descended to the second and then the first, he realized there were no guards at all in the building. He decided they were likely called out to the gates to prepare for an invasion, and the city was probably depending on street patrols to prevent break-ins.

The offices, it turned out were on the first floor. Rezkin found the one labeled *Governor* and let himself inside. The room was larger than he expected and in complete disarray. Books, scrolls, and papers were stacked atop every flat surface. A few maps decorated the walls, one of them hanging limply from a single pin. The desk held several stacks of books and ledgers plus a few items that seemed to serve no purpose. A letter lay half-written in front of the chair. After shuffling through a few piles of papers, Rezkin realized there was an order to the chaos. One pile on the right corner of the desk was outgoing correspondence, while a larger pile that leaned precariously was incoming. A third pile held reports regarding recent attacks by vuroles and other wild creatures. Rezkin was about to move on to a fourth pile when something caught his eye. The word *dragon* was scratched across the top of a page, and it was followed by two columns of names—one for the survivors and the other for the dead.

Nothing else in the pile was of interest, so Rezkin moved on to the next. Eventually, he came to a list of the city's prisoners. Five were listed, but none of them mentioned a clan name, and neither were any of them sent to the quarry. Rezkin felt a mounting emotion, and the vagri began to heat. His first instinct was to stifle the feeling, but thoughts of power had him reconsidering. It took him a few minutes to decipher what it was he was feeling. Frustration and ... desperation. The latter was a new emotion for him, but one he felt acutely and on Tam's behalf. He *needed* information if he was going to find Tam. Rezkin resolved then to take a more active role in getting what he needed. He snatched one of the maps off the wall and left the office in haste.

He surveyed the streets for any movement. Based on what he could see from the hill, the nicer homes were located on the northern side of the city. He turned that way but continued his surveillance. He finally caught sight of one of the city's morally challenged residents exiting a building through a broken window. It was not hard to find the destitute if one knew where to look. Rezkin descended on the man and had him pinned against the wall before he knew he had been caught.

"What? W-who are you? What do you want?"

The man's putrid breath made Rezkin's stomach churn. He ignored it and said, *"Where does the governor live?"*

"I don't know nothin' about the governor except his name—Rias Ardmore."

The information was of no use to him since Rezkin already had the man's name.

He growled, *"Do you have a master?"*

"A master? I don't know what you mean." The man slipped beneath his grip, and Rezkin found himself holding the man upright.

"Who do you serve?"

"I don't serve anyone. I'm just a beggar, nothing more."

"And a drunkard," Rezkin muttered. Moonlight glinted off his dagger as it migrated toward the man's throat. *"Who leads the underworld in this city?"*

"Ah—you want Trag. I don't know him, but I know where you can find him."

Rezkin released the man with a shove and said, *"Take me to him."*

The man stumbled to catch his balance and then continued stumbling as he led Rezkin through the streets. Rezkin might have wondered how this man could avoid the city guards if any had been present. As it was, the streets were silent and still save for the two of them. The man abruptly stopped in front of a narrow townhome sandwiched between another townhome and a bakery. He pointed. *"In there. He lives there."*

Rezkin ignored the drunkard as the man lurched into the darkened alley and disappeared. He refocused on the building in front of him and considered his many options for egress. Trag was a mystery, and Rezkin liked to have the upper hand. Therefore, he elected to slip into the home unseen so that he could riffle through the man's belongings. If he truly was a criminal overlord, did he have minions posted at the doors and windows? Was his home fortified with black-market spellcraft? Rezkin wanted more information besides that given by a street drunkard.

Rezkin slinked through the shadows to round the row of buildings so that he could approach Trag's home from the rear. The alley behind the townhome was as clean as an alley could be. Each home had a clothesline running from one side of the alley to the other, and Trag's was no exception. Rezkin inspected the items left to dry on the line and deduced that they all belonged to one or more males of the same size.

The rear door was locked, of course, but Rezkin made short work of it. As he stepped across the threshold, though, he felt the familiar tug of a ward, a weak one, but a ward nonetheless. Using his will to bend the ward inward, Rezkin found an edge and stepped around it into the narrow home. He entered a hall that separated the kitchen from an open doorway that led to the cellar. Beyond that was an office to one side and a sitting room to the other. Rezkin searched both rooms but found the most interesting missives in the lower drawer of the office desk. It seemed that in addition to other black-market dealings, Trag was in the business of trading information, and the most recent messages received were from none other than the army sitting outside the city's gates.

Next, Rezkin made his way up the stairs to the second level only to find both bedrooms empty. A floorboard creaked at the other end of the hallway, where a door opened to a washroom. A middle-aged man with a saggy belly and spectacles shuffled from the room. He wore a long nightshirt, slippers, and even a nightcap, and he blinked lazily as he adjusted his glasses.

Rezkin waited for the man to notice him, and when he did, he did so with a shout. The man ducked back into the washroom with surprising efficiency and reemerged with a dagger.

"*You dare break into* my *home?*" said the man, his gaze sharpening to a point.

Rezkin leaned lazily against the wall to throw the man off and said, "*Are you Trag?*"

The man paused. "*You don't know?*" He frowned, then nodded slowly. "*Tragon Dimwell, City Accountant.*"

"*City accountant? I am not here to see an accountant. I am here to see the man in charge of what passes for a criminal underworld in this city.*"

"*I don't know what you're talking about.*"

Rezkin nodded toward the dagger in the man's hand. "*I believe you do.*"

Trag glanced at his own dagger and licked his lips. He seemed to be in a struggle between his two identities, a struggle that Rezkin was beginning to understand all too well.

With a burst of speed, Rezkin closed the distance, disarmed the man, grabbed him by his nightshirt, and threw him into one of the bedrooms. Trag tumbled to the floor, and Rezkin shoved him into the corner away from anything he might effectively use as a weapon.

"What's going on here? Who are you, and what do you want?"

Rezkin kicked a short stool over in front of Trag and perched upon it like a predator sizing up its prey from above. He flicked a dagger into one hand, then a second into his other hand, and leaned toward the now quivering man.

"You have a reputation, Trag. Tell me, how does the city accountant become the master of the city's underworld?"

Trag pushed his spectacles higher on the bridge of his nose and lifted his weak chin. *"I assure you that I have no idea what you're talking about."*

"You do or you do not. Either way, I am not leaving until you tell me what I want to know or you are dead. If you give me too much trouble, we'll make it both. Are you ready to answer my questions?"

Anger suffused Trag's expression as his beady eyes filled with menace. *"You will pay for this. Who are you?"*

Rezkin waggled the dagger in front of Trag's gaze. *"Ah, uh. You are to answer my questions. Firstly, what do you know of the army outside the gates? Why are they here, and what do they want?"*

"How should I know? I am just an accountant."

Rezkin spun the dagger nicking Trag's left cheek. The man shouted and slapped his hand over the tiny, bleeding gash. *"That was a lie. You see, that is the* wrong *kind of answer. You* want *to stick with the* right *kind of answers."*

Trag licked his lips and said, *"Okay, they're Ashaiian, and they want something, obviously, but I do not know what."* The man licked his lips again, and Rezkin could see the hunger that entered his gaze. *"Ah, maybe I could find out for you—for the right price."*

Rezkin flicked the dagger in his other hand scoring a matching mark across the man's right cheek. Trag growled and wiped at the wound with his other hand. *"I-it is some kind of weapon that they believe is somewhere in the city. I do not know what it is or where it is, I swear!"*

Rezkin spun both daggers at the same time barely missing Trag's fleshy face. *"You have already lied to me twice, so, you see, I do not believe you."*

Trag's eyes widened as he tried to shrink into the wall behind him and away from Rezkin's daggers. *"Look, I do not know any more about the weapon, but I do know things—things you might use to get the information you seek."*

"For that, I might let you live."

With another lick of his lips, Trag said, *"I know about the governor's wife. She has been exchanging notes with someone on the outside. They promised to let her boys and her live if ..."*

The man trailed off, and Rezkin saw the hunger once again invade the man's gaze. Rezkin pressed the tip of one dagger to the soft flesh beneath the man's chin. *"If what?"*

Trag blinked, and his fear once again consumed his greed. *"If she kills her husband. That is what the missive said."*

"You saw it for yourself?"

"Of course. My man brought it to me before delivering it since it was such a high-profile recipient."

"And I suppose you felt no duty to warn the governor?"

"The governor suspects what I do—there are rumors, of course—but he has no proof, and I am not about to give him any to save his hide when he would as soon throw me in prison."

Rezkin considered ending this blubbering man here and now. He could see little use for him, and there seemed to be nothing redeemable about him either. If he did that, though, the threads of the meager criminal elements in the city would be left flailing in the wind without order. He ultimately decided it was perhaps more efficient to leave the man alive for the time being. He abruptly stood and crossed the room toward the entrance. *"I'm the Raven, and you serve me now."*

The man's expression flashed with recognition of the name, and his face paled. *"The Raven? Come from Ashai?"*

Rezkin ignored the question and said, *"Where is the governor's home?"*

"It's not as though the governor's residence is a secret, not that I would protect him if it were." Tragon smoothed his nightshirt, smearing blood over the white linen as he stood on shaky legs. He gave Rezkin directions then seemed bolstered by the distance Rezkin had made between them. He said, *"Mayhap you came with the army outside our gates?"*

Again, Rezkin ignored the man as he turned to leave. *"Remember, you serve me now. Should you receive orders from me, I expect them to be followed."*

"Yes, yes, I understand. I'll not argue with you." Despite the fearful tremor in the man's voice, Tragon did not seem to take him seriously, and no one had ever tasked the Raven with taking care of anything. He wondered if he was losing his touch and worried that it might have something to do with *feeling* things.

Rezkin let it be as he left the townhome and made his way through the city toward the governor's home. He hid behind a couple of topiaries as the city guard passed him by without notice. It had only been since he neared the governor's mansion that the patrols had appeared. The house had a ward of moderate strength surrounding it, but that did not deter Rezkin. He slipped through the ward and then a ground-floor window at the rear of the house. The window dropped him into the kitchen, and he could hear the snoring of the house staff through an open doorway. He continued toward the stairwell where he scaled the banister while avoiding the steps, which were sure to be creaky. Once at the top, he headed for the most ornate door. As it swung open, Rezkin could see that it was a bedroom, and it was occupied.

Upon the bed, the soft glow of the fire in the hearth illuminated the dusky skin of a young woman whose auburn hair flowed freely down her bare back. Her bottom half was draped in silky bed covers, and she sat astride a naked man who appeared to be at least fifteen years her senior. The scent of mind-numbing incense was heavy in the room, and the lovers did not notice Rezkin as he slinked into the darker shadows. Rezkin waited only a few breaths before acting, and had he not arrived at that time, he would have been too late. He darted across the room, the dancing blue swirls of his blade flashing in the golden firelight. *Bladesunder* arched down and across knocking the woman's knife from her hands and lodging it in the wall beyond the bed.

The woman yelped as the man beneath her pushed her from him and bounded out of bed. Rezkin spun to arrest the man's shouts before they began. With a knife poised at the man's throat and *Bladesunder* caressing the woman's hair, the room fell still.

"*Rius Ardmore?*" Rezkin said just loud enough for the man to hear.

With wide eyes and lips pursed in a shocked *O*, the man quickly nodded. The woman struggled to cover herself with the bed covers, but her gaze was glued to *Bladesunder*'s vicious point. "*Please,*" she whispered, "*spare us.*"

"*Quiet, now,*" said Rezkin as he kicked the woman's discarded nightdress toward her.

Rius's lips waggled soundlessly before sound emerged. When he did finally speak, he said, "*Who are you? What do you want? If it is money, you are welcome to take it. Just do not hurt us.*"

Rezkin circled *Bladesunder*'s tip in front of the woman who had quickly donned the nightdress. He said, "*She was about to kill you.*"

Rius shook his head. "*She is my wife,*" he murmured. "*She would never.*"

"*Your wall décor says otherwise,*" said Rezkin as he tipped his head toward the knife he had liberated from the woman's murderous grasp.

Rius's eyes widened as he finally focused on the weapon lodged in the wallboard. "*What?*" he shouted.

Rezkin tisked and tipped Rius's chin up with his knife point. "*Careful, Rius, or you will wake your staff, and I shall be forced to kill them.*"

Rius's pained gaze dropped to his wife, who stood more than a head shorter than him. Rezkin could see a multitude of questions dancing with the flames reflected in the man's eyes, but in the end only one word escaped his tight lips. "*Why?*"

The woman stepped back until she bumped into the bed. "*I-I had to. The Ashaiians said they would let the children and me live if I k-k-killed you."* Her words ended on a hiccup as tears streamed from her pale eyes.

Rius's distraught expression morphed into resignation. *"I understand, my love. I do not blame you. If my death meant that you and the children might live, then so be it."*

It was at that moment that Rezkin realized the governor's true weakness was not in fear for his own life but for that of his family. Suddenly, the woman was much more valuable.

"Enough," said Rezkin, regaining their attention. *"In answer to your question, I am the Raven."*

The governor squinted at him. *"The Raven of Ashai? You are here because of the army, then? It is strange that you should be with them. I had heard you supported the so-called True King."* He glanced at his wife then said, *"Despite the present circumstances, I am glad that you are here."*

Rezkin was sure that was the first time those words had been uttered about the Raven, and he certainly did not expect them from the governor. It was apparent the man was too distracted by the notion of his wife killing him—or perhaps it was the prospect of losing his family—for him to focus on the true threat. Rezkin said, *"I want information on the quarry."*

Rius blinked, then his gaze seemed to sharpen before he said, *"The quarry, is it? I know not why you would want information on that godforsaken place, but I suppose some of your ilk may be there."* He paused, then said, *"Word has it that you have made clear your support for the True King of Ashai. Is this true?"*

Rezkin tilted his head back and said, *"Why do you want to know?"*

"Because the Ashaiian army is outside my gates, and I doubt they will be leaving until they get what they want."

"The weapon."

"Is that what they are calling it? Of course they would try. Everyone knows their king is mad. Should we expect more from his followers?"

"What is this weapon?"

Rezkin allowed Rius to back up until he leaned against the bed. He reached over and took his wife's hand in his own. Then he inhaled sharply and straightened with resolve. *"If you take care of that army out there, I will give you all the information you desire. I will even give you the so-called weapon."*

The man's wife looked at him in alarm. In a harsh whisper, she said, "Rius, please just tell him what he wants to know."

"Or I can just take what I want from your bleeding hide," said Rezkin

It appeared that Rius had suddenly found no small amount of courage as he said, *"Dead men cannot speak."*

"I never said you would be dead."

"Even so, whatever you would do to me cannot be worse than what they will do once they get in here—and they will get in here. I doubt the walls will last the morrow. I have heard of your exploits—taking on entire guilds in a single eve. This cannot be much more difficult."

Rezkin's gaze found the fire poker, and he considered the many things he could do with it to make the man talk. The fact that Rius was a presumably innocent man played on his mind, though. Rezkin had not had enough time to gather anything incriminating on the man, and torture—well, he had to think. Was he the Raven or the Rez? The Rez, the identity he had been assigned since birth, would not stop at torture or concede to the man's presumed innocence. He would do what was needed to get the job done, regardless of the cost. The Raven, however—his own creation—had only ever tormented the corrupt.

Rezkin stood from his chair, picked up the fire poker, and began stirring the coals with it. As the tip grew red and then orange, he mulled over his choice. The Rez or the Raven? Torture or a deal? He lifted the poker and examined the white-hot tip, then his gaze slid to Rius. *"Torture would be easier,"* he mused aloud. The man swallowed hard and pulled his wife closer.

The tension in Rezkin's shoulders released as he hung the poker back on its rack. Then he headed for the door.

"W-where are you going?" sputtered Rius.

"I go to dispatch an army."

. . .

Rezkin was headed toward the gate when Azeria appeared at his side. "You followed me?" he said.

"It is our prerogative to keep an eye on you."

It frustrated him that she had been able to pursue him without his knowledge. She had a number of decades beyond his years, though, and she had obviously spent it learning warcraft. He would have respected her less had she been lacking.

"Is everything to your satisfaction?" he said, not truly caring for the answer. He had stopped within sight of the front gate, although still too far away to be seen by the numerous guards and militiamen who were gathered there.

"No, it is not," she said. "I thought you would kill the governor."

"I did not."

"Why?"

Rezkin watched as one of the militiamen, a small-man no older than fourteen, dropped a sword that was too heavy for him. He turned back to her. "The governor is not my enemy. He is merely a man doing his job."

Azeria, too, watched the small-man as he fumbled with the sword. "So now you will take on the army by yourself?"

"I am not by myself. You are here."

"But you did not know that."

Rezkin pointed to the small-man. "Would you rather *he* do it?" Then he waved to the lot of them. "Look at them all. They are unprepared for this fight. The Ashaiians may be disorganized, but they are trained fighters, and they have mages."

"This is not your battle."

"Of course it is. These people are under threat by Caydean, and I aim to defeat him."

"You cannot do that by fighting every backwoods battle you encounter."

"I am fighting this one. You may help or get out of my way."

Azeria took another look at the sorry lot that was the entire fighting force of the city of Gauge, then said, "Very well. I will help you, but if Entris asks, I am telling him I did it for the practice."

Rezkin nearly laughed. It was an odd feeling at any time, but most certainly in the moments preceding a battle. "There is one more thing." She looked at him questioningly and he said, "I want to kill as few of the Ashaiians as possible."

"What? You want to go to battle against a foe without killing them? What madness is this?"

"I am the true king of Ashai, and these are my people. If I kill them all, I will be king of a graveyard."

She sighed in irritation before saying, "I will not kill anyone who does not try to kill me."

Rezkin nodded. "Fair enough." Then he stepped out of the moon's shadow. "Keep your hood up and follow me. Act like you belong here."

Azeria muttered, "Because I do not look suspicious at all wearing a hood in the dark."

"They are not looking for people on the *inside*," replied Rezkin.

Her voice was heavy with disgust. "These humans are oblivious."

Rezkin skirted the largest group of militiamen to access one of several ladders that led to the catwalk along the top of the wall. Bowmen, most of whom were probably civilian hunters, dotted the walkway, but Rezkin ignored them as he continued toward the front gate. He stopped when he had a good vantage of the opposing army. To their credit, most of the Ashaiians were asleep, he assumed in preparation for a dawn attack, although it was equally likely they were passed out from consuming too much drink. Either way, Rezkin was going to make sure that when dawn arrived, the order to attack never came.

He leaned closer to Azeria so as not to be overheard. "Can you open a pathway down there?"

"Without being detected? Impossible."

He drummed his fingers across the rough wood atop the wall. "What about inside the armory tent? You have been there."

"Yes, I can open one there, but the power will be felt. They will likely think it is a mage attack."

"Actually, that is good. It is closest to the command tent and the tents belonging to the officers."

"That is a good thing?"

"Yes, because they will be the ones to investigate, and we can dispatch them without upsetting the rest of the camp."

"What about the human mages and the Sen?"

"Only two mages were mentioned earlier. We can handle them."

Azeria gripped her hilt tightly as she said, "I am not prepared to battle a Sen. There could be daem'ahn. We should bring Entris."

"Entris is still seriously injured. Besides, he is busy searching for the weapon."

"Which you will have if we are successful. The governor promised to give it to you."

"I do not trust the governor at his word. Do you?"

"No, I suppose not."

After descending a ladder, they secluded themselves in a vacant farrier's shop near the wall. Rezkin was waiting for her to open a path when she looked up at him and said, "This is an ill-conceived plan."

"Sometimes long, drawn-out strategies prevail. Other times, one must plan for the moment. This is the right moment. In a few hours, it will be too late. The orders will have been given."

"You truly believe that if you can prevent the order to attack from being given, you can prevent the battle and save lives on both sides?"

"That is my intent."

She shook her head as though he were daft, and then began opening the pathway. The scent of lightning filled the crisp air surrounding them, and the shop was lit from the other side of the tear that hovered in the air before them. It was smaller than before and did not reach the floor.

"Quickly," she hissed.

Rezkin dove through the hole, and Azeria followed, tumbling onto him as the tear disappeared. The sides of the tent flapped harshly in an absent wind then quickly settled. Rezkin could hear people calling to each other from outside the tent. He pushed Azeria off him, took to his feet, and drew his Sheyalin blades. Azeria drew her short swords as she righted herself. They shared a quick glance, then bounded out of the tent.

Rezkin did not get a good look at the first man to attack before the man was impaled. He noted the officer's insignia as the man slid off his blade, and Rezkin refocused on the next attacker. Another man farther away started to raise the alarm, but Azeria quickly silenced him with a dagger.

"He was not attacking you," Rezkin muttered as *Kingslayer* clashed with another blade.

"He might as well have been," she argued as she kicked a militiaman away from her then rendered a second unconscious. "If he had raised the alarm, more would come, and more would need to die." The first man had somehow lost his sword, but he came at her with a tree branch anyway. "Seriously?" she sputtered as she stepped to the side and smacked her pommel into his temple. The man hit the ground with a thud.

Rezkin and Azeria both looked around and realized no one else was coming at them. In a matter of seconds, they had taken out everyone who had heard their arrival. He said, "We should move them inside."

"Do not bother," said Azeria as she pointed toward a couple of robed figures dashing between tents, heading in their direction. "The mages are coming."

"I doubt they have seen us, yet. Let us hide and surprise them," said Rezkin.

Azeria moved to hide behind a wagon while Rezkin ducked back into the armory tent.

A moment later, the first mage appeared on the scene. "What is this?" she shouted.

Then a man rushed into the tent holding a glowing mage stone. He jumped back and snapped a ward around himself as Rezkin leapt for him. The ward had little effect, and they both tumbled to the ground. Rezkin got the upper position as ineffective spells battered against him.

"Wait, no!" cried the mage as Rezkin's dagger flashed in the moonlight, streaming in through the open flap.

Before Rezkin could open the mage's throat, though, he was

abruptly pulled away from—or, rather, *thrown* from him. Rezkin tumbled into the open and rolled to his feet. He could see that Azeria was locked in a heated battle with the other mage, but he did not have time to assess her condition. His confusion over his own situation lasted only seconds before the truth was revealed. When the mage stepped out of the armory tent, his eyes were blacker than night, and he wore a sadistic grin that shined brightly in the silvery light. He thrust his arms forward, and black tendrils shot toward Rezkin.

"Daem'ahn!" shouted Azeria, her voice strained.

"I know he is," replied Rezkin as he darted to the side to duck behind a barrel of water. The inky blackness smashed into the barrel, and the wood blackened and crumbled releasing the now-putrid water with a crash.

Azeria's teeth were clenched as she said, "No, I mean *mine* is daem'ahn."

Rezkin spared a glance for the female mage and sure enough her eyes were also black, and she was wielding a dark power that Azeria struggled to combat using her many decades of experience.

Rezkin launched a throwing dagger toward the male mage, hitting his mark, although the mage did not go down. Instead, he laughed and began building another attack. As the inky ball of black power grew before him, Rezkin closed the distance. He knew it was better to fight the demon with power, but he did not know how. Instead, he relied on what he did know, and he knew many, many ways to kill.

The mage grinned over the top of his monstrous black ball before he hurled it toward Rezkin's oncoming form. Rezkin abruptly dropped to the ground and slid into the mage knocking him from his feet. In the same moment, Rezkin sunk his serrated dagger into the mage's chest, then he got to his knees and sliced *Bladesunder* across the man's neck taking his head from his body.

Rezkin breathed heavily over the body as he assessed the situation. Just as he spied Colonel Whitner and a squad of soldiers heading their way, Azeria screamed. He looked to his right to see her gripping her side, but she was infuriated. She shoved the female mage backward with a blast of air then jumped on the woman. Rezkin was about to go to Azeria's aid when he realized she did not need his help. The mage fell to the ground, with Azeria atop her, then began convulsing. Azeria gritted her teeth as she rose above the woman and then stabbed her short sword down through the woman's heart. The mage's convulsions lasted a few more seconds before they finally stilled. Azeria fell to her side and kicked the mage several times, taking her anger out on the corpse. Then she rose and gingerly made her way over toward Rezkin.

Colonel Whitner and his men paused to take in the battle scene before he shouted for the men to attack. At the same time, the blast of a horn broke the still night, and the city's gates opened. A rush of guards and militia flooded the Ashaiian encampment and chaos ensued. Rezkin and Azeria took down the colonel's men in tandem as they made their way toward the colonel. Just before they reached him, Colonel Whitner turned tail and ran. He was headed toward a large tent screaming, "Berringish!" when Rezkin's dagger landed in his back. Azeria and Rezkin circled the tent and waited near the flap. When no one emerged, Rezkin darted inside with swords raised. The tent was empty save for a disheveled cot and a locked trunk.

Azeria sent a gust of hot air at the trunk, which blasted the lid open sending chunks of wood and a few papers into the air. Rezkin quickly shuffled through the trunk's contents, which included a few items of clothing, a cloak, and two vessels wrapped in burlap. The vessels were marked with the same glyphs Rezkin had seen on those that had contained demons like the one in Ferélle. After explaining to Azeria what they were, he smashed each of them on the ground. By the time they exited the tent, the Ashaiians had sounded the retreat. Without their officers to pull them together, Rezkin doubted many would survive, and those who did would not form any sort of organized force. If anything, they were likely to be picked up by the Verrilian army on their escape toward the north to the sea.

Rezkin felt a pit in his chest. After a few minutes, he identified the feeling as disappointment. He had hoped to spare as many of the Ashaiians as possible. Still, he had prevented the slaughter of the people of Gauge. The thought that plagued him was, what had happened to Berringish?

With one last fruitless search of the tent, Rezkin turned to Azeria and said, "Let us get back to the city before the guards pull back. Our efforts will be much more difficult once the city is repopulated and order is restored."

Azeria nodded, and they efficiently cut their way through the throng of battling soldiers back into the city. They had only just made it to the main throughfare, now lined with torches and burning piles of refuse, when they were descended upon by their comrades.

"Azeria!" called Entris from a sideroad.

Azeria grabbed Rezkin's sleeve then pulled him toward the dark roadway that led toward the north side of the city. When they were within close proximity, Nanessy surrounded them in a ward to prevent the escape of light and then created a glowing orb that hovered over her palm. With eyes wide with alarm, Nanessy glanced up and down the street at the battles that had pressed into the city. Apparently, not all the Ashaiians heeded the call to retreat, and none of their commanders were left alive to reel them back into compliance. Entris, on the other hand, appeared as stoic as ever, but he surveyed Azeria's condition with a sharp, critical eye.

"You started a war (*irritated*)," he said as his attention shifted toward Rezkin.

"We disarmed the Ashaiians by taking out their leadership. We prevented the slaughter of the inhabitants of this city."

Entris focused back on Azeria. "How was this decision made? Did he consider his actions (*concerned*)?"

"You mean was I mad?" said Rezkin.

Entris nodded without shame. "I do." Then, looking back to Azeria, he said, "How did he convince you to participate (*cautious*)?"

Rezkin thought for sure Azeria would voice her doubts about what she had called an "ill-conceived plan," but instead, she said, "While similar actions by someone else might have been considered rash, his actions were premeditated and with considerable purpose (*sincere*). If the governor was truthful, then the weapon is ours."

An atypical, pained expression passed over Entris's face as he said, "The *weapon* belongs to no one. Come. I will show you."

The streets farther from the front gates were quiet and lit only by the moonlight. Entris led them past several rows of buildings and a square full of open stalls that were closed for the night. It was only when they neared a large building that a loud rustling reached Rezkin's ears. It was the sound of thrashing combined with a muffled cry.

"What is it?" Rezkin whispered.

"You will need to see for yourself," said Entris as he opened a door, the lock already having been smashed.

Two torches were propped near the center of the room, barely illuminating the space around them and leaving numerous shadows around the storehouse's perimeter. Inside were stacks of pallets and crates containing mostly food stores, but it was the large creature in the center just beyond the torches that captured their attention. A beast about the size of a horse yanked and clawed at massive chains that wrapped around its body and wings. Its long neck was bent over until it nearly touched the ground where a shorter chain wrapped around its maw and cinched it to the floor. The juvenile dragon tried to cry out, but its mouth was secured shut so tightly that the chains were biting into the still soft scales and causing blood to seep to the floor.

Entris held out his arm so that they would stop at the edge of the room. He said, "I believe this is what has awoken the drahg'ahn in the mountain."

"You believe this is her offspring?" said Rezkin.

"I do. It is very young. You can see that the scales have not yet hardened. Someone probably stole one of her eggs, and it hatched here, perhaps within the past few months."

"We should kill it," said Azeria.

"It is only a baby!" replied Nanessy.

Azeria said, "It is drahg'ahn. It will get bigger and live for a very long time. It is vulnerable now. In a few months, it will be near impossible to kill."

"Quiet," said Rezkin in a hushed voice. "Do you hear that?"

"Yes," said Azeria. "What is that?"

Rezkin peered through the dark as he tried to focus his hearing past the thrashing of the creature and rattling of chains. Beneath all of that, he heard a droning sound. No, it was a voice—a voice that rose and fell with a lilting cadence.

"Someone is here," he said. "Spread out and find him."

The others did as Rezkin said. Entris and Nanessy went to the right of the dragon, and Rezkin followed Azeria around to the left. The chanting grew louder as they rounded the pitiful creature that occupied the room's center. Rezkin could barely see Nanessy and Entris on the other side of the room converging with them. There in the dark recesses between them was a man bent over a painted vessel that sat on the ground. He was chanting something in a disjointed language that barely carried to their ears. The man abruptly looked up and scowled at them.

Rezkin launched a dagger at the man before he could say another syllable. The man jumped back as the dagger sliced through his tunic sleeve. "Berringish?" he said.

The man glanced Rezkin's way but said nothing. Then another voice in the shadows cut through the din. "Master," it hissed. "This way."

"No! I must finish this," Berringish growled.

Azeria tried to move in on him, but she was repulsed by a power they could not see. Entris ran to her side as Nanessy lobbed a fireball into the darkness. The fireball collided with the invisible force and was snuffed out as it released an acrid smoke that caused Azeria and Entris to cough. The chanting continued, and black tendrils snaked along the ground toward the dragon. As the tendrils climbed its legs, the dragon began to groan and jerked against its chains.

In that moment, Rezkin made a decision to cut their losses. He ran toward the dragon, deftly avoiding a swipe of its tail as he drew the black blade. He grabbed hold of the power inside him that he had come to know as his vimara and yanked on it as the black blade descended. It smashed into the first chain link with a glimmering spark of green lighting. The link exploded in a shower of bright green sparks. Rezkin rounded the creature as its freed wing flapped wildly. He swung at the next link, fueling his strike with the raw power of his vimara and released that one as well. The chains crossing the beast's body fell loosely around its feet, but its head was still secured to the floor by its muzzle.

Rezkin inched closer to the dragon's head as its bulky body pivoted and jerked against the restraints. The dragon's tail lashed wildly at him and then it stilled. It watched him with a bright yellow eye. The predator's gaze was calculating, as though it knew he would release it, and it was prepared to seize the opportunity to punish him for its imprisonment. With a deep breath, Rezkin prepared himself for a quick retreat then swung with all his might against the chain that cut so deeply into the beast's face.

The dragon screamed as it reared backward, finally able to stretch its neck toward the sky. It flapped its wings and whipped its tail wildly. It seemed to notice then, the black tendrils snaking up its legs. It snapped at them and danced away with an angry fury.

Berringish screamed, "No!" as the beast separated itself from the floor, breaking the link between itself and the tendrils. The dragon's wings flapped wildly as it struggled to gain inch after inch of height. Then a magnificent wind filled its wings, and Rezkin glanced over to see Azeria's power filling the air. Caught on the updraft, the beast soared toward the ceiling and broke through the rafters with a wicked screech. A loose length of chain caught on one of the broken pieces, and the dragon yanked and squawked as it tore pieces from the ceiling. Rezkin and the others took cover where they might as the dragon continued raining roofing down on them. When it finally wrenched free, the remainder of the roof collapsed.

Rezkin opened his eyes to see that he had been protected by a ward that he did not remember casting. In fact, he was certain it did not belong to him. It had the feel of Azeria, of all people. After pressing the wreckage of the roof away from him, he caught his feet and turned to find his companions doing the same. Nanessy had illuminated the area with a glowing ball of blue light. Rezkin quickly examined the area where Berringish had been, but the Sen and his assistant were already gone. He doubted they would be easy to find. The Sen seemed to possess a power unlike any he had previously encountered.

"Is everyone okay?" he said.

"You set it free," said Nanessy.

"I figured it was better than allowing Berringish to take control of it using a demon."

"I am not sure that he would have been successful," said Entris. "The drahg'ahn are descendants of daem'ahn and ahn'tep. They have a natural resistance to invasion by another daem'ahn."

"Yes, but this one was young," said Azeria. "It may not have had the strength to fight it off. There is no telling what would happen to a daem'ahn possessed drahg'ahn. I doubt the Sen could have controlled it like he intended."

"Then we now know that Berringish is willing to try anything to gain power," said Rezkin.

"He is intelligent, though" said Entris. "To be able to capture a youngling like that one and to have the resources to force a possession on one would take extensive planning and immense power. If he had succeeded, he might very well have been unstoppable."

"Where did he go?" said Nanessy.

"He escaped during the battle," said Rezkin. "For now, though, we must find the quarry and save Tam. We can worry about Berringish later."

15

Tam headed toward the tool cart but did not make it more than a few feet before Guent hurried up to him. The man grinned, exposing several gaps between his remaining teeth, and handed Tam a pickaxe.

Tam hefted the axe and said, "Thanks."

Guent, an Ashaiian wanderer unlucky enough to be picked up by slavers, ducked his head and said, "No problem, Master, sir."

As Guent hurried away, Uthey tugged on the chain that connected them. "Come on, *Master, sir.* Your rocks are waiting."

Although Uthey had said it facetiously, it was not uncommon those days for many of the slaves to refer to Tam as *master* or *boss.* He figured it was better than the *other* name they had given him. In the aftermath of the cave-in that had killed a guard and that Tam and Uthey had survived, some of the men seemed to think that Tam possessed power over the rocks. Tam did not bother to correct them, since no one would believe the truth. He had tried to explain it to Uthey, but his partner had only shaken his head as if Tam had finally lost his mind for good. Perhaps he had, he thought. He had neither seen nor heard from Goragana or his *lessers* since the day of the cavein, and he had begun to wonder if any of it had happened at all. The only thought that gave him pause was that since that time, the pains in his head had given him less trouble, and his nose bled only half as often as it had.

As they turned down one of the tunnels toward where they had been making progress the previous day, Milo stepped into the torchlight. "Hey, Answon demands your presence."

Uthey growled, "*Demands*, does he?" Then he turned to Tam and, in Gendishen, said, "*We cannot cave to a demand. Let's go.*"

Tam shook his head and stepped around Milo. He said, "Tell Answon ... You know what? Don't tell Answon anything. So long as he continues making demands, we will be ignoring him."

Milo hurried to keep up with him while lugging a stack of heavy sacks. "What am I supposed to tell him, then? That you are ignoring him? He will kill me for that message."

"Why give him a message at all?"

"He will kill me *without* a message, too."

"If he's so intent on killing you, why do you continue to work for him?"

"I don't work for him. I'm a ... what do you call it ... free agent. Truth be told, I like you better. You don't threaten to kill me."

"Then stop carrying his messages."

"No, he threatens to kill me."

Tam sighed. They were getting nowhere. A moment later, another man—Tam did not know his name, although he had seen him lurking around the barracks—came up to him. "Montag wants to speak with you," he said.

Tam stopped and released a chuckle. "Answon, Montag. Is Demetrus hiding around the corner?"

Both men turned to peer at the intersection with worried eyes.

"I do not see what is funny about that," said Milo.

Tam's grin fell. "Perhaps it's not, but laughing feels better than screaming." He elbowed Uthey in the side. "Isn't that right?"

"*I am not sure what you are saying,*" grumbled Uthey. "*But they do not look like they are laughing. Why are you?*" Although his Ashaiian had improved since they were stuck together, he still had trouble translating when people were speaking quickly.

"And I thought you were the jovial one," Tam muttered. He looked at the two messengers and said, "If Answon or Montag or even Demetrus want to see me, they can come find me in sector four. I'll be there all day. Breaking rocks. Just like every other day."

Milo inched a little closer and lowered his voice. "Have they told you anything lately?"

"Has *who* told me anything?"

He glanced at the other man then said, "The rocks. Are they speaking to you?"

Tam rolled his eyes and pushed past Milo making his way to sector four. When he arrived with Uthey at his side along with Milo and the other man—he really needed to learn his name—on his tail, Demetrus was, in fact, awaiting him. Demetrus cracked his scarred knuckles and took a step forward. Six of his own men were at his back, and he had the confidence of a lord backed by a dozen knights.

Tam said, "What do you want, Demetrus?"

Demetrus said nothing but flicked his fingers and pointed toward Tam. In the next moment, pure chaos erupted. The men did not stop to ask if the messengers were on Tam's side. They simply attacked, and Tam and Uthey were stuck in the middle of the fray. Tam gripped his pickaxe in two meaty fists as he swung it upward from the left toward the first man to move on him. Uthey met the attack of another man wielding a shovel, holding him back for the moment.

Tam did not take his gaze from his opponent as he used his other senses to keep track of the rest of Demetrus's crew. Instead, he called into the meager light of the torch, "Demetrus, this is between you and me. Let's settle this between us."

Again, Demetrus said nothing, but Tam imagined him sneering through the growl he released before leaning back and settling against the cave wall to watch. Tam toppled forward as someone—either Milo or his attacker—stumbled into him. His breath left him with a punch to his kidney, and he sent an elbow back into the assailant's face. Then he kicked forward at another attacker just as his neck was yanked to the side. Uthey's attacker was tangled in the chain and using the advantage to keep Uthey within his reach. Tam slammed the butt of his pickaxe into the base of the man's skull causing him to tip forward into Uthey before hitting the ground either unconscious or dead. Tam had no time to find out as he was immediately grabbed from behind in a tight choke hold. Not a second later, someone crashed into his feet and he and his attacker were pitched to the floor.

Tam looked up from the tangle of limbs and chain into the irate stare of Demetrus. The man's jaw ticked just before he pushed off the wall and picked up a fallen pickax. He looked like a demon as he hovered over Tam wielding the pickax in the flickering torchlight.

"I am done with this," said Demetrus just as the pickaxe sailed down toward Tam's chest. Tam had barely heard him through rush of blood in his ears and the unidentified grinding that seemed to be coming from all around him. He blinked grit and moisture from his eyes, then looked up when the axe never fell. The hold on his neck loosened, and Tam scurried away from the brawlers as they stilled. He was furiously coughing and dragging himself to his feet to the sounds of someone screaming. When he realized everyone, friend and foe alike, had frozen and was staring at him, he wondered if he was the one that had been screaming. Then he noticed their gazes were settled behind him, and he spun to find the source of their terror.

Demetrus was there, absorbed into the wall as if the rock had grown around him while he fought its clutches. His face was a stoney mask of agony frozen in time and immovable. Tam took a step backward then remembered the enemies at his back. Their gazes shifted from Demetrus to Tam, and, in a flurry of flying limbs, they disentangled themselves and ran from the tunnel. As they tried to make their escape, they collided with a gathering of slaves and masters who had come to investigate the commotion. By the time they were close enough to see anything, Demetrus had completely disappeared into the rock and there was nothing to witness.

The slave masters took one look at their bloodied faces and, blessedly, elected not to whip them, merely hollered at them to get back to work. Only Tam, Uthey, and Milo were left in the tunnel, and they quickly collected their tools and began working. Tam felt heat on the back of his neck and every time he looked over, he encountered the dark stares of Milo and Uthey. He tried, at first, to ignore them, but after a while the sense of unease became too much. When they were finally permitted a break around midday, Milo disappeared into the throng while Uthey was not so lucky.

"What?" Tam huffed.

"I said nothing," replied Uthey.

"I can feel your anxiety."

"Is that another of your powers?"

"I don't have any powers. You know that."

"Then I think I have caught your madness."

Tam tugged at his filthy hair in frustration. *"Look, that back there, it wasn't me. I didn't do that. It was the rocks."*

"Right. The rocks ate the man of their own accord."

"They did!" Tam insisted. *"They were protecting me because they made a deal with my king, or emperor, or whatever he is now."*

Uthey said nothing as he sat on a boulder staring at everything *except* Tam. Tam groaned and plunked down onto the gravel to rest his weary muscles. He closed his eyes to the feel of a soft breeze caressing his face. He must have dozed off because when he came to, he was surrounded by scruffy, bedraggled men. He quickly got to his feet, worried that he was about to incur the wrath of Demetrus's men. Instead of attacking him, though, the men began introducing themselves, each one offering him their services. One particularly large Sandean went so far as to pledge him fealty so long as Tam took him along during the escape. By then, word had gotten around about Tam's plans. Even the guards were aware of his designs, and they badgered him about it with scornful laughs at every opportunity.

By the next day, everyone had heard about Demetrus's fate, and although the slavers suspected Tam had something to do with it, they could not find a body or witnesses that said anything other than that the rocks ate him. At one point, a mage was brought down from the quarry's rim to check that Tam indeed had no vimaral power. After two days of Demetrus's absence and rumors of Tam's involvement,

Tam's *army* had grown to nearly thirty men. By the third day, Answon and Montag, together, requested Tam's presence at a meeting of the sect leaders.

"All right, I'm here. What do you want?" Tam said.

Answon and Montag shared a look, then Montag said, "We want to know what happened to Demetrus."

"You already know what happened to Demetrus. *Everyone* knows what happened to Demetrus."

"Aye, we know the rumors, but we want to hear it from you. Did you make the rocks eat him?"

Tam considered lying and telling them that he had, in fact, caused Demetrus's unusual demise, but since he was incapable of replicating the feat, he decided it would be a dangerous bluff. He said, "No." Answon and Montag shared a smug look that said he had confirmed their suspicions. Then he added, "The rocks did that on their own. They were protecting me."

Beside him, Uthey groaned and muttered, *"I've told you how crazy that sounds. It would be better to admit it was you."*

Answon said, "What power do you hold to make the rocks do your bidding?"

"It is not *my* power. It is the power of my king. He made a deal with the fae for my protection."

Answon did not laugh. His dark gaze was assessing as he said, "Your king would make a deal with the fae for *your* protection?"

Tam paused. He had no idea what deal Rezkin had made. All he knew was that his safety was included in it. At least, that's what a rock monster had told him. "He did," Tam said with confidence.

Answon said, "Your plan—are you depending on the rocks to help you escape?"

"They have offered as much."

"This is ridiculous," growled Montag. "I cannot believe we are listening to this."

"I want in," said Answon. Tam's shock was apparently evident because Answon said, "I have considered what you said. I am not a slave. I will not be satisfied with being a slave. I would rather die than go the rest of my life without knowing freedom." He turned his attention to Montag. "Will you?"

Montag said, "You realize if this fails and we survive, we will both be stoned to death by our own men."

Answon looked back at Tam. "If you get us out of this quarry and this king truly does come for you himself, then I will serve him as well."

16

Rezkin peered down into the quarry from his perch in a tree overhanging the cliff's edge. There was only one obvious way down, and it appeared to be the only way out, as well. He was not deterred, though. His only concern was that his efforts would be in vain and that Tam would either not be there or was already dead. Surely by that time the hole in his mind had taken his sanity if not also his life. More than even death, Rezkin dreaded what he might find if Tam were still alive.

After scrambling down from the tree, Rezkin retraced his steps to join his companions. "I am going in," he said.

"You would go down there alone?"

"There is less chance of being caught. Besides, the rest of you are too obvious. There are no women down there, and no one is wearing a hood. There is no way to hide what you are."

"What is your plan?" said Azeria.

"I will get caught."

"You mean to go down as a prisoner?"

"It is the way of least resistance. Most of the prisoners are not chained. Once I have found Tam, I will bring him back out with me."

"How?" said Nanessy.

"We will scale the walls if we must."

Entris said, "From what you have said, he may not be in any condition to be scaling walls."

"I doubt Tam could do that anyway," said Nanessy. "We are talking about Tamarin Blackwater, Rezkin, not *you*."

"Tam is stronger than you think."

"He *was* stronger," she replied. "He has been a prisoner for months. He will be weakened and ill."

"If it comes to the worst, then you kill the mages and guards up top, and I will kill all those in the quarry. Then you can raise us up on the lift."

"You speak of killing with such ease," said Nanessy. "What makes you think we are capable—"

"—or *willing*," said Azeria.

Nanessy nodded.

"These are slavers," said Rezkin. "You said you oppose slavery. It is time to stand up for that which you believe."

A half hour later, Rezkin stumbled into the clearing on the opposite side of the quarry and rocked back on his heels as he took in the scene. Three mages sat around a table playing stones, and a half dozen guards occupied posts or were lounging in the shade. A squat building sat at the cliff's edge, and the lift was secured at one side.

"*Hey!*" he called in Verrili, knowing the guards were all Ashaiian. "*Can you help me? I seem to be lost.*"

Two of the guards rushed forward and grabbed him roughly while a third came around and patted him down for weapons. His hair was a disheveled mess, he had not shaved in a couple of days, and he wore a rough, homespun shirt and pants he had acquired in Gauge, along with a pair of worn boots, one of which had a hole in the toe.

"*Hey, hey, now. What's the big idea?*" he said as though he did not realize he was speaking to the enemy.

"Shut up," growled one of the guards who shoved him toward the table. "Well? Is he a mage?" the man said.

One of the mages looked up from his gaming pieces. "What do you want me to say? I'm not a reader. None of us are."

"But you can feel power or something, right?" said the guard.

The mage rolled his grey eyes. "Only if he's actually using it. But look at him. No respectable mage would look like *that*."

"Maybe if he's trying to get into the quarry, he would," said the guard.

Rezkin had to give the man credit. He was not completely stupid.

"Why would he *want* to get into the quarry?" said a second mage, this one with mousy brown hair and a thin scar on one cheek.

The guard shrugged. "Mayhap he wants to break someone *out?*"

"What's going on here?" said Rezkin, still speaking Verrili. *"Where are you from? You're not the normal guards, are you?"*

The mage with the scar chuckled. "I think you're giving him too much credit. Just send him down the lift and put him to work."

"What if someone misses him?" said the guard.

"He's Verrili," said the first mage. "Sooner or later, they're all going to be slaves anyway."

Rezkin visibly gawked as he rode the lift down into the quarry. He was trussed up like a pig after having put up a fight at the top for appearance's sake. Every so often he mumbled a protest past an aching cheek. One of the guards had socked him good in the jaw. The minor pain was nothing he could not handle, though.

Once Rezkin landed in the quarry, one of the guards shoved him out of the lift with a strong kick to the ribs. Rezkin rolled out then scrambled to his feet while doubled over holding his side. The guard grabbed him by the back of the neck and yelled in his face, "You. Are. A. Slave. Now. You understand me?" as if raising his voice would help a Verrili man understand him better.

"What's happening to me? I don't understand," cried Rezkin.

"I've got him," said a man who approached cautiously. He was obviously Verrili, and Rezkin wondered if he was not one of the former slave masters of the quarry from the time before the Ashaiians were in charge. His suspicions were confirmed when the man wrapped an arm around his shoulders and directed him toward a barracks. *"Stay quiet, okay? I'm Jerril. You call me Slave Master Jerril, okay? Look, these Ashaiians, they think we are all slaves like the rest of this lot, so you'd best be careful around them. Where did you come from?"*

Rezkin lowered his voice to match that of the Verrili slave master. *"I was fishing in my boat upriver when it sprung a leak. I came through the woods looking for help. What are the Ashaiians doing here?"*

"They invaded a few weeks ago. They've taken the quarry and who knows how much else. Did you not see any before you came here?"

Rezkin shook his head. *"I heard there was some battle to the south but didn't put much stock in it."*

"Well, they're here now. I was a slave master when they came. They made me a deal that I could continue working for them. I help keep the slaves in order, and I don't get beat on; but truth is, I'm not much better off than these other poor sots."

"I just want to go home to my wife and son," said Rezkin.

"I think you'll not be getting there for a while unless we can take the quarry back."

"Who are these slaves? Are there others like us? What of Ashaiians? Any Ashaiian slaves?"

Jerril's face scrunched. *"There are some Ashaiians who came through before all this. What do you care about the Ashaiians, though, eh?"*

"I just thought maybe they were spies."

"Spies? Nah, that lot have it worse than we do. The Ashaiians—those up there"—he pointed toward the top of the cliff—*"don't care if other Ashaiians are down here. They figure they must've been refugees. You know the Ashaiians are at war with themselves. Nah, we're all just slaves to them."*

Jerril stopped beside an empty barracks. *"You stay here. No work for you today since it's almost quitting time. The bell will be ringing soon, and the others'll come back. You're lucky to get here on shower day. The smell is worse by the end of the week. Just keep your head down and do what you're told, okay?"* Jerril shook his head sadly and said, *"Welcome to the quarry."*

Rezkin surveyed the barracks, which was empty save for a few scraps of fabric here and there. The whole place wreaked of body odor and waste. He rounded the back of the barracks and found the source of the latter foul smell. Instead of a row of latrines or outhouses, he found an open pit.

The sound of a bell echoed off the quarry walls, and after several long minutes, people started entering the pen that surrounded the barracks. The men were filthy from the sweat and grime of the caves, and at first, it was difficult to tell one from another. One by one, each stopped under a cistern that was held up by stilts and pulled on a chain. A bucket of water crashed down atop their heads, and then they moved on for the next person to "bathe." Rezkin realized that Jerril's idea of a *shower* was severely lacking.

Rezkin watched each man, hoping to find Tam, but he never showed. He stopped a man who was walking by and said, *"Has everyone gone through?"*

The man looked him up and down, then said, *"I not speak Verril."*

Rezkin let the man go. He decided it would appear more suspicious if he suddenly spoke the man's language than if he just found another person to ask. He stopped a second man and posed the same question.

"Yeah, we're all clean. Can't you tell?" the man said with a snort.

"I'm looking for someone. I did not see him go through."

The man shrugged. *"Could be he's on the other side."*

Rezkin followed the man's gaze, and he realized that across the quarry was another barracks and another cistern. A plethora of feelings suddenly suffused Rezkin. He stopped himself from pushing them away, and instead examined them. He felt disheartened that he had not found Tam in this group of men, yet he was still hopeful that Tam was not dead. There was a chance, after all, that Tam was in the other group.

"Hey, you new here?" said the man he had just been questioning.

"Yes, I just arrived," said Rezkin.

The man nodded. *"I'm Makon. You are?"*

"Ren."

"Well, Ren, I'll show you the ropes. Then you're on your own, but you'll owe me."

Rezkin nodded and followed Makon around as he showed him

where to eat, where to relieve himself, and where to report to in the morning. Makon pointed out a few people Rezkin should avoid and a few others who could manage to get him a few select supplies smuggled in by the guards. After Makon showed him where to sleep, the man left him to his own devices.

Rezkin did not attempt to sleep that night, certainly not with so many threats surrounding him on all sides inside the barracks. Instead, he went into *eskyeyela*, the meditative sleep he had been taught at the northern fortress that, thanks to the shielreyah at the citadel, he now knew to be a sacred ritual of the Eihelvanan. According to Entris, it was apparently used to help replenish their vimara when they could not sleep, but it also helped to connect them with the power on a deeper level. Rezkin knew, now, that the river-like thread of filaments in varying colors that he saw during eskyeyela was, in fact, a visual representation of his own vimara, and that the music he heard was an auditory interpretation of that power. Apparently, each person's tune was different and personal. Rezkin had always found comfort in the music of his vimara, and he did so then as well.

He was deep in *eskyeyela* when a soft voice broke through the soothing harmony. It took a little longer for the accompanying image to invade his thoughts, but once he could see it, he was glad for it.

Azeria lay at his side beneath a swaying rowan tree. Her silver-eyed gaze met his own, and she appeared peaceful and relaxed. She smiled at him and brushed a lock of his hair from his face.

"How are you?" she said.

"I am well. I have not found him yet."

"You will. I have faith in you."

"You do?"

She smiled fondly. "Always."

He took her hand and held it to his lips. "Are you really here?"

She patted him playfully. "Is there another like me? Of course I am me."

"But you are so different here."

"How am I different?"

He brushed a finger down her cheek as he held her soft gaze. "You seem to like me here."

She pulled him down until his lips met hers. Warmth spread through his chest, and his stomach turned with a strange, jittery feeling. She pulled back and said, "You are very likeable."

"Not many would say that about me."

Her fingers danced over his still-wet lips. "You do not need many to say it. Only one."

Rezkin stirred awake to find that the vagri on his chest was burning him. He held it away from his skin. It quickly cooled, but it had taken on a dim glow he had not before seen. The glow did not dissipate with the heat, so he quickly shoved the vagri back into his shirt.

In the dark, Rezkin could hear a few people tossing around. Some coughed and others groaned or grunted. Then the bell was ringing. Rezkin stood with the others, nearly all of whom made some sound of protest as they shuffled out of the building. Most trudged toward the pits to relieve themselves then gathered at the entrance of the pen. Once the gate to the pen was unlocked, they all spread into the yard grabbing carts and taking up pickaxes, hammers, and shovels. There did not seem to be any order to it as each person grabbed what was closest.

Rezkin grabbed a pickaxe and followed the others into the cave. His gaze roved the scraggly, disheveled men. With such poor grooming, it was difficult to tell the slaves' faces apart. He realized he would need to get closer if he were to recognize Tam. He wondered if, perhaps, Tam would come to *him*. Throughout the day, Rezkin shuffled from one tunnel to another, working his way into varying groups of men as he avoided the prying eyes of the slavers. They had a brief respite at midday when they were given water and a meager meal of corn mush and lentils. Then they were back in the mine hacking away at the rocks.

"Hey, anyone tell you what to do down here?"

Rezkin turned to find Jerril standing behind him. The man carried a whip, but it was wound in his hand, and it did not appear as if he intended to use it at that moment.

Rezkin shrugged. *"I break away the rocks."*

"Yes, but do you know what you're looking for? Do you know what to do with them?"

Although he had already figured out what do to, Rezkin shrugged again and looked at Jerril dumbly.

Jerril shook his head and came forward to point at a thick white layer. *"You put the white rocks in that pile over there."* He bent and picked up a small fragment from the ground. *"You put these shimmery ones in that cart. You find anything else, put it over there."* He pointed to a pile of white stone. *"Got it?"*

Rezkin nodded knowing that was all the information he would get out of Jerril. Jerril probably did not even know anything about the rocks. It was no matter. Rezkin already knew the mine was mostly known for its limestone, used in building, and copper ore; but none of that mattered. He was only there for Tam. After Jerril sidled away, Rezkin continued hammering the rocks while plotting his next move. Another slave moved up beside him a little too close for comfort, and Rezkin took a few steps to the side. After a minute, the man closed the distance again.

Rezkin turned to see a man who appeared to be of mixed Pruari descent looking at him with amber-colored eyes. *"What do you want?"* said Rezkin.

The man grinned but not in a friendly way. *"I want to know what you're looking for."*

"What are you talking about?"

"You don't know who I am, do you?"

"Should I?"

"If you'd been here more than a day, you would. I am Answon. I am one of the sect leaders."

"Sect?"

The man glanced over Rezkin's shoulder, apparently checking for guards, then said, *"There are politics down here not unlike those above. The sect leaders own everyone. You do not yet belong to a sect. I can tell a wary* man when I see one, though. You have been all over these caves today. You are up to something."

Rezkin decided that this man, who saw much, may have seen Tam. He said, "It is true. I am looking for someone. I believe he was sent here sometime in the past couple of months."

"Many men have come here in that time, and many of them have died as well. If your friend lives, he will not be the same as when you last saw him. Best to let him go."

"What do you want?" said Rezkin.

"What makes you think I want something?"

"If you truly are a sect leader, I doubt you chat up newcomers for the sake of conversation."

Answon grinned again, his white teeth shining brightly in the light of a single torch. "No, you would be correct. You seem friendly with Master Jerril. How do you know him?"

"I do not know him. He brought me into the quarry. That is all."

"Yet he takes the time to explain things to you."

"I was captured by the Ashaiians, but I didn't do anything wrong. I'm Verrili, and I'm not supposed to be here. Jerril knows that."

"Ah, I am Verrili, as well, but you do not see him trying to help me." He took a step toward Rezkin. "That's because you lowlanders stick together, and you believe the mountain clans are worse than the dirt beneath your shoes." Answon spit on Rezkin's shoe to punctuate his point.

"I have nothing against the clans," said Rezkin. "In fact, I was in the company of the Archebow Clan not two days ago. We were searching for several of their clan members who went missing in Gauge."

"Is that so? The people of Gauge have always been accepting of the clans, if not exactly friendly."

"Perhaps, but it was not the people of Gauge that were the problem. It was the army of Ashaiians at their gates."

Answon's face registered pure shock. "The Ashaiians have taken Gauge? Why would they want it?"

"I doubt they succeeded. It's a long story. The point is, I'm looking for someone. Can you tell me if you've seen him?"

Answon appeared distracted, but he said, *"What is this friend's name?"*

"He is an Ashaiian named Tamarin Blackwater. He goes by Tam."

Answon's expression abruptly shuttered, and Rezkin knew the man recognized Tam's name. Rezkin was relieved to confirm that Tam was, at one point, actually in the quarry. Whether or not he lived was still to be discovered. Answon glanced behind Rezkin again. He said, *"A storm is brewing. You had best choose the right sect. Your friend, Jerril, will not be of any help when the thunder begins."*

Answon made to step past him, but Rezkin reached out and snagged the man by the collar. At the same time, he placed his foot behind the other man's heel and shoved him, forcing Answon off balance and tipping him into the wall. Using his forearm, Rezkin applied pressure to Answon's throat while simultaneously locking the joint of the man's right hand. The great sect leader Answon could not so much as sneeze without Rezkin's permission.

Rezkin stared icily into Answon's wide eyes. *"You will tell me where Tamarin Blackwater is now."*

Answon tried to swallow and failed. Rezkin eased off the man's neck so that he could choke out a response. *"The stone mage knows. I'll take you to him."* Answon's gaze slid to the end of the tunnel then back again. *"But we have to be smart about it so the guards don't catch us."*

Rezkin applied just enough pressure to the man's larynx to make the warning clear then released him. Answon rubbed his throat then turned down the tunnel. He did not so much as glance Rezkin's way again. Rezkin knew Answon had the information he needed. The fact that he was a sect leader was of no consequence. Rezkin was not interested in taking over the quarry. He wanted only to find Tam and get out of there. He hefted his pickaxe and followed Answon down the tunnel. The sect leader entered the main cavern ahead of Rezkin. Answon strode up next to another slave and began pushing the cart with him toward the mine entrance. Rezkin waited a moment for them to get far enough ahead that he may not be seen then tossed his pickaxe into another nearly full cart. He called to a man who was gathering rocks and beckoned him to help. They pushed the rickety metal bin toward the entrance then abandoned it in the yard where other men were unloading them into larger piles.

With a quick glance, Rezkin spied Answon just across the open expanse between the two sections of the quarry. Rezkin was about to follow him when the slave master approached. Jerril said, *"Hey, what are you doing out here? You were working in the tunnels."*

Rezkin grabbed a chunk of white stone and started carrying it toward the larger pile. He did his best to shrug and said, *"I got tired of that and decided to try this for a while."*

Jerril chuckled. *"This is not a workhouse. You cannot switch jobs just because you want to."*

Rezkin grinned back at the man. *"I never knew you could switch jobs in a workhouse. Why did I clean the latrines for so long?"*

Jerril laughed heartily. *"I do not care where you work just as long as you are working, but the other masters will care if they catch you."*

Rezkin shook his head. *"They do not see me. I look the same as any man here."*

Jerril's eyebrows reached for the sky. *"Not like any man here. These are weak and tired. Beneath those rags you are strong. Tell me, friend, are you a fighter?"*

The slave master walked closer and leaned in conspiratorially. *"If you want to earn favor with the guards, you will fight for me."*

"Fight where?"

"In the pen. After work hours. There are always fights. Some of us place bets. It's the only business happening around here. Choose a sect. I don't care which one. Then ask to be a fighter. I will bet on you. If you win, both you and your sect leader will see rewards. It is a good way to gain status here—if you win." He grinned maliciously. *"Sometimes even if you lose."*

"You mean throw the fight?"

Jerril shrugged. *"Sometimes, under the right conditions. You have to make a name for yourself first. Say, what is your name, anyhow?"*

"Ren."

"All right, Ren. I'll be keeping an eye out for you. If you lose me money, you and I will have a very different relationship. Understand? In the meantime, get back to work."

Rezkin unloaded the cart for the next few minutes as he waited for Jerril to move away, all the while keeping an eye out for Tam. Although many men accompanied the carts out of the mines, none of them were Tam. By the time Jerril was out of sight, Answon had disappeared into the darker interior of the encampment. The quarry lay in the shadow of the cliffs, causing the sky to darken quickly, and most of the lanterns lit only the working areas. The bell rang just as the sun disappeared, and the stars broke through the twilight. The moon, however, had not yet found the way to brighten the deep hole, so the slaves ambled through the pen in the dark with only a few torches to prevent them from tripping over each other.

Rezkin's gaze swept the crowd for both Tam and Answon as he joined the food line. A prisoner to Rezkin's left muttered in Gendishen, *"Can't they make anything besides this gruel?"*

Rezkin said, *"Do they always ring the bell so late?"*

The man gave him a disparaging scowl but answered anyway. *"Sometimes I think they forget to let us stop working. It wouldn't surprise me if they made us work through the night. What do they care? It's dark in the tunnels anyway."*

The man on Rezkin's right huffed. *"But then when would we process the leaves?"*

"The leaves be damned," said the man on the left. *"I say we burn them all. Mayhap we'll die happy from the smoke."*

"What leaves?" said Rezkin.

The man on the right said, *"Some of us work the night shift at the tables."* He nodded into the dark toward a section of the quarry Rezkin had not yet visited. *"We process parabata leaves."* He held up his hands to show they were stained a greyish purple. The crazed look in the man's eyes suddenly made sense. He was high on *ink*.

"Why do you work at night?" said Rezkin.

"The leaves bake in the sunlight. It's easier to make us work in the dark than to put up tents, I suppose."

"Where do the leaves come from? I thought they grew only in Pruar."

"So far as I know, they do. I guess that's where they come from."

Rezkin looked at the grey slop in his bowl and wondered if the cooks laced it with *ink* to keep the workers energized and compliant. Then he considered that perhaps they only laced the morning porridge since drugging them at night would be counterproductive. The food was hardly edible, but he had eaten worse. After a while, a fight broke out in the yard, and Rezkin used the distraction to slip into the dark and pad his way across the gravel inner yard toward the other barracks. He passed a pit on the way that had the cloying smell of death and decay, and Rezkin knew it was the hole where they tossed the bodies of those who succumbed to the devastating effects of the quarry.

The second barracks was identical to the first, and the men were just as miserable and downtrodden. Few even glanced his way when he entered the gathering area of the pen. In fact, most had their attention on the fight that was occurring there, except that the fight had become a brawl concerning at least five participants, none of whom were Tam to Rezkin's relief.

Just as he was approaching the barracks, Rezkin caught sight of the man who had gotten away. Answon glanced toward him then turned around the corner. Rezkin approached on silent feet. When he rounded the side, he surprised those who lay in wait for him. The first man belatedly leapt forward bearing a broken axe handle. As it swung downward, Rezkin sidestepped and jabbed a second man in the throat. Then he elbowed the first man in the temple before ducking a punch and sweeping the legs out from beneath a third man. The second man, having recovered his breath, grabbed for Rezkin, but Rezkin wrenched him forward and behind as he issued a hard punch to the man's kidney.

The first, now blocked by the second, growled and pushed his partner out of the way before barreling forward with his club. Rezkin grabbed the man's wrist as he spun to the side causing the man to lose hold of the club, which Rezkin claimed. He clubbed the third man in the face before bringing the weapon up into the first man's gut. Then he kicked the first man in the jaw sending him sprawling into the third. The second man jumped back into the fray, but not for long. Rezkin bludgeoned him in the back of the head, rendering him unconscious. Then he kicked the third man in the side of the head to the same effect. By the time Rezkin was finished, all three men lay in an unmoving, bloody pile.

Answon backed away with hands raised. *"Okay, okay, peace! I will take you to him. I will take you to the stone mage."*

"That is what you said the first time. You had best not be wasting my time. I find it hard to believe there is a mage down here."

Answon shrugged. *"He says he's not a mage, but he's definitely something. Come."*

With all senses on alert, Rezkin followed Answon into the dark barracks where they were met by a crowd gathered around a central figure who was barely visible in the low light. Answon called out for people to move as he pushed his way through the throng. Most moved out of the sect leader's way quickly, and those who did not were moved *for* him and none too gently.

As Rezkin grew closer, the stone mage drew to his feet, and so did the man to whom he was connected by a thick chain. Despite the dark, the stone mage seemed to recognize a potential threat when he saw one because he raised his pickaxe as though he intended to put it through Rezkin's head.

"Come no closer," said the stone mage.

Rezkin said, "If you raise your weapon against me, you had best know how to use it."

The stone mage faltered. "R-Rez?"

"'Tis I, Tam. I've been looking for you."

Tam abruptly dropped the pickaxe and threw his arms around Rezkin's shoulders. Rezkin allowed it, knowing Tam was not a true threat to him. "Rez! I'm so glad to see you. I knew you would come!"

Rezkin patted Tam's back, then looked at him in the dim light as they pulled apart. "Of course I came for you, Tam. You are my best friend."

Tam suddenly appeared cautious as he released Rezkin and leaned toward the man to whom he was connected. He said in Gendishen, *"You can see him, right? He is really here?"*

"Aye, he's here, but I couldn't say who he is," said the man. He abruptly

cleared his throat and stepped forward. He, too, spoke in Gendishen. *"I'm Uthey, Tam's partner in everything we do"*—he chuckled as he hefted the chain that linked them—*"but who are you?"*

Tam turned to Uthey so abruptly that he nearly fell over. *"This is him! This is my friend, my king."* Tam turned to Rezkin. *"Or is it emperor? I heard someone was taking over the Souelian. It was you, wasn't it? I knew it!"*

"This?" said Uthey. *"This is your emperor? The one you've been going on about? He is nothing but a slave like us."*

"No," said Tam, shaking his head so adamantly that his chain rattled. *"Don't you see? He's disguised."* He said this last word in a drawn-out, hushed stage voice as though it was a secret between him and *everyone* gathered around them. "I'm so glad you're here, Rez. I *really* need your help. The headaches, the nosebleeds, the constant influx of *everything*—I can't take it anymore. I'd be dead if not for Goragana."

Rezkin's blood felt cold as he said, "What do you know of Goragana?"

Tam abruptly grabbed Rezkin's shirt in both hands and said, "I'm telling you, Rez, he talks to me. The *rocks* talk to me. And they can move all on their own."

"Okay, Tam, but what did Goragana *do*? Did you make a deal with him?"

"A deal?" Tam shook his head, then wiped his nose, and Rezkin could see the dark liquid staining his hand. "No deal. He said the deal was already made by the *shattered one*. That's you, Rez. I can see it now. The light—your aura, I guess—is all around you, and it's so broken. How did you get so broken, Rez?"

Tam wiped his nose again, then looked at his bloodied hand appearing confused by what he saw. He turned back to Rezkin, picking up a previous line of thought as though nothing else had occurred. "Goragana helped slow the bleed, Rez, but I need it to stop. Where are the healers?"

It was obvious that Tam's mind was not all there, and Rezkin hoped that healing the hole the healers had induced would repair him.

Tam swayed again, and Rezkin worried that they were out of time. Entris and Azeria were beyond the quarry walls, and Rezkin wanted Tam fixed immediately. For all he knew, the stress of the escape could be Tam's end.

Grabbing Tam's head between both hands, Rezkin said, "The healers are not here, but I am going to help you, Tam. I know how to do it now."

"Really? You finally found your power? I can see it flowing through your broken aura."

Rezkin's voice lowered as he growled, "Everyone out. Now."

An icy chill suffused the air, and those nearest him jumped to do his bidding, dragging those on the outskirts with them as they exited the barracks. Even Answon departed, pausing only once at the doorway to glance back into the nearly vacant room. Once they were alone, Rezkin looked at Uthey. "You will kneel there and not move a muscle. Do you understand?"

Uthey backed away a step but looked to Tam before kneeling as Rezkin demanded.

"Okay, just keep focusing on my power," Rezkin said. He recalled what Entris had told him about healing. Rezkin had all the requisite knowledge from his mundane healing studies, and he knew how to access his power. The one issue that had held him back from healing Entris was his inability to feel compassion for the male. Rezkin could tell by the heat against his chest and the dragging sensation that came with every breath that his worry and fear for Tam would be enough to make the connection. He hoped that the knowledge and skills he had at his disposal would be sufficient to heal something as complex and delicate as a hole in his friend's mind.

Rezkin, for once, embraced the elation at finding his friend and the sadness of seeing him in such a state as he reached for his fluxing vimara. He envisioned the liquid river of white in his mind, mentally splitting it into multiple-colored filaments. Then he plucked at the silvery adamantine power of healing and the amber power of life. He could hear the melody of his vimaral music as he wove the threads into a single rope and began pouring them into Tam's mind.

Tam's eyes widened, and he sucked in a breath as Rezkin continued his ministrations. The light of his vimara illuminated the recesses of Tam's mind, and Rezkin easily identified the gaping hole that consumed much of it. The hole seemed quite a bit larger than what his healers had first described, and Rezkin wondered how much of the damage would be permanent. The silver and amber rope separated into hundreds of smaller silver and amber threads, and Rezkin began stitching the hole with the filaments. Once it was closed, the scar flashed brightly then was gone. Rezkin searched for additional damage to Tam's brain but found only a few small lacerations that needed repair. When he was finished, he pulled away and closed off his vimara.

Rezkin was immediately on alert. People were surrounding the barracks. He could feel them moving in on him, and he knew he needed to kill them before they succeeded in their devious plans. He bent and retrieved the pickaxe Tam had dropped and surveyed the dark recesses. Uthey had not moved, but Rezkin knew the man was merely waiting for the best opportunity to strike. Rezkin was preparing to spring into action when Tam's voice cut through the paranoid fog that had invaded his mind.

"Rez, you did it! I can feel the difference. The sounds and lights and everything that was so blindingly brutal are all gone! I knew you had power. I mean, we knew that as Tieran's cousin, you should have had power. No one can deny you're the True King."

Rezkin gripped the pickaxe tightly in one hand but released the other to pat Tam's shoulder. "There is much for us to discuss, but for now, you may rest. Here, allow me to remove those shackles from your necks."

"You can do that?"

"Of course. There are few bindings that elude me," he replied with a bit of chagrin as he recalled the way Entris had trussed him in power. Rezkin reached inside his boot and pulled out a set of lockpicks he had stowed there in case the slavers had chained him as they had Tam. He motioned Tam toward him and set his hands upon the shackle around his friend's neck. He felt the enchantments in the metal that would normally prevent anyone from removing them without the key. Rezkin created a small potential ward and wrapped it around the enchanted metal sealing away the enchantments. It was a technique that Journeyman Wesson had assured him was impossible, but Rezkin had known it to work on many occasions. Then he pushed into the potential ward, creating a hold where the lock was located and through which he could use his picks to free the two men. As the chains fell away from first Tam's and then Uthey's necks, the two men stretched and stared at each other. For months they had been chained together learning to move as one, and now they were free to move beyond the limits of the short chain. Tam rubbed his neck but said nothing as he slowly moved farther from Uthey than he had been in months.

"Thanks be to the gods, the Afterlife, the Hells or wherever you hail from," muttered Uthey.

Finally, Tam found his voice. "Thank you, Rez. I thought I would die in those chains."

"I know not how you will die, Tam, but so long as I breathe, it will not be in chains."

Tears flooded Tam's eyes, and he swallowed hard as he gave a curt nod.

Rezkin hefted the pickaxe and said, "Come, let us depart this place."

Tam reached out and grabbed Rezkin's arm. "Wait, it's almost time."

"Time for what?"

There was a loud *crack* followed by a deep rumbling. Through the open doorway, Rezkin's could see the ground and walls of the quarry shaking violently, and massive boulders split from the rock face to tumble into the quarry floor and shatter. Someone called into the darkness, and the bell began ringing furiously. Rezkin, Tam, and Uthey ran out of the barracks. Around them, the slaves erupted into what at first appeared to be anarchy, but it quickly became clear that most of the men seemed to know where they were going and what they should be doing. Several stormed the gate to the pen and began pushing against it. Then someone produced a pickaxe and began hacking away at the lock. As soon as it popped free, the gate was shoved open, and men flooded into the larger yard where they scrambled for tools.

Tam gripped Rezkin's shoulder and said, "I've got this, Rez. This is our escape. I planned it all out, and now it's time to go. We need to get to the mine."

Rezkin stepped to the side as someone nearly ran into him. The man ended up tripping over his own shoes instead. The man looked up at Rezkin from where he was sprawled and grinned. Rezkin recognized the man as Makon, the slave who had shown him around when he had arrived. Makon said, *"Get moving, newcomer."* Then Makon was up and running away again.

With Tam and Uthey on his heels, Rezkin made for the carts where the men had left their tools at the end of shift. Rezkin passed the pickax to Tam, and Uthey grabbed the last hammer. Rezkin was left with the remaining shovel. The balance was not ideal for use as a weapon, but he had been trained for such tasks. He hefted the shovel with ease as they ran toward the mineshaft. The clash of weapons and shouts of injured and dying men reached them in the darkness as a team of slave masters filled the space between them and the mouth of the cave. Rezkin had no trouble bashing in the head of the first guard who accosted him, nor the second. He sliced, smashed, tripped, and stabbed at people as they got in his way.

Rezkin avoided the sting of a whip as it lashed toward his arm and turned his focus on the whip-wielder. He gritted his teeth and said, *"Out of the way, Jerril. We're getting out of here."*

Jerril's gaze danced around wildly. He said, *"I'll let you go, but not him"*—he nodded toward Tam who still stood near Rezkin's side—*"and not the rest of them."*

"You are just as much a prisoner here as we are," Rezkin said. *"You think the Ashaiians will thank you for getting in our way? You'll be punished for allowing the uprising to happen, and you'll be lucky if they only make you a slave."*

Jerril swallowed hard. *"The other slaves know me. They will never let me escape with them."*

"Hide or fight, Jerril, but if you get in my way, you're dead."

Jerril held up his hands, one still holding the limp whip, and backed away into the darkness. Rezkin, Tam, and Uthey continued into the mines, following the rest of the men who had already made it there. The chain of men hiked into and out of the caverns and through passages both cut and natural. Sometimes they crawled, and sometimes they climbed and had to help each other lest the passage become clogged with bodies. Hours later, a cool current of air stirred Rezkin's hair, and he knew their trek through the caves was nearly at an end. When he stepped into the night air under the stars, he was on the pebbled beach of a large lake. The water appeared black with only a sliver of moon to light the shore. There were no lights to indicate dwellings around the lake, only the occasional glint of ripples along the water's surface.

The escapees who had already made it out of the tunnels gathered around Tam. Most had collapsed from fatigue, although a few knelt as though in supplication. After a while, one of the men in the crowd shouted in Gendishen, *"Stone mage, tell us where to go. What do we do now?"*

Another echoed the question in the Ashaiian trade dialect and a third in Verrili. Rezkin surveyed the dark figures as he awaited the reply. When finally it came, his surprise was only surpassed by his satisfaction.

"Do what you want," said Tam in Ashaiian trade dialect. "I am not your keeper."

"But we owe you our lives. I am yours to command," said one of the men speaking Gendishen.

"You owe me nothing," said Tam, also in Gendishen. *"I intended to escape. I merely brought you with me."*

Rezkin shoved several men out of the way to reach Tam's side. He said, "Others came with me to rescue you. I need to retrieve them. I will return before dawn. Are you okay with them?" He tilted his head toward the crowd of tired slaves. A few had wandered away, some were taking the opportunity to bathe in the lake, but most were now laying on the ground hoping for a good rest.

"I'll be fine. Some men here are loyal to me. Maybe more now that we've escaped. I can handle trouble if it arises."

Rezkin nodded. "I know you can."

Tam's confident smile was worth the all the troubles they had endured in reaching him. Even though the hole in Tam's mind was now gone, Rezkin could not shake his guilt. How much damage had it done? How had it changed Tam? Tam seemed to be in high spirits, which was impressive considering the months of captivity and torture he had endured. That combined with the constant torment and threat of death from his own mind had surely had an impact on him. Rezkin considered these thoughts and more during his trip back to retrieve his companions. The trip over the surface was much faster than it had been in the caverns despite the hills and forest. When he finally arrived back at their encampment, Nanessy was first to greet him.

"Rezkin! You have returned—and you are glowing."

"I am?" he said in alarm.

"Well, not *you*, exactly, but that *thing* under your shirt."

Entris and Azeria strode up next to Nanessy, and all their gazes were focused on his chest. He patted the vagri under his shirt and said, "Yes, it does that now."

Entris and Azeria shared a look, but Nanessy said, "We saw the battle down in the quarry and thought it was your signal to take out the guards and mages up here. It was not as difficult as I expected. They were not prepared for an assault, and Entris and Azeria have amazing control of their power."

Rezkin thanked them then noted that Nanessy was covering her nose.

"What?" he said.

"Rezkin, I do not mean this to be rude, but you stink."

"I know," he replied. "Believe me, the slaves from the quarry are far worse. I came to retrieve my things so that I may bathe in the river."

"You found Tam, then?" she said. "You are done with the quarry."

"I found him. He is well enough but—"

"But what?"

"I had to heal him. I could not wait for you all to get there. He looked as if he might die at any minute."

Entris said, "You were capable of healing him? You made the connection?"

Rezkin nodded but did not look at the male. "Yes, I did what I could, but perhaps you could take a look at him."

"Where is he?" said Azeria.

Rezkin picked up his pack and paused as he grinned. "He organized and successfully implemented an escape from the quarry. He and dozens of men are resting beside a lake about an hour's walk from here. His attention lingered on Pride and the other beasts of burden as he scratched the shaggy scruff he had grown on his face. "It is too bad we do not have more horses. We will again have to double up."

Azeria, who had been on lookout, pointed the tip of her bow at Rezkin and said, "I am *not* riding with you."

17

Rezkin placed the relay device back into his pocket and then returned to his companions who were resting beneath the swaying boughs of a willow tree several paces from the lake's edge. Although the Eihelvanan wore hoods to hide their ears, nothing could detract from their stunning eye colors. Rezkin now understood that the icy brilliance of his own eyes was due to his Eihelvanan blood more so than his human parentage, although from what he had been told, Bordran's had been the same.

Rezkin glanced at the motley group by the water. Most of the slaves who had escaped the quarry with Tam had already left to find better fortunes, but a small group of his most avid followers remained on the beach.

Rezkin drew his gaze away from them and approached his companions, noting Tam's puzzled expression.

"So, let me get this straight. Your parents were human, but you're an elf?"

"The correct term is Eihelvanan," Rezkin replied. "And so says Entris."

Tam was crouched on the ground with his arms crossed over his knees, and he glanced around regularly as though hearing things that no one else could. Rezkin wondered if the mysterious sounds were real or if they were all in his friend's head. He glanced at Uthey who sat next to Tam. Aside from their initial celebratory separation, they had not parted since Rezkin had returned. Uthey spoke limited Ashaiian, but Rezkin and Tam were able to communicate with him in Gendishen. When Rezkin spoke to the others, Tam translated seemingly without thought. Tam's odd movements and strange behavior did not seem to bother Uthey, and he was taking the presence of the Eihelvanan in stride.

Rezkin turned to Uthey. *"What are your plans henceforth?"*

Uthey appeared uncomfortable under Rezkin's scrutiny. He said, *"Tam told me you were the True King of Ashai. And now we hear you are an emperor. Is it true that you're also the ruler of Gendishen?"*

"It is."

Uthey rubbed the back of his neck that had been entrapped by the shackle and said, *"As a citizen of Gendishen, I am at your disposal. However, I must tell you that I am already under oath to serve General Blackwater, here, in his army."* Uthey said this last as he pounded on Tam's back and laughed boisterously.

Rezkin raised one eyebrow and glanced at Tam. *"General Blackwater? What army is this?"*

Tam rolled his eyes and nodded to the sorry group of men still dozing by the lake. *"Uthey swore that if our escape was successful, he would serve in my army. They swore it, too. It was all in jest."*

"Maybe for you it was," said Uthey, *"but I would've done just about anything to get out of there."*

Rezkin took another look at the men on the beach. Although they were weary from weeks or months or even years of servitude in the quarry, they were strong from the hard work. Some of them might even have been soldiers or mercenaries like Uthey at one time. Regardless, they were loyal to Tam, and Tam was loyal to Rezkin; therefore, they were *his* men now per *Rule 45*—collect, maintain, and maximize resources.

Rezkin drew his gaze back to the present and changed the subject. "I just spoke with Farson."

"Farson?" said Tam with a groan. "I've not seen him. Where is he?"

"He is not here. He is on the ship near the Isle of Sand. They were searching for you."

"Then how could you speak with him?"

Rezkin held up the relay device and said, "I created these. They are like smaller versions of the mage relays. Farson has one, so I was able to speak with him through it."

"That's amazing! Can I see it?"

Rezkin handed over the device. After Tam had examined it for several seconds, Entris asked to see it. As he and Azeria muttered over the device, Rezkin said, "The Ashaiians are patrolling the Verrilian coast in force. It will not be possible to meet with the ship for extraction."

"What are we going to do?" said Nanessy. "Should we head for Ferélle?"

"No, I think not. We are presently far to the west, and we do not have enough horses. With so many Ashaiian troops in Verril, it would not be wise. Pruar is closer, and it does not appear that Ashai has forces there."

"Pruar is the wrong way!" said Tam. "I thought we were finally going back to Cael."

Azeria said, "I can open a pathway to Caellurum."

Rezkin shook his head. "These men are not mages. From what you have told me, it would be difficult to take them through the pathways, and we cannot abandon them. Besides, I am not going back to Cael. Journeyman Wesson is on assignment in Ashai. I will take the ship north from Pruar and meet him."

"*You* will go?" said Tam as he leapt to his feet. "Are you abandoning me *again?*"

"I am not abandoning you, Tam. You have a different destiny."

"Like what? Go back to Uthrel and watch drunkards stumble down the street? Get kidnapped again and sent Maker knows where?"

Rezkin could see the hurt in Tam's eyes, and he was once again doused in the guilt of having inflicted such pain on his friend. He placed a hand on Tam's shoulder and said, "I will give you a choice,

Tam. You may come with me, if that is what you wish, *or* you can fulfill a greater need."

"What *greater need*? I've just been through the Hells, Rezkin, and none of it was helpful to our cause. Of what use could I possibly be?"

"You are to be my general in the East."

"Your *what*?"

"You will lead the Gendishen army in our fight against Caydean's tyranny."

"What are you talking about? I am no general."

"You are. You planned and executed a successful rebellion against an overwhelming oppressor and led your people to safety. You have the loyalty of your men."

"My *men*? There's, like, ten of them. That's not an army."

"No, I will provide the army. You will provide the leadership."

"I've never led an *army*. I've never even been a soldier. Please, Rezkin, choose someone else."

"I need someone I can trust. You are a capable fighter, you have studied history and strategy, and you speak the language. You will be assigned strikers and officers who know what they are doing. Heed their council. Besides, you have something else of value far greater than experience in the army."

"What would that be?"

Rezkin glanced at Entris and Azeria who did not bother to hide their interest in the conversation. "You have the ability to speak with the ahn'an."

Tam's eyes widened. "Isn't that what you called the fae?"

"Yes, you have already developed a rapport with the Ancient called Goragana. This relationship will be pertinent in the coming war. We will need the strength of the ahn'an to fight the demons. You already command their power, Stone Mage."

Tam's face paled. "I never called myself that. You know I'm no mage."

"No, your power is not your own. You command the power of others more powerful than yourself."

Tam ran a shaky hand through his hair. "I wouldn't say I *command* it," he mumbled. Then he said, "Why Gendishen?"

"As I said, you speak the language. Besides, there is a vacancy. The former king, who led the army personally, is dead."

"Wait, you want me to fill the role of the *king?*"

"Only in part. You will share the responsibility with Drom Nasque who has been taking care of the other affairs of the crown. The military is your purview."

Rezkin looked down at his travel clothes then surveyed his companions and the wilds around the lake. "I am sorry I cannot provide you with a formal ceremony at this time. Do you accept your post?"

Tam gaped at him, and although he said nothing at first, Rezkin could see the thoughts warring in his eyes. Finally, Tam closed his mouth and swallowed. With a nod, he said, "I do."

"Kneel," said Rezkin.

Tam glanced at Uthey and then to the other men who seemed to sense something was happening. They gathered themselves and, as Tam knelt at Rezkin's feet, they joined the others on the scene. Rezkin withdrew *Kingslayer* and rested it on Tam's shoulder.

"I hereby assign to thee the title of Sword Bearer and grant unto thee the rights and privileges of magistrate, governor, and general of Gendishen. This Sheyalin blade, dubbed *Kingslayer*, is vested into thy care to be wielded appropriately in carrying out these duties."

Rezkin could feel the power of the enchantments in the blade buzzing as he turned the sword toward Tam hilt first. Tam looked up at him in awe as his fingers wrapped around the hilt, and Rezkin felt as though a cord snapped inside him. Although he still felt a subtle connection to the sword, *Kingslayer* no longer belonged to him. It belonged to Tam.

Rezkin handed over the scabbard, and soon, *Kingslayer* hung from Tam's hip. The men approached to congratulate Tam and to find out what great event had just happened. Tam became overwhelmed and excused himself from the group. He had stopped about fifty yards down the shore of the lake when Rezkin rejoined him.

"What is wrong, Tam? Have I done something to offend or upset you?"

Tam shook his head. "I didn't know you were going to do that. I don't think I'm worthy."

"The swords are mine to dispense, and I believe you are."

Tam turned to him with unshed tears in his eyes. "Is this because you feel bad about putting a hole in my mind?"

The guilt slammed into Rezkin hard, and the vagri started to burn his skin. "No. I do regret that, and I am sorry for it. I cannot make amends for what I did to you. I can only try to do better. This, however, was earned. You have come far since first we met, and your loyalty is without question. I can think of no one better to carry this noble Sheyalin."

"Except *you*," said Tam.

Rezkin grinned, and he found that it was genuine. "I have only two hands and had three swords. Is it not better to put it into the hands of someone who will use it?"

Tam's gaze slid up to the hilt of the black blade that was strapped across Rezkin's back. "It *is* very impressive."

"*Kingslayer* or the black blade?"

"Both. You have not named it then?"

"No, a name has not presented itself to me as of yet. Perhaps when it reveals its potential."

"Potential?"

Rezkin nodded. "It is a unique blade made of mage material. I think it may prove to be greater yet."

Wesson took a deep breath, then cast the sigil spell that would identify him. He had never had cause to cast the spell, but he had watched his master do it on several occasions. Although the land was dark in the night, the walls of the Mage Academy were alight to his eyes with enchantments. Many of the spells used constructive power to prevent unwanted visitors, but there were plenty composed of destructive that would have severe consequences should someone tamper with them.

Wesson had no reason to do so. He was not in hiding, exactly, although his companions were presently engaged in clandestine efforts to acquire information about kingdom affairs that might be helpful to their cause. Wesson, however, had no reason to think that he might have been identified as being in Rezkin's retinue. No one knew who he was. At least, no one who might have recognized him since leaving Ashai.

Wesson waited a long while before the door finally opened, and when it did, he was surprised to find that Archmage Genevera, herself, had answered. Despite her youthful looks, she was a commanding woman with an air of sophistication and a bearing befitting royalty. Her long, brown hair was braided over one shoulder, and her charcoal mage robes replete with colorful tabards appeared pristine.

Wesson bowed and said, "Greetings Archmage. I did not expect *you* to heed my summons."

"Journeyman Seth, how could it be anyone other than myself? You know you made quite the impression at the Battle Academy following your exam here."

Wesson was unsure how to respond. It was clear she had risen in the night to answer his call herself because she saw him as a significant threat, hence the multitude of wards surrounding her person in addition to those on the academy itself. He was suddenly unsure about the task before him. Although Rezkin had bade him to recruit his acquaintances first, Wesson had decided to go for a more direct approach. Now, he wondered how he would ever convince the archmage of his sincerity and the rightness of his cause. Not knowing what to say about his previous actions, he decided not to address her concerns at all. Instead, he said, "I have come seeking an audience with you."

She tilted her head and looked upon him with a soft gaze that spoke to the many years she had lived beyond those of her looks. He could feel a tightening of her wards and the development of new spells behind them. Alarm surged through him when it occurred to him that she was preparing to attack. He held her gaze and slammed up several wards of his own, though he was not sure if he could hold off the archmage for even a moment should she unleash her fury.

She pursed her lips then traced her power over his own, and he knew she was searching for the slightest crack in his defenses. He was nearly certain she would not find one, but his confidence waivered. She seemed to notice and smiled.

"Before I grant you entry to our hallowed halls, I must ask you, Journeyman Seth, whom do you serve now?"

Wesson hesitated, not because he doubted his loyalty or his cause, but because a wrong answer at that moment would likely be the end of him. He prepared himself as best he could for the worst and said, "I have sworn fealty to no one, but I serve the True King of Ashai, Emperor of the Souelian."

Her eyes flashed with interest. "And you know this emperor personally?"

"I do. I asked him to send me here, into the heart of Caydean's realm so that I might speak with you, to encourage you to take up our cause. You should know the truth of things before choosing which side to serve."

"We are the Mage Academy. We are not required to serve either side."

"The academy, itself, no, but your people are already being drafted into Caydean's army. Eventually, he will not be satisfied with your reticence and will force you into service, if he has not already."

He could see that he had struck a nerve when her expression shuttered, and he hoped Caydean had not already gotten to the archmage. If so, his own time in the world would not be for long.

Genevera stepped to the side and motioned to the open doorway. "Please, come in, Journeyman Seth. We should not speak of such things outside the walls."

On the other side of the wall were at least a dozen mages prepared to attack. Genevera waved her hand, and the number of spells they held immediately dropped. Based on the results of his apprentice exam, Wesson would have been surprised with such a showing of force. After what he had done at the Battle Mage Academy, though, he knew it was warranted.

Genevera lead him through the vaguely familiar hallways toward her office where a sleepy-eyed assistant awaited them. She did not smile upon seeing Wesson as she had the last time he had seen her. Instead she dropped her gaze to the floor as if she would rather not garner his attention. Apparently, news of his destructiveness had spread.

As Genevera rounded her desk, she motioned for him to take a chair and said, "You are wearing the wrong robes, Journeyman."

Wesson tugged on the grey threads and said, "I am a generalist, as *you* declared when I passed my apprentice exam."

She gave him a disparaging look. "I had thought that by demeaning you to such a title, you would be encouraged to accept your rightful place."

Wesson shifted uncomfortably. "My employer does not require me to kill. He allows me to use my power how I see fit and only asks that I serve him loyally so long as I am in his service."

"You have truly sworn no oaths to him?"

"None."

"I find it hard to believe that a rebel leader such as he would permit an unbound mage in his close company. The fact that he has endeared himself to you proves his cunning, though."

"He *has* endeared himself to me. In fact, I consider him to be a friend, and if I were forced to swear fealty to anyone, I would be proud to call him my liege. He is a worthy leader. But you are wrong in one major respect. He is not a rebel. He *is*, in fact, the true king of Ashai. Not only was he named Bordran's successor but also he is a rightful heir to the throne."

Genevera's studious gaze sharpened. "How so?"

"He is a prince of Ashai. He is King Bordran and Queen Lecillia's third son."

"Impossible. The third child died at birth."

"So everyone was told, even Lecillia. I performed the test myself using Lecillia's own blood, freely given. He *is* her son."

"How did you get Lecillia's blood? My sources say that no one at the palace has seen her in months. There are even rumors that Caydean killed her."

Wesson shifted uncomfortably. He was not sure how much he should reveal since he did not yet know who held the archmage's loyalties. Then again, Caydean already knew Lecillia was no longer in the palace. It was everyone else who was being duped.

"Lecillia escaped the palace and sought refuge with the True King. She has since been reunited with her father, King Moldovan, who has also recognized the True King as his grandson and passed to him the crown of Ferélle."

Genevera sat back in her chair. "That is not how I heard it happened. It is said the red castle was a bloodbath, that the usurper killed Moldovan and most of his court and claimed his throne."

Wesson held up a finger and said, "There are bits of truth in that story. It *was* a bloodbath, but only because someone *else* tried to seize the throne, and the True King destroyed him and his followers, after which Moldovan crowned him king freely."

The archmage tapped her desk thoughtfully, then said, "And the Leréshi queen? Did he force her to accept his rule?"

"On the contrary, it was she who offered *him* a deal he could not refuse. I know him well enough to say confidently that he did *not* desire that union, nor did he go there seeking the throne."

She did not look entirely convinced. "I have heard so many stories —stories of the infamous Dark Tidings raging across the Souelian claiming kingdom after kingdom—stories of stolen princesses, civil wars, and of prophecies fulfilled. Everything we are told is of the death and destruction left in his wake. It is said that he holds a great and terrifying power that only our King Caydean can overcome. If I did not know your true strength, I would fear that he has bespelled you, Journeyman."

"With all due respect, Archmage, what you hear are Caydean's carefully constructed lies. It is he who has brought actual demons into this world. He seeks to sow chaos at every turn, and it is only by the grace and skill of the True King that we will be able to stand against him."

She did not flinch at the mention of demons, and Wesson wondered if she already knew of them or if she thought he was prone to hyperbole. Instead, she focused on something else he had said. "You speak of grace. Has this *destroyer* any grace?" She leaned forward, and her professional demeanor slipped away, her gaze filled with an indescribable need. "Tell me of the True King, himself. Tell me of the man beneath the mask."

Wesson nodded and thought for a moment before speaking. "Being the third son, you should know, he is young, not much older than me, in fact; but he is knowledgeable and wise beyond his years. When he speaks of nobility and choice and duty, people listen and are inspired to be better. There is a darkness in him, something deeply ingrained, that makes him more capable than most; but he contains that darkness and shares with his people the goodness, the right-eousness of a king blessed by the Maker—or the gods, if you prefer.

"In truth, I do not know if he thinks of me as such, but I feel myself fortunate to call him friend, for he is valiant and protective of those he holds close. He lives by a code—a set of rules. He says that rule one is to protect and honor your friends. He is a king—no, an emperor—and yet he places his friends above himself. I think he does the same with all his people, in a way."

"Yet he sends you here, into the heart of Caydean's territory."

"As I said before, I requested it. He offered to send me to one of his kingdoms to be raised, but I insisted—"

"Raised?"

Wesson swallowed hard. For all the confidence he had discussing Rezkin, he had decidedly less when it came to his own concerns. "He has made me the king's mage. The other mages, the masters, believe I need to be raised to the status of mage to hold the position."

A small smile threatened at the corners of her mouth. "A smart and cunning man, indeed. He holds the one who could perhaps be his greatest adversary close."

"It is not like that," Wesson protested. "He values me. He trusts me."

"And does not ask for your fealty?" she said with a raised eyebrow.

Wesson straightened. "No, he has not. In fact, he has voiced his preference that I do not give it."

"How odd, but it keeps you happy, does it not?"

Wesson did not need to admit aloud that it was true. The archmage and he both knew what it meant to him not to be bound by someone else's expectations.

"What I am hearing is that this marauder shows you his true self, his darkness, but you are satisfied to accept it because he puts on a good show for the people; and you praise him for it, no less."

"What? No, that is not what I am saying."

Genevera weaved her fingers together and looked upon him with a kind but pitiful expression. "It seems this usurper has a certain and unyielding charisma to have pulled the wool over *your* eyes, Journeyman. I think Ikestrius would be disappointed. *Honor and protect your friends.* I have never heard a more obvious attempt at placation." She reached toward him as if to take his hand that he had not offered. "Open your eyes, dear boy. Of course you would feel valued. You were always a loner, were you not? The small boy run out of his home by angry villagers wielding pitchforks. You always had trouble finding acceptance with your peers. I do not say this to hurt you, but you need to *see*. After Tica—"

"Do not speak of Tica," Wesson blurted in a rush. He suddenly felt like he had made a terrible mistake. While he had thought the archmage was open and inviting of his views, she was truly digging for information on the True King. And he had served it up on a silver platter.

He stood and rounded his chair, then gripped its back as he faced her. "Can you not see the truth? Caydean is a *monster*. He killed his own father and brother. Even now he is tearing families apart for his draft so that he can, what? Go to war with our neighbors? We had *peace*! No one was fighting us. And what about all the noble houses he destroyed after the King's Tournament? There was no plot against him. No one questioned his claim to the throne."

She raised her eyebrow again. "Except this True King? Did you not say he was the rightful heir? Do you not think he has been plotting this for years?"

"No, he was not! I mean, I was with him when he found out about that. He did not even know he was related to the royal family. *I* performed the test!"

"And you think it was coincidence that he came upon you, arguably the most powerful mage of our time? No doubt he offered you generous riches to be his mage."

"No, you have it all wrong!" Wesson said as he tugged his locks in frustration. "I can see how this all looks to you, but none of it happened how you think. What you have been told is *lies*. Please believe me, Archmage. You *must* understand. You are on the *wrong* side!"

Genevera rose from her desk and, even though they were about the same height, Wesson had the distinct feeling that she was looking down on him. She came around the desk and approached slowly before placing her hands on his shoulders in a too familiar, motherly way. "*You* need to understand, Journeyman. The Mage Academy is not beholden to the king. It stands as a kingdom unto itself. So long as our people stay within these walls, Caydean's draft means nothing. We need not choose a side at all. *You* do not need to choose. You are safe here. You are home."

Wesson liked the idea of being safe at home for about the length of a heartbeat. He backed away from her embrace and said, "No, this is not my home. My *real* home, my family, is in danger. Do you think Caydean will be satisfied with your reluctance to serve him? If he cannot get to us here, he will go after everyone we care about. We have seen it before with the nobles."

A flare of uncertainty entered her gaze, and she dropped her hands. "I know what you say is true, but you do not understand the consequences of our involvement in this war. Our power could destroy the world beyond its ability to sustain *life*, much less return to any semblance of peace. We must not become involved."

Wesson balled his fists. "And the Battle Mage Academy? Will they be satisfied to *not get involved?*"

Genevera pursed her lips. "No. Despite my efforts to convince him otherwise, Battle Master Rhone has accepted Caydean's call to arms." A hard edge entered her voice. "Those battle mages are so eager to employ their training they forget about the cost." She smiled at him sadly then. "It gave me hope that you were not with them. But it seems you have chosen to fight on the other side—*against* them."

"I do not wish to fight against my brethren, some of whom I call friends. I had hoped to go there next to convince Rhone not to side with Caydean."

She scoffed. "Rhone is set in his ways. You know this. He would never listen to you."

"No, but he does fear me."

She gave him an inscrutable look. "Do not underestimate the battle master. His skills are practiced and honed. You are still young and untested."

Her words felt like a punch to the gut. He said, "I am not untested. I have seen battle."

"I thought so," she said kindly but sadly. "For so many years you steadfastly refused your calling, refused to become a battle mage, refused to kill; but you *have* killed, have you not? I can see it in your eyes. They are haunted with the ghosts of your victims. You said your king did not require it of you; however, you have not only killed in his name, but he has convinced you that doing so was of your own choosing."

Wesson swallowed the bile that rose in his throat, focusing on the burn as it was suppressed. "I did kill of my own free will, but I did so to protect others—*only* to protect."

"Those who you protect are *his* people, are they not? What of *your* people? What of Ashai? Will you kill them all?"

Blinking tears from his eyes, he said, "I do not *want* to kill anyone!"

She stepped toward him, her majestic robes floating about her. "And you do not have to, Wesson. Stay here with us. Help protect the academy. *These* are your people. With all our power and enchantments, you need never kill anyone again."

She must have seen his distress on his face because she did not press him further. Instead, she said, "Please, you need not decide now. Stay here and rest. Decisions like these should be made on a clear mind and a full stomach."

Wesson glanced out the window at the midnight sky and nodded. He needed rest. Somehow, the archmage had gotten to him. Already, he was doubting all that had happened over the past year. He knew Rezkin was cunning, but was he so deeply cunning that he had planned all of it? Their meeting in the road, the offer of employment, the revelation of his birthright? Had Rezkin manipulated everyone into thinking it was their idea to follow him? The mysterious island, the discovery of power unlike any they had known, the appearance of *demons* in their midst—was it all Rezkin's machinations? Wesson had to ask himself, was Rezkin capable of it? The resounding *yes* echoed in his mind long after he had been shown to his room.

As Wesson sat on his bed, he rubbed his face. His mind felt foggy and unsettled, and he could not shake the feeling that something was not right. But what was it? Was it something to do with the archmage? Or was it his place in Rezkin's subterfuge that was troubling him? Without bothering to undress, he lay back on his bed trying to clear his mind. His worries would not stop, though, and that night he slept fitfully. He was visited by a dream from long ago, one that had haunted him ever since.

Standing atop a hill overlooking a cloud-shrouded valley, rivers crossed every which way; but through them no water flowed, only fire. Streams of yellow, red, and blue flame whipped the air. The heat lashed his face as his loose hair began to sizzle. The putrid smell of burnt hair was swept away on a tide of ash.

"Caw!"

Above, a lone branch reached for the valley from a dead tree, a raven upon its bough.

"Caw!" the raven called, and the land did answer.

Across the valley lay not rivers but cities. Dozens of cities under siege, fires flaring, buildings toppling. Soldiers flooded streets, and men, women, and children died together and alone.

"Caw!" the raven cried, and the cities shuddered.

Shadows fell from roofs and slinked from alleys, swarming the soldiers and submerging all in darkness.

A turbulent wind abruptly struck from behind, and salt and moisture clung to his skin. He spun to catch its source and there lay a vast ocean. Across the grey-blue expanse stood a forest of palaces, and as he watched, each fell beneath the shadow.

"Caw!"

18

Wesson awoke to a pounding in his head. He reached up and pressed his palm to his temple. His head throbbed, but he realized after a minute that the pounding was not *in* his head. It was outside his room ... *somewhere*. The sound seemed to echo around the building, through the halls, and even within the wards. He could feel within the power of the academy a thrumming, like lute strings wound too tight and plucked to breaking. He slipped on his boots and hesitated a moment to tie them before heading for the door only to find it locked.

He frowned down at the latch wondering why anyone would bother with a mundane lock. When he tried to unlock it via his power, though, a spell blocked him. As he unraveled the spell, another immediately took its place. When it was released, two more took the place and then four. Every time he broke the enchantment, two more took the place of the last. The pounding grew louder, and alarm shot through him. If he kept trying to break free, he would be locked in the room indefinitely.

Refusing to be undone by panic, Wesson gathered his power in a compact spell with big repercussions. Upon applying the token that would activate the spell, the door burst from its seat in the frame and crashed against the opposite wall. He stepped into the corridor to find the academy in an uproar. The sound wards on his room had prevented him from hearing all but the pounding that struck once more before abruptly stopping. At the same time, the walls shook, and debris rained down from the ceiling. Several students rushed by him, worry constricting their faces, and he reached out to snag one of them by the robe.

"What is it?" he said. "What is happening?"

The apprentice glanced down at Wesson's generalist attire, snatched his own robes from Wesson's grip, and said, "Are you daft or just deaf? We are under attack." Then the student turned and ran away with his friends.

Wesson stood there for a moment considering his options. If the Mage Academy was under attack, it could only be Caydean's forces. He wondered what power they could possibly be wielding to break through the academy's wards as they were. Surely the battle master would not allow his battle mages to attack their brethren mages. At no time in the history of Ashai had such a war between mages been fought. There were laws and traditions and treaties in place to prevent such an end. If Caydean was attacking, though, this could be Wesson's chance to draw the mages to his side. He just needed them to survive.

With an urgency he felt deep in his gut, Wesson ran toward the epicenter of the disturbance. As he got closer, the way became more treacherous as the ceiling was partially collapsed in places and students and masters ducked and dodged the debris that was falling and strewn about the floor. Wesson clambered over a pile of rubble and tumbled down the other side as he narrowly avoided an explosive ball of nocent energy. A darkness in his well surged to the surface as he acknowledged that only a natural battle mage could have created such a thing. His knees scraped over rubble, and his generalist robes made it difficult to crawl along the floor. He headed toward the nearest wall and pressed himself up against it as he got to his feet.

Wesson's gaze landed on a pile of broken wood and stone a few paces down the corridor, and he was sickened by the sight. There, half buried beneath the detritus was a young man just as broken as the materials that lay atop him. His eyes were open, but they stared at nothing, and neither did he move, nor even to take a breath. Wesson's own gaze lost focus for but a second. Deep inside, it felt like something was crawling up the side of his vimaral well. It was fueled by his anger, and Wesson felt fear but not for the chaos of his surroundings. He feared himself and what might he do when he found the enemy.

The mage lights lighting the corridor flickered, and Wesson knew something big was coming. Something was drawing on the power of the academy, and he needed to be prepared. He swallowed down his nausea and moved farther down the corridor. By now, most of the students had already evacuated, and he could see ahead where some of the masters were gathered behind what was once an intricately carved, solid banister that surrounded an atrium that opened to the lower floor. Wesson dove behind the wall as another blast shook the building. The mage nearest him glanced over, her face pale and sweaty beneath a tangle of blond hair. Wesson recognized the woman as Master Licentia. She had been his friend Tica's supervisor at the academy. He remembered her as being a dominant woman who accepted no excuses but laughed easily. She was not laughing now, and her confidence was clearly shaken.

"I know you," she shouted over the clamor. "You need to get out of here. This is no place for you."

Despite the turmoil, Wesson felt a pang of embarrassment. Of course, she would remember him as the stunningly average mage with a lackluster performance, but, like most mages, she did not know the true nature of his power.

"What is happening?" he shouted back. "Is it the battle mages?"

"Yes, at least, some of them are. Others look to be *ours*."

Wesson risked peeking over the barrier to get a look at the first-floor foyer below them. A couple of battle mages were already in the building amongst a group of mages dressed in red robes. Wesson had never seen red robes on a mage, and he did not know what it meant. More commotion came from outside the building, and he knew a larger force was moving in on them.

A light suddenly flashed so brightly that Wesson was momentarily blinded. Once his vision cleared, he looked toward the light's source to find Archmage Genevera standing at the top of the stairwell. Streamers of lightning snaked outward in a cloud around her, and every so often, one would strike out at one of the red mages with combustive force.

"We need to back her up," he said as he tugged Master Licentia's shoulder hoping she would follow. He kept low as he ran along the banister, calling to those he passed to follow. Most ignored him, but a few fell in line behind him. By the time they reached the top of the staircase, he had half a dozen mages in tow. These were not battle mages, though. They were life mages, architects, engineers, and academics. Although all of them would be competent in casting wards and spell slinging, they were not accustomed to war. They were masters, though, and he only a journeyman generalist. Once on the staircase, the others ceased listening to him. They moved forward to assist the archmage, keeping enough distance so as not to be struck down by her spells. Wesson surrounded himself in wards of his own design, strange things that combined constructive and destructive energies. Then he ran down the staircase to stand at Genevera's side.

Genevera looked over at him, and if she were surprised to see him standing within her sphere of power, she did not show it. It appeared that nearly all her attention was on maintaining the spells that were keeping the enemy at bay in the foyer. She turned her attention back to those in front of her, and Wesson saw a hardness enter her gaze. He, too, looked and that was when he saw someone he had not expected. The man in black moved to the forefront and met Genevera's fierce challenge with a scowl.

"Berringish," said Genevera. "Why have you attacked our academy? This is a school of learning, a center of research and advancement. We are not a threat to you."

"It is a center of resistance," said Berringish, his steadfast gaze sealed to the archmage. "I warned you, Genevera, that if you did not bow to my authority, I would destroy you."

"To *your* authority? Do you not mean Caydean's?"

"The mages serve under *me*."

"You are not one of us, Berringish. I always knew you could not be trusted. You hold no power here. Caydean cannot usurp the leadership of the archmage."

Berringish grinned malevolently. "No power? I will give you one more chance to kneel at my feet before I obliterate you and all who follow you." He waved his battle mages forward. "I do hope you resist."

Genevera did not hesitate. She blasted the battle mages back with the thunderous clap of lightning followed by an enormous sphere of power that held the energy of a monsoon. Part of the ceiling over the atrium collapsed sending a massive cloud of dust into the foyer. Genevera quickly turned to Wesson.

"I was wrong, Journeyman. Please, get our people to safety. They will need your strength. I will hold them off."

"No," blurted Wesson. "I can help you. We can fight them together."

She placed a hand on his shoulder and said, "There are few I fear in this world, and I admit now that you are one of them. Berringish is not like us. We may have the strength to best him together, but our people will suffer before the end. What I have admired about you most is your regard for life. Please, Journeyman, put their lives first. Save them."

It went against his better judgment to do what the archmage asked of him, but Wesson had no time to mull over the potential consequences of what he was about to do. Instead, he turned back to the mages that had followed him onto the staircase.

"We need to protect the students while they escape," he said. "Archmage's orders!"

The mages looked to Genevera, but she had already turned back to the enemy in the foyer. As they ascended the stairs, the steady vibration of wielded vimara thrummed through Wesson's chest in tune with the many explosions. Wesson's stomach churned with something else, though. At first, he thought it was the misery and guilt that came with abandoning the archmage, but eventually he realized it was the sense of another power being wielded. It was a power akin to the darkness that simmered just above the surface of his awareness. Wesson tried to shake the feeling as they sprinted through the corridors collecting any students and mages they passed. At the end of the hallway, a clutch of initiates ran past, and a red-robed mage emerged in their wake. One of the students in the rear fell under the mage's spell, and it was a gruesome sight to behold.

The mage turned her head toward them, and Wesson saw then that her eyes were not her own. They were filled with an inky blackness that Wesson knew to mean one thing. A bubble of power surged out of him before he realized what he was doing. A dark, smokey power slammed into the mage, pressing her against the wall as it insidiously dug its way under her skin. She screamed as black lines covered her body as if tendrils of tar were filling her veins. Another of the mages with Wesson lobbed a fireball her way, and the black power ignited causing the mage to burst in a shower of blood and flesh that coated the corridor.

Wesson's stomach lurched, but he did not have time to be sick. People were screaming and dying in the corridors, and the echoes of their torment assailed his ears. He and the other mages herded the students down a stairwell to the lower level where they intended to make their escape. Most of the students would have gathered in the dining hall, as was the designated safe area for an event such as this. Outside the dining hall was an impromptu barricade of shelves, books, and furniture in addition to chunks of the fallen walls and ceiling. Several mages manned their posts at the barricade expecting a fight.

Wesson skidded to a halt as the other mages rounded the barricade and headed into the dining hall. Mage Licentia paused to look back at him.

"Come," she said.

He shook his head. "No, I cannot leave her there to die. I need to go back and help."

She scowled at him and hissed, "There is nothing a *generalist* journeyman can for the archmage. Do as she commanded."

Wesson swallowed hard. "I am more than a generalist, and she needs me. Go. Get the students out while there is still time."

Then he turned and ran toward the foyer all the while scolding himself for such folly. The archmage would be furious with him for ignoring her command but only if she lived. When he finally made it to the site of the battle, the foyer was almost completely destroyed. A gaping hole existed where the outer wall once stood, and most of the second floor had collapsed into a mountain of rubble. The blasts of power were no longer emanating from within the building, though.

Wesson scrambled to the top of a pile of debris that nearly blocked the corridor save for a few feet of space near the broken ceiling. From there, he saw that the archmage had managed to force the enemy out of the building and onto the lawn. She stood several paces outside the academy surrounded by a swirling vortex of wind and lightning. Her hair and robes billowed in the wind as she commanded the forces of nature with the strength of her vimara and a willpower of stone. Before Wesson could wedge himself through the gap, Berringish raised a talisman and released a power unlike anything Wesson had ever felt. It washed through Genevera's wards and power unimpeded. Genevera's arms flew out sideways, and her back arched before she abruptly collapsed in a heap.

When the archmage's power abruptly ceased, an eerie calm settled over the scene. Wesson struggled to hold himself back as his instincts screamed at him to run to her, to help her. Berringish dropped the spent talisman to the ground where it crumbled to ash and calmly stepped up to Genevera. He looked down on her prone form then shoved her body with a heavy foot. She shifted and Wesson could see her face clearly. It was contorted in agony and frozen there with her eyes open and unseeing. She did not move or blink, but it was Berringish's reaction that told him that Genevera was dead. The man simply turned and walked away from her without so much as a backward glance.

Berringish's forces were significantly fewer than what they had once been, going by the number of black and red-clad figures littering the ground. With only a handful left at his call, Berringish said, "Find any stragglers and kill them. We shall deal with those who escaped later." Then he turned to a weaselly man who scurried up next to him. With a bow, the man handed Berringish a goblet.

"It was a success, Master?" said the weaselly man.

"Yes, Armas. With the archmage dead, there is no longer a threat near Kaibain. Send notice to the generals. Our forces move west in a few days. We shall break the rebellion *before* it joins with the Torreli and Sandean forces."

Wesson took one last look at the archmage's broken body then turned and hurried back down the corridor to make his own escape. His companions would soon be hearing about the attack on the academy, and he did not want them assuming him dead. On his way out of the building, Wesson employed some of the stealth spells he had been working on since meeting Rezkin. Once in the city, Wesson made a beeline for the first clothesline he saw. Unfortunately, it held mostly women's clothing, and he was not about to make that mistake again. He opted to wait for the *second* clothesline on his route, from which hung an assortment of men's work clothes. They were all too big for him, but it was not uncommon to see young men wearing hand-me-downs in the poorer districts, so Wesson figured he was safe rolling them at the cuffs. At least he was not so obvious. It was no longer safe to be a mage in Kaibain.

Wesson balled up his mage robes and stuffed them in a burlap sack he snagged from a pile behind a tavern then headed for the safehouse. It was a squat building with multiple egresses, which had pleased Striker Kai. The fact that it was nested between two alleys behind the other buildings was a bonus. Wesson glanced behind him then passed the first passage that would take him to the refuge. Once he was sure no one was following him, he slipped into a narrow crack between two buildings and shuffled toward the rear. As he neared the safehouse, he saw that Corporal Namm was sitting outside the door on a rickety chair dressed in work clothes much like those Wesson had stolen. His feet were propped on a crate as he whittled a wooden nub into a figure Wesson could not yet identify. Namm completely ignored Wesson as he entered the building.

Wesson stepped through the doorway to find Striker Kai seated at a table in quiet discussion with Waylen and Fedrin. They all looked over as Wesson approached, each of them eyeing his new apparel.

Although none were used to seeing him dressed as a mundane, only Kai seemed to recognize that something was wrong. Before Wesson could say anything, though, he was suddenly assailed by a flurry of fabric and flesh.

"My sweet Wesson is back!" cried Celise as she threw her arms around him.

As Wesson attempted to disentangle himself from the overzealous young woman, he caught the smirk that stole across the striker's face. Wesson had insisted Celise stay on the ship, but his so-called *matria* had other plans. She refused to be parted from him, and it had taken all his fortitude to keep her from following him to the Mage Academy.

Wesson turned from Celise, who remained halfway wrapped around him but did not wait for Kai to ask questions. He said, "The Mage Academy was just attacked by Caydean's forces. The archmage is dead. Everyone else is dead, captured, or in the wind—I think mostly the latter."

"What?" said Celise. "You could have been killed." Deepening her hug, she said, "You are not to leave me again."

Kai's expression darkened. "None of my sources indicated the Mage Academy was a target."

"The archmage refused to take a side," replied Wesson. "I guess Caydean saw that as cause enough." He raked a hand through his hair dislodging small bits of debris and dust. Then he walked over to the table with Celise in tow and sat heavily in one of the dining chairs. Celise sprawled across his lap as if it was where she belonged. He said, "There were a couple of battle mages, but most appeared to be regular mages. Their eyes were black."

"Demon-possessed?" said Waylen.

"So it would seem. It makes sense, I suppose. There was a man in charge who I recognized. His name is Berringish."

"The king's advisor?" said Kai. "Wait. Did you not say the last time you spoke to Rezkin through the relay that Berringish had been in Verril?"

"Yes. They prevented possession of the dragon, but Berringish got away. The archmage warned me about him once. I think she never trusted him. He is not a normal mage."

"How so?" said Fedrin.

Wesson glanced at Fedrin and Waylen, unsure if he should say the next part in their presence. Kai seemed to understand because he asked them to wait in the adjacent room, which held little more than an old lamp and a mattress that had seen better decades. Wesson asked Celise to go with them, but she refused to release him from her viselike grip. Wesson leaned closer to Kai and whispered, "Remember what Connovan said about Rezkin's old masters? He said there had been *three* to start. The third, Berringish, stayed behind to train Caydean. Both Connovan and Rezkin have said that Berringish is *Sen*, and the Sen are capable of calling forth *demons*."

"Ah. You believe Berringish is responsible for the demon possessions. It seems simple, then. Take out Berringish and we take out the demons."

Wesson shook his head. "I doubt Berringish would tie the demons to his own life force in any way. If we kill Berringish, that could stop *more* demons from coming into our realm, though. It will not be easy. He is extremely powerful. The power he used went straight through the archmage's wards. It was like he took the life right out of her."

"Can the Sen do that?"

"I do not know. Rezkin may know more about them." Wesson sat back in his chair and sighed, while Celise lazed against him. "For now, I think we need to go west, and we must make haste. Berringish is planning to break the rebellion. He said something about Torreli and Sandean forces."

"Aye. So I have heard. My sources say that Torrel and Sandea have joined forces and are moving for the western pass. It is believed that they intend to join up with whatever rebel forces have gathered in the west."

A bolt of alarm shot through Wesson. "How far west?"

Kai shrugged. "Somewhere between Maylon and the coast, so they say."

Dislodging Celise, Wesson abruptly stood as if he could make for the coast that second. "We must get there before Berringish."

Kai looked at him thoughtfully. "Right, I nearly forgot you were from the west. We cannot put our personal needs above the needs of the empire."

Wesson swallowed his protests and instead agreed. "I know, but in this case, my personal needs are congruent with those of the empire."

Kai considered him another moment then nodded succinctly. "Very well. We shall make haste."

19

The path to Pruar was an arduous one. Western Verril was largely uninhabited, and no roads connected the two kingdoms. The relationship between Verril and its western neighbor was strained, and no trade occurred by land save for the black-market import of parabata leaves and its product, the deleterious but intoxicating drug known as *ink*.

Entris and Nanessy continued to share a horse, and Rezkin was surprised to feel a sense of disappointment that Azeria would not ride with him. It was an odd feeling to want someone to get within his guard, yet he could not deny that he wanted it. He found himself staring too often at her cloaked figure hoping to catch sight of her face beneath her hood. Somehow, he *missed* the sight of her. He had not seen her in his dreams again since the night he spent in the quarry, and he wondered if she had ever truly been in them at all. Besides her odd behavior the one time he had asked about them, she never let on that she shared the dreams. Rezkin felt disappointed that it had all been in his head alone.

With frequent stops for the men on foot, reaching the border of Pruar took a little more than a week. Passage was rough and tiresome over the forested hills, but the delineation was obvious when the terrain turned to relatively flat savannah that Nanessy mentioned looked much like western Ashai. The wildlife was plentiful and unlike anything Rezkin had seen in his travels. One such beast stood between him and the first water source they had found that day. It was nearly midday, and the horses and men were already nearly spent.

Rezkin stared at the blob. It was like a sack of potatoes wrapped in grey leather with four stubby legs and a snout that narrowed to a point. Although it was as tall as a horse and twice as wide, it did not appear to be aggressive. Still, Rezkin was cautious as he steered Pride around the creature. The beast flapped its tiny winglike ears but otherwise failed to acknowledge their presence as it rooted around in the dirt. Once past the bulbous creature, Rezkin guided Pride to the river's edge. The river, although shallow and show-moving, appeared less safe than the plains. Monstrous creatures with scales, claws, and rows of razor-sharp teeth were collected in groups along its banks.

"What are they?" whispered Nanessy.

"I have never before seen these creatures," said Rezkin.

"They're called fithyers," said one of Tam's men named Lo'an. "They're supposedly related to alligators. We have them in Sandea." Lo'an was a large, hard man built like a boulder. As soon as he had his hands on a blade, he had shaved all the hair from his face and scalp save for his eyebrows. The man's hands were stained greyish purple from having been forced to process parabata leaves into *ink*. Rezkin had been keeping a close eye on the man to ensure he did not cause trouble, but so far, Lo'an had borne his withdrawals with admirable resilience.

"Will they attack us?" said Nanessy, eyeing the deadly creature as though she already knew the answer.

Lo'an nodded. "They're fast runners, but they prefer to stay near the water. They're not picky. Anything that ventures near will be eaten."

Nanessy nodded and said, "Well then, I think one of these is in order." A semicircular ward appeared around the group blocking out the fithyers but allowing the men and horses to reach the water.

Entris and Azeria made their way farther upriver, presumably to refresh themselves in private since they still had not revealed their true nature to the men. Rezkin wanted to go with them. He had begun to feel a sort of kinship with the Eihelvanan, as though he might even *belong*. Acknowledging that feeling came with its own pains, though. Azeria did not think he belonged. Rezkin rubbed his chest as he considered that perhaps she was right.

"Rez?"

Rezkin looked over at Tam who was cooling his feet in the river. "Yes?"

"I just wanted to say that I am sorry about you and Frisha."

Rezkin wondered what had prompted such a thought but did not ask. The truth was, he had not thought much about Frisha since he had met the Eihelvanan. He still cared about her, and he realized that he always would, but she was not his and never would be. He was still confused about how they had ended up together in the first place. Had he ever truly wanted her? He had found her to be attractive, and he appreciated her forthright nature, but he had never felt about her the way he felt about—

He stopped himself from pursuing that line of thought. Feelings would only weaken him. They would make him go mad.

He looked back at Tam and said, "She is happy with Tieran."

"At first, I was surprised to hear that, but then I realized they have a lot in common." Tam grinned mischievously. "They're both spoilt."

Rezkin thought of his cousin and Frisha together and smiled. "That they are." It no longer bothered him that Tieran had claimed Frisha's heart. If anything, he felt mostly relief.

With his mind churning, Rezkin stared across the plain. After a moment, he saw a spurious movement. He focused on the spot, and seconds later, he saw it again only closer. Then he realized what he was seeing. It was a person running toward them. He was being pursued by several large, spotted cats. As the runner neared, Rezkin saw that he was only a small-man of perhaps fourteen years. He carried a spear and a large satchel and wore garments made of hide and leather. A string of sharp teeth hung from his neck, and his head was shaved on the sides so that only a thick braid of black hair trailed across the center of his scalp and down his neck.

Rezkin withdrew the black blade prompting others in his party to go on alert. When the small-man was within a dozen yards of them, he skidded to a stop, his eyes wide with alarm. Tam's men were shouting at the boy to hurry, to not stop, but he did not listen to them. The five leopards closed on the boy. Then they were past him, and the boy fell back behind the line of over-sized felines. The leopards spread out to surround the men with their backs to the river. Nanessy extended their shield ward to surround the men and horses. The leopards slowly stalked closer. The largest one sniffed at the ward, then took a step and slipped through it as though the ward did not exist. Then the leopards were all within the ward, and Nanessy was preparing new spells.

"*Who are you?*" shouted the small-man in Pruari. Although it was apparent that he was *with* the leopards and not running from them, he did not enter the shield ward. "*You do not belong here. You must go back the way you came.*"

Rezkin said, "*We are not tesias. We are not your enemy.*"

The small-man pointed his spear at Rezkin. "*You look like tesias. You do not belong on the plain. Go back to where you came from.*"

"*We cannot do that,*" said Rezkin. "*We seek passage across the plain to the sea.*"

"*The sea is too far. Go back!*"

Rezkin lazily swung the black blade, and the small-man's gaze followed its movements. Then Rezkin said, "*We are going to the sea with or without your consent.*"

The rumble of the leopards' growls reverberated in Rezkin's chest. He lifted his sword in preparation for a fight and was not disappointed. A leopard on his left leapt at him. Rezkin swung his sword like a club, striking the leopard with the flat of the blade. It yelped and crashed to the ground as another of the cats came at him.

The small-man pointed at the other men and said, "*Get them! They are not armed.*"

Nanessy launched a javelin of light at one of the leopards. It fell back from the blast but quickly recovered. As Rezkin swiped at a cat that was attempting to claw his way past his sword, another sprung out of the grass at his back. Tam jumped at the cat with his blade bared and managed to score its side before it retreated. The cat yowled as it limped away, and a sudden, blasting wind flattened the grass and threatened to topple the lone tree on the bank. A new ward formed between the leopards and the men, and the large cats began to pull back as the ward expanded. Rezkin turned to see that Entris and Azeria had rejoined them, and they were both casting their power into the melee. Entris's ward held as the cats rebounded off it, and each time it seemed to grow stronger.

The small-man looked as though he was at a loss. He spoke to the cats, but his voice was too low for Rezkin to hear. Abruptly, one of the leopards began to change. Its face flattened, its legs lengthened, and its tail disappeared. The spotted yellow and black fur retreated into its dark skin, and soon enough, a man was standing before them. Practically his entire torso and upper arms were covered in tattoos. The small-man handed the tattooed man a hide that he carried in his satchel. The man wrapped it around his waist and turned to face them.

"You are trespassers," said the man.

"We mean you no harm," said Rezkin. *"We are only passing through."*

The man pointed toward a woman who lay prone in the grass. Another woman was crouched over her. The latter had donned a leather wrap provided to her by the small-man, but the woman on the ground was severely injured with a gash up her side from her hip to just under her breast. Both women were similarly tattooed to the man.

"Is this no harm?" said the man.

"You attacked us," said Rezkin.

The man scowled at Rezkin but then turned his attention to the injured woman. His expression was filled with compassion and worry. She was young, perhaps in her early twenties, and she appeared to be suffering greatly.

"We can heal her," said Rezkin.

The man grabbed the small-man's spear and pointed it toward Rezkin. *"You will not touch her."*

The woman who was tending to the inured female hissed and practically growled at the male. *"Tisaya, be quiet. He is right. We attacked them."*

The man known as Tisaya looked at her as though surprised to hear her speak. The woman was a bit older than the other two. Although her face was young, her bearing spoke of years of experience.

"Come," said the woman to Tisaya, *"help your sister."*

As Tisaya moved to the injured woman's side, the older woman stood to face Rezkin and the others. Her gaze paused on the hooded figures of Entris and Azeria, but she quickly sought Rezkin's attention. *"Forgive us. My nephew and niece act before they think. I am Anana. We are of the Virero Tribe. Ahnja is injured. We must return her to our healers."*

"We will not stop you," said Rezkin. *"Go."*

She ducked her head then said, *"We would ask that you come with us."*

"Why would we do that? You attacked us. There will be more of you in your village, and we will be at the disadvantage."

"Unlike my nephew, I do not believe everyone not of the tribes means us harm. Our spirit hides are difficult to damage; but his blade cut deeply"— she nodded toward Tam—*"and your wards are strong. You could have overtaken us—killed us, even."*

"It is as I told the small-man. We are not your enemy."

"No, I think you speak truth. Please, be our guests tonight. The sun is hot, and your men look tired. Can they not use the rest?"

Rezkin glanced at the weary men then looked to Entris and Azeria. "She wants us to go with them to their village. We are invited to be their guests this night."

"What sense does that make?" said Nanessy. "First they attack us. Now we are guests?"

Tam still gripped his sword as he stepped up beside Rezkin. He said, "Rezkin, they're animals."

"Yes?"

"No, I mean, they're *animals* that turn into *people*. What are they? What makes you think we can trust them?"

"These are the omessa people, and I believe they are the legendary leopard men from the historical reports of past military campaigns into Pruar. It was never clear if they fought *beside* the leopards or if they *were* the leopards. It seems we now have our answer. They are said to be highly effective in battle."

Tam frowned and muttered, "They didn't seem very effective. They gave up awfully quick."

Rezkin eyed *Kingslayer*. "Most people are not equipped with a Sheyalin."

As Tam looked down at his sword, Entris approached Rezkin. Keeping his voice low, he said, "You wanted to find Gizahl. These people may have information about him."

Rezkin was genuinely perplexed as he said, "Why?"

Entris shared a look with Azeria but merely said, "It is complicated."

Rezkin did not trust the leopard people who had attacked them, and he was not particularly interested in visiting their tribe. The prospect of finding Gizahl, the ancient Eihelvanan who may hold the key to preventing his madness was promising, though. Rezkin sheathed his sword and nodded toward the Pruari.

"What reason could you have for inviting us to stay with you?"

Anana lifted her chin and smirked. *"You may or may not be enemies, and you bear dangerous weapons. It is easier to keep an eye on you as our guests. It is in your best interest to come. The savannah is dangerous at all times but especially at night."*

"Fair enough. We will come with you on the condition that you give us your oath that no harm will befall our people."

Anana seemed, at first, unwilling to grant such an oath, but she eventually said, *"I vow, as a tribe mother, that your people will come to no harm at Virero hands so long as they remain peaceful."* She rolled her shoulders. *"I cannot speak for the other tribes, though. If you are not with us, you may become their prey."*

"*Then they will die,*" said Rezkin with the confidence of a warrior who could follow through on his promise.

"*It is best not to make enemies of us,*" she said. "*The omessa people are many.*"

"*Not as many as the tesias,*" said Rezkin. Her confident expression faltered for the first time as he mentioned the city dwellers who had been attempting to subjugate the omessa people for more than a millennium.

"*No, the tesias are many more, but they dare not come this far from their cities. You are safest with us.*"

Rezkin glanced again at Entris then begrudgingly accepted the invitation. It turned out they were not far from the Virero village. Less than an hour's walk placed them in the midst of a culture steeped in animal worship. The people possessed varying shades of dark skin clothed in leather and the fur of their prey, and their dark hair was shaved, plaited, knotted, and woven in a multitude of styles. Jewelry made from bones, teeth, and even shells was common, but more so were the extensive grey-purple tattoos that covered most of their exposed flesh. Their homes were framed in the tusks and bones of animals larger than any Rezkin had ever seen, and the patchwork of pelts and skins that lay over them spoke to the variety of prey in the plains. The most frequently seen pelt, by far, was the pale golden yellow of a lion, and all the larger huts bore a lion head, either male or female, over the entrance.

"Wow, they must really like lions," said Tam. "Odd since they're leopards."

Nanessy replied, "I would venture that they *hate* lions. They are killing them, after all."

"The golden haired one is correct," said a woman who had just emerged from the largest of the huts. "The lions have been our enemies since the dawn of omessas."

"You speak Ashaiian," said a surprised Nanessy.

The woman, clothed in the pelt of a striped short-furred animal, nodded. "I do. I am Eseyi, the Tribe Mother. I attended the Mage Academy in Kaibain when I was young."

"Oh, you are a mage!" replied Nanessy.

She nodded and turned her attention toward Anana as she switched to Pruari. *"What are they doing here?"*

Anana hissed as she glanced at her nephew. *"The young ones attacked them before I could stop it. Ahnja was wounded. I invited the outsiders here to keep an eye on them. I have given them an oath of safety in our tribe. This one speaks Pruari."* This last she said with a nod toward Rezkin. It was an overt hint to the woman to watch what she said, but Rezkin did not take offense.

Eseyi frowned and surveyed the group of people and leopards. Finally, her worried gaze settled back on Anana. *"Where is Ahnja now?"*

"She is at the healers' hut. She will survive, but she will think twice before attacking a man with a sword."

"A sword cut her?"

"A Sheyalin. She did not recognize the blue marks."

The woman looked up at Rezkin still mounted on his horse. "You have a Sheyalin?"

"I do," Rezkin said, then nodded toward Tam, "but it was his that cut the young woman. She should not have attacked us."

The woman's gaze paused on Tam's hilt. Rezkin's felt her probing power slide over the weapon then disappear. "Two Sword Bearers in one group? What is it you seek?"

"We were merely traveling to the sea where we will meet with our ship," said Rezkin.

She nodded, then looked at the two hooded figures behind him. "And who are they?"

"I will introduce them later in private, if you do not mind, Tribe Mother."

Eseyi nodded then looked to Anana. *"Take them to the grand hut. They may stay together. The women may be my guests, if they prefer."*

They were led to a large, empty tent, but it was quickly filled with furs, a small table, and four chairs. As omessa men and women came and went from the tent, Rezkin dismounted then turned to Nanessy and Azeria. "You two are invited to stay with the tribe mother, but it would be best if we remain together. These people have given us no reason to trust them."

Nanessy glanced at Tam's men who were making themselves comfortable. Although a few had attempted to flirt with Nanessy, they mostly kept to themselves. Tam spent his time split between the two groups. For her part, Nanessy spent most of her time at Entris's side, and Rezkin noted that she was, more often than not, smiling happily.

She wore that same smile now as she looked at Entris and said, "I do not mind."

Azeria muttered something in Fersheya under her breath. Although Rezkin could not understand it, Entris certainly did because he gave her a long, scathing look. It was the strongest expression Rezkin had seen on the male's face since they had met.

Rezkin looked to Azeria to see if she had a problem staying in the hut, but it was obvious her mind was elsewhere. Her sour expression softened ever so slightly when she saw him staring. Pride nudged his shoulder from beyond the tent flap, and Rezkin awoke to his surroundings with a jolt. He had somehow lost awareness, and that sent a surge of alarm through him. He shook his head to clear it as one of the tribal men led him and Entris to a pen where they could tend to the horses.

As they were brushing down the horses, Entris said, "She will never accept you."

Rezkin paused and looked over at the male. Although he was pretty sure about whom Entris was speaking, he asked anyway. "Who will not accept me?"

"You know who—Azeria (*irritated*). She is discerning, and you are young and weak."

Rezkin did not know why, but he felt inclined to argue with him. "If I am so young, then I have time to become stronger."

"If you were one of us, you would be too young for her (*earnest*)."

"But I am not one of you."

"No, and you never will be, despite your potential power. If Azeria could not accept *me*, she will certainly never accept you."

"She did not accept you because she did not love you."

Entris was quiet for a moment, then he said, "Perhaps you are right, but she will never love you, either. She does not even respect you."

"What makes you think I want her love?" said Rezkin, and he wondered why it had taken him so long to raise the point.

Entris was quiet again. He narrowed his eyes at Rezkin then something seemed to shift behind his gaze. His voice was barely above a whisper when he said, "Perhaps if I train you."

"What?"

Entris cleared his throat and raised his voice. "Perhaps if you are a Spirétua, in truth, she will respect you enough to give you a chance." He nodded once, firmly, as if he had made up his mind. "I will train you (*determined*)."

"Why would you do that? I know you wanted her to marry you."

"I care for her—deeply (*sad*)—but I only ever wanted her to be happy (*earnest*)."

"You do not believe she will be happy with *me*."

"No, but she has not found happiness with any of our men. Perhaps she could with you—*if* you could match her strength."

"She hates me."

"Do not be deterred by her words. I do not believe she is being forthright with her feelings."

"I thought it was considered deceitful to hide one's feelings in your culture."

"Sometimes our feelings are not obvious even to ourselves."

Rezkin did not argue the point. *Feelings* were not something with which he had much experience. He was sure Entris understood them better than he, although he thought the male's view might be skewed by his interest in both women. He was only glad Entris had not challenged him to a duel over one of them, which, according to the tales, happened commonly enough amongst love-struck men.

Rezkin finished seeing to Pride's needs and followed Entris out of the gate. The omessa people did not ride horses; therefore, the pen was not meant to hold a battle charger. The fence was sturdy, though, so he thought it would suffice. A giggle from behind him caught his attention, and Rezkin turned. A small-woman—a *girl*—of about eight years was standing beside the pen near where a small-man pumped water into the trough. The girl giggled again and looked up at Rezkin through her lashes. She wore a coy smile on her face and a pink flower in her hair.

She held similar flower up for him and said, *"I like your eyes. They are blue like the sky."*

Rezkin glanced at Entris who urged him on with a nod. Rezkin took the flower and said, *"Your eyes are lovely like the golden grass on the plain."*

The girl looked down with a cross expression then glanced toward the small-man behind her. *"Onti says they look like the lion's hide."*

Rezkin presumed by her displeasure that this was considered an insult. He said, *"It is also the color of the sun, and the sun is strong and powerful."*

The girl smiled up at him and then shouted, *"Hey, give it back!"* as the small-man grabbed the flower from her own hair. He ran away from her with a cackle, and she chased after him.

Rezkin turned to find Azeria standing behind him. Her arms were crossed, and she wore a bitter expression. Rezkin did not know what upset her this time, but Entris was watching her with interest. Rezkin held the flower out for Azeria who appeared surprised as she took it from him. Then he started walking back toward the tribe mother's hut.

Azeria and Entris kept pace with him, and Azeria said, "What did you say to upset the girl?"

Rezkin frowned as he looked at her. *"I* did not upset the girl. The small-man upset her."

"Oh. What did she want?"

"She said she likes my eyes. I returned the compliment. What difference does it make?"

"We are potentially in enemy territory. Every interaction could be pertinent."

Rezkin shook his head. "The only thing pertinent I got out of that conversation was not to compare anyone here to a lion. It is considered an insult."

A man who had been present when they met the tribe mother was waiting for them outside the hut. He ushered them inside, and Rezkin found that Nanessy and Tam were already seated between two of the four leopards who lounged lazily on the piles of furs. Neither Nanessy nor Tam looked particularly comfortable seated amongst the large felines. The tribe mother and another woman, who appeared to be younger by a decade, were seated across a short table from Nanessy and Tam.

The tribe mother clapped her hands together so that the bangles on her wrists clinked and said, *"Make room for our guests."*

The leopards rose and moved to the perimeter of the tent before settling again. Then Eseyi motioned for Rezkin, Entris, and Azeria to take their seats.

"It is time for formal introductions," said the tribe mother. "As I have already introduced myself, I will begin with Jeina"—she motioned to the woman next to her—"the spirit walker of the Virero Tribe."

"Spirit walker?" said Nanessy.

"She is what you might call a shaman. She bears the power of what you would call a life mage, but she was trained in tribal magic. Hers is the old way." She then nodded toward the leopards. "These are the female elders. They rarely take human form any longer. It is your turn."

Rezkin was about to introduce himself, but Nanessy stalled him with a hand on his wrist and spoke first. "I should do the honors, if you do not mind. I am Mage Nanessy Threll, and this is Rezkin, Emperor of the Cimmerian Empire, more commonly referred to as the Souelian Empire."

"We have heard of you," said the tribe mother. "You are the destroyer."

"Why do you call me that?" said Rezkin. "I have destroyed nothing."

She passed her fingers over the table as if pointing to places on a map. "You go from kingdom to kingdom destroying the reigning monarchies and instilling your own rule. You have created chaos on the Souelian."

Rezkin did not care for the portrayal that was so much like that of the Eihelvanan, but he did not bother to argue the point. He nudged Nanessy with is elbow and she hesitantly continued. "And, this is Tamarin Blackwater, General of the Eastern Army." She paused looking at Entris, obviously unsure what to say.

Entris and Azeria shared a look then lowered their hoods. "I am Spirétua-lyé Entris, and this is General Azeria of the Eihelvanan."

The Eseyi's gaze did not stir from Entris for a long while. Finally, she said, "I know what you are. You bear the cold power, do you not?"

"I do," said Entris, then he tilted his head toward Rezkin, "and so does he."

"I thought him to be human, but you say he is one of yours?"

"More or less," said Azeria with a sideways glance at Rezkin.

Jeina, the spirit walker, said, "There are stories of your kind from long ago. I thought they were myth, but I see now that you are real, so perhaps the stories are as well."

"What do you know of the cold power?" said Rezkin.

Jeina produced several cups from a lidded basket beside the table. She set one in front of each of them and then poured a pink liquid into the cups. She motioned for them to drink as Eseyi spoke.

"Not all of our people have spirit animals. Jeina and I, and a few others, cannot change because we bear the vimara of the mages. Those who change bear the cold power."

Rezkin looked over at Entris in surprise. "They are Spirétua?"

Entris tilted his head. "Not exactly. It is complicated."

Jeina raised a finger and said, "The story goes that long ago a pale-skinned warrior with the pointed ears of a wolf came to Pruar. His power was so great that it had sustained his life for many millennia. By the time he came to the savannah, he was tired and ready to give up on the life he had lived. He could not bear to end his own life, though; so, instead, he made a deal with the gods. In exchange for his great power, the gods granted him a spirit animal to keep him company and to take his mind from the worries of man. He was happy again. He found great joy in the simplicity of life on the plains. Between the animals and the people, he never needed to be alone. It is said that as a man he would lure women away from their tribes and seduce them; and that is why his many children and their children and their children's children were born with spirit animals."

"What happened to him?" said Tam.

"It is said that after a time he grew tired once again and that he gave himself over to the animal. He forgot his true nature and became one with the wolf. Sometimes, a great wolf, larger than all the others, is seen on the plain. Some believe it to be him."

Rezkin looked to Entris. "Is the story possible?"

Entris nodded. "It is not common, but it does happen that a Spirétua who has lived beyond the years his mind can endure will trade his power for the spirit of an animal; but, the people of the omessa tribes are the only people, human or otherwise, in whom the ability has been passed down from generation to generation as far as I know."

"And you think that Gizahl has something to do with these people?" said Rezkin.

"I think it is possible that Gizahl came to Pruar in search of a long-lost friend or that he perhaps intended to join him."

Rezkin looked to the tribe mother. "Are you familiar with the name Gizahl?"

The tribe mother took a sip of the pink liquid and said, "No, I have not heard of it, but if he was seeking the Great Wolf then he would have gone to a different tribe."

"What do you mean?" said Nanessy.

"The wolves are in a different tribe."

"Oh, you only have one type of animal here."

"We are born with our spirit animals, but we do not choose them. We are a tribe of leopards, but our children are not always leopards. When they reach the age of majority, they go to live with the tribe of their spirit animals, and the leopards from other tribes come here."

"Except for the lions," hissed Jeina.

"No," said Eseyi, sadness overtaking her, "the lions kill any leopards born to them."

"That is terrible!" said Nanessy. "They kill their babies?"

"They are our enemies. They would not increase our numbers with their young."

Rezkin said, "So if we wish to find Gizahl, we need to find the Great Wolf."

"Perhaps," said the tribe mother, "but it is unlikely he will welcome you. I doubt he even remembers how to speak. He has been only a wolf for many centuries—*if* the tales are true."

20

The plains were loud at night. Out in the dark, animals busied themselves with the age-old activities of predators and prey. Beasts roared as their victims screamed, but those were not the most disturbing sounds. It was sounds of the hunt that kept Rezkin listening intently. Pack animals yipped and chirped at each other, sometimes over great distances, as they closed in on their prey. It sounded as though they were laughing at their victims' fear. Rezkin was reminded of a conversation he had with his master long ago when one of his own victims had accused him of being cruel.

He had asked, "Master, what is *cruel?*"

Master Peider had replied, "No, Rezkin, we are not cruel. Cruelty is when one takes pleasure in the pain and suffering of another."

"No," Rezkin had said. "I do not feel pleasure in this. I feel nothing."

He had not laughed then. He had merely shoved a blade into the man's skull without a second thought. That man had died then, just like the prey on the savannah, except that Rezkin had not eaten the man. No, that man's death had not been for the purpose of survival. It had been for justice. At least, that is what he had been told. Someone somewhere had been the judge, and Rezkin had been the executioner. It had not been the first time Rezkin had killed, and it certainly had not been the last; and Rezkin had not been lying. He *had* felt nothing at the time. But now he felt something. Thinking back on the event had drawn out a sadness in him—not for having killed the man, but for the necessity of it. The man was a rapist and murderer. He had deserved to die, but his victims had not. Rezkin felt something in that moment that he could not identify for certain, but he thought perhaps it was pity.

He shook himself to be rid of the feeling then rose from his pile of furs, grabbed the black blade, slipped past his sleeping companions, and exited the hut. The village was not exactly bustling with people that late, but there were numerous leopards stalking the dark. The light from the perimeter of torches used to deterred other animals from nearing the huts glinted off the felines' eyes. Rezkin wondered, for a moment, what it would be like to take the form of an animal, to have a simpler purpose.

As he strode through the village, he noted that at least two of the large cats were following him. When he reached the edge of the village, though, he did not stop. His pursuers did, however. He walked into the open savannah, his path lit by the moon and stars, and drew the black blade. There he began practicing his sword forms, adjusting them for the length and weight of the blade. He rolled and jumped and spun as his blade sliced the air. It was on one such turn that he caught sight of a massive ball of fur surging at him. He raised his sword just in time to block a sharp bite to his neck, but it knocked him to the ground. His grip on his sword held, but with the feline atop him, the blade was too long to be useful in such close combat. He dropped the blade and withdrew one of the many knives he had secreted about his person.

The cat lunged at his face, and he could see little more than the massive teeth lit by the moon. He sent a powerful punch into the beast's face and shifted his hips in an attempt to toss it off him. The cat's claws dug into his flesh, though, maintaining its hold on him. He stabbed the knife into its ribs. The blade did not sink in as he expected. In fact, it was deflected beneath his grip so that he lost hold of it. He quickly replaced the lost blade with another, and this time, he stabbed toward the beast's face. The large cat recoiled, withdrawing its claws, and this time Rezkin was successful in extracting himself from beneath the animal.

As he launched himself to his feet, Rezkin grabbed the black blade and thrust it between himself and the large cat. Now that it was farther away, he could see that this was not a leopard. It was a lion. The lioness leapt at him, but this time he was ready for her. The black blade sliced through the air, and blood and entrails splattered across Rezkin and the ground as the lioness was cut nearly in two.

Rezkin was searching the dark for any other movement when he heard a loud clacking sound emanating from the village. It quickly spread until there was a chorus of clacking drowning out all other noise. Then he saw people and animals running all over, and many of them were fighting and dying. Leopards and lions clashed in a flurry of claws, teeth, and fur.

After taking a second to collect his knives, and with the black blade in hand, Rezkin ran into the fray. At the edge of the village, he found a lion and leopard in heated battle. As he ran past, he sunk his blade into the lion's back and kept running. He was headed toward the hut where his people had been sleeping when a burst of light and a loud explosion rocked the air. He noted that a ward was raised around the hut and the lions were unable to get past it. Rezkin silently chided himself. He had not even considered using his power to battle the creatures. When his life was threatened, he had fallen back on his training and depended on his fighting prowess and his blades. He might have avoided the deep gouges to his chest had he erected a ward during his practice.

Rezkin jumped back as a phantom loped by him. It looked like a leopard except that it seemed to lack a corporeal body. It was light and shape and form, but when it attacked a lion, it did so with the brutality and strength of a real cat. Rezkin looked past the melee around him to find the source of the spirit cat. Jeina stood out in the open, a soft glow like that of the spirit leopard surrounding her. Her eyes widened as Rezkin charged toward her, and she ducked in time to avoid being crushed by a massive male lion with a dark, shaggy main and the largest claws Rezkin had seen.

Rezkin placed himself between Jeina and the lion, this time remembering to raise a ward around the spirit walker. The lion roared at him as if warning him away, but Rezkin was not deterred. The black blade was effectual against these shapeshifters, and so was the cold power of the Spirétua. Rezkin was not practiced in using his power in close battle, though, so he depended on that which he knew best. He danced with the lion in a deadly show of strength and power as he wielded his black blade with the skill of a swordmaster. The lion swiped its claws through the air and snapped its massive jaws. Rezkin advanced toward it just as Jeina's ghostly leopard attacked the lion from behind. With a quick slash and stab, the lion was dead.

Another lion nearby bellowed into the night so loudly it shook Rezkin's chest. Then all the lions were roaring in synchrony. Rezkin assumed it was the sound of retreat since they abruptly scattered into the night.

Rezkin paused as the leopard made of light moved toward him. It quickly passed him by, though, and surged at Jeina. Then it leapt *into* her, and she shook as she absorbed it.

"*What was that?*" he said.

"*It was my spirit leopard, Shioni,*" she said. "*I cannot shift, but I was able to use my power to bond with her. It is the old way. Thank you for protecting me.*"

Rezkin nodded and looked over to see his companions outside the hut where they had been sleeping. Tam's men were unarmed and remained behind Entris's shield ward, but Entris, Azeria, Tam, and Nanessy stood outside it with a pile of dead lions at their feet.

"Rezkin, you're injured!" said Nanessy as she ran up to him.

Jeina's gaze dropped to his injured chest. "*You should see our healer.*"

Azeria stalked up to him, her expression a mask of apathy. "This is not bad. I can do it, although I do not know if I should. You would not heal Entris."

Rezkin could tell that it had very much bothered her when he had refused to heal Entris, and for some reason that bothered *him*. He said,

"I *could not* heal Entris. I would have had I control of that power at the time."

She briefly met his gaze but then looked away as she placed her hands on his chest. He felt the familiar tingle of healing energy flow through him, although this time it seemed to be accompanied by something more. It was as though another power was mixed into the healing. It paused upon recognizing his power, as if it was asking for permission. He decided to allow it, and somehow it felt ... intimate. He wondered if it was only in his mind, but then he caught the slight flush to Azeria's cheeks. It was in that moment that he felt another new sensation: pleased satisfaction. He quite enjoyed the feeling, and he momentarily wondered if having *feelings* might just be worth it.

"What was that?" he said.

She would not meet his gaze as she said, "I healed you. You should thank me."

She started to turn away, but Rezkin grabbed her hand. This time, she looked at him in surprise. "Thank you," he said, and he could see that she knew it was about more than the healing. She had done something else to him; he just did not know what it was yet. It surprised him that not knowing what she had done did not bother him. In that moment, he was only glad she did it.

The moment was broken when Jeina said, "*There is the tribe mother. I must go to her. Please remain near your hut for now.*"

Rezkin and his companions stayed in the hut as requested until the sun broke the horizon. It was not long before they were summoned to the tribe mother's hut. When they arrived, she looked beyond exhausted. She invited them to sit around the table as they had before, but this time she did not offer the pink liquid. This time it was a darker brew with a slight purple tinge.

Rezkin sniffed the liquid and said, "Is this parabata tea?"

Eseyi nodded. "It is very mild. It will give you energy after a long night." Rezkin eyed the tattoos of the man who brought in a tray of food and set the cup down, which drew a wan smile from Eseyi. She said, "You do not approve of the use of parabata? I do not blame you. It was not meant to be used by any but the omessa."

"Do you not worry about addiction? About the damage to your bodies?"

Eseyi shook her head as the man sat down beside her. "No, you misunderstand. The omessa are not affected by parabata in the same way. It has been used by our people since we became a people."

The man ducked his head and said, "I am Torat, mate to Eseyi. I was hunting when you arrived yesterday. Eseyi taught me your language." After they exchanged greetings, Torat said, "To change from human to animal takes vast amounts of energy. We cannot change often, usually only when our power is at its height when the moon is at its fullest. *Ink* fuels our change, though. We cover ourselves in many tattoos so that we can change at will. It burns away quickly and does not harm us.

"The tesias discovered our *ink* and what it could do to them. They stole it and began selling it to the rest of the world. There are many among the tesias who blame us for their misfortune. We understand that *ink* has done much harm to many people who are not omessa. This makes us sad, but we can do nothing about it. It was the tesias who stole it from *us*. Even now, we must hide our parabata crops because the tesias take all that they find. It is becoming more and more difficult for us to produce."

Nanessy said, "Without the parabata, you will only be able to change during the full moon? That will make you vulnerable."

Torat nodded. "Yes, we are merely human in this form, but our spirit animals are stronger than mage spells and blades." He eyed Rezkin's sword. "Most blades, anyway."

Rezkin did not need to think long to know what to do. For nearly a year, his thieves in Ashai had been stealing and storing all the *ink* and parabata leaves they could find. He looked toward Entris and said, "We will seek out the Great Wolf to find Gizahl." After Entris nodded, Rezkin turned his attention back to the tribe mother. "And we will convince you and the other tribes to fight with us against a great enemy that threatens all our lives."

Eseyi frowned at him. "What great enemy?"

"King Caydean of Ashai is using demons to control people and take over the Souelian."

"What does this matter to us?"

"It is only a matter of time before he sets his sights on Pruar. I seek to stop him."

"If this king wishes to take Pruar, he will have to fight the tesias. Distant kings care nothing for the omessa people. Why would we fight beside the one known as the destroyer?"

"Because I have something you want very badly—parabata. I have warehouses full of it and the *ink*."

The tribe mother narrowed her eyes at him. "How is it that you have so much parabata?"

"That does not matter. What does matter is that it is in Ashai. If you want it, you will need to come with me to get it."

Eseyi wore a sour expression as she considered his proposal. Finally, she said, "If you find the Great Wolf and convince him to unite the tribes in your cause, we will fight beside you."

Torat looked at his wife with disgust and anger. "I will *not* fight beside the lions."

"You will fight beside the Great Wolf," Eseyi countered. "That is my decision."

Torat was obviously displeased as he followed them out of the hut, but none of his displeasure seemed to be directed toward Rezkin or his companions.

Rezkin paused beside Entris and said, "I could trade my power for a spirit animal? I could become like them?"

"Yes, it is possible," replied Entris.

Torat smiled showing two rows of straight white teeth. "Well, maybe not like *me*. You might become a wolf or a hawk." He glanced to the sky where one such bird soared overhead. "There are many kinds of spirit animals."

"How do I know what I would become?"

"You do not. The spirit chooses you. Give me a few minutes to

collect my hunters, and we will take you to the Wile
the wolves."

They gathered their horses while they waited
hunters. Azeria narrowed her eyes or pursed her li
every time Rezkin glanced her way. Finally, she said,
wish to trade the power of a Spirétua to become an a

"I did not say I would, I only asked if I *could*. A
people, I am destined to go mad with my power. Per
for a spirit animal, I could avoid that fate."

She shook her head. "Or you could end up becomi

This time Rezkin frowned. "Can they become prey
only heard of predators."

A laugh sounded from behind them. Torat said, "T
spirit animals, but there is a horse tribe. Horses are no

"No, but they are powerful," said one of Torat's me
younger, and he smiled like Torat.

Torat said, "This is my son, Remy. He can al
language, but the others cannot. If you need to speak
speak through him or me."

Soon, it did not matter, though. The hunters co
back to them because they were in the form of leopa
ards ran fast across the savannah, but they were lim
men who were still on foot. It was just past midd
finally reached another village. At its entrance was a
that had been roughly carved into the shape of a wolf.
stopped beside the stone wolf and chuffed. A few se
wolf pounced on the lead leopard, who Rezkin pre
Torat. The two tussled for a minute before they beg
each other.

A woman in a short, woven dress approached and
pelts at the leopards. Although they did not seem conc
their nudity, Torat and his hunters used the pelts to w
themselves once they had changed back into humans
became a young woman who greeted Torat and
enthusiasm.

"This is my daughter, Tiseyi. Obviously, she is a wolf, so she must with the Wilepa Tribe."

Nanessy said, "I'm sorry. I know how difficult it is to be separated m your family."

Tiseyi grinned. "I am only glad I did not become a lion."

Torat released a low growl. "They would have killed you before epting you." Tiseyi turned curious eyes on Rezkin and his compan- s. Torat patted her on the head and said, "Not now, Tisi. I will plain later. For now, we must see your alpha."

Tiseyi nodded then turned toward the village. As they walked, she dated her father on the happenings of her tribe and complained out a man who was apparently showing her too much attention.

"I will skin him alive if he touches you," growled Torat.

Tiseyi laughed. "Don't worry, father. I already threatened him with e same. He knows his place."

Torat kissed her on the forehead and said, "Of course you did. You e my daughter."

Although the village looked much the same as that of the Virero Tribe, is time, they were not led to a hut. At the center of the village was a arrow pit containing the charred remnants of a large fire. Beside it was a ble long enough to seat a dozen people. At the table sat a man with fine hite hairs streaking his hair and beard. He had several large rings in his ars, and multiple necklaces of beads and bones adorning his neck. His attoos were more extensive even than those of the other hunters, leading ezkin to wonder how much time this man spent as his spirit animal.

The man did not stand as they approached, but instead invited hem to be seated at his table. Torat sat across from him, but the rest f his hunters found seats on the ground. Rezkin and his companions ll sat on one side of the table, while Tam's men joined those on the ground.

After a quick greeting, the man said in Pruari, "*What have you rought me, Torat?*"

Torat lifted a hand toward Rezkin. "Alpha Osolo, I have brought to you the *Destroyer*. He speaks Pruari, but his companions do not."

Osolo rocked back in surprise. In the Ashaiian trade dialect, he said, "Do you speak truth, Torat? Why would you bring the Destroyer to *my* village?"

Torat slapped his hand against the table a few times, a foreign gesture to Rezkin. He said, "He ended up in our village, and we could not have him destroying ours alone." He laughed at Osolo's dismay and said, "Relax. He does not come for your tribe—not exactly. He seeks the Great Wolf and an alliance."

"The Great Wolf does not speak to outsiders."

"He does not speak to *anyone*," said Torat. "But the Destroyer will not be deterred."

"Actually," Rezkin said, "I seek a man named Gizahl. The Great Wolf may know where he is."

"*And* you want an alliance," said Torat.

"That too."

"An alliance against what?" said Osolo.

"The Ashaiians and their demons," said Rezkin.

This time it was Osolo who laughed. "Demons do not exist. They are tales used to frighten children from going into the dark alone."

Rezkin caught Osolo's eye. "They most certainly do exist. I have fought them myself. What you call my *destroying of kingdoms*, I call liberating them from the demons' control. King Caydean and his ilk are using the demons to gain control of the Souelian. Everyone is at risk, even the omessas."

"What of the tesias?" said Osolo. "Are they controlled by these demons, as you say? I will gladly go to war against them."

"I do not know if Caydean has gotten to anyone in Pruar yet. It is difficult to know who has been possessed until I am confronted, and I have not yet been to your cities."

Osolo scowled. "They are not *my* cities. No omessa would betray their tribe to go to one. Besides, the tesias will kill a lone omessa. That is why banishment is our worst punishment. A lone omessa is a dead omessa."

"Except for the Great Wolf," said Torat.

"The Great Wolf has power unlike ours," said Osolo. "He can afford to be alone."

Entris abruptly lowered his hood, and Azeria followed his lead. He said, "We would appreciate help to find the Great Wolf. He is *our* kind (*earnest*)."

Osolo was speechless for a moment. Eventually, he said, "What are you?"

"We are the Eihelvanan," said Entris, "and we seek our kin."

Osolo looked between Rezkin and Entris. "You look like kin, but the Destroyer's ears are normal."

Entris scoffed, "My ears are *normal* for an Eihelvanan. His are stunted."

"His are human," said Azeria, not bothering to disguise her disgust.

Osolo said, "You say the Great Wolf is one of you? An Eihelvanan?"

"Yes, he was long ago. And so is Gizahl. We need to find them."

Osolo sighed. "Many seek the Great Wolf. It is a matter of honor to find him. Only two in our tribe have been successful in this generation, and they did not get close enough to speak with him even if he *could* speak."

"We will get close enough, and if he retains the ability at all, he *will* speak with us," said Entris with complete confidence.

"Very well," replied Osolo. "It will not hurt to send out a party, and it may even raise the young hunters' spirits. They have become anxious with boredom since the lions have not attacked recently."

Torat growled as he seemed to do every time the lions were mentioned. "They attacked us last night. None of ours were lost, but our *guests* were able to kill several of theirs."

Osolo glanced around the table with a guarded look. He muttered, "That is surprising, but perhaps it should not be. You *are* the Destroyer."

21

The savannah was a haunting vision of swaying blues, greys, and blacks in the dark. The large moon cast an eerie light over everything igniting the ripples in the water as silver ribbons. Osolo claimed that, despite the dangers of the savannah in the dark, it was easiest to find the Great Wolf at night. The alpha and his hunters were blessed with the night vision of primal predators. The leopards were at the fore, though, since their feline ability to see in the dark was greater still. Entris had shown Rezkin how to cast his power in a way that made the night light up to his eyes, and he had shared this ability with their other companions. Most of Tam's men were now armed with spears or bows, thanks to the omessas. The former slaves had been surprised to finally see Entris and Azeria for what they were but were no more disturbed by the revelation than they were that men could become animals. Despite the unusual circumstances, no one protested as they set off on their adventure.

The way was, apparently, too dangerous for the horses with the risk of broken legs, so Rezkin and his companions were on foot. They traversed the marshland that consisted of soggy mud speckled with clumps of grass. He looked up from his precarious footing on a sodden mat and glanced into the distance. A silvery wolf slipped through the tall grass. They had been warned that wolves were not native to the savannah, so any wolf seen was one of the omessa. The same could not be said for many of the other animals, though. The owl that was hooting in the distance to his right could just as easily be wild as it could a scout for another tribe.

The leopards led them to a path over a stream that was relatively shallow with larger boulders and pebbles to step across to the other side. Rezkin did not see any of the strange water creatures that had threatened them the previous day, but he knew they were there. He, Entris, Azeria, and Nanessy kept tight wards around themselves and the other men, but only his and Entris's would preclude attack from an enemy omessa.

Nanessy was just about to step from a rock onto the bank when her ward lit in response to a strike. She chirped but otherwise maintained her composure. She whispered into the dark, "Snake."

Rezkin was once again glad for the wards as he considered how difficult their night would be if someone was attacked by a venomous snake. They were in a marshy land halfway between the stream and a grove when something large shifted between the hillocks. Rezkin narrowed his eyes as he tried to focus on something that caught his attention. He heard a hiss and a yip up ahead, and then the omessas were on alert. The ground seemed to shift all around them, and their wards began flashing with impacts at their feet. Then something massive surged toward them.

The black blade snapped outward, flickering with green lightning as it struck something black and sleek at about head height. Behind him, something else moved. It shifted toward Tam's men, and a few arrows pinged off the creature to no effect. Tam shouted that something else was on their other side, and Rezkin knew they were surrounded. They had walked right into a trap, and he still could not see exactly what was attacking them.

Nanessy cast a spell, and a stream of flame surged toward the monster. The flame was abruptly stoked by a gale created by Azeria, and it crashed in an inferno against the beast, lighting its face. At first, Rezkin thought it to be another dragon, but then he realized the truth to be almost as terrible. It was a giant serpent large enough to swallow them all whole, and its body wound through the marsh all around them. After two more attacks, on their shields, Rezkin identified at least three of the creatures.

The wolves and leopards were not within the protective shields, and Rezkin did not know how long the wards would hold since their spellcasters were also expending energy to fight the beasts. He took a calculated risk and dropped the shield around himself before jumping into the muck. He landed on the back of one of the creatures and held on tight as it reared and squirmed. He gripped the snake with his legs as he rose up and plunged his sword into its body. Red liquid sprayed across him as the head of the creature snapped toward him. Rezkin released his hold to fall onto another of the grassy mats and swiped his sword across the beast's face. One giant, glassy eye burst, and the snake began violently flailing. Rezkin rolled to his feet, slashing and stabbing with abandon as both the injured snake and a second focused on him.

Meanwhile, Entris and Tam were focused on the third snake that was nearer the front of the group and targeting the majority of the omessas. Rezkin caught glimpses of the two battling the beast with swords in hand while power surged around them. Rezkin could not focus on them, though, because he was in the midst of a chaos of his own making. He had successfully gotten the creatures' attention, and he was in the fight of his life. He was staring at the sinuous belly of one of the creatures, about to plunge his sword into it when another blade cut through. As the serpent fell, Azeria slid onto his grassy platform. She said nothing but turned to slash at the creature on the other side that was preparing for an attack.

In the distance, Rezkin heard a sudden yelp echoed by a several vicious growls, and he knew that at least one of the wolves was down. A moment later, three leopards leapt onto the back of the snake Rezkin was fighting. As their claws dug in deeply, Rezkin hacked and stabbed. The snake was just about to sink its fangs into one of the leopards when, with a final valiant effort, Rezkin's blade swept clean through the beast's body. More blood sprayed over them painting

Azeria's white hair red as she cast her power at the second snake. Several stakes of broken wood impaled the creature just before a spear drove into its side.

Rezkin looked over to see Tam's man, Lo'an, gritting his teeth as he tried to yank the spear from the serpent. Soon enough, several of Tam's men, a handful of leopards, and Rezkin and Azeria had managed to take down the second snake, and they turned their attention to the third. Just as they reached it, the beast fell under Entris's blade, but there was no celebration in the victory. One of the leopards and two of the wolves were dead with a third gravely injured.

Abruptly, Torat was in human form towering over the injured wolf. His pained wail was heavy enough to detract from the fact that he was nude. He grabbed the wolf and held her close as he cried, "Tisi, no, stay with me, pup. Please, Tisi, stay with me."

Remy was beside Torat in no time, also clinging to the unconscious wolf. Along her side was a single, large puncture wound. Rezkin did not think or wait for permission. He pushed the two men out of the way and grabbed the wolf. His power entered Tiseyi's body in the same way it had Tam's mind, only this time, Rezkin was not as careful. There was no *time* to be careful. Tiseyi had been bitten, and venom was surging through her system. Somewhere around him, he could feel a jostling and hear the boisterous growls, but he was fully invested in Tiseyi, and he could no more respond to them than he could raise a dead wolf to life. But Tiseyi was not yet dead. He still had time, time that was dwindling with every breath.

Rezkin's power crashed through the she-wolf's body seeking the venom that threatened to end her. He could feel the paralysis that was making it hard for her to breathe. He loosened those muscles and pushed his power into them to get them moving again as he gathered the toxin and filtered it from her blood. Then he was pushing the venom out of her, back through the wound through which it had invaded. The jostling stopped, and Tiseyi's body relaxed, but he could feel her slipping away. He began tugging, pulling on her lifeforce. It did not want to respond, so he pulled harder. Then he heard a shout. It was loud and directly in his ear.

"No!"

But Rezkin kept going. He pulled so hard on her lifeforce trying to drag it back that he thought his own might jump from his body and follow hers.

"Stop!" the voice yelled.

Rezkin did not stop. He gripped Tiseyi's lifeforce within his power and held it there. It struggled against him as if it wanted to leave until it finally relented and began to spread through her body again. Once he was sure her lifeforce had a hold, he released it and watched as it suffused Tiseyi's body. Then he pulled his power from her and slowly became aware of his own body once again. He was shocked to find that he was surrounded, and it looked as though his people and the omessas had been battling between them. Torat was being held back by Osolo and another of the alpha's men, and Azeria stood over Rezkin with her swords drawn. Entris was at his side, his hand gripping Rezkin's shoulder as he spoke harshly.

"Come back. Stop this," he said.

"I am," said Rezkin. "I am back. What happened?" It disturbed him greatly that he had been oblivious to his surroundings, particularly with so many hostiles surrounding him. The only other time he could recall being so dissociated had been when he was engaged within the crystal in the battle against the first demon on Cael.

Entris scoffed and stood. "You went too far. You should have let her go."

"She would have died."

"Yes, but her death would have been better than the life you have given her."

"What does that mean?"

At that moment, Tiseyi opened her eyes and looked up at Rezkin. She remained in her wolf form, and her wild, canid eyes did not stray from him. Rezkin felt as if a connection had grown between them.

"Can you stand?" he said.

She looked at him as if she could not understand his words, then she shifted and yipped in pain. Although he had pulled the venom from her body and restored her lifeforce, he had not healed the wound at her side completely.

"I am sorry," he said. "I should fix that—"

Entris's hand landed on his shoulder again. "You have done enough. We shall speak of this later. I will finish the healing." Entris laid his hand on Tiseyi's side, and after a moment, she skittered to her feet. Entris said, "I think it best we move quickly."

Once Tiseyi was standing on all fours again her father and brother joined her. They flanked her on either side as she gingerly moved to join the rest of the wolves. They left the marshland, but Tiseyi continued to fall behind the others until, eventually, she took a place padding along beside Rezkin.

Once they were within the grove, the other wolves spread out sniffing the ground like foxhounds on a trail. One yipped and the others shifted in that direction—all but Tiseyi who kept her head low to the ground as she kept pace with Rezkin. They traversed the grove in discordant fashion, a unit of warriors, wolves, and leopards all seeking a single enigmatic being that did not want to be found.

The wolves led them along a small stream that grew as they ascended an ever-steepening slope. Eventually, the stream became a cascading river, and upon reaching a cliff at the edge of a plateau, it was a thrumming fall of water that crashed onto a rocky base. One of the wolves closest to the cliff suddenly lifted his head and released a haunting howl. Then, from the depths of the plateau, came an even deeper, mournful drone. It was a howl that reached for the heavens and threatened to pull them down atop everyone. The other wolves joined the fading wail stirring something primal within Rezkin. It was an instinct he felt deeply but pushed away. It was the instinct to run.

Something soft brushed against his hand, and he looked down to find Tiseyi leaning into his side. She appeared interested in the cry of the wolves but did not join them. Instead, she leaned into him further before laying down and placing her head on her paws. Rezkin felt a new sensation stir within him—concern. He glanced questioningly at Entris who merely shook his head in disapproval.

The drone of wailing wolves abruptly ceased, and the wolves and leopards gathered around the pool to drink and rest. Osolo approached cautiously in the dark. He spared only a quick glance for Tiseyi who still had not moved. He said, "From here, you must climb. Up there, beyond the fall, is a cave. The Great Wolf is there, but I cannot say for how long. He was not happy to hear us coming."

He looked down at Tiseyi and said, "What did you do to her? She does not respond to me as she should. I am her alpha."

Since Rezkin did not actually know what he had done to her, he hedged. "We can discuss this later. For now, we go to find the Great Wolf."

Rezkin started for the cliff, and Tiseyi and the others followed. A ledge that would have been invisible in the dark without his power, provided a path up the cliff face, but it was too narrow for the wolves to follow safely. Even so, Tiseyi tried to pursue Rezkin up the cliff in her wolf form. When it became clear she could not make it, she began to whimper. The sound pulled at Rezkin, but he did not turn back. Eventually, she was left behind, and he and his companions continued without the omessas. Rezkin wondered how the Great Wolf had gotten into the cave. Did he truly spend all his time as an animal, or did he secretly change when no one was there to see?

The cave was nearly sixty feet from the ground, and the ledge became slippery as they neared the waterfall. Rezkin's footing was sure as he reached the cave entrance, and he reached back to assist Nanessy who was not used to such treacherous adventures. Tam, Azeria, and Entris followed them into the cave, but the rest of Tam's men had been ordered to remain at the cliff's base with the omessas. The passage was not deep, and as soon as they set foot inside, they could already see a faint light at the other end. The way scended on a steep slope, much of which was covered in loose talus. They emerged from the cave beside a placid pool illuminated by the moon and stars and surrounded by a smattering of trees and other brush. Frogs croaking from lily pads snapped up glowing fireflies as they signaled to potential mates. At the water's edge awaited a lupine beast at least three times as large as the other wolves.

Rezkin gripped Tam's shoulder. "You and Nanessy stay back."

Then he nodded toward Entris to take the lead. Azeria slipped around him and went next. Her snow-white hair was stained red from the serpents' blood, and she looked like a herald of death in the moonlight. The wolf lifted his muzzle and sniffed the air before releasing a warning growl. Then Rezkin sensed a flair of power emanate from Entris. It called to his own power, so he permitted an answer. The growl ceased, and the wolf scented the air again. This time, he rose to all fours and padded forward with a predatory, loping gate. Entris and Azeria drew their weapons, as did Rezkin, while the giant wolf circled them. It stopped in front of Entris and suddenly the hair along its spine rose in a sharp ridge. With its head lowered, it bared its lengthy canines at them and released a deep growl. The growl ended in a single word. "Why?"

"You can speak in this form?" said Entris. The wolf growled again, and Entris answered. "We mean no disrespect in disturbing you, Great Wolf. We came to find Gizahl. We had reason to believe he may have sought you out."

The wolf's voice was fierce and dark as he said, "You disturb my peace to find another?"

"Yes and no. We have another purpose in seeking you."

"I will not speak to your blades. Put them away."

"You meet us with hostility then insist we sheath our own claws? Have you forgotten all our ways? We are not your enemy."

The wolf released a chuff that sounded like a laugh. "You think your pitiful steel will stop me? I could eat you all if I wanted."

"Perhaps," said Entris, "but both he and I wield the power of the Spirétua, the power you forsook. And he wields a blade greater than steel. You had best not test us."

The wolf turned his violet eyes on Rezkin. They were not the eyes of a wolf, nor the eyes of a man. They were Eihelvanan, which Rezkin hoped meant something of the male was left within the beast.

"What is he?" said the Great Wolf. "Is he a halfling? Is he yours?" This last he said as he swung his giant head toward Azeria.

"(*Appalled*) He is not my *child*," she said.

The wolf chuffed again as he padded around them. "A lover then."

"No—"

"It is no matter. Gizahl is not here. He is changed. Speak your other request."

Rezkin said, "We seek to unite the omessas against a common enemy."

"Human concerns are no concerns of mine."

"The omessas are your people—your progeny."

"I care nothing for human enemies. My progeny are strong and can prevail against anything the humans bring at them."

"We do not fight a *human* enemy," said Rezkin. "One of the Sen has joined with the Ashaiian king to bring demons into this realm. Already we have encountered them in several kingdoms. It is only a matter of time before they come here."

At this, the wolf stopped and turned toward them. "Daem'ahn, you say?"

"Yes," said Entris. "You may be a wolf now, but you were once Spirétua. It is your duty to fight against the daem'ahn no matter your form."

The ground thrummed as the Great Wolf dropped to lay on the ground. He said, "I have no inclination toward war. The life of an animal is simple survival. Politics and treachery and greed are things of men."

"Perhaps," said Rezkin, "but demons do not discern. They will spread through the lands leaving chaos in their wake. Even here."

A gust of hot air slapped them in their faces as the Great Wolf released a giant sigh. "I knew I should have killed you all before you spoke."

"You will help us then?" said Entris.

The Great Wolf got to his feet and headed toward the cave, where Tam and Nanessy anxiously waited. "I cannot ignore the daem'ahn." He paused and turned back. "Why do you seek Gizahl?"

Entris sheathed his sword and said, "This one is a human-born Spirétua. We hoped that, in his wisdom, Gizahl may know of a way to stave off the madness."

The Great Wolf huffed. "He is not mad already?"

"No, I am not," said Rezkin, "and I would prefer to keep it that way."

"Very well. You can find Gizahl with the omessas."

"What tribe?" said Entris.

"The lions."

The sun rose early over the flat savannah, but most who had been in the hunting party the previous night slept late into the morning. Rezkin had risen long before the others, and by midday, he could feel his energy waning. Entris had assigned to him several tasks that would presumably hone his vimara, but the more he used his power, the more tired he became. The vagri that hung around his neck, however, had acquired enough of his power to not only glow but to begin to vibrate with a pulsating hum. Rezkin began to wonder if Entris was right and he should remove it, but something deep inside him actively resisted the notion. In fact, the mere thought of removing the vagri made him sick to his stomach. He worried that he had become addicted to the vagri's effects such that it had created in him an unforgiveable weakness.

Still, he could not bring himself to remove the stone. It remained warm even now as he sat astride Pride gazing at the village in the distance. Mounted on the horse to his right was Nanessy and to his left was Azeria. Entris had joined Tam and his men on foot while nearly the entirety of the leopard and wolf tribes were hunkered in the grass in animal form. The scouts had already captured three of the roving lookouts, and they were reasonably sure the lions were not yet aware of the omessas' presence. They could surely see Rezkin, Nanessy, and Azeria as they rode forward. It was a calculated risk for the three of them to approach the village on horseback. The lions would not expect them to be accompanied by the other omessas, but they might equally mistake them for tesias.

They rode slowly, as if beleaguered from a long trek, and Azeria remained hidden beneath her hood. Rezkin caught sight of a lioness padding through the tall grass toward the village ahead of them. She broke into a run as soon as she reached the clearing, and a few minutes later, a score of lions stalked near the village edge. Soon enough a tall man wearing a fitted wrap of pelts over his torso and hips slipped through the sea of felines. Rezkin noted the spots on the pelt and knew the leopards would be incensed. He hoped they kept their senses long enough for their plan to work.

"Tesias are not welcome here. Who are you, and why have you come to our village?" said the man in Pruari.

Rezkin pretended not to understand. "Does anyone here speak Ashaiian?"

The man growled and said, "What do you want, *brika?*"

Rezkin knew *brika* was Pruari for outsider or foreigner, which meant his ruse had worked. The lions did not mistake them for tesias. He said, "We are looking for someone. We believe him to be in your village."

The man raised his spear and said, "If he is here, then he does not wish to be found by *you*. Go away before we eat you."

"You are cannibals?" Rezkin said as if the idea was appalling, which it was.

"We do not eat our own kind, but you are not like us. You are mere humans. We are lions, and for lions, your meat is as good as that of your horses."

"Are you not also human?" said Rezkin. "Or have you all decided to give up your humanity to live like animals?"

"How we choose to live is none of your concern. Leave now. I will not give you another warning."

"We do not require another warning, but we do require an audience with Gizahl."

Only the hardening of the expression on the man's face gave him away. The man had been surprised to hear the name, but he knew it. He raised his spear and chuffed, and the lions attacked as one. Rezkin felt his disappointment deeply as he took the front leg off the first lion to leap at him. Although Tam was at a disadvantage on foot, his Sheyalin bit deeply into the hide of another lion that had come at him and Nanessy. With the sudden eruption of violence, the horses balked.

Pride gnashed and stomped and kicked the lions as their sharp claws scored his armor and dug into his exposed meat, but he was trained for battle such that Rezkin maintained control. Even though they were shielded with wards, the other two horses bolted, sending Nanessy and Azeria to the ground. The latter hit with considerably more grace than the former, but both recovered quickly.

The pandemonium grew as the leopards and wolves entered the fray. Growls and snarls and the screeches of death filled the air in a cacophony written of hate and violence. The black blade flashed with green lightning as it descended on the neck of a dark-maned lion poised to attack one of Tam's men. The sword cut through the golden hide with ease before slicing into another. A lioness immediately jumped at Rezkin, and he knocked her away with a powerful burst of vimara he had failed to contain. Rezkin immediately felt the loss of energy but continued to fight with as much vigor as he could muster.

Tiseyi pounced on the lion that had attacked Rezkin before it could recover its feet. Her vicious growls were accompanied by the tearing of flesh as her fangs ripped into the lion's neck. The lion was much larger than Tiseyi's wolf, though, and although it was bleeding heavily, it quickly gained the upper position. Rezkin leapt forward and plunged his sword though the back of the lion's neck. Then he worked to pull the limp beast from atop the she-wolf who had luckily escaped with only minor injuries. The lions were severely outnumbered, and before long, what remained of their fighting force was gathered in a tight pride in the center of their village, surrounded by angry wolves, leopards, and men.

Rezkin called for the omessas to stand down, but years of resentment spoke louder than his voice. It was only when an enormous male lion sauntered into their midst that they faltered. His mane was as dark as the fertile soil, and his eyes were as golden as his hide. He stood nearly a head taller than the other lions, and his paw alone could probably crush a man's skull beneath it. He carried a length of blue fabric in his mouth as he strode into the middle of his pack. He abruptly began to morph into the form of a pointy-eared male who was tall and broad but significantly smaller than his lion form. He donned the blue fabric like a toga and turned to face Rezkin and his comrades.

"I am Gizahl. You need not kill them all. What do you want of me?"

Entris dispensed with his hood and stepped forward. "Why do you use these people to attack us (*angry*)?"

Gizahl shrugged. "Why not?"

"Look around," Entris said, using his sword to point out the macabre destruction of life. "There was no need for these people to die (*disgusted*)."

Gizahl ignored Entris's protests and said, "I do not know you, young one. Who are you?"

"I am Entris, Spirétua-lyé from the Freth Adwyn."

Gizahl eyed Entris as though he did not believe him but then redirected his attention toward Azeria. "And you?"

Azeria removed her own hood to reveal her striking features, so different from those of the Pruari. "I am General Azeria, Pathmaker."

He nodded as though it was expected and looked toward Rezkin. "Who are you? Are you human or Eihelvanan? I cannot tell."

"Apparently, I am both," said Rezkin. "And that is why we have come to find you."

"Why?" Gizahl said, although his tone implied he did not care about the answer. "I did not sire you, did I?"

"No, my father was King Bordran of Ashai."

Gizahl stroked his chin thoughtfully. "I do not recall the name (*disinterested*)." Then he shrugged and said, "Go away. I am busy."

"Busy with what?" said Azeria. "Your tribe was practically slaughtered."

"Oh, they are not *my* tribe. They are merely animals (*disgusted*). I cannot help it if they worship me."

"Those *animals* can hear you," said Osolo upon approach.

"What do I care?" said Gizahl. "The only one of them that spoke the common tongue is over there in pieces (*bored*)."

"I will tell them what you think of them," said Osolo.

Gizahl chuckled. "You are their enemy. They will not believe you."

Rezkin considered Gizahl's words and knew them to be true. The lions worshipped Gizahl, and nothing anyone else said would change their view of him. It occurred to Rezkin that there might be a way to change that, but he had to do so without Gizahl knowing. He sought the vimara at his core and began giving it shape in the way that Entris had instructed. This shape, however, was something new, something he was not sure was possible. He impressed his will upon the vimara and spread it out to encompass everyone gathered in the village center. Then he sifted through the multitude of languages stored in his mind and pushed the knowledge into the power stream. In that moment, the entire village began to understand the words spoken in the common Ashaiian trade dialect. The villagers did not seem to notice that they were listening to a foreign tongue, and Rezkin wondered if he had somehow imparted his own feelings of comfort with the language on them. He did not know how to make the effect last, so he continued to hold the power as they spoke.

"I am omessa, at least," said Osolo, "while you are an outsider."

Gizahl scoffed and raised a finger. "Correction, I *was* an outsider—long ago. I have been a part of this tribe for more than a century, though, and I know this. These beasts believe only what they want to believe just as you believe your so-called *Great Wolf* cares for you."

"He is our father," said Osolo, "and we are his children. You, however, are a *brika*. You may be capable of the change, but you are not one of us. I am starting to believe that *you* are the reason for the hostility between the tribes. You do not belong here."

Gizahl released a low rumble that was more lion than man. "Your tribes grew weak (*pity*). With the power of your transformation, the tesias were practically powerless against you. You became complacent. It was through my *encouragement* that you regained your fighting prowess. You should be thanking me."

"Encouragement?" said Torat, stepping up next to Osolo. "You mean war. We should *thank* you for killing our people? For forcing us to kill each other?"

"These lions were eager for a fight. I had to do very little to encourage them. A few exaggerations, a few lies, and they were ready for blood. You leopards and wolves were always ready to accommodate them. The horses and hawks and hyenas just ran away. They have no spine at all (*disappointed*)."

The villagers appeared to grow concerned to Rezkin's eyes as they looked between each other hoping to find some clarity, but Gizahl was not paying them any attention. Many returned their pleading gazes to Gizahl as if he might provide them with the comfort and reassurances they sought.

Rezkin said, "What lies did you tell these people to make them want to kill their kin? Even you cannot be so powerful as to instigate an entire century-long war."

"What difference does it make to you?"

Rezkin shrugged. "None, I suppose. Entris told me you were powerful, but I fail to see it. I doubt you have it in you, yet you stand here taking credit for something in which you had little part."

Gizahl lifted his chin. "When I found these people, they were weak and apathetic. The other tribes did not give them the respect they deserved, yet they did nothing to *take* that respect." He shook his fist in the air. "*I* gave them a reason to fight, and they became strong again."

Rezkin rolled his eyes and shook his head. "More lies. What reason could *you* have possibly given them?"

Gizahl grinned. "I only sowed a bit of hate between the tribes. Men and women alike will fight for the lives of their children. And when those children are dead, their thirst for vengeance has no limits."

Rezkin surveyed the expressions of those gathered around them as he said, "Are you saying you killed their children?"

"Only those who were not lions. Those would only add to our enemy's numbers. I had only to blame their deaths on the other tribes, and war was inevitable."

Several of the villagers cried out as many leapt to their feet. Gizahl appeared startled at the sudden outburst and even more shocked that anyone would rise against him. A number of the warriors surged toward him, and it took a shield ward from Entris to prevent the angry lions from tearing Gizahl apart.

"Enough, Gizahl," shouted Entris. "You will no longer antagonize these people. As Spirétua-lyé, I order you to return to the Freth Adwyn."

Gizahl pursed his lips as he stared daggers at Entris. Then his gaze landed on Rezkin, and he grinned. "If I return to the Freth Adwyn, you will not get what you want. Did you not seek me for a reason? It seems my time here is done. Ensure my escape, and I will tell you whatever you want."

Rezkin could tell by the look in Gizahl's eyes that he had no intention of being forthcoming regardless of the outcome. He shared a look with Entris, and he knew the Spirétua-lyé understood this as well. Still, it did not hurt to ask.

"We want only information. How do I stave off the madness of those Spirétua born to humans?"

"Ah, that. Yes, I do know a way, but that information will cost you."

"Fair enough. If you tell me, I may feel inclined to let you live."

This time Gizahl did laugh, boisterously. It was odd to see one of the Eihelvanan so expressive, but Rezkin supposed Gizahl had lived a long time, much of it with humans. The male said, "You could not kill me if you tried."

Entris said, "No, but together we could."

Gizahl smirked at Entris. "You would kill one of your own—the oldest of our race—for a human born? Even the syek-lyé would take exception to that (*confident*)."

Entris gritted his teeth. "Very well, Gizahl. General Azeria and I will return you to Freth Adwyn where you will remain in custody until the syek-lyé says otherwise. Perhaps he will take mercy on you if you provide the information we require."

Gizahl rolled his eyes—a very human-like gesture—and said, "I will not tell you because you cannot make me."

"You are acting like a youngling," said Azeria.

Gizahl shrugged. "Perhaps I have grown so old that I have come full circle. I will say this, though. What you seek is an ancient way. It is both alive and dead. Both possible and impossible. You possess the knowledge, and you lack the knowledge to make it happen."

"Great," muttered Azeria. "He now speaks in riddles."

"No, not a riddle," said Gizahl. "Merely a fact." He pointed to Rezkin. "Perhaps this one has already solved the mystery, though."

Bands of light abruptly wrapped around Gizahl, only these were darker than those that had bound Rezkin upon meeting the Eihelvanan. These were a vivid red, like glowing blood, and Gizahl did not seem pleased. In fact, Rezkin saw the moment the ancient Eihelvanan's confidence faltered. His expression soured, and his shoulders slumped like a small-man sent to bed without his dinner.

"We shall return quickly," said Azeria. "The path will not be long. Do not leave this place."

Rezkin nodded and watched with the same awe he always felt as the rent formed in the air. Azeria, Gizahl, and Entris disappeared and the rip with them. As soon as Gizahl was gone, Rezkin released the power that was sustaining the language translation to the various tribe members.

"Where did they go?" said Tam.

"She opened a pathway straight to their home. It is difficult to explain, and I doubt I would do it justice."

A few hours passed, during which time Rezkin spoke with representatives from the various omessa tribes. Getting them to come to terms with each other was proving to be more difficult than getting them to agree to go to war with him. It probably did not help that, as he spoke with the tribal leaders, Tiseyi lay at his feet gnawing on the leg of a dead lion. By the time Azeria and Entris returned, the tribes had managed to agree on only one thing, and that was that they all wanted—no, *needed*—Rezkin's parabata. It had been a long time since Rezkin had checked on his stores of the drug, but his people had been intercepting all black-market *ink* and parabata entering or traded within Ashai for nearly a year. He figured it was enough parabata to sustain the tribes for at least twice as long.

When Entris and Azeria finally stood before him, Rezkin was seated at a small table surrounded by the most vocal tribal members who had participated in the battle. The lions were subdued, having lost their *great leader*, but one in particular voiced his hatred for the other tribes with vehemence.

"They do not deserve our help," said Bratu. He was a tall man with the lean muscle of a runner. His hair was cropped short, and his skin was a bit lighter than most of the omessas so that his *ink* showed vividly in contrast. In addition to the dark purple, he had several red tattoos adorning his chest and shoulders.

"Why do you hate us so much?" hissed Torat. *"It is your tribe that attacks us. You kill your own children if they are not born lions."*

"That is not true!" said Bratu. *"It is your people who kill our children when they are sent to you."*

"You lie," cried Torat. *"We have never killed a leopard or any omessa outside of battle."*

Bratu spread his arms wide, and Rezkin was glad the man had the sense to cover himself with a leather loin cloth. Many of the omessas who had changed wore nothing at all, but at least the leaders had covered themselves. Rezkin knew it had nothing to do with propriety or decorum. Being naked in human form before one's enemies left one with a sense of vulnerability. Or so he had been told. His own nudity had never bothered him. Still, he had found that he preferred not to see other men's genitalia on display; and, more recently, he had been experiencing discomfort with seeing the women exposed.

"Then who is killing our children?" said Bratu.

Azeria strode over to stand next to Rezkin. "What are they arguing over now?"

"They are arguing over who has been killing the children of the lion tribe who are not born lions. The lions insist it is the other omessas, and the others believe it to be the lions themselves."

Azeria eyed the wolf at his feet, and Rezkin was nearly certain he saw a flash of irritation cross her otherwise placid visage. She said, "Were they not paying attention? Gizahl told us he had lied to the lions about killing their children."

Rezkin nodded. "As Gizahl said, some people hear only what they want to hear." Then he turned to the two arguing and switched to Pruari. *"You heard what Gizahl said. By his own words, you heard him take credit for killing the children."*

"But he was our leader," Bratu said. *"Why would he do this to us?"*

"He wanted you to war with the other tribes. He wanted you fractured. It was how he maintained power."

A mourning wail went up in the crowd of lions, and it was followed by several others. The people of the lion tribe had lost many young ones to Gizahl's treachery.

Osolo turned to Bratu. *"This is your fault. You turned from the Great Wolf to follow your own leader. The Great Wolf is our great father, not the lion."*

Bratu looked as though he would attack Osolo, then his shoulders slumped. *"You are right. We believed that a great lion spirit would lead us to prosperity above the other tribes. We were ... jealous ... that the great spirit should be a wolf. We should not have turned from him."*

At that moment, a large savanna hawk landed on the post of a nearby animal pen. The hawk abruptly began to elongate and morph into a lithe woman with creamy brown skin. Her hair was plaited into many long braids that covered her breasts and reached to her waist. She stalked toward them with a sensuous gait and smirked at the men's appreciative stares. She stopped before Rezkin and tossed her braids over her shoulder before stroking one hand down her side to rest on her hip.

"I am Fetari, Tribe Mother of the Disoni Tribe."

Rezkin was surprised that this woman was the leader of her tribe. She looked to be in her late twenties at most. He started to rise, but she reached out and stopped him with a hand on his shoulder. Rezkin prepared his muscles to react should she attack him. He knew from experience that this was not the kind of woman to be trusted. Then again, he was not sure what a trustworthy woman looked like.

She said, "Don't get up. I know who you are, Destroyer." She pointed toward the sky. "We have been watching since you arrived in Pruar. You are impressive in battle, but I am most captivated with your ability to bring these tribes together. For many decades, it has been impossible to get them to speak in this way."

"It took the spilling of much blood to make it happen," said Rezkin.

She shrugged one shoulder causing her exposed breasts to bounce before his eyes. "If you had not captured the great lion, more blood would have flowed—blood of the innocent." She paused and looked at Entris and then Azeria. Azeria shifted closer to Rezkin, and Fetari smirked. Looking back at him, she said, "You and your companions possess great power, yet you do not come here demanding our fealty. You seek to buy our assistance with your parabata. I respect this." She brushed her fingers across his jawline. At his feet, Tiseyi released a low growl but continued gnawing on her bone. Fetari said, "We accept your deal. The hawks are at your service."

Fetari turned, and her gaze seemed to undress Entris as she passed him. Then her womanly curves became wings and feathers, and she soared back into the sky. As she flew away, several more hawks took her place watching the people on the ground as they circled overhead. Rezkin had not paid much attention to the birds and other small animals that had surrounded them on the savannah, and he chided himself for the oversight. He would need to be more vigilant. Animals that were really people was a new concept to him, one that he now added to his mental list of potential threats. Although his masters had not taken into account threats of the Eihelvanan, shielreyah, ahn'an, dragons, demons, water monsters, and spirit animals, he was still alive. His training was thorough enough to accommodate shifting dangers. So long as he maintained his *Skills* and followed the *Rules*, he would survive. His *Rules*, however, seemed to be changing over time to accommodate both new hazards and his friends. Already, he was breaking several to use his vimara, an act which could literally drive him mad. Rezkin reached up and touched the pulsating vagri, feeling both comforted that he had it and disturbed that he *needed* it.

The talks finally ended when the sun was setting, and the leopards and wolves parted to return to their own villages. Rezkin and his companions accompanied the leopards as they rejoined their tribe, and he was only mildly surprised that Tiseyi joined them. She was, after all, the daughter of the leopard tribe mother and father. Once they arrived, though, she remained at his side rather than with her family. She also did not shift back to her human form, and he realized that something was definitely wrong.

"Come, Tiseyi, leave him be," said Torat as he tried to get his daughter to vacate the hut in which Rezkin and his companions were staying. Tiseyi ignored her father as she sat at Rezkin's feet. Torat looked to his wife and said, "What is wrong with her. Why will she not come?"

Eseyi shook her head. "I do not understand either. Tiseyi, please shift so that we may speak with you." Tiseyi stood, turned her back to them and sat back down. Eseyi's tone became harsh as she said, "Tiseyi, he is the Destroyer, the emperor of his people. You cannot stay here with him. He desires to be alone with his people." When Tiseyi did not respond, she said, "You shift now, or I will have Jeina force the shift on you as if you were a stubborn cub."

Rezkin glanced at Entris who wore a noncommittal expression, but there was judgment in his eyes. It was obvious that Rezkin had done something to the she-wolf when he had healed her, but Entris was apparently letting him figure it out for himself. Rezkin felt like a small-man again under his masters' tutelage.

Rezkin turned his focus back to Tiseyi and knelt on one knee. He met the she-wolf's gaze and said, "Please, Tiseyi, will you shift so that your parents may speak with you?" Tiseyi whimpered and nuzzled his hand before meeting his gaze again. She seemed to behave more like a true wolf than a human within a wolf. "Please?" he said.

Finally, her body began to crackle as she became the young woman he recognized from the previous night. A livid red mark, not yet healed, broke the sinuous lines of the *ink* tattoos on her side. She held his gaze for a moment and then Azeria was standing between them holding up a lengthy hide for her to wrap around herself. Tiseyi took the proffered hide and did as Azeria bade then looked to her parents.

Eseyi came forward and took Tiseyi's hand. "Come, daughter. Leave this man be."

"No, mother, I cannot leave him," protested Tiseyi.

"What? Why not?"

"Because he is my mate."

Eseyi's eyes widened, and she looked at Rezkin. He was certain his own surprise was written across his face. She looked back at Tiseyi and said, "He cannot be. He is not omessa. He is not your mate."

"Yes, mother, please understand," Tiseyi pleaded. "I can feel it." She pressed her mother's hand to her chest and said, "In here, Mother. The pull is so strong, I cannot fight it. I do not *want* to fight it. It is impossibly hard for me to stand here in this form. My wolf *needs* to be with him."

Azeria abruptly rounded on Entris. "What is the meaning of this? Why does she think she is his mate?"

Entris glanced from Azeria to Rezkin, then met Eseyi's questioning gaze. "He used his vimara to save her life. She should have died, but he pulled her back from the edge, and she accepted him. He bonded her vimara to his. She was in wolf form when it happened, so the bond is strongest with her wolf."

"What does this mean for her?" said Eseyi.

"It means that if she is to have any semblance of a normal life, she must stay with him. It seems this is a one-way bond. Only she will suffer if they are parted."

Tiseyi turned to Rezkin and took his hand in an all-too-familiar way. "Please, you cannot send me away. I will not survive it. You must let me stay with you. My wolf needs you. *I* need you."

Torat grabbed Tiseyi by her other arm and tugged her toward him. His face was contorted in anger as he berated her. "What has happened to my strong, independent daughter? Since when does the great she-wolf beg of a man to keep her?"

"Please, Father, he is not just any man, and he is not my master. He is my mate. I know he is. I am still your strong daughter, but I know I will be stronger *with* him." Her eyes were pleading as she looked at Rezkin. "But he does not need *me*, so I must beg. I will serve however I must in order to stay near him, but one day he will see that I am not only a worthy mate but that he is lucky to have me."

Rezkin backed away from Tiseyi, from everyone. The vagri became a slow burn as feelings washed over him. Once again he was pushed into a bond with a female that he did not choose. He looked to Azeria, but her stoic expression gave nothing of her thoughts away. The sensations that flooded him were not unlike those he felt in the face of a futile battle. He was ... *overwhelmed*. The *Rules* dictated that

374

he should retreat when he could not win, and that was what he would do. He skirted the others and backed toward the entrance. Tiseyi attempted to follow, but her father held her back with an iron grip. She whimpered as Rezkin backed through the opening to leave the tent and the unwinnable battle behind.

Rezkin threw himself into his senses as he walked, ignoring the feelings in his chest, and identifying every possible angle of assault. He monitored the corners, checked the shadows, and surveyed the darkened sky. He made a mental note to inquire if any of the omessas were bats. Once he had found an adequate open space between the huts and within the torchlight, he tossed his shirt aside and drew the black blade. It swung through the air in far-reaching arcs of power and grace. He twisted back and forth, ducked and jumped and rolled, all the while slicing the air into thin strips of nothingness.

After a while, Tam appeared at the edge of his makeshift practice yard with *Kingslayer* drawn and ready. Rezkin advanced on him and the two fell into a silent battle between student and master. Then suddenly, Tam disappeared and Azeria was before him. A fire ignited in his chest as his own fighting spirit rose to the challenge of battling the faster opponent. He pushed himself until all his reserves were empty and he was merely standing with his sword hanging at his side. Azeria approached then, sheathing her swords as she breathed heavily. They stood silently breathing for several minutes before Rezkin finally said, "I will not be forced to mate another."

Azeria was quiet for a moment. Then she said, "No one said you had to mate her. But she is mated to you. You can either accept her and gain a strong ally or reject her and allow her to wither and die."

He looked at Azeria in surprise. "You speak in favor of allowing her to remain with me?"

She did not meet his gaze as she said, "There are many kinds of bonds in this world. This one is not unlike the one you have with the vagri. It does not need to be one of romantic intimacy."

"But she says I am her mate."

"Perhaps you are *now*, and perhaps you will agree to fulfill her needs in that way; but that does not mean you cannot claim your soulmate."

"My soulmate?"

She shrugged and looked down at the ground. "Perhaps. Sometimes a connection is drawn between two people before they have even met. This connection cannot be broken no matter who comes between them." Her tone changed and her jaw clenched as she said, "Sometimes they do not even want the connection that is forced upon them."

At hearing the vehemence in her voice, an icy chill suffused his heart. Rezkin no longer felt overwhelmed. He felt … nothing. He was filled with the cold emptiness with which he was long familiar. "I see. I will not be forced into any connection with another, nor will I force one upon someone else." He sheathed his sword and grabbed his shirt from the ground where he had thrown it.

Azeria said, "What will you do?"

As he shook out his shirt, he said, "I pulled her back. She did not want to come, but I kept pulling until she finally agreed. I did not realize what I was doing at the time. I did not heed Entris's warning. Now that it is done, it is my responsibility. She will remain with me, but I will not be hers. I will find a way to fix this."

Rezkin returned to the large tent where he found Tiseyi awaiting him. As soon as he ducked through the tent flap she jumped to her feet, but she did not rush him. Instead, she stood looking pensively at him. Rezkin glanced around to see that the tent was otherwise empty then he closed the distance between them.

Before he could say anything, Tiseyi said, "What is the cause of your distress? Do I displease you? Are you not attracted to me? Because many men from several tribes have desired to be my mate. I do not remain unmated for lack of options."

"No, I am sure you do not," said Rezkin. "It is not a matter of attraction. You are a beautiful woman and a good fighter. I respect you for your independence and strength. But I cannot be yours."

"You already have a mate?"

"No—"

"Then you desire someone else? It is the white-haired one, yes? I have seen the way you look at each other. With time, you will see that I am the better choice, and you will forget about her."

Rezkin did not bother to correct her assumptions about him and Azeria. In fact, he refused to think too deeply on the subject. Instead, he said, "It was wrong of me to force this bond upon you. I did not know what I was doing at the time, and I would like the opportunity to fix it, if you will let me."

Tiseyi's eyes widened. "You would destroy our bond?"

With a frown, he said, "Do you really *want* this? To be bonded to me and I not to you? Before your ordeal, would you have chosen me as your mate?"

Her lips opened with a response that did not come. He could see the uncertainty in her eyes as she seemed to be searching his for answers. Finally, she said, "I did not know you. I cannot say if I would have chosen you eventually, but I cannot say that I am entirely displeased. You are handsome and strong and a capable leader. I have seen how brutal you can be, yet I also sense a kindness in you. I think you will be a good mate."

"No, you have *not* seen how brutal I can be, and none of those qualities would make me a good mate. This forced bond is unfair to both of us but especially for you. You deserve to choose where your loyalties lie. I do not believe this bond cannot be undone. Will you allow me to try?"

Tiseyi took both his hands in hers, and Rezkin allowed it. She said, "I will allow this because you have asked. What do you wish me to do?"

All the while he had been practicing in the yard, Rezkin had been mulling over a way to break the bond. He did not know if it would work, but he knew he had to try. He said, "I think you should shift to your wolf form since that is the form you were in when the bond was established. Then lay down, and I will do the rest."

Then, with Tiseyi curled on the ground, Rezkin sat and opened his mind to the vimaral river that surged through it. He heard the melody of power shifting around him as he plucked at the various strands of color. Somehow, none of them seemed appropriate for his cause and yet they *all* did. He pulled at the combined white light and wrapped it around himself then around Tiseyi. With a gentle push, he pressed the power into her body. After a moment, he felt an answering tug from her own vimara. Like a fish on a line, as soon as he felt the tug, he snagged it, wrapping it in his own power.

The vagri on his chest heated, and he could see its glow even from behind his closed lids. Rezkin slid his vimara around and over Tiseyi's, and he felt her shudder at the intimacy of it. Eventually, he came to a juncture where the vimara split. One bundle of her power stretched out toward him to tangle with the vimara at his core. Rezkin presumed this to be the bond that had formed between them. He plucked the strand, and it vibrated in tune with his own melody. Somewhere in the distance, he could hear another song that was not his own.

With deft control, Rezkin began picking apart the strand of power that was the bond. As he plucked and pulled, releasing strands, more strands grew in their place. His frustration mounted when it seemed that the bond was only getting thicker and tighter, and he eventually gave up on that approach. After taking a steadying breath, Rezkin dove back into the bond, and this time he turned toward his own vimara. He grasped a tendril and sent it shooting into the thickened bond, wedging it between the filaments such that it split nearly in two. Tiseyi whimpered, and Rezkin could feel her discomfort vibrating down the bond. He dug into one of the thick strands, tearing with the strength of his will. Something else, another power, seemed to be fighting against him, and he wondered if it was Tiseyi's doing. As he pulled, the strand began to fray. In the distance, Rezkin could hear the pained wail of a wolf, and agony and terror flooded the threads that connected them.

Rezkin started to back away, but as he did so, the threads began to heal themselves. He braced himself and threw his will back into the effort, wrenching and tearing at the filaments. Suddenly, the large strand snapped, the ends of which unraveled along the bond to smack into each of their cores. A searing yelp sounded from Tiseyi, and pain slammed into Rezkin so hard blackness stole across his conscious mind.

When Rezkin came to, several people were hovering over him. Tam was attempting to shoo them away with a warning that Rezkin might attack them upon gaining consciousness. While Tam and Entris pulled other hazy figures away from him, Azeria came into focus. She scowled and slapped him in the face.

"What is wrong with you?" she snapped.

Rezkin tried to sit up, but his mind spun with a dizzying fog. "I was trying to break the bond," he muttered.

Her expression became blank. "Did you?"

Rubbing his head, Rezkin said, "Part of it, I believe."

"Impossible," said Entris from somewhere to his left. "No one can break that bond."

Rezkin shrugged. "We will have to ask Tiseyi."

Azeria glanced up then looked down at him again. "She is unconscious. What did you do to her? She was in excruciating pain."

The now familiar pang of guilt flooded him, and Rezkin sat up more quickly than his head and stomach would have preferred. He turned his gaze toward Tiseyi to find her parents scowling at him from where they held her unconscious wolf.

"What did you do to our daughter?" hissed Eseyi.

"I did not intend to hurt her. I was attempting to break the bond between us."

"Of course you would try to ruin something like that, *Destroyer*," hissed Eseyi. "You have no respect for the sacred mate bond. You do not deserve her."

Torat laid a hand on his wife's shoulder. "She is not *dead*, Eseyi. Let him explain."

"I thought you *wanted* her free," said Rezkin.

Eseyi swallowed hard. "Not at this cost. Did you not hear her pain?"

"No, I mean, I did once, but—"

379

"But you did not care," growled Torat.

"No," said Rezkin, getting to his feet. "I did care, but I thought I could do it. I wanted to set her free, and I did—partially."

"What do you mean, partially?" said Eseyi.

"Truthfully, I am not sure. We will find out more when she wakes."

"*If* she wakes," said Eseyi.

Torat replied, "She will be fine, my love. She is strong."

"Why do you defend him?"

"I am not defending him. I am showing confidence in our daughter. She can handle anything he throws at her."

When she came to a short time later, Tiseyi shifted to her human form and tears began streaming down her face. She sat up and quickly looked around until she found Rezkin. Then she merely stared at him as he stared back. She wiped her tears then said, "I feel as though something is missing." She tapped her chest. "In here."

"Is the bond broken?" Rezkin said.

She shook her head. "No, not completely, but—"

"But what?" said Eseyi.

Tiseyi turned to her mother as if just realizing her presence. "I still feel a connection to him, a bond, but it does not feel the same. I feel close to him, but I do not feel as though I *need* to be with him. I do not think he is my mate."

"He never was," snapped Eseyi.

"No, I see that now." She stood on shaky legs. She wrapped a blanket around herself and closed the distance between herself and Rezkin. She looked up at him with hope in her eyes. "I *know* you now, even more than before. I think something you did changed the bond. I can feel your feelings. I know your desires."

A chill suffused Rezkin. He did not like Tiseyi knowing anything about him that he did not intentionally share.

She tilted her head curiously as though picking up on the feeling. Then she glanced toward her parents and back to him. "I know that you want the best for your people, and I know that you have been truthful with us. Your desire for a mutually beneficial alliance with the omessa tribes is genuine."

"I have not lied to you."

She nodded as if she truly did know. Then she said, "This connection we have is special. I wish to remain with you."

Rezkin was disappointed that he had not broken the bond completely, but it seemed to be an improvement of sorts. There was one concern for which he needed reassurance. "I am not your mate."

Tiseyi smiled. "No, you are not, but we can be friends."

Rezkin tilted his head in thought. He had not added to his official list of friends in some time. He had not considered that he would ever need to, but this situation seemed extraordinary. He slowly nodded and said, "Very well. Friends it is."

22

Tiseyi loped at his side as Rezkin led Pride on foot over the cracked, rocky terrain. Her paws barely touched the rocks as she covered the ground with more grace than the rest of them put together. Her dark coat, which looked like charcoal bearing flecks of silver, stood out against the pale, weathered rocks. She leapt over a gully then turned and happily waited for him as he climbed the side with Pride in tow. Unfortunately, the gully was dry and the last time they found a water source had been hours before the sun had reached its zenith. Northern Pruar was more desert than savannah, and even that late in the fall it was hot beneath the unrelenting sun.

Rezkin tipped his head back to watch the hawk that kept pace with them overhead. Its wing dipped, and the bird dove into a lazy spiral before straightening and ascending on an invisible current. This time, Rezkin was fully aware that the raptor was omessa. In fact, three of the birds were on their trail, leading the way and ready to take word back to the rest of the tribes should he need them. Rezkin looked back to the men who were making their way across the shallow gully, and he reached down to give one a hand. The former slaves were tired, but still, they did not complain. Nothing but their honor was keeping the men with the party as they made their way across northeastern Pruar.

The omessas, on the other hand, twenty in all, had no problem navigating the rough terrain. A combined force of wolves, leopards, and lions plodded across the broken earth with the ease of the animals they emulated.

About an hour later, a mirage overtook the horizon. It shimmered blue and silvery grey and stretched for as far as Rezkin could see. It took him a moment to accept that it was not, in fact, a mirage, but the ocean, and directly in their path was a port city.

"Thank you," shouted Tam as he waved his hands in a worshipful gesture to the hawk that had guided them true. He and Uthey patted each other on their backs as they enjoyed a momentary celebration of good fortune. Rezkin shared in their joy at finally reaching the city but did not fully understand the boisterous display. Tiseyi groaned and looked up at him with worried eyes.

"Do not fret," he said. "I will not allow any harm to come to you in the tesia city."

The she-wolf brushed against his leg as she continued padding across the broken terrain. He glanced over at Azeria and Entris who were also eyeing the human city with concern. They would have to be particularly careful not to be seen since there was no telling how the humans would react to the presence of beings of a mythical race. They had only their hoods and enchantments at their disposal, which he thought might not be enough in such a crowded city..

He pondered their dilemma for a moment before asking, "Can you not make yourselves appear human?"

Azeria gave him a vicious scowl, but Entris said, "It is difficult to change our nature."

"You do not have to change your nature. Can you not place an illusion over yourselves?"

"I am not good with creating illusions," said Azeria. "It is not one of my strengths."

Entris said, "I can create such an illusion for a time, but Azeria would need to stay near me to reap the benefits as well. It would become unstable with distance."

"Show me how," said Rezkin.

Entris looked back to see that Tam and his men were far enough behind not to overhear their conversation. Then he said, "I have been considering this. Gizahl did not give us the answer to your problem. It is best for you not to use your vimara."

Rezkin's gaze slid to Azeria, but she did not look his way, nor did she give away her thoughts. He said, "I have considered it as well. It is unacceptable to remain weak in a skill in which I could excel. I must learn to use my power to its full extent."

"You know what will happen if you do."

"No, I know what you *think* will happen."

"You are intentionally being difficult. It has always been so—in *every* case."

"Gizahl seemed to think I already knew the answer. I must only figure out what I know. Besides, it is not your problem."

"It most definitely *is* my problem. *I* will be the one who must kill you when that happens. I do not wish that fate upon either of us."

Rezkin did not wish for that fate either, but he was driven to pursue the knowledge and skills of the Spirétua. Creating an illusion would be a small step toward that goal. He looked at Azeria again and considered that it was only logical to give her the best chance at survival. With *two* of them able to cast the illusion on her, she would have a greater chance of going undetected in the human city. Once again, he said, "Show me."

When they finally reached the city named Ki'kyo, Rezkin asked around until someone could give him directions to reasonable accommodations. It seemed most of the inns were located along the main thoroughfare that passed through the market beside the docks. Eventually, he was able to find lodging for everyone, including the omessas who had taken on their human forms and donned clothing similar to those the tesias wore. He gave Tam money to purchase clothing and supplies for his men since they were all wearing the thread-bare rags they had worn at the quarry. Nanessy offered to help Azeria find apparel that was more common for human women and even suggested mage robes, but the female refused.

When Rezkin saw that everyone was settled and Pride was seen to, he headed for his own room. That is when the innkeeper called to him without looking up from his books. *"No dogs in the inn. It can stay in the stables with the horses."*

A middle-aged woman in the colorful garb of the tesias strode up behind the man. *"That's not a dog! That's a wolf. What's a wolf doing in here?"*

Rezkin said, *"She is with me."*

The innkeeper straightened and finally looked down at the canid. *"A wolf comes into the city and we kill it. It's either a wild animal or an omessa."*

The woman sniffed. *"Same thing. They know better than to come here, though."*

Rezkin said, *"As you can see, I am not an omessa, and she is mine."* Tiseyi brushed against his legs and looked up at him, and he considered that he should have worded that last differently. He did not want her to think he was staking a claim on her. *"She is well-trained and will not cause any trouble."* He adjusted the purse that hung from his belt so that the heavy coins clinked together, then said, *"Or I can take my business elsewhere."*

The innkeeper looked to the practically empty common room and sighed. *"Just don't be bringing it down here with the other guests. And clean up after it! I don't need wolf scat all over my floors."*

Rezkin nodded and headed toward his room. He had tried to get Tiseyi to stay with Azeria and Nanessy or the other omessas, but the she-wolf just huffed and followed him into the room. The bedroom was a small affair with a moderately sized bed, a dirt floor, and a single wooden chair in the corner. After checking the room for traps and poisons, he sat in the chair and pulled out the mage relay device he had created. He first made contact with the ship that had been waiting for their call off the coast and ensured they would be docking on the morrow, then he shucked his clothes and weapons and lay down in the bed. He considered that the bond could be a ruse and

Tiseyi could attack him in his sleep, so rather than sleep, he entered a deep mediation. Still, he meditated with a knife under his pillow.

When he roused himself before dawn, it was not to the soft fur of a wolf laying by the door but to a woman clad in one of his shirts sleeping in the chair across the room. He shifted and she was instantly awake. She smiled over at him and tugged the edge of the shirt down to cover more of her legs. "You wake early," she said.

"I train in the morning," he replied.

Tiseyi smiled coyly, but she did not move. "I thought perhaps you were eager to see a certain elf. I know you desire the white-haired one."

"I do not—"

"You cannot hide it from me. I can smell your interest in her. I know your feelings and desires, remember?"

Rezkin said nothing as he retrieved clean clothes from his pack. Tiseyi raised one eyebrow and looked at him expectantly. As he began dressing, he replied, "Azeria is an accomplished warrior, and I respect her. That is all. And neither does she desire me."

Tiseyi seemed to struggle with something before she finally said, "I do not believe that. She wants you. She must only accept it."

As Rezkin looked over at her, a glint of the morning's first light fell across her flawless, bronze skin. He considered that she was an attractive woman, yet she did not draw him to her as did Azeria. Still, ever since he had attempted to break the bond between them, he had felt a closeness to her, a sense of familiarity, as if she were a distant part of him. Somehow, it made him inclined to confide in her; only, regarding Azeria, he had nothing to confide.

He said, "You are reading too much into things."

Tiseyi rolled her eyes and strutted over to a table that held a pitcher and basin. She said, "You are stubborn, but I believe you will relent. No one can remain so distant from everyone. It is inhuman."

"Perhaps I am less human than previously thought."

"From what I have heard, the elves are even more sentimental than humans. You will come around. At least, I hope you do. I cannot bear to feel this coldness from you. It is disturbing."

Rezkin said nothing, and by the time he was dressed, Tiseyi had washed and transformed back into her wolf form.

Not long after the sun rose, the ship called in from port using the relay Rezkin had created. He gathered his entourage and boarded with haste. After a quick celebration of Tam's return and a debriefing, Rezkin assigned Shezar, Marlis, and Yerlin Tomwell to accompany Tam and his men back to Cael and then on to Gendishen. They were able to acquire passage to Uthrel on a Gendishen trading vessel. Farson, Jimson, Reaylin, and Nanessy, along with the Eihelvanan and the omesessas, were to accompany him to Ashai. The voyage would not be a long one, thanks to the direction of the currents and Nanessy's power over water. Rezkin had originally planned to disembark secretly near Port Manai so as to land that much closer to the King's Seat in Kaibain, but Journeyman Wesson had informed him through the relay that the Mage Academy had been sacked, and a large contingent of the king's army was moving toward northwestern Ashai. Rezkin decided to confront this contingent and hopefully contain the threat before it spilled over the border.

The first few days north of Pruar had been quiet as they only encountered a few Pruari fishing boats. The closer they got to Ashai, though, the more frequently they observed scouts. After successfully avoiding the Ashaiian warships near the port city of Cerrél on the southwestern coast, their ship continued north along the coast toward the smaller, northern city of Port Gull. Wesson had requested their presence in the small village of Benbrick that lay upriver a little more than halfway to Maylon. Rezkin did not know the significance of Benbrick, but he was willing to accommodate the would-be battle mage who had already proven himself.

Rezkin was at the railing watching the coast pass by when Farson approached.

"You have been accumulating some strange allies. Is the wolf really a woman in disguise?"

Rezkin glanced around to make sure Tiseyi had not snuck up on him. She was quite stealthy in her wolf form. When he was satisfied that she was not near, he said, "Yes and no. She is both, really."

"We should have known about the shape-shifters," Farson grumbled, mostly to himself. After a moment of silence, he sighed. "Despite your collection of allies and kingdoms, we have not made much progress on defeating Caydean."

"I disagree," said Rezkin. "It has become apparent that this war is much larger than one man sitting on a throne directing his army toward a battlefield. It began decades ago, before I was even born, and it is not about the kingdom of Ashai. Ashai is only the breeding ground for a more devious plot, one that was not Caydean's doing. I now believe that the Sen Berringish is responsible, at least he was in the beginning. It was he who brought the demons to our lands, and now Caydean has taken up his mantle. We have prevented the enemy from gaining footholds in three kingdoms, and keeping the dragon out of their hands was a major triumph. We were only lucky to have been there when we were."

Farson huffed. "Luck. I do not believe in luck."

Rezkin turned to face the man who had helped raise him. He said, "I have made the decision to learn the way of the Spirétua."

"Even if it will drive you mad?"

"Even so."

Farson was quiet for a moment. Eventually, he said, "I fear nothing in this world, not demons, not dragons, not Caydean—nothing but *you*, because I know what you are, of your capabilities. My fear was potent when I believed you to be intent on destruction, but I no longer believe that to be your cause. I do not, however, know which to fear more—you with clear intent or you with your mind addled."

"I am not the most dangerous being in the world."

Farson appeared pained as he said, "You are the most dangerous to me."

Rezkin did not know what to make of his former tutor's confession. He said, "You are a striker. It is your duty to care about the welfare of Ashai. I assure you I will acquire the maximum *Skills* available to me and do my best to see that Ashai survives this war so that it may prosper again."

Shaking his head, Farson said, "It is not the welfare of Ashai that concerns me, Rez."

"What then?"

Farson grumbled, "You could not understand." Then he turned and strode away, and Rezkin was left wondering after him. He glanced over to see Azeria watching him with a perplexed expression.

"What is it?"

"Your mentor is a strange one (*confused*). His facial expressions are contrary to the feelings he claims."

"How so?"

"He claims to fear you, yet he looks upon you as if filled with concern *for* you."

Rezkin chuckled feeling genuinely humored. "Farson? Worried *for* me? If so, it is only because he fears the consequences of my failure."

Azeria pursed her lips. "Not so. He said it was not your kingdom with which he concerns himself. I believe he loves you."

Rezkin frowned. "Have you been speaking with Nanessy?"

She looked at him curiously. "No. Why?"

"Never mind." Changing the topic, he said, "Our destination is the village of Benbrick. We shall be there in about two days' time. In the meanwhile, I shall be training with Entris. Will you join us?"

She appeared surprised that he would ask. "I am not Spirétua."

"No, but you use your power in a similar fashion. You may have some unique insight."

"Very well. If you wish it, I shall join you."

He held her gaze and said, "I do wish it."

Wesson stared at the village. It was nearly midday, and the main road into town was desolate. A shutter creaked, a dog barked, and in the distance, he could hear the racket of the mill down by the river. As he looked on, a few people left what he remembered to be the general store and entered a tavern that had been built since he had last been home.

"It looks so much smaller than I remember."

Waylen glanced his way. "It could not be any smaller. How old were you when you were last here?"

"I was twelve," said Wesson as he kicked his horse to get it moving again. He directed it down a dirt path that led away from the village center.

"Why did you leave?" asked Corporal Namm who rode behind him. Celise rode at Wesson's side, and it had taken some convincing just to get her to accept her own horse.

Wesson's shoulders tensed, and he hedged. "I had to leave. I came into my power early." He nodded down the roadway. "This is the way to my home—or, rather, what *was* my home. My mother and her husband still live here. Both of my stepsisters are married now. One lives in Vogn and the other in Maylon. I have never met them."

Waylen said, "So you have not been home since you were *twelve?* Not even to see your mother?"

Wesson shook his head. "No, it was not safe."

"I cannot say as it is any safer now," Kai grumbled from behind where he rode beside Dennick Manding.

"No, perhaps not, but that is why we are here," said Wesson. "The Torreli and Sandean forces will converge with the rebels in this vicinity, so this is most likely where Caydean's forces will attack."

"If the rebels are near, should we not have seen them by now?" said Waylen.

Kai said, "The buildup of the Ashaiian army in the central hills pushed the rebels to the west nearly a year ago. They have had plenty of time to establish a foothold in the area. I would not be surprised if the whole village was full of rebels."

"Not likely," grumbled Wesson. "The people of this village were not exactly the sort to dedicate themselves to a greater cause."

Kai said, "Is that truth speaking or resentment?"

Wesson swallowed a growl and said nothing. Although he had been left with little good to say about the village, it was not fair to disparage them *now* without cause.

Pushing aside his thoughts, Wesson focused on the ride. It was not long before his family home came into view. The land around it was mostly prairie, although the backyard butted up against the small, wooded area that lined the creek. The front gate that had been in need of mending when last he was there had been replaced and appeared to be freshly painted in white. A garden-lined path led up to the front steps that were decorated with boxes of calla lilies along each side.

Wesson dismounted and left his horse with the others who would wait outside the gate while he announced their presence. Celise, at least, understood his desire to greet his mother alone. He felt odd as he approached the front door. This was his home, the one he had shared with his mother for years following his father's death; yet he stood poised to knock as if he were merely another guest. The door opened before his knuckles struck the wood, and then Wesson was wrapped in a woman's arms. He inhaled her familiar scent as he gripped his mother tightly. She broke their embrace and leaned back to look at him as he did her. He was surprised to find that he was actually a few inches taller than she was.

A tear threatened to dip from her lashes. "My dear Wesson, look how you have grown. My boy has become a man."

Wesson took her hand from his face and pressed a kiss to it as he said, "Hello, Mother. I am filled with joy to see you well."

Her smile faltered just barely as she glanced behind him then took in his odd clothes. "What are you wearing? Should you not be wearing mage robes? Has something happened?"

He patted her hand and said, "I shall tell you of it later. I have brought guests. I hope you do not mind. We have come a long way in a short time."

"Of course," she said, waving toward the others. "Please, bring them in. I shall have cook prepare some refreshments."

Wesson smiled at remembering cook. She was a hard woman with a warm heart, and she had scolded him as a child as much as she had praised him. He had learned quickly to avoid her when she was carrying her wooden spoon.

As the others made their way to the front steps, his mother said, "I am afraid Grayth is not here right now, but he will be home this evening. I think you will like him."

This time, it was Wesson's smile that dropped. He had never met Lord Grayth Prisitus. His mother had married the man shortly after Wesson's impromptu departure from home. The union was born of a business arrangement, unlike his mother's first marriage, which had been for love. In all her letters over the years, his mother had never spoken ill of Lord Grayth, and Wesson was led to believe the man treated his mother well.

Wesson heard the patter of small, soft slippers up the pathway before he was once again wrapped in the embrace of a woman.

Wesson sighed and said, "Celise, this is my mother, Lady Urmela Prisitus."

Celise did not pause as she moved in front of him and straightened her spine. She stared down his mother as she said, "I am Celise, a matria of House Erisial. I have claimed Wesson Seth as my first consort. I greet you, Matrianera Urmela, with respect; but, if you wish to challenge my claim, you should know that I have a strong champion."

Wesson's mother stared at Celise with wide eyes. Then her gaze dropped to Celise's barely-there clothing before finding Wesson once again. Wesson could feel the heat warming his face as she avoided his mother's probing gaze. He swallowed hard and said, "This is Celise of Lon Lerésh. I do not recognize her claim, but she will not leave me be."

Celise flinched and peered up at him with pained eyes, but she merely took his hand and said nothing. A small smile crept across his mother's face, and she nodded toward Celise cordially. "It is a pleasure to meet you, Celise. I would not think of challenging your claim to my son. In fact, I think it is lovely that he has met a daring young woman such as yourself."

Wesson frowned, but Celise beamed at his mother before turning her luminous smile on him. She danced on her tiptoes as she gripped his hand tighter. Kai strode from behind and laid a heavy hand on his shoulder before gracing his mother with the courtliest bow Wesson had ever seen.

"Greetings, Lady Urmela. I am Striker Zankai Colguerun Tresdian." With a wink, he said, "Everyone calls me Kai. It is a pleasure to meet you."

"A striker?" said his mother, turning back to him. "Are you in trouble again?"

Kai raised one eyebrow at him. "What kind of trouble would you get into that your mother thinks would garner the attention of a striker?"

Wesson huffed. "Nothing." Then, ignoring the striker's mirthful gaze, he introduced Namm, Fedrin, and Dennick.

For the next couple of hours, Wesson's companions regaled his mother with tales of his least brag-worthy moments. They carefully steered away from anything that might worry her, and they had not yet mentioned anything regarding his involvement with war or kings or faraway kingdoms. His mother was a bright, well-educated woman, so she surely knew there was plenty they were not telling, but she seemed to enjoy the stories anyway. She paid particularly close attention to whatever Celise had to say, which mostly revolved around Wesson and her plans for him. Apparently, they were to have many children in their future, which also pleased his mother. Wesson was seeing his mother for the first time through the eyes of a man, rather than a boy. Where once he had seen a lady who ruled their home with unquestionable authority and an iron tenacity, he now saw a woman —one who had strength and dignity but also faults and flaws. He thought he loved her more now than he ever had.

It was near dinner time when her husband Grayth finally arrived home. Wesson was less than thrilled to meet him at first, but after a while, he realized that his years of concern had been wasted. The man was soft-spoken and considerate, and very little seemed to stir him. They were all seated around a long table on the back lawn when Kai caught Wesson's eye during a lull in the conversation.

Wesson tamped down his mounting anxiety and cleared his throat. "Mother, there is something we need to discuss, and I am afraid it is quite urgent."

She nodded knowingly. "I was wondering when you would finally get to the reason for your sudden visit."

He was momentarily taken aback. "I need a reason?"

"Son, I have not seen you in seven years. The last time I heard from you, you had just acquired a job and were traveling in the east. Now you show up out of the blue with a most unique retinue. I know you are up to something, and it must be important."

Wesson released a breath. "Right. Well, it seems fairly quiet out here, but I am sure you have heard of the turmoil in the east."

She nodded, her expression somber. Wesson did not miss how Grayth's hand wrapped around his mother's as they both looked at him. Wesson swallowed the lump in his throat and continued. "King Caydean has basically declared war on the world. He has upended the great houses, declared his own people to be enemies, and sent troops into other kingdoms."

Grayth leaned forward and rested his elbows on his knees as he stared at Wesson. The man's grey hair and soft blue eyes made him appear aged, but his stern expression and tense bearing spoke of strength. "Son—"

Wesson winced at the title.

"I need to know something right now before you say anything else." He glanced at the striker then looked back to Wesson. "Are you a rebel?"

Wesson's anxiety spiked. He had no desire for war to break out here and now in his own home with his mother stuck in the middle. He had to be strong, though. He had to show them both that he was, without a doubt, on the side of right.

He lifted his chin and said, "I am quite more than a rebel. My loyalty is to the True King of Ashai, Emperor of the Souelian; and I am the King's Mage."

His mother's hand covered her gasp, and Grayth sat back. Both continued to stare at him as though none of his companions existed. Finally, Grayth said, "The King's Mage? How can that be? You are barely more than a boy."

"I may be young, but I am powerful." He looked to his mother. "The employer I told you about nearly a year ago is the True King." He nodded toward Kai. "The striker, here, and the others all serve him.

Caydean's forces are moving this way to intercept the rebels before they can join with the Torreli and Sandean forces that are moving down the coast. They will be here in a matter of days. I came here to save my family and my home, but I will fight beside the rebels if they are willing to stand openly against Caydean."

After a moment of what appeared to be deep contemplation, Grayth slowly stood and made to leave the table. Kai also rose and, with his hand on his hilt, made it clear he was ready to put down any resistance.

"I must speak with someone," said Grayth, eyeing the striker.

"I am afraid I cannot allow that," said Kai.

"Relax," he said, glancing toward Wesson. "I have no intention of outing you to the army." After a brief pause, he added, "I am a rebel."

Grayth backed up a few steps before turning and walking toward the barn. Wesson nodded at Kai's glance, and the striker followed Grayth. Wesson's mother looked at him with trepidation.

"He answers to you?"

Wesson shrugged. "Technically, he only answers to the True King, but I was placed in charge of this mission."

"He will not hurt him, will he?"

Wesson watched as the two men led their horses from the stable and checked their tack. He shook his head. "So long as he is telling the truth, no. Did you know he was a rebel?"

"He does not speak of his business, and I do not ask, but I had my suspicions. Grayth is a good man. He can see wrong when it is before him, and what Caydean has been doing is wrong. It is abhorrent, actually. Of course, the *official* tales make his actions sound somewhat reasonable, but we hear the rumors even out here. Most people are not fooled, although there are some in town of whom you should be wary."

"Of course." He paused as his heart began to race, then he finally asked the question that had been plaguing him. "Diyah?"

His mother's gaze softened. She glanced at Celise, then said, "Wesson, you should know that Diyah is married."

Wesson's heart stuttered. Although he had suspected it, he had never truly accepted that she would not be his. "When?" he choked out.

"About three years ago. Her father insisted she marry as soon as she turned sixteen. She already has a child, and another is on the way."

Children. Diyah had children. He had never even considered that she might already have started a family. His next word was nearly as broken as his heart. "Who?"

"Wesson, we do not need to speak of this now—"

"Who?" he insisted.

"Tomlin."

Just hearing the name caused Wesson's stomach to flip. Tomlin Holcom was everything Wesson had once hoped to become. He was a good man with a golden conscience, the kind of man people naturally respected and fell into line behind when they needed a leader. He helped the needy, volunteered at the Temple of the Maker, and was slated to be the next town mayor. If Wesson had been forced to choose anyone besides himself for Diyah, it would have been Tomlin. He was surprised, though. With their age disparity, the two had never been close when he had known them, and he was amazed that Diyah's father, who was more familiar with a tankard than his daughter, had managed the match. He wondered if Diyah, herself, had arranged it.

Wesson simply nodded and hung his head. After a few minutes, Celise slid into his lap and wrapped her arms around him. Although he had not accepted her claim and was obviously mourning the loss of another woman, she had the strength to support him when he needed it. For that, at least, he respected her.

It was well after dark when Kai returned with Grayth and another man Wesson did not know. Wesson had been trying to decide how to explain to Celise that they would not be sharing the single bed in his room when he had been summoned to the study. Kai introduced the stranger as Payton de Voss.

"Payton *de Voss*?" said Wesson. He knew the name belonged to Reaylin, and he wondered if there was any relation.

"You know me?" said the man who surveyed the home as if he had never seen it. Although he had a strong bearing, his eyes were shifty, like those of a man accustomed to being watched.

Kai gave Wesson a subtle shake of his head, and Wesson cleared his throat. "Ah, no, I have only heard the name."

Payton nodded is if it were expected, but he did not pause in his perusal. Suddenly, the man's gaze met Wesson's, and it was unnerving. "I'm told you're Dark Tidings's mage."

"The True King," replied Wesson.

The man grunted. "We shall see." He had a way of speaking that was low and quiet and a bit slurred. Wesson thought if he had not been listening so intently, it would barely have been intelligible. Payton's gaze briefly dropped to Wesson's clothes then found his face again. "They said you're a battle mage. You don't dress like it. That's smart, but I'm surprised one of your station would deign to wear the clothes of a mundane."

"You have a problem with mages?" said Wesson.

"No, I don't have a problem with *them*. It's them has a problem with *me*."

"Why would that be?"

Payton scowled as if Wesson should know the answer. "'Cause I'm not *special* like you. 'Cause I'm a poor man from a poor family in a poor land. 'Cause I don't got your education or status. What other reasons does one of you need?"

"I do not think like that—"

"Of course you do. You all do. But it's me is showing you all now. The weight of this kingdom is on the shoulders of a poor mundane and thousands of others like me. Caydean don't understand. He can't. It's in his breeding. But when a better man sits the throne, the kingdom will stand strong on the backs of simple men."

Wesson narrowed his eyes at the man, an expression that did not go unnoticed. He said, "Who would this better man be? You?"

Payton abruptly barked a laugh that nearly made Wesson jump. "*Me*? A king? That would be the day. Even a simple man like me knows a king needs to be smart and cunning and knowledgeable. No, the throne belongs to men like you, men like Caydean, except *not* him because he's lost his wits. He's a cruel man with cruel means. Mayhap this Dark Tidings'll fill the void. Maybe he won't."

It finally dawned on Wesson who this man really was. "You are the leader of the rebels."

Payton nodded once. "I am."

"Why are you in Benbrick?"

"Same reason as you, I expect." Payton looked around the room and nodded at Grayth. "Well, maybe not exactly same as you. It seems you have other reasons for being here, but mine have nothing to do with family. Don't see as I have any of that left. As you know, we've been hoping to join forces with the Torreli and Sandeans. When we heard the king's forces were moving west, we vacated the hills near Maylon and settled ourselves around these smaller villages. When the king's army gets here, we'll be ready to fight alongside our new allies."

"They are only allies until they become your enemies," said Wesson. "What do you think Torrel or Sandea want to get out of this? Both will be vying for the throne, and what is left of Ashai will be torn between the two once their truce has ended."

"We won't let it get that far. We will fight *with* them, then we'll fight *against* them until a new king sits the throne."

"If there are any of you left," said Wesson. "And what did you plan to do about the throne? Were you just going to let the dukes fight it out amongst themselves?"

"The way I hear it, the seat belongs to the Duke of Wellinven."

"I doubt Lord Haden Nirius will be taking the throne—"

"No, not him. The son."

"Tieran?"

"He's the rightful heir after Prince Thresson."

"Prince Thresson is assumed dead."

"You know what they say about assumptions."

Wesson tilted his head as he looked at the man anew. "Do you know something about the missing prince?"

"Can't say as I don't. Won't say as I do," muttered the man.

"Yet you assume he will not be taking the throne."

"I know he won't. The way I see it, though, even a bad leader can't do worse than a mad one. Caydean has to go."

"You should know, then, that Tieran Nirius has sworn fealty to the one you know as Dark Tidings. He did so because it was proven that he *is*, by both blood and bond, the True King." Wesson paused as he waited for the information to sink in. Payton sounded like a simple man, but if he was truly the rebel leader, he had to be calculating and deliberate. When the man merely nodded and hummed under his breath, Wesson said, "I find it hard to believe that the rebel movement could be built on a promise of a better future without at least some idea of who would be king."

A spark lit in Payton's eyes, and Wesson thought he looked somewhat bemused. The rebel leader said, "Leaders rise and fall in war. The truth is in who survives. The right man will reveal himself before the end. If you are as powerful as they say, mayhap *you* have designs on the throne."

"*Me?* No, that is not a responsibility I would ever desire. A king must deal with realities harsher than I can stomach."

Payton's expression soured, and his gaze turned hard. "Those don't sound like the words of a powerful, tried and tested battle mage."

"It is no secret that I abhor violence and especially killing," said Wesson. "And I have those feelings *because* I have been tried and tested."

"Hmm, we shall see," the man muttered again. Then he looked toward Kai who was leaning against the wall by the door. "Your intel is a bit behind," he said. "My sources claim Caydean's army will be here tomorrow."

"Tomorrow!" cried Wesson. "That cannot be. I was sure we made better time than that."

Payton turned back to him. "It seems you were only just ahead of them. This home is surrounded by my people. We were concerned that you were forward scouts, but I am convinced that you are, at least, not with Caydean."

Wesson looked to Kai, and the striker nodded. It seemed he had been aware of the rebel forces surrounding the house but had not thought it important to inform Wesson.

Payton took a few steps toward the doorway then turned back. "We plan to hit them from the shadows. We will pick off the smaller groups on the fringes and then attack from the rear once the Torreli and Sandeans begin their frontal assault."

"We cannot wait for foreign forces to arrive," Wesson said in dismay. "Benbrick will be inundated by then."

"We don't have a choice. Our numbers are limited. We count a number of mages amongst us but could use your help protecting our people from mage attacks."

"Mages? Where did they come from?"

"Some have been dodging the draft for months. Others stayed just ahead of the army after the Mage Academy was attacked. We even have a few trained battle mages who refused to serve Caydean."

"I had no idea," said Wesson. "I would like to meet with them —tonight."

Payton nodded. "I figured you would. The striker seems to think you'll be a good leader for them. You'll give them someone to unite behind. I'm only trusting you because Grayth trusts you. If not for him, I'd have killed you before you knew we were coming."

Something dark stirred within Wesson's chest as he rankled at the threat. Through gritted teeth, he said, "You would have failed and died for trying." The heat with which he spoke surprised him almost as much as the words.

Payton grinned. "Now that sounds more like a battle mage."

23

Frisha could not say how long they had been traveling, whether days or weeks. She spent most of her time tied up in the back of the wagon beneath the tarp, and she did not know which direction they were going or their destination. The one time she had asked how much longer it would be, she had received a slap to the face from one of the men. The mistress had ignored her altogether since they had left the coastal safe house, and Frisha had the impression that if she made too much trouble, they would dispense with her. She figured they had no reason to keep her alive now that she had been replaced with an exact duplicate. She found herself having sympathy for Brandt's plight after having been copied. She wished she had been kinder to him, or at least more understanding. It was not Brandt's fault that he had a duplicate. At least *his* duplicate had not been found to be a threat. Frisha worried for her unwitting companions, and her jealousy reared its ugly head whenever she thought of Tieran with that other woman, the *golem*.

The bright light of day was suddenly snuffed, and Frisha was cast into darkness beneath the tarp. The transition had been too quick for a transition to night, so she figured they must be in the shade. The sounds changed, and the creak of the wagon and clomp of hooves echoed around her. Were they in a tunnel? Perhaps a cave? Chill air ruffled the tarp, and Frisha shivered. She tried to swallow, but her throat was parched. Her tongue and lips equally had no moisture, and her tears had dried up days prior. Wherever they were, it was windy and arid.

The tarp was ripped from the back of the wagon, and Frisha struggled to sit up. Her aching body, which was low on sustenance as well as warmth and moisture, refused to cooperate. One of the men jumped into the wagon and dragged her by her bound hands to the end where another man grabbed her and threw her over his shoulder.

Frisha's eyes slowly adjusted to the dark. It turned out they *were* in a cave. Small sconces lined one wall, which lit a pathway farther into the cavern. The mistress had already started down the pathway when one of the men called to her.

"Mistress, what do we do with her?"

The woman could not be bothered to stop, but she called back as she continued down the pathway. "She stinks. Give her a bath, then put her in the cell."

The man grumbled under his breath as he moved down the pathway. He turned into a side chamber and settled Frisha on her feet. Frisha's mind spun as she tried to get her bearings. After removing her restraints, he pointed to a half-barrel filled with water and said, "Get in there."

Frisha looked at the water longing for a drink but abhorring the idea of bathing in front of the man.

"Now," he barked, "before I throw you in."

Frisha jumped then stepped onto a stool and slid into the frigid water without removing the sack dress she had been given upon kidnapping. The man handed her a cake of soap, which she used liberally to scrub her hair and body. As she did so, the man rummaged around in a trunk to one side. Eventually, he pulled out a simple, homespun dress that was only marginally better than what she was wearing. He handed her a towel and the dress then stepped into the main corridor with a grumble about stuck-up women.

Frisha dried herself and donned the drab, grey dress, but she had no shoes or coat, and she continued to shiver as the man called out for her to follow him. Frisha ran her fingers through her hair as she stumbled behind the man. The cave was not like the caves she had visited on the coast with their dripping stalactites, stalagmites, pools, and columns. This one was dry with naturally smooth, rounded walls and corners. Besides the barrel in which she had bathed, Frisha saw no other water. She had never seen anything like it, and under other circumstances, she might have thought it beautiful.

The reality was anything but, though. They came to a chamber that was only half covered by ceiling, the rest open to the sky. Bars had been placed along one side of the rounded chamber together with a locked gate. The walls, the bars, and the gate were all covered with runes. Inside the cell were a few nooks with blankets, a couple of wooden benches, a water barrel, and several buckets, but Frisha saw no prisoners. Frisha's guide said something to a guard who sat outside the cell, and the woman moved to open the door.

As the keys clanked in the lock, the guard said, "Stay back or I'll have them beat you again."

Frisha was confused for a moment since she could not see to whom the woman was speaking. Then a figure unfolded from a shadowed corner in the cell as Frisha was thrust inside. The gate slammed behind her, and the keys jangled again as the lock was secured.

Suddenly, the guards were no longer the threat that most concerned her. Someone was *in* the cell with her, and it was obviously a man. The large figure moved into the light as he neared. He wore ragged clothes that looked as if they had once been quite fine. The dark hair on his head and face had grown long and appeared choppy as if trimmed quickly with a knife. The way he stood with poise gave him an air of dignity that belied his unkempt appearance.

Frisha backed away as the man closed the distance between them. The man glanced toward where the guards had once stood, but they were gone now. He returned his hazel gaze to Frisha and then bowed.

"Milady, please do not be fearful of me. You will come to no harm by *my* hand. Allow me to introduce myself. I am Thresson."

Frisha's eyes widened, and her mouth dropped. "Thresson? *Prince* Thresson?"

"Ah, I am remembered. One and the same, I am afraid."

"But you have been missing for almost two *years!*"

"Has it been that long? It seems I have been here for an eternity. And your name, milady?"

"Frisha. Frisha Souvain-Marcum."

"Marcum? As in General Marcum?"

"Yes, I am his niece and heir. At least, I *was.* I'm not sure there is anything to inherit now."

"Then I am in good company. Welcome to my humble abode. Please, make yourself comfortable. Choose any seat you like. I have a feeling we will be here for a while."

Frisha gave the prince an awkward curtsey then moved away from the bars. She slid down to sit against one wall as Thresson sat opposite her on the ground.

"It is good to have someone to talk to," he said. "I have been alone here for too long."

"But you are a mage. Can you not use your power to free yourself?"

He smiled sadly. "No, I am afraid not." He motioned toward the inscribed bars that made up one wall of their cell then pointed toward the walls that were adorned with similar symbols. "The runes prevent me from accessing my vimara in here. I cannot cast." He was quiet for a moment, then he said, "I have so many questions. What has been happening in the world? I know only what I hear from *them.*" He tipped his head toward where the guards had exited. "No, first, tell me how you came to be here."

"It was a trick," said Frisha as she went on to explain how she had been replaced by the golem. "What about you? Everyone out there thinks you're dead. What happened?"

Thresson released a breath then squinted up toward the sky that could be seen through a hole in the ceiling. "I had escaped at first, or so I thought. One of the strikers at the palace warned me of Caydean's intention to have me killed. He got me out of the palace. I went willingly, of course, but it turned out it was a ruse. The striker was loyal to Caydean, and I had been lured into a trap, same as you. At least they did not bother to replace me. Perhaps they did not have the means to do so at the time. I cannot imagine how terrible it would be to have someone else living my life, fooling everyone I know."

Frisha swallowed as tears threatened to spill over her lashes. "I am trying not to think about it, but it's impossible. What terrible things will she do in my name, in my body? People will think *I* am doing them. Even if I could escape from here and prove that she is not me, they will never look at me the same. She will ruin me."

Thresson reached over and took Frisha's hand in his own, giving it a squeeze. "Perhaps someday you will have the chance to redeem yourself. Until then, try not to think about it. It will only drive you mad."

"Is that how you deal with it all? With *this*?" She motioned toward the cave around them.

Thresson gave her a sad smile. "When I was a young child, Caydean would do horrible things to me. Sometimes he would inflict injuries, but most of the time it was only my pride that suffered. Even then, I knew that he was not worthy of my regard. I vowed to never let him beat me, to never surrender. So *this*, this is one more trial I must endure. I will never let him win."

Wesson paced in the shadows just beyond the torchlight as he looked up at the white columns bathed in moonlight. The mayor's home was the largest building in Benbrick as it was also used for several other functions. It seemed that this mansion, as stately as one could expect to find in such a small village, was now home to not only the mayor but to his protégé and his protégé's child and wife—a wife named

Diyah. Wesson had for so many years longed to see her, but these were not the circumstances about which he had dreamt.

He released the caramel-colored strand of hair he had been tugging and wiped his moist hands on his grey robes that he had donned for the occasion. Kai had pestered him to wear his battle mage apparel, but Wesson refused. He still feared the darker power that gripped him every time he thought of something happening to his mother or friends. He was certain that if he let it loose, it would destroy more than his enemies—it would destroy *him.*

"Ready?" said Kai who stepped up beside him.

Wesson inhaled a sharp breath as a soft hand slid into his own. He glanced down at Celise on his other side and said, "You should not be here. It could be dangerous."

She looked at him with a smile too innocent for a Leréshi and said, "Do not worry, my Wesson. The striker will protect us."

Kai chuckled and said, "She still does not know what you really are, does she?"

"Does anyone?" Wesson mumbled, and Kai looked at him thoughtfully.

"Perhaps you are right, but I think Rezkin knows. He chose you for a reason."

"I cannot see how. I have done so little for him."

Kai rubbed a hand over his beard and said, "I do not believe that to be true. I think you ground him."

Wesson looked at him with wide eyes. "*Ground* him? I am about as far from grounded as a person can get. I am a mess inside."

Kai smirked. "You balance each other." Then his expression sobered, and he took a step forward. "Let us get on with this."

Beyond the grand entry of the mayor's home were multiple rooms connected directly rather than by a central corridor. They first passed through a sitting room, then an office, then a smoking room, then into a place the butler referred to as the great hall, although it was not much larger than any of the other rooms. The difference was that this room was empty save for a few narrow tables along the perimeter and a half dozen high-backed chairs pressed against the walls. Gathered in a cluster at one end of the room were sixteen mages dressed in the robes and panels indicative of each individual's status. Two mages wearing black stood to one side, and Wesson knew these to be the battle mages. Only one wore the silver-trimmed, black panels of a natural battle mage, the silver indicating an affinity for nocent power. The other wore grey panels with brown and blue trim indicating he was a *trained* battle mage with crystallis and aquian affinities. The quality and style of their panels indicated that they were both journeymen.

Wesson, flanked by Kai and Celise, moved to the center of the room where Payton awaited him. The rebel leader cleared his throat, and despite his gruff voice, the sound easily carried to every corner. "Everyone, this is Mage Wesson Seth, the one I told you about."

Wesson said, "It is Journeyman."

Payton gave him a disparaging look and turned back to the crowd that was fraught with whispers. "He claims to be king's mage to the emperor of the Souelian."

There were several gasps in the crowd, and he heard more than one person mutter *destroyer*. A dark-haired, olive-skinned woman stepped forward, and the knowledge in her gaze belied her apparent youthful age. She said, "This journeyman is only a boy, and he is dressed as a generalist. Why should we follow him?"

Payton shrugged and stepped aside, presumably to allow Wesson to make his own case. Before Wesson could speak, though, Celise stepped in front of him. "I am Celise d'Erisial, and I am Wesson's matria. You will show him respect. He is a good man." He knew her aggressive stance was meant to be intimidating, but he doubted anyone was focused on her words with so much skin exposed. Her dress may have been acceptable in Lon Lerésh, but the more conservative people of Ashai were unlikely to take her seriously, just as they did not take *him* seriously.

Wesson exchanged a look with Kai who took Celise's hand and pulled her back behind Wesson. With a force of will, Wesson kept himself from fidgeting as he took in the disapproving stares. He said, "Your concerns are valid, Mage Regala." The woman's eyes widened as she was seemingly surprised that he knew her name. He nodded. "Yes, I know you. I remember you from when I tested at the academy."

She narrowed her eyes at him as if trying to remember. Then she nodded. "Yes, I recall it was a less than stellar performance."

Wesson nodded. "That is true. I tested using constructive power, but the truth is, my greatest natural affinities are in nocent and pyris."

"Impossible," said Regala. "If that were true, you would not have been capable of wielding constructive power."

"No," said the other natural battle mage in the room as she stepped forward to join Regala. She was a young woman with auburn hair and dark eyes set above a strong nose. She said, "I remember you now. You came to the Battle Mage Academy about a year and a half ago. Rumor said it was you who decimated the central tower and the land to the west."

Wesson nodded again. "That is also true. I was assured, though, that the battle master was going to do everything in his power to make sure people forgot me."

The natural battle mage smiled. "The *official* story was that it was an earthquake, but anyone who was there at the time will never forget the truth. The rumors were so rampant, the battle master threatened to expel anyone caught spreading them." She turned to the others and said, "He is obviously in disguise." She turned back to him. "That is smart considering how close Caydean's forces are."

Wesson exhaled sharply. "I do not ask that you follow me. I ask that you follow the True King, the Emperor of the Souelian. He is coming."

"Here?" shouted someone in the crowd.

"Yes, he will be here soon, and he is prepared to lead us all to victory against Caydean's forces."

"How will he do that?" said another. "One man cannot defeat an army."

"It is not just one man," said Wesson. "He has his own people, and he will fight alongside the rebels and *you*, if you will accept him. Look, I have seen his proof. He *is* the rightful heir to the throne of Ashai; and, truth be told, he cannot be worse than Caydean."

There were a number of nods and grunts as people agreed with the last sentiment. One man said, "I heard that he sacked Gendishen. He killed the king!"

He was followed by another who claimed Rezkin had used some kind of power over the mind to force King Moldovan of Ferélle to turn over his throne.

"He seduced the Leréshi queen," said a third, "and now he is their king as well."

"He cannot be trusted," said a male voice.

"No, don't you see?" said the first. "He was powerful enough to claim three other kingdoms. Perhaps he *can* defeat Caydean."

Wesson did not attempt to correct their assumptions about Rezkin since they had reached an advantageous conclusion. Still, Regala stared at him with a distrustful gaze. She crossed her arms and raised her voice above the others. "None of that explains why we should follow *you*, though, *Journeyman*."

"Does it not?" called a loud, familiar voice from the doorway.

Wesson spun on his heel to meet the gaze of a man he respected as a father. "Master Ikestrius," he said.

Ikestrius nodded in greeting then strode forward to stand beside Wesson facing the crowd. His short, black robes and loose, black pants were pristine, as usual, as were his grey panels that bore white, blue, and brown stripes on the trim. Ikestrius's gaze was wise yet slightly unnerving as he stared at Wesson. Then he said, "It is good to see you again, Journeyman. You have not grown."

As a smile stretched across his former master's face, Wesson ducked his head. "No, unfortunately not," he muttered. "But I have changed."

Ikestrius took in Wesson's grey robes then said, "Perhaps, but not enough if you intend to lead this group."

"But now you are here," Wesson blurted. "*You* would be a better leader."

Ikestrius slowly shook his head. "No, I do not know this emperor of whom you speak so highly. Besides, in sheer power, you are the superior mage, here. I can see in your eyes that you have gained experience in our time apart. I look forward to hearing the stories." Then Ikestrius turned to the crowd of mages. "You know who I am, but you may not know that Wesson, here, was my student for six years. In that time, I came to know him to be an honest, forthright individual. He is young, true, but he is also compassionate and knowledgeable. He possesses an unparalleled power to be revered and, more importantly, feared. If he says the emperor is our True King, then I am inclined to believe him. Either way, I guarantee you do not want to be his opposition."

The other mages looked at Wesson again, this time with more thought. Regala's lips were pursed as her gaze roved over him appraisingly. He knew she could not see his power, but to him it looked as if she were trying. She said, "So you think we should follow him out of fear?"

Ikestrius huffed. "Have you heard nothing I have said, Mage Regala? You should follow him because he is deserving of your respect *and* fear."

Wesson could not remove his gaze from Ikestrius as the man spoke such words in support of him. He had never known his master to be forthcoming with praise. It was so uncharacteristic that Wesson almost wondered if the man had a hidden agenda. Then Wesson felt guilty for thinking so cynically of his former master when the man had just honored him with such high praise.

Wesson was roused from his thoughts by a commotion at the door. A second crowd of people were crowding through the narrow entry, some of whom were being pushed from behind by someone trying to get to the front. The newcomers fanned out at the opposite end of the room, which seemed to be shrinking by the second. As Wesson's gaze traversed the angry and disgruntled faces, he nearly groaned aloud. All the anxiety he had been somewhat successfully subduing since returning to his mother's home returned with a vengeance. His stomach lurched, and he was forced to swallow the bile that surged up his throat. For a moment, Wesson was not the emperor's battle mage, honored by his companions and feared by his enemies. He was a small boy, lost and scared as he ran from the mob who would hang him in the square for the entire town to see. He was a killer, slaughterer of lambs and boys, wearer of blood and decimated flesh.

The men who had been pushing through the crowd were finally revealed as they crossed the open expanse to meet Wesson in the space between the two groups. The first man's steps were large and determined as he closed the distance. One arm was raised in a sign of aggression while the other hand yanked a sword free from its scabbard. Wesson had been around enough warriors by then to know that the man did not know how to hold a sword properly, but that did not deter him. He looked as though he would eagerly take Wesson's head from his body, and Wesson could not really blame him. It was only the second man's grip on his arm that kept him from plowing into Wesson. They stopped only a couple of paces from him, and Wesson knew the threat was real. He felt no shame in erecting a protective ward around himself and Celise who still stood near Kai behind him.

"You!" shouted Onus Willam. "You killed my boy, and now I will finally have justice."

The second man, Dowen Ambs, placed his hand on Master Willam's shoulder and tried to speak sense into him. "Onus, he is a mage now. He'll kill you."

Master Willam shrugged off his friend and shouted, "He's guilty! He needs to hang!"

Several people in the crowd shouted their agreement, and Wesson felt as though he had been punched in the gut. These were the townspeople, the people of Benbrick, the people with whom he had grown up. To hear them calling once again for his death was disheartening, to say the least. Their hateful words were the echoes of his nightmares, and Wesson's guilt kept him silent. He glanced up at Master Ikestrius who raised a brow with a look that said enough. Wesson was on his own. He was no longer a child, and these people held no authority over him. He had considered innumerable times what he might say if he were ever confronted by Moulden's parents, yet now that he was in the thick of it, his mind was blank. He *had* killed Moulden, and no amount of reasoning would change that fact.

Master Willam's sword glanced off the enchanted barrier that separated him from Wesson. "Have you nothing to say while you hide behind your magic shield? Come out and fight like a man, you murderer!"

Wesson's spine straightened as angry words began to filter through his mind. He said, "It is true. I did kill Moulden; but I am not a murderer. Your son was a bully of the worst kind. He *and* his two friends, I might add," Wesson said with a glare for Master Ambs, "attacked *me*, and Moulden might have killed Diyah if I had not stopped him." Wesson looked past Master Willam to the townspeople. "If my power had not presented itself then, we might *both* be dead. You all know who Moulden was. He enjoyed terrorizing others, especially those who were too small or weak to put up a fight." He looked back to Master Willam. "Moulden's fate was sealed by his own actions."

Master Willam slammed his sword against the barrier again and said, "He was only a boy!" This time tears filled his eyes, and his chest heaved as if he had been fighting this battle for the past seven years.

"For that, I am sorry," said Wesson. "He did not have a chance to better himself, and that will always weigh heavily on me. I did not choose to kill him, and I would not have if I had control of the power. That lack of control was not my fault, though, and neither were the circumstances that lead to your son's death."

Master Willam seethed and gripped his sword harder before throwing it across the room to clatter against the wall and onto the floor. Then he stormed out the door with Master Ambs on his heels.

Wesson looked to the rest of the crowd. They had gone silent, but their stares spoke volumes. This time it was Master Ambs's son, Bryce, who stepped forward. Bryce and Siguey had both been damaged in the incident that had taken their friend Moulden's life, and they had been lucky to survive. Bryce had apparently acquired a limp, though, and Wesson wondered if that had also been his fault.

Bryce looked down at his feet as he stood with his hands clasped behind his back. When he looked up, it was not anger that stirred his features but sorrow. "Wesson—I mean Lord Seth, er, Mage ... ah, I wanted to say I'm sorry. What happened, I know it wasn't your fault.

Master Willam knows it too." He glanced back at the crowd. "We all know it. We were wrong to attack you and Diyah. Maybe I shouldn't say this, but I'm glad you came into your power then. Moulden was out of control. We all were. I've thought a lot about what happened." He ducked his head and blinked a few times before finishing. "You're not wrong when you say we might have killed you."

Wesson did not know what to say. He had never heard Bryce speak anything but a nasty remark with a sneer. It had been seven years, though, and much had changed in that time. Wesson knew he had changed, but he felt most of that change had happened in the last thirty seconds. Bryce's words released something inside him. The terrible, nagging guilt that had followed him from his home snapped like a thread leaving behind an empty pit devoid of feeling. Wesson knew it needed to be filled, but he had nothing with which to fill it. He thanked Bryce and then the silence stretched on before it began to fill with the voices of the townspeople who had begun to discuss the happenings amongst themselves.

A soft voice called to him, "Wess," and he was filled with warmth and not a small amount of sadness.

He looked up to see a beautiful young woman coming toward him. Her strawberry blonde hair was tied back in a loose braid, and her brilliant blue eyes drew him into their emotion-filled depths. She carried on her hip a small child with pale yellow locks and bright blue eyes like her mother's. The child's legs wrapped around her middle just above a protruding belly where he knew she carried another of her children.

Wesson immediately dropped the shield ward. His mouth went dry, but he managed to whisper, "Diyah."

She smiled sweetly then looked at Bryce. Bryce nodded toward Wesson then backed into the crowd. Diyah returned her attention to Wesson and said, "You look good."

"You more so," he said, and he realized he was staring. He cleared his throat and said, "I never heard from you."

Her smile fell. "I-I didn't know where to find you."

He felt the blood drain from his face. "I wrote to you every week."

Her expression was troubled as she said, "Wesson, I haven't heard from you since that day we went to the market. I didn't receive any letters." Then tears dripped onto her cheeks, and she said, "My father. It had to be him. He probably burned them." She wiped her face and then looked at him curiously. "What did they say?"

Wesson's mouth hung open, and he quickly closed it. How could he sum up seven years' worth of his heart's confessions in only a few words? Just then they were joined by the last person Wesson wanted to see at that moment. Tomlin Holcom strode up and put his arm around Diyah. His smile was just as broad and welcoming as it had always been, and he greeted Wesson with enthusiasm.

"If it isn't my favorite mage and lord," said Tomlin. He held out his hand and said, "It is really good to see you again."

Wesson swallowed hard and reached out to take Tomlin's hand. "Of course, it is good to see you, too, Tomlin."

"Hey, Wess, I've wanted to thank you so many times for saving my girl." He looked down at Diyah with admiration then stroked his daughter's golden curls. "I don't know where I'd be right now without them."

Diyah grinned and pushed Tomlin playfully. "Oh, you'd be right here with some other girl."

Wesson thought he might be sick as Tomlin leaned down and kissed Diyah's cheek. "Never," he said. "There is only you."

Just then, Wesson felt a pressure on his back, and he looked down to find Celise with her arm wrapped around him. Tomlin's eyes widened, and he appeared noticeably uncomfortable as he took in Celise's appearance.

"Hello," said Celise. "I am Celise. I am Wesson's matria."

Diyah glanced between Wesson and Celise then said, "Matria?"

Wesson groaned and said, "It is, ah—"

"I am what you call … his wife," said Celise.

Wesson started, "No, I—"

But Tomlin did not wait for him to get far. He slapped a hand on Wesson's shoulder and said, "Congratulations, Wess. You've done well."

Diyah elbowed Tomlin in the ribs but smiled. "Yes, congratulations. I'm very happy for you."

Wesson simply groaned and looked at Celise. She gazed at him with such sweet sincerity and innocence that he did not have the heart to argue in front of them all. Her finger tipped his nose, then she abruptly kissed his cheek. Wesson felt heat spread from the spot, and he knew his face had turned red.

Diyah handed the child in her arms to Tomlin and stretched her back. Then she said, "About the letters?"

Wesson shifted his feet and glanced at Celise. Given the circumstances, he decided it was best not to divulge the romantic sentiments. Instead, he focused on that which had plagued him the most over the years. "I, ah, had hoped for your forgiveness."

She looked at him curiously. "Forgiveness for what?"

He wiped his sweaty palms on his robes. "For the lamb."

Diyah grimaced. "That was terrible, wasn't it? I'll never forget it, but forgiveness is not necessary, Wess. You didn't mean to do it. I always knew that."

Surprise tore through him so savagely it took with it an enormous weight. Between Bryce's words and Diyah's forgiveness, the heavy guilt that had held Wesson back was abruptly released. He felt truly free for the first time. As he looked at Diyah now, with her child and husband fueling her smile, Wesson suddenly felt as though things were the way they were meant to be, and the curse of the darkness inside him was far less daunting.

Diyah abruptly grabbed Wesson's hand and squeezed with both her own. "Wess, I am afraid. They say the king's army is coming *here*, that we are going to be attacked. I have always had faith in you. Please, you're the smartest person I know, and you are a mage now. I believe you have the power to save us. Will you do it?"

Wesson gazed into her fearful eyes and said, "I will do everything in my power to keep you and your family safe. You have my word." Then she smiled at him, and the world could once again breathe.

A rising din drew Wesson's attention back to what was happening in the the room. While the two groups filling the space that seemed to have shrunk did not merge, those within the groups mingled amongst themselves. Wesson could tell by the frequent glances in his direction that most of their conversations revolved around him. Over the next several minutes, the mage group seemed to split into two factions. The smaller one formed around Mage Regala who was speaking with Ikestrius, while the larger included the two battle mages. Wesson thought he should be anxious as he awaited their decision, but in fact he felt quite calm. Somehow, knowing that Diyah did not hate him and that most of the townspeople did not blame him had alleviated most of Wesson's fears.

Wesson stood a little taller as the natural battle mage approached. She said, "I am sorry we were not properly introduced. I am Journeyman Elantra Dewin, and I am at your service." She waved to the group of mages behind her. "They have also decided to follow you." With a grin, she said, "Despite the battle master's efforts, your reputation precedes you, Journeyman Seth."

Wesson maintained a professional bearing as he nodded appreciatively. "Thank you, Journeyman Dewin. I appreciate your faith in me."

"You're welcome, and, please, call me Elantra. My brother is Journeyman Dewin." Her expression became solemn. "He chose the other side."

"I am sorry to hear that. Perhaps we will be able to change his mind."

She shook her head sadly. "I doubt it. He practically worships Battle Mage Rhone. He called me a traitor when I ran from the academy."

Wesson was saved from the need to say something that did not sound trite when Mage Regala approached. She said, "We have been discussing some of your feats. I had no idea you were the one to deal with the ship in Maylon."

"That was *you*?" said Elantra.

"Be that as it may," continued Regala, we will not put our services under the leadership of a journeyman. Battle Mage Ikestrius assures us that, despite your youth, you are worthy of the title of mage should you accept it. If you want to be our leader, you will do so immediately."

Wesson took a deep breath, then reached into his pocket. He withdrew a small, gold disc. It was a token given to a journeyman upon being raised to the status of mage. This particular disc had been given unto him by Reader Kessa while she breathed her dying breaths. He held the disc in his open palm for Mage Regala and the others to see. When Wesson explained when and how he had come by the disc, she nodded her head.

"Very well, I recognize Reader Kessa's assertion that you have earned the rank, Mage Seth. If anyone could be sure of such a thing, it was she. We shall go over our plans when we see you on the morrow at dawn."

Wesson said nothing and only nodded. As Mage Regala and the other mages filed out of the room, Elantra looked at Wesson curiously. "If you already had that,"—she nodded toward the disc in his hand—"why did you not use the title?"

He shook his head. "I did not endure the normal trials. It was bestowed upon me during the worst of circumstances. I did not feel that I was worthy."

"And you do now?"

He tilted his head in thought. He was still not completely sure that he had earned the title, but he also did not feel guilty for owning it. He said, "I do not feel that I am *un*worthy of it."

Wesson felt a tug on his hand and turned to find Celise smiling at him. He was suddenly struck with how beautiful she was. It was as though he was seeing her for the first time, and he was mesmerized. Her barely-there green top and skirt hugged every luscious curve, and her mahogany mane of thick, wavy tresses framed her perfect heart-shaped face. The way the natural candlelight reflected in her intelligent eyes had him spellbound. With a sharp inhale, Wesson was struck with the realization that this brilliant, inviting smile was reserved only for him. He had always known that Celise was attractive, but he could not fathom how he had never noticed just how gorgeous this woman was before now.

"Come, my Wesson. You have many worries, but we will enjoy tonight together."

For once, Wesson had no desire to turn her down.

The sun shone brightly as it crested the horizon. The ground was damp with frost, and the air had the crisp bite of late autumn. Wesson stepped through the back door to the kitchen and smiled as Cook handed him a hot cup of coffee.

"Thank you," he said to her. "You are a lifesaver."

Cook patted him on the arm and rolled her eyes. "You are as petulant this morning as always."

Wesson frowned and growled, "I am not petulant. I am sleep deprived."

Cook cackled brightly as she went back to preparing their breakfast. "Whose fault is that, hmm? Will you be blaming that cute little wife of yours?"

"She is not my wife," he mumbled.

"Oh? She had best be your wife after all the ruckus you made last night." She leveled him with a stare, and Wesson could not help the blush that formed.

Kai entered the room with a bark. "If Celise is your wife, does that not make Rezkin your father-in-law?"

Wesson groaned. "Please, not you, too."

Kai's grin lasted only a second longer before he became serious. "We got word this morning from the scouts. The first wave of the Ashaiian forces will be here in a matter of hours. A second contingent is not far behind."

Wesson's eyes widened. "*Two* contingents? Why so many?"

Kai shrugged. "I guess they want to make sure no one survives. We also got word that a galleon has docked at the river. I expect that will be Rezkin. I have sent someone to fetch him."

Cook pushed a plate in front of Wesson and pointed to the small kitchen table. "Sit," she said as she placed another plate in Kai's hands. "Who is this Rezkin?" she said. "Your father-in-law."

Wesson's mother entered the kitchen on the heels of Cook's question. "Yes, Wesson, why is he coming here?" said Urmela.

"Firstly, he is *not* my father-in-law. Secondly, he is the emperor of the Souelian, True King of Ashai."

Urmela's face went pale. "The emperor is coming *here*? Today?" She shook her head. "Oh no, Wesson, we are not ready for such an esteemed visitor. He cannot come here."

"Do not worry, Mother. Rezkin does not expect or care for all that pomp and foolery. He is as much at home in the stables as he is at court."

"Surely not. You said he is the son of King Bordran and Queen Lecillia. He should be used to the fanfare."

"I told you, he was not raised like that. He has had an *unusual* upbringing that even *I* do not understand. All will be well."

24

R ezkin's gaze roved over the quaint homestead. It was an attractive dwelling that was larger and more refined than the others he had seen in the area, and it had a peacefulness to which Rezkin was unaccustomed. It did not surprise him that this was the place from which the journeyman had originated. Someone so steeped in goodness and right had to come from a place like this. The world outside this home had a hardness that, Rezkin knew, had tried to bury the journeyman. Wesson was strong, though, and he had prevailed in spite of his hardships.

Once in the yard, Rezkin dismounted and passed his reins to Kai who greeted him with a salute befitting the striker. He introduced Kai to the Eihelvanan and Tiseyi, although the striker seemed confused about why he was introducing a wolf. Rezkin figured he could get into that later. He glanced around the yard before heading for the group standing outside the back door. Wesson stood with a wellbred couple who were in their middle years. He assumed these to be the journeyman's mother and stepfather, and he was not disappointed upon introduction.

"Pardon me, but I cannot believe the king is here at my home," said Lady Urmela. "It is such an honor to have you here."

"Thank you. I am honored to be here," said Rezkin, swiping his cloak to the side as he offered her a courtly bow. He wore his black Dark Tidings armor over a tunic that was embroidered along the trim with green and gold lightning bolts, and his long, black cloak hung like a regal cape behind him.

Urmela preened as she glanced up at her husband who seemed a bit more discerning—or perhaps *distrusting*. He bowed politely, but his hard eyes and quiet disposition indicated to Rezkin that the man was not fully convinced of his purported position.

Urmela's expression changed as she turned back to him. "They said Caydean's forces are nearly here. How close are they?"

Rezkin did not get a chance to answer because another man took his words.

"I can answer that," said a tall, rough-looking man who strode up from the pathway. "Looks like they'll be passing by a half day's walk to the east of here near the ruins of Garten Knoll. Hopefully none will venture this way." The man came to stand only a few feet from Rezkin, and he did not offer a respectful greeting of any sort. Instead, he held out his hand, as if between equals, and said, "I'm Payton de Voss. I hear your name is Rezkin."

Rezkin was not fooled by the man's nonchalance. His carriage was a matter of pride but also a test of sorts. In the man's pale gaze, Rezkin could see the fear riding his mind hard, yet his gruff voice did not quaver. Rezkin did not take the man's hand. Instead, he waited as Farson and Kai moved in to stand on either side of the man with swords drawn.

Farson growled, "You will respect your king. Kneel now or I will make you."

Payton met the striker's hard gaze but eventually dropped his eyes. Just then Reaylin approached. She stopped with wide eyes only a few paces from the group. "Daddy?"

Payton's head swung her way, and the shock that stole across his face was genuine. "Reaylin? Y-you're alive!" He held his arms open, and she ran into his embrace to grip him tightly. "I thought you were d—I thought the worst, my girl. Where have you been?"

When Reaylin finally did speak, her words came out in a rush. "I'm here, Daddy. I'm sorry. I shouldn't have run away like that, but I didn't think you'd let me go. I went to join the army, but they wouldn't have me."

Payton abruptly pulled back, and holding her firmly by the shoulders, he growled, "The army? Why would you join Caydean's army?"

She shook her head as tears filled her eyes. "No, it wasn't like that."

Payton held up his handing stalling Reaylin's explanation. He looked to Rezkin and said, "Would you please excuse us? I have not seen my daughter in years, and we have some things to discuss."

Rezkin was not particularly inclined to grant leave to Payton, but he could see the discomfort Reaylin was experiencing plainly written on her face. He nodded, and the two moved several paces away. Even so, their excited voices carried, and he was able to hear most of their conversation.

Payton muttered something too low to hear, then Reaylin said, "I was going to spy on them. I was going to be your man on the inside, you know?"

Payton hugged her tightly to his chest again and said, "That was a terrible idea. I wish you had told me. I wouldn't have let you go."

This time it was Reaylin who pulled back. She stomped her foot and said, "See, Daddy? That is *exactly* why I didn't tell you. You have never accepted me as a warrior." She crossed her arms over her chest. "You spent all your time training with your rebel soldiers and never had time for me, just like you never had time for *her*. You think I'm weak like mother."

Payton's eyes widened. "You think your mother was *weak*?"

"She *was* weak, but I am nothing like her. You need to open your eyes and see who I've become."

Payton raised a finger. "Now listen here, young lady. Your mother was one of the strongest people I've ever known. She wasn't a warrior or a soldier, but she was strong of will and mind. She was a healer, and she died helping those who needed her."

Reaylin's eyes widened, and her jaw dropped. "Momma was a healer?"

Payton's expression turned from one of fury to guilt. "She was. I'm sorry I've never spoken of her, but the loss was just … it was too much. I threw myself into the cause so I wouldn't have to think about it. I guess I wasn't thinking about you, too. I'm sorry for that." He inhaled sharply and straightened. "But I never thought she was weak, and I don't think *you're* weak. You don't need to run off with some harebrained scheme to prove yourself to me or anyone else. There's no telling what kind of trouble you'll find."

Reaylin chewed on her lip as her gaze darted to the people around her then settled on Rezkin. She gave him a tentative smile then turned back to her father. She said, "I think it's too late for that. I have so much to tell you, but now isn't the time. You, um, might want to give Rezkin a little more respect. He's scary skilled beyond your imagination, and he really is the True King."

Payton looked down at her with a disapproving glare. "You've gotten yourself wrapped up with this lot, eh?"

She nodded emphatically. "It's a good thing, too. He saved my life. He's saved a lot of lives. I wouldn't be here if not for him."

Payton's hesitant gaze slid to Rezkin, and he seemed to mull over his options. As far as Rezkin was concerned, he had none. He either submitted or was *discharged* of his duties. They were actively at war, about to go into battle, and he no longer had the luxury of allowing potential enemies to remain at his back while they considered their options. Reaylin's father or not, he was the rebel leader, and Rezkin would have his fealty.

Reaylin's father took one more look at her pleading expression then returned to stand before Rezkin. He cleared his throat and ducked his head. His posture was submissive as he approached, but he did not go so far as to bow.

"I, ah, suppose I owe you an apology. You saved my daughter's life, so she says. I owe you a life debt."

Rezkin quirked an eyebrow. "More accurately, *she* owes the life debt."

Payton scowled and snapped, "I'll owe it if I say I owe it." He seemed to catch himself and quickly said, "I'm sorry. I am not used to speaking to the noble sort. She says you're the True King. I'll be expecting to hear more of it, but for now I'll accept it."

Rezkin shook his head. "I'm afraid that will not be good enough. Caydean's forces will be here soon, and there is no more time to mince words. You are either with us or against us."

"Oh, I'll stand with you. Anyone who stands against Caydean is a friend of mine."

"And after?"

Payton dropped his gaze again then glanced at the strikers and mages and then his daughter. With a heavy exhale, he said, "On my daughter's word, I'll accept you as the True King, but I can't speak for my men. I lead them. I don't own them."

Rezkin nodded curtly. "You have twenty minutes to convince them. Striker Kai and Captain Jimson will go with you."

"Reaylin?"

"She stays here. She is a valuable member of my retinue, and I will not have you absconding with her. I think you will find that she would be greatly bereaved if something should happen to the captain, so you had best make sure he returns unharmed."

Payton returned his attention to his daughter who blushed furiously as she shared a look with Jimson. Payton's bewildered expression turned to a scowl as he directed his ire at the captain. Jimson did not look perturbed in the least as he stood erect in his immaculate black and green uniform, the corners of his lips raised only slightly as he looked fondly at Reaylin.

Rezkin shook his head. He found that he was pleased Jimson's interest in Reaylin was finally returned, but he had bigger issues. Namely, the double contingent of soldiers, mages, and battle mages heading their way. He waved his hand toward Payton, effectively dismissing him as he turned to Wesson.

"We have much to discuss, Journeyman."

Wesson tugged a lock of his hair and said, "It is *mage* now."

Rezkin nodded as he followed the mage into the house. "Good, the other mages will be pleased."

"You should know I did not go through the normal trials—"

"Wesson, the only person insisting you are anything but a mage is *you*. Just accept your place."

"Right," said Wesson as he led Rezkin and his coterie into the sitting room. There were few places to sit, but they made do by bringing in extra chairs and benches from the other rooms. Wesson said, "I think there is something I need to do. I will return shortly. Cook should be here in a moment with refreshments." Then he disappeared through the doorway.

Just as he had promised, a portly woman appeared with a tray laden with eggs, meats, breads, and jams. She returned a second time with another tray containing a jug of fresh juice, a pot of coffee, and several mugs and glasses. A few minutes later, Mage Wesson returned, only he was changed. No longer did he wear the drab, grey robes of a journeyman generalist. He was bedecked in black. A short tunic-style robe that stopped just above the knees was draped over loose black trousers, and his black panels, bearing a thick silver stripe beside a thinner red one, were cinched at the waist by his belt.

Rezkin dipped his chin in greeting and said, "Battle Mage."

Wesson's severe visage did not change as he replied, "Emperor." The battle mage abruptly shifted forward upon noticing how Entris and Azeria crowded in behind him, each gripping the hilts of their swords. The crackle of mage power infused the air as the three began building upon each other's distrust.

"Who are they?" said Wesson, eyeing the cloaked strangers.

Rezkin grappled with his own internal power as he prepared to assist the battle mage should it be required. "*They* are two of the Eihel-vanan. Battle Mage, meet Spirétua-lyé Entris and General Azeria."

Wesson added a few more layers to his shield ward and said, "I would say it was a pleasure to meet you, but it appears you are preparing to attack me."

Entris's vivid gaze tore from the battle mage to meet Rezkin's. "He must be eliminated."

"He is on our side," said Rezkin.

"For now," replied Entris. "He is no doubt drawn to you because of the nature of your power and because of the chaos you create. Despite your heritage, you, like he, are a product of mayhem."

"We have discussed this, and you are well aware that I disagree. My training was more ordered than the lives of the outworlders. The battle mage, too, has been trained in order as evidenced by his ability to wield both destructive *and* constructive power. He is not to be harmed. Just as he has protected me and mine, he is under my protection."

Entris's attention returned to Wesson as his power flared, and although other mages would not have been able to detect it, Wesson's darker power appeared to respond. A lash of inky blackness snaked out from him before dispersing into a smokey layer of protection between them. Wesson's eyes widened as though he were surprised by what had just happened.

"What was that?" he blurted.

Rezkin said, "I believe that was your power responding to a threat from the Spirétua."

Entris nodded, his expression as grim as ever. "Your daem'ahn recognizes the threat I pose."

"*Demon?*" shouted Wesson. "What demon? I am not possessed, I swear!"

Entris narrowed his eyes. "You pretend as if you do not know?"

Azeria hissed, "Why are you speaking to it? Just dispense with it before it attacks."

Wesson turned to the female. "I am not an *it*! And I am not a demon, either."

"You are," said Entris. "The destructive power you call nocent is a remnant of a daem'ahn ancestor. Most have very little and are only vaguely influenced by the power. Those who are possessed wield more of it and are overwhelmed by the chaotic drive of the daem'ahn. You, however, are not possessed, as you say. You are the product of the physical joining of a human with a true daem'ahn. You carry the pure nocent power of the daem'ahn with which you were joined; yet your human *will* has been strong enough to overcome the daem'ahnic instincts."

Wesson spun to stare at Rezkin. "What are they saying? That I am an *actual* demon?" He shook his head furiously. "I swear, it is not true. I am not evil."

Entris said, "Daem'ahn are not evil. They do not seek to inflict pain and terror for pleasure. They are products of chaos. It is simply their nature to destroy order. As Spirétua, it is my duty to destroy *you* before you wreak havoc on this world."

Wesson stared at Rezkin as if he might have an answer. Something in the battle mage's gaze told Rezkin that he knew Entris's words to be true, even if he did not want to believe them. Rezkin met Wesson's gaze and said, "Is this truly the source of the great and terrible destructive power you have feared for so long?"

Wesson merely looked at him as if at a loss for words. Urmela abruptly appeared in the doorway. She rushed to stand beside her son. She gripped his hand and looked into his eyes. "It is," she said.

Wesson's breath left him in a rush. *"What?"*

She rubbed his hand between her own. "I am sorry, Wesson. It is true. It was your father's doing. But you are a good man. You have never been what they think you are."

Wesson pulled his hand from hers and backed away. "You need to tell me what you are talking about right now, Mother."

Urmela wrung her hands together as she glanced at all the serious faces. She slowly sat on the divan across from Nanessy and said, "Your father used to work at the palace, as I told you. One day he came home early. He was in a panic. He had witnessed something he should not have. I did not find out until much, much later what it was. Your father said he stole something that held terrible power and that it could not fall into the wrong hands. We stayed in Kaibain for a few months to defer suspicion then came here to Benbrick.

"It was not until the night before you were born that I found out what your father had stolen. I did not completely believe him, but he was absolutely convinced that Prince Caydean's tutor had summoned a demon. He said it was a very powerful demon and that it was intended for the prince. It made no sense because he specifically said the *third* prince, when there were only two. But, apparently, since there was no third prince, the tutor was going to put it into Caydean. Before he got a chance, your father stole the vessel in which the demon was contained."

Wesson's face was pale, and he looked as if he might be sick. "What then?"

Urmela's eyes filled with tears as she said, "Your father said he did not know how to destroy the demon, so it needed to be hidden. Before I knew what he intended, he had broken the vessel and somehow guided the demon to my womb."

"He placed the demon into his own unborn child?" said Nanessy.

Entris said, "The soul is not completely in this world until birth. Since the daem'ahn's essence already inhabited him prior to birth, the daem'ahn must have been pulled into this realm by the soul when it settled. The two beings fused into one. That is why he is both human and daem'ahn, and it explains why his human will is strong enough to withstand the that of the daem'ahn."

Urmela blinked furtively as she stared at Entris. Then she swallowed and said, "You were born the next day, and I tried not to think about it. You were always such a good boy—sweet and gentle and compassionate. I thought maybe it was all a mistake and that the demon was destroyed or lost. Then, when you killed that boy—" At last, she broke into tears. She stood and stepped toward Wesson. He allowed her to close the distance and take him into her arms as she cried. "I am so sorry. I love you no matter, Wesson."

Rezkin stepped to their side and met Entris's thoughtful gaze. "The battle mage has the right to prove himself through his choices, and he has. He is not the threat you think him to be. In fact, I believe we are fortunate that the demon's power is contained within someone with such honor and character. He is an ideal vessel. That being said, it is my belief that Berringish, having failed to place *this* demon into Caydean, summoned another to finish the job, only that one is a true possession since Caydean was already a boy when joined with it."

Azeria said, "Perhaps if we remove the daem'ahn from this Caydean, he will be a better king."

Kai cleared his throat and said, "I can guarantee that would not be the case. He was a monster even as a young child, *before* the possibility of possession. No, his madness stems from something else."

"The striker is correct," said Entris. "I believe Caydean is a human-born Spirétua. He has likely gone mad due to his power."

"How is that possible?" said Nanessy. "It would not have affected him as a child. Mages do not come into their power until near adulthood."

"Human Spirétua do not *come into* their power like mages. They are born with it, as are all the Eihelvanan. It would have started driving him toward madness since birth."

"But Rezkin is not mad," said Nanessy.

Entris shook his head. "No, but he was trained to suppress his power. He did not know he had it, and his limited usage was, from what I can tell, of a passive nature. Caydean would have experienced the power with or without training in how to use it; but if Berringish knew Caydean was Spirétua, he likely began training him immediately. His innate power combined with the daem'ahn possession would have destroyed his mind long before he reached adulthood. Unfortunately, as Spirétua *and* daem'ahn, he will be that much more difficult to defeat."

Just then, Payton entered the room. He said, "Our people are in place. It looks like Caydean's forces will arrive at Garten Knoll near midday tomorrow."

"What of the Torreli and Sandeans?" said Rezkin.

Kai, who followed Payton, said, "Scouts have reported that they have not yet passed Zigharan's End. Should they invade now, and should we do nothing, they will meet with Caydean's forces in about a week far to the north of here."

"It is best we do this on our own," said Rezkin. "Joining with the Torreli and Sandeans should be a last resort. While they claim to be allies to the rebels, I do not trust them not to turn on us before they turn on each other."

"You think they will try to lay claim to Ashai," said Farson.

Rezkin nodded. "They would not otherwise expend the resources. If we can defeat Caydean's army here, they may think twice about invading."

25

Rezkin dismounted far enough from the rebel camp that no one would detect Pride's presence in the waning illumination of the sun as twilight encroached. Then he silently made his way through the thick copse along an embankment to the south of the camp. A dry creek bed that would afford them enough cover to mount a surprise attack cut across the field. The land beyond the creek bed was a flat plain of high grasses, short shrubs, and a few small copses here and there. A modest hill that gradually steepened was the only break in the otherwise unimpressive topography. At the top of the hill were the ruins of a once illustrious estate that had been famed for its glorious gardens. Most of the rebel troops occupied either those ruins or the copses while others would be hidden within the grasses themselves. It was far from an ideal location for an ambush using such insurrectionary tactics, but if they succeeded then Caydean's primary forces would be disabled.

No fires were permitted in the camp that night. They would not want the enemy scouts to find them before the ambush. Rezkin quietly flitted between rebel groups listening and watching for signs of betrayal. Rezkin felt no confidence in Payton de Voss's assurances that all his people were trustworthy. The mages, too, were a curious sect. Although some seemed to genuinely respect Battle Mage Wesson, many of them only begrudgingly followed him thanks to the insistence of his former master, Ikestrius, that Wesson was worthy of his leadership role. Rezkin searched the field for Ikestrius and found him presumably setting blast charge spells where they would do damage upon activation during battle. A handful of mages were assisting him as they spread out around the base of the hill.

Rezkin returned his attention to the men around him before he set to climbing the hill. It was at that moment that he saw something odd. A man wearing a vest and a slouchy cap was crouched over something on the ground. The man looked up frequently as if checking to see who might be looking. Rezkin assumed the man did not see him hidden in the darker shadow of a tree. The man checked his surroundings one more time, then stood. As he did so, a bird squawked and struggled in his grasp. The man immediately ran up the hill toward the ruins, and Rezkin took after him in haste. Just before he reached the top, where, by the morrow, a large contingent of rebels would be placed, the man released the bird. Rezkin drew his crossbow and fired. The bird's flight was abruptly arrested, and it tumbled from the air to crash into the ruins. The ruins were quiet as the moon rose to bathe them in silvery light, and Rezkin quickly covered the distance to where the bird had fallen.

Rezkin picked up the dead bird and wrenched his crossbow bolt from its body. Then he inspected the bird's leg where he found attached to it a rolled scroll. He held the small missive up to the moonlight so that he could read its message. It was a warning to Caydean's forces detailing the rebels' location and approximate numbers. Rezkin dropped the bird and pocketed the scroll before rounding the crumbled wall that separated him from the remainder of the ruins. He drew *Bladesunder* as he stalked the abandoned halls and corridors of the ancient estate searching for the spy. He paused upon hearing the slightest whisper of clothing then a footfall. His quarry was on the other side of the wall to his left. Rezkin's steps were silent as he kept pace with the sounds that echoed off the stone. The steps paused, and a second set of steps joined the first.

"Is it done?" whispered a voice from the other side of the wall.

"Yes, it's off," said a second voice, a little louder than the first.

"Sshh," hissed the first. "Keep our voice down. Are you sure it made it? I thought I saw something fall."

"Yes," huffed the second with impatience. "It's a bird. Birds don't just fall out of the sky. Are you sure we'll be okay? What if Caydean's men don't recognize us? We'll be killed with the rest of them. What if we're caught?"

"Will you stop worrying so much? Nobody's gonna catch us. They're all too busy worrying about their own hides."

"But Payton—"

"Don't you worry about Payton. He thinks we're all blindly devoted to the rebel cause."

"What about this True King? There's something about the way he looks at you—like a viper about to strike."

"What are you going on about? He's got better things to be doing. Come one. Let's get back to the camp before someone finds us up here."

It was too late, though. Rezkin had already found them, and he was not about to let them go. He backed up then sprinted forward before bounding off a side wall to catch the broken edge of the top of the wall. He pulled himself up and over then dropped onto one of the men. *Bladesunder* sailed through the air to cut off the second man's cry before it started. Then he stabbed downward to impale the first man through the top of his skull.

Rezkin was wiping the blood from his blade when a woman's seductive voice reached his ears. "You should have let them live." Rezkin's body went rigid at the interruption. He had not heard anyone approach. Then he relaxed when he realized who had spoken to him. Azeria unfurled herself from a shadow. Her white hair glowed like a cloud as she crossed the space between them, and her silver eyes reflected the light of the moon as if they were filled with moonlight themselves. She said, "We could have questioned them, found out what they knew (*disappointed*)."

Rezkin stepped over the dead bodies to join her. "They were

merely grunts. I doubt they knew anything useful, and their presence would have upset the rebels' morale. If they found out spies were in their midst this entire time, they might not have the courage to follow through with the plan."

"Should they? The plan may be compromised (*cautious*)."

"I do not believe it to be so. The information in the missive implies Caydean's forces do not yet know of the rebels in the area."

"Then we are fortunate that you caught it."

"Indeed."

Azeria tucked a strand of stray, wind-tousled hair behind her ear and met his gaze. "You are not what I expected."

"How so?"

She glanced over the sea of silvery grasses before returning her gaze to him. "Entris and I watched you for weeks. Your actions were often cold and violent (*disturbed*). I thought them to be evidence of your madness. It was not until I spoke with you that I learned how calculated your actions were and continue to be. Yes, you killed these two men without hesitation, but you were not without reason or just cause (*earnest*)."

"They were traitors, spies."

"Yes, exactly."

Azeria seemed to want to say more, but her words were apparently trapped. Rezkin glanced back at his fresh kill and frowned. Azeria was used to killing and death. She was a warrior, a general, but he wondered if what she had to say was best not said over a couple of bloody corpses. Rezkin held his hand out, motioning for her to join him at the edge of the ruins. Her feminine figure swayed gracefully as she led, deftly stepping over chunks of rubble and picking her way around cracks in the foundation. Rezkin realized he enjoyed watching Azeria and not because he was watching for signs of an impending attack. He could not help but appreciate her beauty.

Once they were beyond the broken walls of the former estate, Azeria stopped. She did not take her gaze from the would-be battle-field that was bathed in starlight as she said, "I do not believe we should fight this battle on the morrow (*anxious*)."

Rezkin appreciated her candor. Few would have spoken against his decision. "Why is that?" he said.

"I bear an ominous feeling; and, about these things, I am usually right (*earnest*)."

Rezkin watched her profile as he searched for hidden feelings, but her expression was as stoic as ever. "You think we will lose?"

"One can win a battle and still lose. According to the scouts, the enemy is formidable. There will be many deaths (*mournful*). Is it worth the risk to fight this battle here and now?"

"This is not the battle I would choose, but it is the one the rebels will fight. They are likely to die either way. We might as well level the playing field."

She finally turned to him and met his gaze. "I am not concerned about losing the rebels."

"You are faster and more skilled than any warrior I have ever seen. You are confident, graceful, and intelligent. You will not fall."

Her bland expression gave way to a frown. "I was not worried about *myself* (*irritated*)."

Although she appeared angry with him, Rezkin could see the warring emotions in her expressive eyes. He stepped closer and reached up to brush a thumb over her cheek. He said, "I will not die, either."

She blinked as uncertainty flashed across her face. Her gaze dropped to his mouth, and Rezkin felt compelled to close the remaining distance. Caution and desire warred for control as he leaned in to brush his lips lightly across her own. Suddenly, Azeria's hands were tangled in his hair, and she pulled him to her, deepening the kiss and pressing her body against his. Rather than pull away, Rezkin wrapped his arms around her and joined her in a heated battle for dominance. His heart raced, and he was swamped with battle energy as the vagri heated to a nearly unbearable level. Never had he felt so invigorated yet desperate.

It was that desperation, that lack of control that caused his heart to freeze. In a matter of moments, he had succumbed to foreign feelings that he did not understand. He had purposely placed himself in a vulnerable position with a superior opponent. His lips stilled, and he pulled away quickly placing Azeria at arm's length. His muscles tensed as she looked at him quizzically.

"Rezkin—"

He took a step back and then another, and her expression turned to one of hurt. Rezkin could not understand the pain in her eyes. What they were doing was wrong. They were both warriors, and neither of them should have opened themselves to the threat the other posed. He took another step then turned and hurried down the hill. With each of his steps, Rezkin felt the tether between them pull taut. The tightness in his chest urged him to turn around and reclaim her, yet his own uncertainties kept his feet moving. He realized that while he had been engaged in the play of tongues with Azeria he had not once thought to guard himself from her. He considered that had she attempted to kill him at that moment he might have let her. The realization should have instilled in him a renewed determination to follow the *Rules*, but he thought he would break every one of them if it meant he could kiss her again. That was when he knew the female would surely be his downfall.

Rezkin followed the dark path back down into the encampment, but he did not look back. They were to go to battle the following day, and he had many things to contemplate that had nothing to do with a pair of intelligent, silvery eyes or soft, pink lips. He needed to focus on the battle ahead and not on the way a certain female made his heart race and his blood heat. Rezkin found Farson surveying a cache of weapons, and the sight of the striker was just enough to douse Rezkin's unnatural vigor. Thoughts of Azeria continued to simmer in the background as he attempted to constrain them and refocus on the field. With an iron will, he forced the thoughts to abate, but in doing so, he felt he had lost something.

He had been contemplating the many wars and battles he had learned about during his training, and he had searched for similarities of circumstance. They were about to do battle on open ground with barely a mentionable topographical or ecological hazard. With the enemy's forces split into two contingents, even a powerful frontal assault on their part would do limited damage and could easily be overwhelmed, especially if the second contingent split its forces to surround them. The rebels' plan to funnel the first contingent into the center then strike the second from behind was a good idea, but he felt that their rearward troops were too weak to be effective. Their spies had confirmed that Battle Master Rhone rode at the front of the first contingent and Berringish led the second. Rezkin had decided his people and most of the rebel mages would attack from the flanks and rear of the second contingent. If all went to plan, this would alienate both contingents and slow the forward progression of the second, thereby enabling the rebel forces to maintain a strong front and reducing casualties.

As Rezkin approached the weapons cache, Farson turned to him. "*You* should be leading this battle, not these untrained rebels."

Rezkin tilted his head as he looked at Farson thoughtfully. Amongst the trees, there was little to light the striker's visage, but Rezkin knew his face well enough. He said, "I was trained to work with what I have in the most efficient manner. The rebels trust Payton and their elected leadership. They will fight for him with fervor. If I attempted to usurp his authority, they would be demoralized. Besides, there is no time to train them to be more effective."

"I do not trust them," said Farson. "What if they turn tail and run?"

"They may. If they do, they will be cut down. Neither Berringish nor Rhone will suffer them to live. If it looks to be falling apart, we will retreat. In a few months' time, we will rally the troops of Gendishen, Lon Lerésh, and Ferélle and opt for a more direct assault on the capital. If it were up to me, we would not be here at all."

"What do you mean, if it were up to you? *You* are the emperor."

"Precisely, and the *emperor* must meet this threat here and now. Berringish and Rhone are distinct threats that must be eliminated. In addition, Battle Mage Wesson was concerned for his family, and he has earned this boon. If I were not emperor, though, I would be doing things very differently."

"What would you do?"

"That is not important now. This is the path we have carved for ourselves. This is the battle we will fight." After a moment, Rezkin added, "I need you to take care of some bodies."

Farson sighed and dropped his head. "Who have you killed now?"

"No one important. Just a couple of traitors. They were attempting to get information to our enemies."

"And you just happened to intercept it."

"Yes. I was in the right place at the right time."

"Of course you were. Why not leave the bodies where they are? There will be plenty more to join them tomorrow."

"I do not want to alarm the rebels. The last thing we need is a panicked exodus."

"Very well. Where are they?"

Rezkin gave Farson the details on where he could find the bodies of the two traitors, then he left with the expectation that his orders would be followed. Although Rezkin still did not fully trust Farson, he accepted that the striker had joined his side—for now. It was the male he encountered after leaving the encampment with whom he truly had to concern himself.

"If you hurt her, I will not hesitate to kill you, madness or no (*earnest*)."

Rezkin stopped a few paces from Entris. "Hurt who?"

"You know who."

"You need not concern yourself with her well-being. Azeria can take care of herself. Besides, you have chosen another, have you not?"

"Whether I have or not is irrelevant. I have known Azeria for your entire lifespan four times over. I care for her, and I will not have you toying with her."

"I do not toy."

"You have said yourself that you have no feelings. She does. She feels deeply—more deeply than you will ever understand. If she is merely a means to some end for you, you had best let her go now. I shall issue no further warning (*determined*)."

As Entris walked away, Rezkin mulled over the many methods of attack he could implement and the likelihood that Entris would prevail. Although Rezkin had gotten faster since training with the

Eihelvanan, he was still not as fast as Entris, and he had yet to master the power of his vimara. Entris had many decades on him in training, and Rezkin knew that nothing less than a surprise attack would overcome the skilled Eihelvanan warrior. Therefore, he felt fortunate that he need not fight Entris, because Rezkin had come to one blatant conclusion. He had feelings for Azeria.

26

"Why did Caydean not kill you?" said Frisha, shifting once again in a futile effort to get comfortable with her seat on the sandy cave floor. Her head and back ached from sleeping on the ground, and the cold that had suffused her bones had not abated with the meager morning light.

Thresson shrugged as he leaned his head back on the rock wall. "I can only speculate. I think it is because he loves the power. Here, I, a prince of Ashai, am at his mercy. He may do whatever he wishes to me, whether it is to starve me or beat me to a bloody pulp; and I can do nothing to him in return. Plus, he loves to brag about his accomplishments. He gets a thrill out of watching the pain it causes me when he follows through on one of his dastardly schemes."

"He comes here personally?"

Thresson nodded. "Yes, sometimes he does not come for months; other times, he visits almost daily."

"But how can that be? I don't know where we are, but I do know we are nowhere near Kaibain.

"I overheard the guards speaking one time when they seemingly forgot about me. According to them, we are in Jerea."

"I don't understand," said Frisha. "How can Caydean be in Kaibain *and* Jerea at the same time?"

"Again, I do not have answer. I presume he has found some method of traveling great distances in a short period of time."

Frisha licked her dry lips as her mind began to run with the possibilities. "Perhaps if we can get out of here, we could use the same method to escape."

"And go where? According to my brother, he has amassed power in most of the kingdoms on the Souelian."

"That is a lie. Gendishen, Lon Lerésh, and Ferélle are under Rezkin's control. He is the Emperor of the Souelian. His seat of power is on the island of Cael. We would be safe there."

"Were you safe?" said a deep voice from beyond the bars. "If you were so safe, how did you end up here?"

Frisha squinted into the shadows trying to discern a figure.

"Ah," said Thresson, "Brother. You are here. Will you not join us? I am afraid I have no refreshments to offer."

"Brother?" said Frisha with alarm. "As in *Caydean*?"

"That is *King* Caydean—soon to be Emperor," the man said with a chuckle. As he stepped into the light, Frisha swallowed her fear. Caydean was as tall and broad of shoulder as Rezkin and had the same stark, black hair and piercing blue eyes. His face was harder, crueler, with severe lines and sharp edges. He carried himself like a predator but lacked the grace of his youngest sibling. His voice was deep and as harsh as his visage.

"So *this* is my brother's mistress? Hmm, I have been told there is beauty in simplicity, but I do not see it."

"What?" said Thresson. "She is not *my* mistress."

"I am no one's mistress!" shouted Frisha.

"No, I suppose not any longer," said Caydean. "He put you to pasture, did he not? Now, I hear you warm the bed of our cousin Tieran."

"I am not warming anyone's bed," said Frisha. "I am a proper lady, and Tieran is my ... well, he is ... he is courting me."

Caydean's lips twitched, and she hoped he did not smile. She thought his smile would be worse than the hateful look he had worn since his arrival. His tone was casual as he spoke, but it held the sharpness of someone teetering on the edge of violence. "Did you know, Thresson, that our traitorous mother's third babe lived?" He paused as he studied Thresson's reaction. Thresson, however, was giving nothing away. Caydean said, "Did you know we have another brother, a *younger* brother? Come now, Thresson, you can be honest with me."

Frisha jumped as Thresson abruptly began choking. He collapsed to his knees as he held his throat, his face turning first red then purple. The choking ended as abruptly as it began, and Thresson collapsed onto his back gasping for air.

Caydean said, "No, of course you did not. That was kept a secret from *everyone*. I only found out after our father's *untimely* demise."

"You mean after you killed him," said Frisha, and then he did smile. Frisha's tongue stuck to her throat as she tried to swallow. Frisha was suddenly ensnared in an invisible web that wrapped around her so tightly she could hardly breathe. Her feet left the ground, and she slid across the cell toward Caydean. With her arms pinned to her sides, her torso slammed against the bars. Then it felt as if a heavy weight was pressing into her from behind crushing her. Her throat constricted as she gulped in air, but her lungs could not expand.

"She is a feisty one," Caydean said as he closed the distance between them to peruse her again. He looked at her as if studying a laboratory specimen. "I suppose she would have to be to keep *him* interested." His gaze slid to Thresson. "He is our brother after all. It is no wonder that he has already made a name for himself." His attention returned to Frisha, and when his gaze caught on the tears that filled her eyes, he grinned. "You see, *this* little bird was betrothed to him, our brother. And when that did not work out, she set her sights on Tieran." He reached up and wiped a tear from her cheek. Frisha could do nothing but endure the brief touch, and it made her feel sick. "I approve of your temerity, *Lady* Frisha, but I am afraid you will *not* be marrying into the royal family. I have no interest in my family's leftovers, and *they* will both be dead." He donned a wolfish grin. "Perhaps Thresson, here, will find a use for you."

The power crushing Frisha against the bars abruptly released, and she fell to her hands and knees. Frisha glanced up through watery eyes to see Thresson scowling at Caydean, but he said nothing.

Frisha pushed herself to her feet and said, "Why are you doing this? What do you want with us?"

Caydean shrugged. "I keep Thresson because it amuses me. *You* might have useful information, which I will thoroughly enjoy getting. Eventually, I will tire of you both. Maybe I will kill you. Maybe I will forget about you and let you starve. For now, you can keep each other warm while I destroy my enemies. I will let your lovers know you have moved on before I cut off their heads. Oh, that is right. They are unaware that you are gone. You have been replaced. No one is coming for you, Lady Frisha. Ever." He smiled again then rubbed his hands together eagerly. "I must go. I do believe a battle is about to begin."

"Are you sleeping?" said Nanessy from his left. Rezkin and his companions were ensconced in the old creek bed to the south of the main camp that afforded enough cover to hide their numbers. Thanks to the scouting efforts of Fetari and her hawk omessas, they knew exactly where and when to meet the enemy.

"I am envisioning battle scenarios," Rezkin replied as his hand came to rest on Tiseyi's head that lay across his lap.

"Oh. That actually makes me feel better," Nanessy said, and he could hear the anxiety in her voice. She had not been trained in battle magic, but that was not stopping her from offering her service. For that, Rezkin respected her all the more. He turned his head and met her worried gaze. "Stay close to Entris."

Her gaze flicked toward the male, who was already beside her. Then she nodded and moved a little closer to him.

Azeria said, "He did not mean for you to sit in his lap (*amused*)."

Her cheeks red, Nanessy started to shift away, but Entris's grip on her arm stopped her. His gaze did not move from the horizon as he said, "She is welcome to sit in my lap if she feels safer there (*encouraging*)."

Nanessy's chin dropped, and Azeria actually laughed. Rezkin had noted that while the Eihelvanan rarely showed emotion on their faces, they were quick to laugh when the feeling caught them. He wondered if he should strive to laugh more. Rezkin quite admired Azeria's laugh. He thought perhaps he would laugh when he lopped off Berringish's head. For some reason, the thought of it pleased him.

It was not long before the heavy sound of footfalls, the creaks of wagons, and the jangling of equipment reached their ears. An enemy scout trudged through the grass not far from the creek bed where they were ensconced, but he took no notice of them. Entris had laid an enchantment over them to muffle their sounds and prevent Caydean's mages from detecting their presence. At least a half hour passed from the time they spied the first scout to the end of the first contingent, which contained primarily foot soldiers and the supply wagons. Many of the soldiers were outfitted with swords—which Rezkin knew to be of questionable quality—light armor, and wooden bucklers. Some carried pikes or halberds, and a great many addition-ally carried short bows or crossbows. Some longbowmen and cavalry were at the rear, but it seemed the bulk of the cavalry were to be found in the second contingent.

Although the hawks had described monsters among the enemy ranks, Rezkin was still surprised by the appearance of other *things*. Throughout the column were dozens of creatures, only a few of

447

which he recognized. A group of thirty or so lizard-like drauglics were clumped around their ukwa, who Rezkin knew to be under the control of a demon by the blackness of its eyes. Although the rest of the drauglics did not appear to be possessed, the ukwa was somehow able to keep them from attacking their human comrades. Also interspersed with the troops were a number of vuroles leashed on thick chains and presumably bespelled for control.

In addition to the drauglics and vuroles, there were other creatures ranging from stout, dog-like beasts with elongated necks to several bull-like monsters with spiked tails and hard plates forming a ridge down their backs. There were even a few tall, willowy creatures that appeared to be a cross between animal and plant. These shot thick vines from stalks where their legs and shoulders might be and then retracted them as they ambled forward shifting from one to the next.

"There," said Wesson from Rezkin's side. "That is Battle Master Rhone, the tall one at the center."

As Rezkin surveyed what little cavalry was present, he realized most of them were not soldiers. They were mages and battle mages. "You believe you can defeat him?" said Rezkin.

Wesson worried at his lip as his gaze flicked back to the battle master. "I have never seen him fight, but he seems to fear me. I took it as a good sign."

"Fair enough," said Rezkin. "Do not unnecessarily risk yourself. This is not a last stand. If we fail and are forced to retreat here, there will be more battles and more opportunities. Lean on Entris or me if need be."

"Right, but once we engage, I doubt he will let me get away. He hates me. But—"

"But what?"

"I am just surprised that he chose to fight for Caydean. The last time we spoke, he seemed concerned about Caydean's mental state."

"Do you think he is possessed?"

"It is a possibility, but not absolutely necessary. He seemed to recognize the danger of *me* falling into Caydean's hands. I thought perhaps that concern would extend to himself. He has always been a king's man, though, so I suppose he would heed his king's call to arms."

When the first contingent had passed, there was a brief respite during which time, the strikers double-checked that everyone knew his or her place. Wesson had crouched low as he made his way along the stream bed to a position more advantageous to attacking the rear of the first contingent. When the second contingent arrived, Rezkin took stock of the enemy troops. The contingent was fully mounted, and most of the soldiers wore heavy armor. Swordsmen and archers rode at the fore while a row of fully armored knights held the center. Many of the horses were battle chargers, and a number of the swordsmen looked to Rezkin to be strikers. Behind them was another group of mages and battle mages, in the midst of whom rode Berringish.

Rezkin had not had the opportunity to truly study the Sen when he encountered him in Verril. The man was of average height and breadth, but he rode with such an air of superiority that he seemed larger than those around him. He wore a sour expression that was hard and disinviting, but his dark gaze continually roved the field. Although he had no reason to believe an enemy lie in wait, the Sen was ever alert and prepared.

Just as the first contingent reached the far side of the hill, a meteoric charge struck the center of the first column causing an explosion that threw men, monsters, and debris in every direction. That was the signal for the battle to begin. A second blast struck the rear of the second contingent startling the horses. While some of the mages and strikers were able to control their mounts, most of the beasts created a flurry of motion. The explosions that followed did little or no damage to their targets as they struck shield wards that sprung up amidst the chaos. From the enemy lines came a massive fireball followed by three more that splashed into one of the nearest copses, causing the rebels stationed there to scatter. A discharge of flaming and bespelled arrows took flight from the allies in the ruins at the top of the hill to rain down on the first contingent that was protected by fewer wards. The drauglics were the first to break ranks as they swarmed the hill, some of them even attacking Caydean's own forces in the process. While the enemy mages and soldiers tried to regain control of their monstrous comrades, the rebels lying in wait in the grasses and amongst the copses attacked.

The rebel attack was the signal for the second round of explosions, which detonated in the field at the center of the second contingent. Rezkin donned the ominous black mask of Dark Tidings as he, Kai, Farson, Azeria, and about two dozen rebels mounted their horses. They, along with the twenty omessas, raced down the stream bed toward a collapsed embankment that permitted them onto the field. Wielding his black blade, Rezkin charged into the rearward cavalry of the second contingent with the omessas on his heels. Green lightning ignited within the blade's inky blackness as he struck his first victim. Based on his fighting style, Rezkin could tell within the first few exchanges that this man was a striker. Before Rezkin could defeat him, though, a second joined the fight. Rezkin guided Pride with his feet as he blocked a slash from the first striker and jabbed at the second. As the second attempted to block the strike, Pride dipped his massive head and bit the man in the thigh. The man shouted as he brought his pommel down onto the chanfron that covered Pride's face, but the ornery horse shook off the impact and bit the man again.

Rezkin was able to best both men within minutes, but something stirred the hairs on the back of his neck as he looked for his next target. Rezkin turned as a leopard lunged at a would-be attacker, sinking its teeth into the man's exposed throat and taking him to the ground. Abruptly and with considerably less effort than in the past, Rezkin brought up a shield ward just as a lance smashed into it. Rezkin gave Pride the command, and the horse kicked out behind him, knocking the knight off his own mount. Before the knight could fully recover, Rezkin had buried the black blade in the man's torso through his armpit. Rezkin quickly surveyed the field for Berringish only to find that the Sen had stolen away with a handful of mages and was making for the ruins at the top of the hill. Between them stood the whole of Caydean's army and the battle master who could be seen lording over the mages from atop his own steed.

As Rezkin advanced, he could see his comrades fighting with fury. Kai was abruptly dragged from his horse, but Azeria was there immediately to back him up. Continuous vimaral attacks by Entris and the mages in the creek bed struck down enemies unlucky enough not to be shielded. The vimaral creatures wreaked havoc on their own forces as much as the rebels, and mages and soldiers from both sides were forced to fend against them. Wolves, leopards, and lions fought drauglics and vuroles as well as men. As Rezkin continued through the throng of soldiers and monsters, he noticed a gap open between the battle master and the rest of his people. Something was forcing him away, separating him from the others. Then Rezkin saw Battle Mage Wesson step into the space.

Wesson triggered his spell just as Battle Master Rhone caught sight of him. The man's eyes went wide upon seeing Wesson, and it was obvious he was recognized and unexpected. Those fighting around them shifted as one like a school of fish around a predator. Wesson stalked forward as Rhone looked around in surprise. They were alone together in a sea of monsters and men fighting for their lives. The spell had done its job in separating the battle master from the pack so that Wesson could fight him without overly concerning himself with the lives of those around him. He doubted Rhone would have been so courteous. The man had only ever seen mundanes as a means to an end—mages, too, for that matter.

"You rejected those robes!" shouted Rhone over the din. "You have not earned them."

Like the battle master was surely doing, Wesson was preparing multiple spells as he spoke. "You have no idea what I have done since I left the Battle Mage Academy in ruins." Rhone scowled at the reminder of what Wesson had done nearly two years before—a feat that Wesson knew to have terrified all those the battle academy had housed. As it should have. It terrified him as well. No one should wield the kind of power he did for destruction. If he had been capable of unleashing that kind of power on Caydean's army, he might have taken them all out in one go. It had been an awakening of a sort—one that he had bottled up and did not know how to release again lest it consume him to destroy the world. He worried that with that kind of power, it was all or nothing.

"We need not fight," said Rhone. "You have obviously come to terms with what you are. You may join us now."

"I will never join Caydean," snapped Wesson. "He is mad, and you know it. I serve the True King of Ashai, as should you. It is not too late to switch sides."

"Switch sides?" Rhone's growl was followed by a mirthless chuckle. "There is only one side in war, boy, and it is the side of the king."

"You are serving the *wrong* king," shouted Wesson. "I swear by mage oath that the one known as Dark Tidings, the True King, the Emperor of the Souelian, is the rightful heir to the throne of Ashai."

Rhone paused, no doubt feeling the effects of the binding spell used during the swearing of a mage oath. For the first time, he appeared unsure. Then his expression turned to one of resolve. "I see that is what you believe, but it cannot be. Caydean is the first-born legitimate son of Bordran. I serve the throne, as do my battle mages. If you do not, then you are an enemy and a traitor."

With that, Rhone unleased an insidious spell that crawled across

Wesson's shield ward, digging into it like maggots to a corpse. They abruptly exploded, shattering Wesson's shield and exposing him to the merciless destruction of the battle master's next spell. It began at his feet, a powerful surge of energy that threatened to suck him into the ground. The earth seemed to move of its own accord as though it would consume him to satisfy its own ravenous hunger. Wesson thrashed against it as he released several spells of his own. Two reproduced his shield wards while the third surged toward Rhone's shield. It splattered against it seemingly without effect.

As Wesson finally extricated himself from the consuming spell, his own spell cast against Rhone's ward began to eat away at the shield like acid. He sent a volley of luminary javelins toward the battle master as a distraction while he generated a spell he had only ever theorized. Before he could release the spell, he was forced to dodge a compressive spell that might have burst his insides despite his shields. The battle master was definitely not pulling his punches. The man meant only to destroy; but destruction was Wesson's greatest curse, a curse that was a blessing during a battle such as this.

As he looked up, Wesson noticed a commotion upon the hill behind the battle master. He could see in the distance that Berringish and several mages had made their way to the top. Apparently, the rebels who had occupied the ruins had been overrun, and the high ground was now in the hands of the enemy. His heart jumped as a bright light burst at at the hill's apex, and in his alarm, he missed reinforcing his shield when the battle master struck at him again. Wesson was blown from his feet with the impact of the spell. Although his ward had absorbed the worst effects of the spell, he was still pained when he landed heavily on his back about ten paces from where he had been standing. He sat up and sucked air into his lungs as he reestablished his shields and squinted into the distance. Rezkin was moving up the hill to intercept the Sen. Wesson got to his feet and returned his attention to his own duel. With his feet firmly planted in the earth, he released the spell he had been holding, his restraint reinforced by his fear of what unleashing the spell might mean. He applied the activation token just as another disfiguring spell surged his way.

Wesson's spell swept forward, and he abruptly hit the ground, throwing his arms over his head. Doing so would do nothing to protect him, though. He was wholly dependent on his wards.

Before the spell was even halfway to the battle master, it began to sizzle and crackle in the air. It appeared as a livid red wall of fractured light as it wrapped around Rhone's shield ward and began collapsing in on itself. Rhone was forced to drop the ward lest he be crushed, and the crackling red spell snapped around him as it continued to collapse. Rhone writhed against it as the spell began to cut into his flesh. The smell of burnt hair and cooked meat began to mingle with the other smells of battle—those of muddied blood, spent entrails, emptied stomachs, and evacuated bowls. Just as Wesson was certain the spell would be the end of the battle master, Rhone defeated it with a powerful burst. As the bloodied battle mage regained his feet, Wesson lobbed spell after spell against him. Rhone knocked them all away as he stepped forward and began a series of motions. It was a kind of ritual magic with which Wesson was not familiar, but it promised to be devastating if permitted to proceed.

"Do not do this, Rhone!" Wesson shouted. "There are people here on both sides. You will destroy them all." Rhone was not listening to him, though, and continued performing the dance-like ritual. Before he was forced to do something he truly did not wish to do, Wesson tried again. "Look around you! Look at these monsters. Surely you have seen the demons! You are on the wrong side."

Rhone appeared crazed while smiling through broken lips. His face and hands were masses of charred and split flesh that oozed with foaming blood. Wesson wondered if the pain of his injuries had consumed Rhone's mind as he began to chuckle lightly. Wesson knew the battle master could not be permitted to finish the ritual, so there was only one thing left to do. He had to destroy him *now*. Wesson took a deep breath then brushed his consciousness over the dark entity that resided inside him. If the Eihelvanan were to be believed, that entity was not only a demon, but truly part of *him*. It was a part of himself he had never wanted to exist, yet it did, and now he needed it.

As soon as he had the thought, the power latched onto his

consciousness like a drowning man clinging to a raft. It yanked and clawed and dragged itself to the fore, and Wesson no longer saw things as he had a few minutes ago. The truth of the battle was clear now, and it was beautiful. There was a certain serenity in the destruction it wrought. It was chaos unfolding, like a blooming flower whose petals were torn away on the wind. Those petals danced on swirling eddies wherever the breeze blew, and the resulting display was no less glorious than the opulent flower from which the petals were derived. Like a red rose in bloom, blood painted the scene in a fall of crimson. The gaping maws of cadavers, stretched in agony, sang a silent chorus that could be heard long after death. And everyone who fell did so with an invitation to join those who fell before them. The invitation was welcoming and open to all regardless of race, creed, or alliance.

Wesson blinked, and all that he had realized had happened in only seconds. The battle master had nearly finished his ritual when Wesson released his innate power. He allowed it to flow freely at first. When the power struck the battle master's ward, it was as if alarm bells began ringing in Wesson's mind. He knew that if he did not rein it in, the power would destroy everything in the field. Pulling back at the last moment, Wesson ensured that only a thin stream reached the battle master. Rhone's expression turned to surprise as the dark power struck him directly in the chest, and then he exploded, his remains showering the field and feeding the blooms of death in a macabre cascade. Wesson's gaze traveled up the hill and stalled. What he saw there made his heart stop.

Rezkin slashed and stabbed as he made his way toward the hill. Nearly as many enemies fell beneath Pride's hooves as did by Rezkin's blade. Behind him on the battlefield, Entris and Azeria and their few mages battled against vimaral creatures and battle mages. To his left, he could see the opening where Battle Mage Wesson dueled against the battle master. From what he could tell in the midst of it, their side seemed to be holding their own, except for the top of the hill.

Berringish and his parade of mages had managed to clear the estate's ruins of rebels and seemed to be attempting some kind of ritual. Rezkin spurred Pride forward with a few heavy kicks to his flanks. The battle charger responded with gusto. Although horses, by nature, were not predatory beasts, Pride, like most battle chargers, seemed to relish the chase.

By the time Rezkin reached the base of the hill, Berringish had established what appeared to be a shrine. The enemy mages were arrayed in a circle, and Rezkin could see an odd device in the center that had the look of a statue, but he was sure had a much darker purpose. Berringish knelt before the statue as he moved his hands and head in a strange rocking motion, and a blue light began to emanate from its top. Rezkin cut down several of Caydean's soldiers who thought to stand in his way as he neared the summit. At the top, Pride was prevented from venturing any farther by the broken walls of the ruins. Rezkin leapt from Pride's back to perch atop one such wall. He ran along its length to reach another. By the time he approached the mages, the blue light had grown to the size of a horse. The nearest mage turned in alarm and cast a spell at him, but it was too late. The enemy mage fell beneath the black blade as a second began sending vimaral attacks Rezkin's way.

The mages shuffled to place themselves between Rezkin and Berringish, and it was only when they began tossing more and more destructive spells at him that Rezkin realized the five remaining mages' eyes had turned black. The nearest one, a woman with fiery red hair, threw a black orb at Rezkin. It was not the first time he had seen this power, and he was certain that if it struck him, he would be dead. He raised a shield ward at the same time that he jumped to the side. The orb skittered off the ward and splashed into the remnants of the wall where Rezkin had been standing. Rezkin rounded the wall and took refuge as three more volleys of black orbs surged toward him.

He risked a quick glance over the wall then chucked a throwing dagger at the nearest mage. As he released the dagger, he coated it in a thin film of power, which allowed it to travel through the mages' wards. The woman's scream was cut short as the knife sank into her chest. A second dagger struck the man who had been standing behind her in the shoulder. He cried out, but the injury only seemed to incense him. Rezkin ducked to avoid several more spelled attacks, one of which rounded the wall to strike his shield from behind. Rezkin released a flap secured to his vambrace, beneath which were several darts and a small tube. Placing the tube in his mouth, Rezkin shot a dart into the first mage to round the wall. Then he dodged an attack by the mage before running a second mage through with his sword. The blood that burbled up through the mage's lips spilled over Rezkin's face as he pushed the mage off his blade. By the time he turned back to the first mage, the man had succumbed to the poison.

Rezkin looked over the wall again to get an idea of where the last two mages were located. Both were gazing up at the light that hovered in the air over the statue. It had begun to separate. At that moment, Rezkin realized what was happening. Berringish was somehow using the device, the statue, to open a pathway. He did not know if Berringish intended to escape or to bring something else through, but Rezkin knew he needed to stop it. He leapt over the short wall and swung the black blade in furious movements as he cut down the last two mages who stood in his way. Then Berringish abruptly turned to him. The man held a sword of his own, and this one was coated in a black, oily substance that writhed as he swung it back and forth before him.

Rezkin glanced at the statue behind the Sen and then up to the pathway that was just beginning to open. Berringish grinned sadistically as he lunged forward. Rezkin parried and stabbed and swept the Sen's blade to the side. Berringish recovered quickly, though, and it became clear that he did not intend to depend on swordsmanship. He released a spell at Rezkin that blasted him backward into one of the half-toppled walls of the former estate. A dark blur suddenly lunged at Berringish. The Sen shouted as he grappled with the huge, charcoal wolf who managed to score a terrible gash down the man's arm. Black ribbons of power wrapped around Tiseyi, squeezing her chest as they simultaneously smashed her into the wall beside

Rezkin. Rezkin climbed to his feet and quickly dodged a second attack. Then Berringish lashed at him with a whip of oily power. When it came into contact with Rezkin's flesh, it felt as though it were seeping the life out of him. The power inside him jumped to the fore, and Rezkin immediately erected a shield ward. Too much strength had been stolen already, though. The shield was weak and wobbly.

Rezkin raised his sword and summoned what power remained within his core. He became famished, and he knew he was drawing on the last of his reserves. Berringish grinned and said, "You are magnificent, as I knew you would be. Most men would be dead already, yet here you stand, ready to fight. Peider and Jaiardun trained you well, but they did not truly appreciate what they had. If I had known that Caydean's assassination attempt had failed, I would have come for you sooner."

Although Rezkin thought that this moment when Berringish started talking would be the perfect time to mount his attack, he was still recovering from the Sen's last attack. Besides that, he wanted to know more of what Berringish knew. "Come for me? To what end?" Rezkin said.

"To use you, of course. With your innate power, your masters' training, and my demon, you would be the most powerful being to ever live."

"Under *your* control, no doubt."

Berringish smiled, and this time it appeared genuine. "Of course, but you would have everything you could possibly want—women to beg for your body, men to grovel at your feet, the power to raze cities, even kingdoms! You would be a demigod, second only to the gods."

"And *you.*"

"Naturally."

"What of Caydean? Is he not the demigod you desire?"

Berringish frowned. "Caydean was a poor substitute. I know that now. He is powerful, yes, but he is mad. His power consumed his mind, and I think he was broken even before that. He is deviant, unpredictable. He will destroy everything and leave me nothing to rule. But with my help, *you* can defeat him and take your rightful place."

Rezkin did not bother to respond with words. Instead, he launched himself at Berringish. With a flurry of strikes, he did not give the Sen enough time to create his life-bleeding spells. Berringish was too slow to avoid a slash to his abdomen, but Rezkin knew it was only a surficial wound. The Sen jumped over a wall as Rezkin backed him deeper into the ruins. Rezkin followed him into what must have once been the great hall as it was a vast expanse of unbroken terrain. In no time, Rezkin had Berringish on the ground, attempting to drag himself away. As Rezkin stepped over him and raised his sword to strike, the newly created pathway released a burst of power which shook the ground, opening a chasm beneath Berringish. He, along with much of the floor of the former great hall, collapsed into the chamber below. Rezkin leapt backward and barely managed to maintain his position above ground. Although he could see nothing of Berringish, a quick perusal told Rezkin that nothing moved in those dark depths, so he turned his attention to the more pertinent rent in the air.

He ran toward the statue hoping to upset the device before anything could come through the pathway, but he was too late. A man stepped from the light onto the cracked and crumbling floor of the ruins, a man who Rezkin had never seen but he would have recognized anywhere. Like Rezkin, he had a powerful build, sleek black hair, and cold blue eyes. This man's features, however, were harder, more brutal, and when he turned his icy gaze, Rezkin saw only malevolence. Those pale blue eyes that first appeared so familiar abruptly became blacker than night as Caydean stepped toward Rezkin. In his grip was a Sheyalin longsword, and his muscular physique was wrapped in the burnished armor of the king of Ashai.

The sound of Caydean's heavy boots crunching through the rubble was drowned out by the crackling of the portal into the pathways. The mad king said nothing as he closed on Rezkin and raised his sword. The black blade met the strike with a flash of green lightning, and then it did so again and again. Rezkin and Caydean danced around the ruins slashing, lunging, and parrying in equal order. Caydean was an excellent swordsman, but Rezkin knew he was better. Given time, he would overcome his older brother. Caydean slammed his blade down forcing Rezkin to leap backward over a fallen pillar. Once the space opened between them, a rumble erupted from Caydean's chest. His was a boisterous laugh filled with sadistic mirth.

"This has been fun, brother, but I tire of this game." Sinuous black lines snaked out of Caydean's eyes and across his face. As they slithered down his neck and beneath his clothing to emerge from his sleeves, they looked like serpents meandering through the grass. The inky black lines erupted from his skin to pass as smokey tendrils in the air. They grew rapidly in size as they shot over the battlefield. Caydean laughed again as the first of the black tentacles claimed its victims. Men began falling to the field in agony as they writhed under the strength of the dark power. Caydean said, "When I am through here, I will go to your pitiful little island and destroy everyone there who thought to stand against me. Then I will crush each of your traitorous kingdoms beneath my boot until not even a maggot lives."

Rezkin ducked and dodged as the inky black tendrils reached for him. His shield only perturbed them for a moment before it collapsed beneath their destructive power. Rezkin was not fast enough to evade the multitude. Several snatched at him as they seized him in their grip. Rezkin's power stirred within him, but as he sought to release it, the insidious power seeped through his skin. The demonic force slid over his own power like oil over water creating a barrier that he could not seem to penetrate. As he struggled to grasp the light within him, the corruption began surging through his body. It first struck at his heart and lungs, gripping and tightening until his chest felt as if it would implode. Then it attacked his mind.

Rezkin blinked a dark film from his eyes. When he focused again, it was not Caydean who stood before him but his masters. Peider shook his head sadly. "You are a disappointment," he grumbled.

Jaiardun scowled. "Our years of sacrifice were for nothing. You are a failure."

Then Rezkin was surrounded by more than a dozen strikers, each and every one of them haunting him from the grave. Striker Adona's brow furrowed beneath an errant lock of golden hair. "This is what I died for?" The other strikers, those who had trained Rezkin throughout his youth, all grumbled in discontent.

Rezkin took a shuddering breath, one that barely wheezed into his aching, tormented lungs, and blinked again. Now only one person stood before him. Palis's pale eyes glistened with anger and pain as he stared down at Rezkin. Rezkin abruptly realized that at some point he had fallen to his knees, and he was now forced to look up at the first of his friends that he had lost.

Palis raised his fist and then pointed at Rezkin. "I stood beside you, and you failed to save me. You let me die on that beach. You may as well have killed me yourself."

Rezkin's chest tightened further. He swallowed hard as he struggled for his next breath. He had not known Palis long, but in the short time they had traveled together, he had found the young man to be selfless and valiant, and he was always quick to smile and laugh. The man who stood before him now was nothing like the *friend* Rezkin had known.

Shaking his head, Rezkin tried to remember what he had been doing before he was visited by the dead. There had been a battle, and evil mages, and ... Caydean. Rezkin closed his eyes and sought the light, the power that could sustain him, the power of the Spirétua. It was there, gleaming beneath the oily sheen of his brother's demonic presence. He battered against the blockade, that crude and sinister miasma that kept him from his power and prevented breath from filling his lungs. A crack began to form, and the tiniest beam of light seeped through. Rezkin grabbed hold of it with all his might and pulled it into his mind, twisting it around and around like a thread on a spinning wheel. The ghostly images cleared from his vision, but what met his gaze was so much worse.

As Rezkin knelt at Caydean's feet, his death imminent, the mad king had turned his attention to the battle. His demonic power wafted across the field inflicting the same debilitating and tortuous effects on the rebel forces. Men and women fell beneath the blades, teeth, claws, and spells of their enemies while they were immobilized by the dark power.

Rezkin knew he needed to help them quickly, but he still struggled to claim his own breath. His body was dying as the power cinched his heart and lungs more tightly. Spots began to form in his eyes, and it was only a matter of minutes, perhaps even seconds before he succumbed to Caydean's superior strength. The screams of those dying on the field and the crackling of the portal were nearly blotted out by the thrumming pulse of blood in his ears. He could continue to fight the battle within to save his own life, or he could fight the battle without to save everyone else. Rezkin had a choice to make, and no more time in which to make it.

Struggling to his feet, Rezkin set his sights on his brother. The darkness threatened at the corners of his vision, but he could see enough to accomplish his goal. He wrapped what power he could wrangle around himself them propelled his body forward. Caydean was not far from him when they collided, but Rezkin had enough momentum to knock the mad king off his feet. Caydean fell backward into the portal, his fingers grasping for purchase against Rezkin's armor yet finding none. Rezkin collapsed atop the statue to which the portal to the pathways was attached. Its power surged through him, competing with the demonic power for the chance to kill him. Rezkin did not live long enough to know which it was that succeeded.

27

Wesson looked up toward the hill just in time to see the second fighter fall back into the portal from which he had emerged. Although he had never before seen the man, his likeness to Rezkin and the power he wielded had led Wesson to the conclusion that he was Caydean, the mad king himself. As Caydean disappeared into the portal, Rezkin had fallen atop the source of the portal's power. The energy surged and snapped erupting in a shockwave across the field that first had to surge through Rezkin.

Wesson ran toward the hill with as much speed as he could muster, but he could only see Rezkin's prone form laying beneath where the portal had once stood. By the time Wesson had reached the crest, Entris and Azeria had joined him. What they found was devastating. Rezkin remained on the ground unmoving with Tiseyi curled up to his side. The wolf whimpered then released a long, agonized howl toward the forlorn sky.

Entris knelt at Rezkin's side as he checked for a pulse. The sounds of battle, the agonized cries of the injured, the pandemonium all evaporated as Wesson looked down on the emperor, on his friend. Wesson could hear only the blood rushing through his ears, and he held his breath in dread-filled anticipation. Eventually, Entris looked up at Azeria and shook his head. Wesson's shock reflected that of the Eihelvanan. Azeria dropped to her knees and grabbed onto Rezkin's armor, flipping him over so that his face was no longer pressed into the dirt. Besides the dirt and bloody splatters from battle, Rezkin looked well, as if he merely slept. Azeria shook him roughly, refusing to accept the truth, and Tiseyi growled and snapped at her.

"Are you sure?" said Wesson, once he was finally able to get sound past the lump in his throat. He had never felt so powerless as he did in that moment. "We had thought him dead once before. He always survives. *Always.*"

Entris seemed to be casting power over the body, but as with Rezkin's power, Wesson could not feel it. When he was finished, the Spirétua-lyé stood and said, "There is no doubt, he is dead. Between the demonic power and that released by the collapsing pathway, he had no chance."

Wesson had a million questions. How had there been a pathway in the first place? Where had it come from? How had Caydean traveled through it? Would Caydean be able to come back? But only one question made it past his lips. "Is there a way to bring Rezkin back?"

Entris shook his head again. "Only the Sen possess that power."

Wesson looked up with hope. "Berringish can do it. He was here."

Azeria cleared her throat, although her voice came out choked. "He defeated Berringish." She pointed toward a massive hole in the ground. "He was there (*despondent*)."

Wesson inched toward the hole and peered down into the dark chamber. A mountain of rubble lay in a heap at its center. "Perhaps he lives. We can dig him out and *make* him bring Rezkin back."

Entris heaved a heavy breath then nodded. "No Eihelvanan would consent to being raised by a Sen."

"He is *human,*" snapped Wesson.

For the first time, Wesson saw Entris's ever stoic façade slip. His eyes blazed with anger, and his jaw clenched as he said, "He is less human than *you*, and now that he is gone you no longer have his protection."

"I do not need his protection," growled Wesson. "But he does need our help. He cannot be dead. He *must* survive."

By then, a small crowd was forming on the hill. The strikers had extricated themselves from the battle, and Kai was standing guard over the body as Farson knelt at Rezkin's head. As the truth set in, Farson released a howl of his own while he tried to pull Rezkin into his arms.

"Get the healer!" shouted Farson. He looked from Wesson to Entris. "Somebody save him. Save the emperor." His voice drifted off, and on a sob, he said, "Save my boy."

Wesson could no longer withstand the sight of so many distraught faces, so many people falling apart at once. He turned his gaze toward the battle that still raged below. With the battle master, Berringish, and Caydean gone, the tide had turned. The rebels were pushing back against Caydean's forces, which were fracturing at the loss of leadership.

Wesson nearly jumped when Entris suddenly spoke from directly beside him. The male was as stealthy as Rezkin. He said, "He has endured it before, the retrieval by the Sen. The marks are visible to all now. Perhaps you are right. His soul may respond." He looked down into the hole and said, "We should search for Berringish." Then his gaze traveled to the battlefield. "With Caydean's power gone, the battle has turned in our favor. It will not be long before what is left of this enemy retreats. Then we will have men to aid us in recovering the Sen if he lives (*hopeful*)."

Entris was right. A couple of hours later, the battle had ended with their side victorious and the remainder of Caydean's forces on the run. The mages had stabilized the ruins so there would be no more cave-ins, and the strikers and Tiseyi stood guard over Rezkin's body as mages and soldiers dug through the rubble in earnest. Every stone had been moved by the time they accepted that Berringish was not there.

"He must have escaped during the battle." Wesson hung his head as the full consequences of what had happened struck him. Rezkin was dead, and he was not coming back. Wesson pressed his palms to his eyes hoping to prevent the tears that threatened to fall. Although there were many atop the hill releasing their anguish, he thought it would not be proper for the emperor's mage to cry in front of everyone.

Wesson walked as softly as possible as he approached the dead emperor, his friend. Kai and Farson stood over him, their gazes hard, but they did not attempt to block him. Tiseyi's head lay across Rezkin's chest, and every so often a pitiful whimper would escape her. Azeria, too, sat beside Rezkin pressed up against his side. She stared at the ground as if completely unaware of her surroundings. It was not a look he was accustomed to seeing on the ever-present general.

Wesson looked up to Farson and said, "You are the closest he has to family here. What should we do?"

"Me? Family?" Farson chuckled through his tears. "He never thought of me as such. You should ask the wolf. She is bonded to him."

Tiseyi looked up at them then turned back to bury her muzzle beneath Rezkin's chin.

"He should be taken back to Cael," said Kai. "He should be buried in his own kingdom."

Azeria abruptly stood. She scowled at Kai then turned to Wesson. "He is Spirétua. He should be entombed in the way of the Eihelvanan." She looked to Entris for support, but Entris merely dropped his gaze then looked away.

Wesson looked back to Farson. "I know you two had a contentious relationship and neither of you were ever truthful about your feelings, but I do believe he thought of you as family."

At first, Wesson thought the striker would not answer, but eventually, he said, "We shall bury him in the ruins where he fell. Garten Knoll will forever serve as a monument to the great emperor of the Souelian, True King of Ashai, who sacrificed himself to save his people." His voice became gruff as he said, "It was a far nobler end than I had expected for him. I underestimated him, something that I will forever regret. I should have … I should have told him how proud I was of him. I should have told him …"

Kai gripped Farson's shoulder. "He knew."

"No," snapped Farson. "He could not have. He was not trained to understand."

"He knew much more than he was trained to understand," said Azeria. She met Farson's gaze and said, "You trained him to be a warrior, but he was Eihelvanan."

As she walked away, Farson looked at Wesson. "What does that mean?"

Wesson shrugged. "I cannot say that I understand them, but I think she is feeling his loss much more than she had expected she would."

"As are we all," said Kai. He huffed, but there was no humor in it. "Lord Tieran will be furious. He has just become emperor."

EPILOGUE

"**D**id you get it?" barked Berringish as he limped into the catacomb that presently served as his home. The walls dripped with moisture, and the air was stagnant, but at least he had not been found by the rebels while he recovered. After dragging himself from the rubble of the collapsed ruins, he had used the last of his strength to erect the barrier that had prevented them from finding him. Now, three days later, the traitors had finally moved off the site, and Berringish was free to implement his plan. Any later and it would all have been for naught.

"Yes, Master," said Armas as he wrung his hands.

"Well, where is it?" he snapped.

Armas jumped as if startled and then scurried back down the corridor. A moment later Berringish could hear the sound of something heavy sliding across the dusty floor mingled with Armas's grunts.

Berringish could not help the rueful smile that played at his lips as the body came into view. Armas had already unwrapped the top half, presumably to confirm the identity, but the rest was wrapped in a green and black flag. The man had been buried in his clothes and armor, but Armas made quick work of those, tossing everything into a pile in the corner. His assistant panted heavily as he attempted to heave the body onto the top of a random tomb, dropping it several times so that it cracked and thudded against the floor.

"Careful, you nitwit. I do not want to have to heal more than is necessary."

"Sorry, Master," Armas said between clenched teeth as he was finally able to leverage the dead weight atop the tomb. He breathed in the dust and cobwebs with a cough before finally positioning the body how Berringish wanted it.

Berringish looked down at the specimen. It was perfect. Much better than that damnable Caydean. This one should have been his all along, no thanks to those meddlesome SenGoka. From the looks of the corpse, Peider and Jaiardun had done their best to destroy him as often as possible. Now that he was dead, he could not conceal the multitude of tattoos that were scrawled across his skin. Up the lengths of his arms, across his torso, and even down his legs were recorded the details of his life and deaths. Each mark and symbol, legible only to him and his kind, communicated something of how he had died, how long his death had lasted, who had retrieved him, and how long he had lived again. There were also marks indicating his many accomplishments as a Goka, which was news to Berringish. He had known the others were training the boy to be a warrior, but he had not known they had considered him to be Goka. It was all the better for him, though. Now that he could finally implement his original plan, he, by virtue of his puppet, would be unstoppable.

Berringish ran his fingers over the cold flesh beneath the man's right ribs where no marks had yet been made. Then he laid a small chest on the tomb next to the corpse and opened it. He collected the three bottles of black, red, and blue ink that would be used to detail these events and took up the tattoo quill. The first marks would record the man's age and the nature and time of his death. When he was finished with those marks, he laid his hands on the man's torso— one on his chest and one on his abdomen. He closed his eyes and ignited his power.

The power of the Sen was different from that of the Eihelvanan and mages. Theirs was the power of the Goddess of the Firmament, Rheina, while his was of the Goddess of Death and Resurrection, Nihko. While he could not say how the power of Rheina felt, he knew well the power of his own goddess. Hers was sultry and inviting. It begged of him to join her while at the same time empowered him to take of her.

"Master."

The muttered word interrupted his thoughts, and he growled as he opened one eye to stare at his assistant. Armas was grinning with elation. The fervor in his eyes would have concerned Berringish on another man, but Armas was an incompetent imbecile.

Armas blinked as Berringish growled, "What?"

"W-won't Caydean be angry?"

In his irritation, Berringish had held his breath—a breath he now released with another growl. "You interrupt me for *this*? What care have I for Caydean's concerns? He is volatile and his insanity makes him difficult if not impossible to control. I need someone whose mind is intact if I am to pull off my plan. This one will take care of Caydean. Besides, he has already accomplished far more in the past few months on his own than Caydean has managed in the last two years. He has already claimed half the Souelian! Now I will make it all *mine* and he will be left to do *my* bidding as soon as I place the demon in him."

Armas wrung his hands again and said, "I saw him fight, Master. Perhaps you should place the demon in him *before* you resurrect him."

"I have told you, it is called a *retrieval*, not a resurrection; and I cannot place a demon in an empty vessel. It requires a soul to latch onto. I must retrieve him first. But before *that*, I must heal him, which requires concentration, so be silent."

Berringish cleared his mind again as he turned back to the task at hand. He sought the center of his power and—

"But won't he cause trouble?"

Berringish sighed. "We have no cause to worry over that."

"Perhaps we should tie him down."

"He will not be conscious for a while after I have retrieved him. There will be plenty of time to emplace the demon. Now be silent or I will ensure that you are no longer capable of speaking. This is the third day. If I do not do it now, it will not be possible."

Berringish concentrated again, this time blocking out all but the cold body beneath his hands. He sent his awareness throughout the vessel searching for damage and was pleased to find that there was very little. The power of the imploding portal had simply been too much for the man's body to handle during Caydean's demonic attack. Berringish was pleased that it had not been the demonic power to actually kill him. That would have made it difficult if not impossible for him to reseat the man's soul. It was another reason for his ire against Caydean. The mad king had promised this one to Berringish, and he knew full well that he was not supposed to kill him using the demonic power. Caydean had betrayed him, despite Berringish's tentative hold over the mad king's demon. It had been one more example of how Caydean had progressively been slipping from Berringish's control.

Berringish sent his healing power into the body that lay naked and prone on the tomb. His kind of healing, that which was forced upon a body, would have been terribly painful for a living being, but this was yet an empty vessel—a temporary setback that would be remedied shortly. With the body healed enough to house a soul, Berringish turned his attention to the retrieval. There, in his mind, he could see the chiandre that would have connected the soul to the vessel at one end and still connected it to the Afterlife at the other. He followed the luminescent line through the darkness, the void, until he finally found the soul waiting too near to the Gate for Berringish's comfort. This one was nearly beyond saving—*nearly*.

Berringish snapped his power around the soul, enveloping it in an embrace that could only be born of a true desire to see it restored. Then he tugged the soul back along the chiandre as he reattached the connecting power to the vessel. He knew that on the outside it would appear as if nothing had happened, but inside this place between the realms of life and death, Berringish felt a massive concussion, like a splinter of the universe breaking away and reattaching itself as the soul settled into its place within the vessel.

Rezkin became aware of his body before he could sense his environment. He took stock of himself yet could not find a cause for his disorientation. He felt the sharp, stinging jab of something like an insect at his wrist but nothing more. The jabbing continued as Rezkin sought a connection with anything around him. Sensation slowly seeped into his body. He was cold—no, *frigid*. Even the hard surface he lay atop seemed warm against the chill of his back. The stinging stopped, and he heard a *clink* like glass. Then there was a muffled sound of fabric and … voices. The sounds slowly morphed into something intelligible.

"Bring the vessel to me, Armas," said a gruff voice.

"Yes, Master," said a second male voice.

The first mumbled, "I do not know how much time we have. He is more *experienced* with this sort of thing than any other I have retrieved."

The name Armas tugged at a memory. Rezkin struggled to place it, but his mind still felt foggy. It was not the first time he had awoken to such a sensation. In fact, it had occurred frequently in his youth. He knew what it meant. He had been healed. But who had done the healing?

Rezkin struggled to open his eyes. With a forceful tug, one lid opened a crack, and he could see a figure looming above him. Rezkin's heart leapt. He could not quite place the face that hovered over him, but his mind screamed *enemy*. The man began to mutter strange words as he held something over Rezkin's torso. Rezkin turned his attention to the object as his other eye finally opened to a slit. With both eyes now functioning, he focused until the object came into view. It was a ceramic pot that was covered in the black script of what looked like jagged, ancient runes, only these were crisp and clean like new. After a moment, Rezkin realized he had seen such marks before on the pots that had contained the demons used in possessions.

Things finally began to tumble into place. The man who stood over him was the Sen Berringish, and he appeared to be attempting to place a demon inside of *him*. Although Rezkin's heart jolted, his body did not follow. Nothing seemed to be working as it should. He was frozen, paralyzed, and he was about to lose what was left of himself. After struggling against his immobile muscles, Rezkin finally calmed himself enough to consider alternative strategies. If trying to force his body to move would not work, he needed another way.

Rezkin shifted his mind into the state of meditation his masters had taught him. There, he looked inside himself for the power that he knew was his. He pictured the river of multi-hued light. He sought the soothing melody of the music that always accompanied it. When he finally found it, the music was slow and faint, and the river flowed lethargically. An external pressure reached his consciousness, and Rezkin could feel the grip of something dark and insipid stealing into him. He knew he probably had only seconds left before Berringish succeeded in his quest to install a demon in his body. Tossing caution to the wind, Rezkin took hold of his consciousness and *jumped* into the river of power.

Rezkin reared up from the tomb and grabbed the man who stood over him. The ceramic pot crashed onto the stone tomb and shattered as a screeching gust swept across Rezkin's bare skin. He snatched a shard of the pot and slashed it across Berringish's neck severing the jugular. Then he lurched to his feet and closed the distance between himself and a second man, Armas. Armas turned to run, but Rezkin was too fast. Rezkin tripped the smaller man, grabbed him by the sides of his head, then wrenched it around until he faced his own back. Then Rezkin stood tall and looked around the dark, dank chamber as his chest heaved in deep gasps of stale air.

Taking stock of his body again, Rezkin felt a sting around his wrist. He looked down to find that he was covered in sharp, jagged runes similar to those that decorated the ceramic pot that had held the demon. Most of them looked to have been there for years, but one blue one that circled his wrist was puffy and red as was a spot over his ribs. Rezkin turned back to the tomb, atop which he had lain as Berringish had tried to claim his body for a demon, and found a box of tattoo supplies in addition to the remnants of the pot. Berringish lay on the floor lifeless in a pool of his own blood. Rezkin searched the rest of the room and found his clothes and armor piled in one corner. His body began to shake as he realized how cold he felt.

After dressing, Rezkin stumbled down the only passage that led from the small chamber and followed it to another larger chamber that held several more tombs. While most of them appeared to be ancient, one in the center looked freshly carved and pristine. The tomb's cover lay atop it askew, but as Rezkin approached, he noted that it held legible script. He had to read the inscription twice before he accepted what he saw. *His* name. *His* titles. This was *his* tomb. Rezkin had died.

Rezkin abruptly regretted killing both Berringish and Armas. He should have allowed one of them to live if only long enough to answer his questions. How long had he been dead? How had he died? Who had buried him? How had his companions fared in the battle? *Why* had Berringish decided to resurrect *him*, of all people?

Stepping closer, Rezkin peered into the tomb in which he had been buried. Inside, he found the black blade, haphazardly tossed aside, and its sheath. That must have been the work of Armas, he decided. No one else would have treated this sword with such irreverence. Rezkin held the sword aloft as he stared into the black void of its blade, that which held the jagged green bolts of frozen lightning. At least he would not be headed into battle unarmed. Then he reminded himself that the blade was not the real weapon. *He* was the weapon.

Reaching back into the tomb, Rezkin plucked from it the stone he had worn around his neck, the vagri that had helped keep his vimara from overwhelming him. The stone was glowing and pulsating as it had of late. As he settled the stone into his palm, he felt it latch onto his power as if desperate for the connection. It flickered brightly and then *snap!* It cracked down the center, and its light was extinguished. Rezkin's disappointment was palpable as he realized the stone was now broken. Despite the large fissure that ran down its middle, though, he could still feel a connection, a bond. The fissure began to grow wider, and the two sides shook. Then, a tiny, clawed hand reached through the gap to grasp at the air, pawing for him. As the tiny hand gripped the end of his finger, Rezkin felt no trepidation, only a rightness.

This truth, this *correctness*, was a new sensation for Rezkin. As he considered all that he had done, all that he had accomplished, he knew that every moment had existed under the pall of predomination. From the instant he was born, his existence had been defined by expectation, tradition, and familial obligation. Every moment of his life, every training scenario, every lesson, had been carefully choreographed to produce a single, predefined entity. Every action and reaction, every thought, had been regulated by the *Rules* and *Skills* taught to him by men who concerned themselves not with his well-being but with the intent for which he had been born. The sole purpose for his being was to serve another, and since that time, he had only added to the layers of duty. The burdens of friendship, governing, ruling had been piled onto the trappings that securely held Rezkin in check. Besides the role of the Rez, designed centuries ago by an ancient king, the new roles in which he had embroiled himself had shackled Rezkin within the confines of responsibility.

With his death, though, those roles had fallen away. Everyone thought he was dead. Would they have begun making plans to supplant him? Such was the nature of anyone in the outworld—everyone could be replaced. How could he think that he was the exception?

As a pain suffused his chest, the tiny creature in his palm turned its scaley nose toward him. His newfound companion blinked at him with cold, blue eyes uncannily similar to his own, and Rezkin knew the little dragon could feel what he was feeling. The creature tilted her head curiously, and he equally knew that neither of them understood the sensation. He had come to know only the pain of loss, and this was similar but different. Was this regret?

Rezkin pushed aside his discomfort and focused on the now and future. Were bonds of friendship and comradery so easily broken by one's demise? He had done his duty to the people he had claimed in creating a place where they could be safe. Now that he was no longer constrained by the outworlders' notions of civility and morality, what goal would he set for himself? What was his purpose in life, or did he have one? Did he *need* one? The question struck him like a physical blow.

He *could* focus on defeating the mad tyrant that was wreaking havoc in Ashai and across the Souelian. Or he could *not*. Should he continue to do as Bordran had designed? Such feelings defied the *Rules*, but Rezkin recognized a stirring of enmity against Caydean for killing him. Could he allow that defeat to stand? Or could he release himself from the bonds of duty and vengeance to become something *else*. With his death had come a sense of clarity. He had always seen himself as a single thread woven through the tapestry of existence; but perhaps he was truly a snag that caused all the other threads to unravel. If that were so, what damage could he do? Rezkin considered that he could be both, and it pleased him to think that he might choose.

No longer was he bound by the designs of crowns and thrones nor guilds and orders. In building his empire, he had changed the world, but he knew that it, too, had changed him. His experiences in the outworld had taught him that the *Rules* by which he had lived were stagnant and confining, and life was fluid, everchanging. In life, he had followed the *Rules*. In this afterlife, perhaps it was time to make his own *Rules*; because the leash that had entangled him had burned away in death. Rezkin was free.

Rezkin will return in *King's Dark Tidings*, Book Six

CHARACTERS

Frisha Souvain-Marcum - Rezkin's girlfriend, General Marcum's niece

Jespia - healer

Rezkin - warrior, King of Cael, True King of Ashai

Brandt Gerrand - heir of House Gerrand, friend of the Jebais

Connovan - former Rez; Rezkin's uncle

Zankai (Kai) Tresdian - striker; loyal follower of Rezkin

Farson - striker; Rezkin's former trainer

Tieran Nirius - heir to House Wellinven

Nanessy Threll - elemental mage; niece of Farson

Wesson Seth - journeyman mage

Caydean - king of Ashai

Tamarin Blackwater - Rezkin's apprentice and friend

Uthey - former mercenary from Gendishen

Answon - sect leader in slave camp at quarry

Probart - slave master in charge of Tam's clutch

Mecca - favored slave and blacksmith

Milo - scarred man, slave in Verril; from Channería

Yin - slave in Verril; from Channería

Timbol Urquin - High Councilor of King's Council (Gendishen)

Henin Vaugh - Gendishen councilor; representative of majority party
Mandis Bent - Gendishen councilor; representative of majority party
Liza Rend - Gendishen councilor; representative of majority party
Asha Candin - Gendishen councilor; minority party leader
Azeria - pathmaker, general
Entris - Eihelvanan Spirétua, 157-yrs-old
Counselor Iraguwey - Eihelvanan counselor
Counselor Rythia - Eihelvanan counselor
Counselor Shohtu - Eihelvanan counselor
Counselor Leyin - Eihelvanan counselor
Brelle - young Eihelvanan warrior
Jao'hwin - Eihelvanan elder warrior
Gizahl - ancient Eihelvanan
Montag - quarry sect leader
Demetrus - quarry sect leader
Goragana - ancient Ahn'an of stone and earth
Brogan - m, member of the Archebow Clan of the Drahgfir
Mountains
Ara - f, member of the Archebow Clan of the Drahgfir Mountains
Mordai - m, member of the Archebow Clan of the Drahgfir
Mountains
Utho - m, member of the Archebow Clan of the Drahgfir Mountains
Garra - f, member of the Archebow Clan of the Drahgfir Mountains
Sessui - f, member of the Archebow Clan of the Drahgfir Mountains
Colonel Whitner - siege of city of Gauge
Lantrik - mage under Berringish's control
Olivus - mage under Berringish's control
Rius Ardmore - governor of Gauge
Tragon "Trag" Dimwell - leader of underworld in Gauge
Jerril - former slave master at quarry
Makon - slave from Verril
Guent - slave in Verril; from Ashai
Lo'an - one of Tam's men
Tisaya - leopard man, Virero Tribe
Anana - leopard woman, Virero Tribe

Ahnja - injured leopard woman, Virero Tribe
Eseyi Virero - Great Mother
Jeina - spirit walker of the Virero Tribe
Shioni - Jeina's spirit leopard, f
Torat - Eseyi's husband
Remy - Torat and Eseyi's son (leopard)
Tiseyi - Torat and Eseyi's daughter (wolf)
Osolo - alpha of Wilepa tribe (wolf)
Bratu - vocal member of Lion tribe
Fetari - tribe mother of the Disoni Tribe (hawk)
Thresson - second prince of Ashai
Onus - Willam Moulden's father (Benbrick)
Grayth Prisitus - Wesson's stepfather
Diyah - girl from Benbrick
Tomlin Holcom - presumed future mayor of Benbrick
Payton de Voss - leader of Ashaiian rebels
Haden Nirius - Duke of Wellinven
Mage Regala - mage among rebels
Elantra Dewin - natural battle mage; journeyman

DEFINITIONS

shielreyah - Eihelvanan warriors who gave up their spirits to guard the citadel

vuroles - wolflike desert creatures that hunt in packs

Eihelvanan - elves

Fersheya - language of the Eihelvanan

vagri - stone Rezkin wears around his neck

yelishila - nostalgia and ennui

saboli - Eihelvanan unit of currency

mirandra - test of Spirétua

leyaghens - stoney fae

uruptee - plant-eating, non-aggressive creature

fithyers - creatures related to alligators

tesias - Pruari of the cities

omessas - Pruari of the plains

Virero Tribe - leopard tribe of the omessa people

Wilepa Tribe - wolf tribe of the omessa people

drauglics - semi-intelligent humanoid, lizard-like creatures

ukwa - tribal leader of the drauglics

Rheina - Goddess of the Firmament; the Realm of Life

Mikayal - God of the Soul/War

Nihko - Goddess of Death, the Afterlife, and Rebirth

chiandre - the soul's connection between the physical vessel/body and the Afterlife

ahn'an - fae (beings composed of the power of Mikayal and Rheina)

ahn'tep - beings composed of all three gods

drahg'ahn - dragon

daem'ahn - demon (beings composed of the power of Rheina and Nihko)

Ro - the innocent as defined by the Adana'Ro

Echelon - governor of a province in Lon Lerésh

Sen - priest of Nihko

Goka - warrior trained in the way of the Goka

SenGoka - warrior priest of Nihko

ABOUT THE AUTHOR

New York Times Best Selling Author Kel Kade is a full-time writer and parent living in a quiet semi-rural town on the outskirts of the Dallas metroplex in Texas. She cohabitates with three crazy dogs, three lazy cats, and one boring fish. Prior to becoming an author, Kel worked as an environmental consultant and later entered a doctoral program to complete research in big data studies of volcanic rock geochemistry and marine research in the Izu-Bonin-Mariana and Central America volcanic arcs.

Growing up, Kel lived a military lifestyle of traveling and living in new places. Experiences with distinctive cultures and geography instilled in Kel a sense of wanderlust and opened her young mind to the knowledge that the Earth is expansive and wild. She has a deep interest in science, ancient history, cultural anthropology, art, music, languages, and spirituality, which is evidenced by the diversity and richness of the places and cultures depicted in her writing. Her hobbies include creating universes spanning space and time, developing criminal empires, plotting the downfall of tyrannous rulers, and diving into fantastical mysteries.

NOTE FROM THE AUTHOR

I hope you enjoyed reading this fifth book in the *King's Dark Tidings* series. Please consider leaving a review or comments so that I may continue to improve and expand upon this ongoing series. Also, sign up for my newsletter for updates or find me on my website (www. kelkade.com), Twitter (@Kel_Kade), Facebook (@read_KelKade), or Instagram (Kel_Kade). Rezkin will return in *King's Dark Tidings* Book Six.

Also, check out my *Shroud of Prophecy* series published by Tor Books. It begins with *Fate of the Fallen* and includes everything from simple foresters to endearing thieves, mysterious reapers, powerful yet flawed gods, dragons, the walking dead, and more!